THE LAND
OF SUMMER

Charlotte Bingham

BANTAM BOOKS

LONDON · TORONTO · SYDNEY · AUCKLAND · JOHANNESBURG

TRANSWORLD PUBLISHERS
61–63 Uxbridge Road, London W5 5SA
A Random House Group Company
www.rbooks.co.uk

THE LAND OF SUMMER
A BANTAM BOOK: 9780553819793

First published in Great Britain
in 2008 by Bantam Press
a division of Transworld Publishers
Bantam edition published 2009

A CIP catalogue record for this book
is available from the British Library.

Addresses for Random House Group Ltd companies outside the
UK can be found at: www.randomhouse.co.uk
The Random House Group Ltd Reg. No. 954009

The Random House Group Ltd supports The Forest Stewardship
Council (FSC), the leading international forest certification
organization. All our titles that are printed on Greenpeace
approved FSC certified paper carry the FSC logo.
Our paper procurement policy can be found at
www.rbooks.co.uk/environment

Typeset in 11/13pt Palatino by
Kestrel Data, Exeter, Devon.
Printed in the UK by
CPI Cox & Wyman, Reading RG1 8EX.

2 4 6 8 10 9 7 5 3

www.rbooks.co.uk

For more information on Charlotte Bingham and her books, see her website at www.charlottebingham.com

For the Duke

ENGLAND IN THE 1880s

Love is not love
Which alters when it alteration finds
. . . it is an ever-fixed mark
That looks on tempests and is never shaken . . .

Shakespeare, *Sonnet 116*

Chapter One

Massachusetts, the 1880s

As always, Emmaline Nesbitt found herself sitting all too demurely on the sidelines pretending not to notice that everyone else was dancing, while next door in the smoking room the man who was to be responsible for the sudden change in her fortunes picked up a fresh hand of cards and wondered whether now might be the time to allow his host to start to win back a proportion of the money he had lost. Normally such a thought would never enter the head of a card player as experienced as he, but tonight he was playing a different game and there was good reason for feeling as he did. He was not seated at the card table just for pleasure, as he would be the first to admit, although there was a great deal of pleasure to be gained for a gentleman finding himself in such opulent surroundings. No, this well-bred, handsome Englishman was here on business, on purpose to try to secure the future of a firm based thousands of miles away back across the Atlantic.

So far it had been good; all the carefully pre-arranged introductions had very soon led to invitations to meetings in New York and Chicago and finally to this house, the principal residence of the Nesbitt family, in Massachusetts. The decision as to whether the Nesbitt & Nesbitt catalogue should carry the furniture, designs and materials of Aubrey & Aubrey Ltd had not yet been taken, but he had the distinct feeling that the scales were tipping heavily in his favour. It might need one more discreet and subtle *coup,* but Julius Aubrey carried more than one trick up his perfectly tailored sleeve, and if he needed to come up with one more match-winning play then he most certainly would, so necessary did it seem to him to land a deal that would ensure the continuing prosperity of everyone connected with Aubrey & Aubrey Ltd, but most of all of himself.

And so the Englishman decided that now was the time to allow his host to stage a dramatic recovery and claw back some of the considerable amount of money he had wagered and lost across the table in the past hour, even though, as Julius well knew, Mr Onslow Nesbitt was a man who possibly carried more spending money in his wallet than most men earn in a year. Yet so much did Julius Aubrey enjoy winning – as much as he hated losing – that for a moment he hesitated, allowing himself to wonder, albeit briefly, how he would feel if he let his host win back most of his money only for the business proposition to founder, leaving him to go back to England empty-handed.

As a matter of fact, he knew exactly how he would feel – very foolish indeed. However, remembering exactly what was at stake and what the alternatives were, he regretfully buried any idea of walking away from the card table a winner and thought instead of the long game, beginning to apply his considerable card-playing skills to making it look as if his host was playing brilliantly, and he himself was not losing quite deliberately.

'Congratulations, sir,' he said to Nesbitt as the final cards were collected up with the losing chips. 'I think that was possibly the most dextrous series of hands played this evening.'

'Most kind of you, sir,' Nesbitt replied. 'Coming from someone who was providing an object lesson in how to play poker, I consider that the highest of compliments. But now, if you gentlemen are in agreement,' he added, stubbing out his cigar and pushing his chair back from the green baize table, 'I think that if any of our marriages are to survive, we should perhaps show our faces once more in the ballroom.'

'I am sorry Mrs Nesbitt did not feel well enough to attend this quite splendid function,' Aubrey remarked to his host as they re-entered the ballroom.

'Mrs Nesbitt is rarely well enough to attend anything, Mr Aubrey,' Onslow Nesbitt growled. 'Other than to herself.'

'A shame, sir. You have my sympathies.'

'Most kind of you, Mr Aubrey, but I don't need 'em. I know plenty of other fine ladies who take to their beds for quite different reasons.'

'I see your charming daughters are greatly in demand,' Aubrey observed quickly, noting the three beautiful Nesbitt girls being danced around the floor by three highly presentable young men.

'My girls are always in demand,' Nesbitt replied, selecting a fresh cigar from a box of Havanas brought to him by a servant. 'All except, alas, my poor Emmaline' – Onslow Nesbitt nodded across the floor in the direction of his eldest daughter – 'or rather the eternal sitter, as her mother calls her.'

'Still can't get her off your hands, eh, Onslow?' a large red-faced gentleman asked his host, adding a nudge for good measure. 'Still can't find a husband for her, eh?'

'Maybe not, Horace,' Onslow replied, lighting his cigar, 'but then perhaps that's preferable to seeing her hitched to that son of yours.'

'I would say you lucky gentlemen are spoiled for choice over here,' Aubrey remarked. 'In England today any young man worth his salt would be charmed to consider taking a young lady with the looks, grace and background of Miss Emmaline Nesbitt as a wife, I can assure you.'

'Is that a fact, Mr Aubrey?' Onslow wondered, eyeing his guest. 'Is that a fact? In that case perhaps you would be kind enough to take her back to England with you?'

Aubrey looked startled for a moment, and then amused. 'I am sure any man would be charmed to introduce Miss Nesbitt to English society,' he said.

'Please, do not hesitate on my account.' Onslow Nesbitt was laughing. 'If you took Emmaline from us you would also take with you the undying gratitude of the whole Nesbitt family, Mr Aubrey.'

Seeing his host distracted by friends who had come up to greet him, the Englishman narrowed his eyes to peer through the throng of dancers at the young woman sitting alone on a chair pulled up close to a pillar decorated with strands of ivy and hand-made flowers. He quickly noted that she had a good figure and a fine head of hair, was dressed well, and sat with great poise and stillness, and as he watched her it occurred to his mischievous mind that here were the makings of a *coup* that might well seal the deal.

From her position on the sidelines, Emmaline had seen the party emerge from the smoking room to stand surveying the dance. The orchestra was playing a tune that she particularly loved, but while her three beautiful and much sought-after younger sisters were getting their chance to show off their dancing skills on the floor, Emmaline had yet again found herself stationed on a gilt chair, her dance card unfilled, her composure belying the humiliation of being once more the only Nesbitt girl not dancing.

She held her dance card high in front of her

17

face, pretending to consult it, as she took another glance at the party of gentlemen still standing at the end of the corridor that led to the smoking room. Among their number was the handsome Englishman who she knew had come over to do business with her father. His re-emergence must, she knew, give hope to those young ladies who had not had the luck to attract any dance partners. Not that Emmaline herself entertained any foolish notions, not by any means. She knew her place all too well. It was on a gilt chair, watching, always watching, as the rest of the world danced by her.

She had, as always, resigned herself to her seat, maintaining her upright stance, trying not to notice that when her sisters danced past her they averted their eyes, as if she was nothing to do with them, so that when she glanced over the top of her dance card and found *him* looking directly at her, surprise made her forget her manners for a moment and she stared straight back at him. She recollected herself almost immediately and dropped her gaze, but out of the corner of her eye she watched with mounting astonishment as he adjusted the set of his tail coat, checked the position of his white bow tie between thumb and finger of one gloved hand, and crossed the dance floor to her side.

There has to be some mistake, Emmaline thought, as she looked to the right of her and the left. Both chairs were empty. *Or perhaps he has brought a message from Papa.*

18

'Miss Nesbitt,' the stranger said, standing directly in front of her, which made even Emmaline realise that there could be no mistake. 'Miss Nesbitt, forgive me. We met briefly before dinner, but since then . . .' Seeing her bewilderment, he started again. 'Miss Nesbitt, I am not sure whether you are aware of it or not, but I am from England, come here to do business in this great country of yours.'

'Mr Aubrey,' Emmaline replied quietly, accepting his hand while finding herself looking anywhere except at his face. 'Of course I recall who you are and why you are here. It is not often that we have visitors from across the Atlantic.'

'Excellent. That makes me a prize exhibit,' Aubrey replied gaily. 'And while I am sure there is little hope for me, I was nevertheless wondering whether perhaps, when you glance at your dance card, you might find that you have just one dance left free, one that you and I might enjoy?'

Despite having spent most of her time on a gilt chair to the side of the ballroom floor, Emmaline knew the ensuing ritual by heart. A young woman must always pretend that her dance card was almost full. No one wanted to dance with someone whom no one else had asked to stand up. It was just a fact.

'I see I have the dance after this one free, Mr Aubrey, the last one,' she said in a low voice. 'No, forgive me,' she added hastily. 'No, that was my mistake. As it happens, by chance – by an extraordinary chance – I have the very next dance free, as it happens.' She peered at her card. 'Yes. Mr Generes was taken home sick, poor fellow.'

'A two-step, I do declare,' Aubrey announced as the orchestra played the introduction. 'I rather enjoy a two-step, truly I do, although considering it takes two people and four legs, surely it should be called a four-step!' He bowed.

Offering her hand to him in the accepted manner, Emmaline rose and allowed herself to be led out on to the dance floor, where her confidence immediately returned, for if there was one thing of which she was quite, quite sure, it was that she could dance.

As it happened, gentleman that he most certainly appeared to be, her dancing partner guided Emmaline round the floor with dexterity, while she herself demonstrated a lightness of foot which seemed to please him. Certainly he had about him an aura of such gaiety and kindness that when the music stopped, and he bowed and thanked Emmaline, she felt overwhelmed with disappointment.

'As you said, there is only one more dance, alas, Miss Nesbitt,' he said, looking rueful. 'And while I imagine there is little chance of your being free, I would give a great deal to have you spurn whoever it is who has the good fortune to have—'

Before he could finish, Emmaline put in quickly, 'As it so happens, Mr Aubrey, this dance is free as well.'

'How very fortunate!' Aubrey exclaimed in

delight. 'Then perhaps we may repeat this last delightful experience? I do so hope so.'

It had taken only a few minutes for Emmaline to quite lose her heart to this man, who seemed to be at such pains to be gallant and charming. From the moment he stood in front of her chair and began to talk to her, she knew that nothing would ever be quite the same again. It was not that she felt she had been swept off her feet, rather it was as if his energy was infusing her with a courage she had never experienced before. As if he could see that she was not by nature a wallflower, but a spirited young woman suppressed by her circumstances, unable to escape from the confines of the gilt chair upon which she had been sitting with such an upright stance, her fan gently waving in front of her face, her eyes carefully avoided by those of her luckier sisters.

She spent the night remembering those two dances as if they were her last on earth, and was amazed when on the following day, preparatory to his departure for England, Julius Aubrey called once more on the Nesbitt household.

Emmaline watched him alight from his hired carriage, as elegant in his morning suit as he had been in his white tie and tails, and assumed that he was calling on her father in connection with the business that had brought him to America.

She turned to Mary, the girls' devoted maid, who was dressing her for the walk she was intending to take, and said, as casually as she could, 'I see that Mr Aubrey is once more visiting Papa.'

'He sure is, Miss Emmaline,' Mary replied, buttoning up Emmaline's warmest coat, and handing her a fur hat and muff as a precaution against the increasingly cold November weather. 'And a handsomer man I don't suppose either of us has seen.'

Mary sighed, and shook her head. Everyone knew that until Miss Emmaline married, none of her poor sisters could. That was the convention in the Nesbitt family. Old-fashioned it might be, but it was a rule which Mr Nesbitt, and Mrs Nesbitt (much more reluctantly, of course), insisted upon. The other three would remain at home until their eldest sister left her father's house. Sometimes it seemed to Mary, and indeed to the rest of the household, that Miss Emmaline was just being downright stubborn in not making herself more apparent to the young gentlemen of the neighbourhood. Although, as even Mary had to admit, Mrs Nesbitt had not exactly helped by always saying of Miss Emmaline, 'Plain, plain, plain, and nothing to be done.'

Old Mary knew very well that if a young woman felt herself to be plain she would always be plain in her mind, and as a consequence, no matter what her features or attributes, she would never behave as though she thought she was worth looking at, and that was a fact. 'And if you don't think you're worth looking at, no one else will,' she would say, though only to Miss Emmaline, since the others were so vain she never had to bother with them.

Mary watched Emmaline disappear down the stairs to the hall, knowing that she would collect the two family spaniels from the dog room, and take herself out into grounds sparkling in the pale winter sunshine. The maid sighed. Walking the dogs, stitching evening purses and playing the piano for hours on end was no life for a healthy young woman. Please God someone would take Miss Emmaline off her parents' hands soon, and then the other three could follow.

No sooner had Emmaline turned her face from the house and headed for the lake than she heard footsteps crunching the frozen snow behind her. Expecting her follower to be no one more surprising than one of her sisters, or a housemaid bringing her a message from her mother, Emmaline turned and found herself once more face to face with the handsome, dashing Mr Aubrey, himself well wrapped up against the elements in a fur-collared winter coat with a brightly coloured woollen scarf tied loosely round his neck. Given how cold the morning, it was surprising to see that he was nevertheless hatless, his thick dark hair standing out against the winter landscape. To Emmaline this only added to his charm, since his fine head seemed to be glistening as fresh snowflakes fell on it, and his face too shone, making him look younger than he perhaps was.

'Miss Nesbitt? Forgive the intrusion.' As the dogs circled round them, barking, he went on, 'I would have sent a note, but there was no one available, given this sudden flurry of snow, to bring one out to you in time. So instead I came in person, which is probably what you did not want at all. Nothing worse than an uninvited visitor, particularly if you are on a walk, enjoying your own company, which I perfectly understand.'

Emmaline smiled. 'I am always happy to walk with someone else, I do assure you, Mr Aubrey.'

'I spoke to one of the maids, and she told me that you were out walking, so on I came, although I suspect she thought it a little forward of me to want to search you out, since we only met last night. She looked somewhat surprised.'

'That is probably because when a gentleman calls here we always assume he is calling on Papa, not us.'

'How very modest of you all. For myself, if someone calls on me I always think it is because they can't do without my company,' he told her gaily.

'One thing, Mr Aubrey, that my younger sisters are not, I do assure you, is modest. We cannot be the least bit shy, if only on account of our names. Our mother, perhaps feeling that she needed to make us stand out against the rest of Boston society, named us Emmaline, Charity, Ambrosia and Ethel. Now, do please say which one of my sisters you wish to call upon, and you will find in me a friend.'

'No, no, Miss Nesbitt, you are mistaken,' her companion told her earnestly, his expression becoming suddenly serious. 'Prior to my departure,

I wished to see *you* once more, not your sisters, however exotically named, I promise you.'

'You are leaving America already, Mr Aubrey? You are returning to England quite soon?' Emmaline asked, not yet willing to believe that this tall, handsome man with whom she had danced all of two dances could have the slightest interest in her.

'Yes, I am leaving America, and travelling back to Europe, Miss Nesbitt. First I must visit the Loire valley on business, then I shall return to England and set myself to tidying up some unfinished affairs in London, after which I shall, er, repair to, er – Somerset,' he told her, his smile widening, and an impish look in his eyes. 'Do you know Somerset, Miss Nesbitt?'

'Somerset? No, I don't think I know Somerset. Is that a state?'

'No, Somerset is what we call a county in England – our island is too small to have states. No, Somerset is a county. The county of Somerset, the place that the Romans christened the land of summer, where they built their villas and grew their vines, and daylight seems to last longer than anywhere else in the world.' He looked down at her with accomplished charm. 'It is indeed a wonderful place, as you may well imagine, for the Romans to have so christened it.'

'It sounds beautiful.'

'It is beautiful. It has every kind of landscape, and we who have lived there for generations believe there is nothing to match it. After the

Romans came King Arthur and his knights, and it is said that King Arthur's Avalon was near Glastonbury in Somerset.'

'The land of summer,' Emmaline repeated, staring ahead of her at some imagined Utopia filled with graceful villas where vines grew, bees hummed, and the countryside was green and fertile.

'It is a place where a man, and a woman, can be happy, I do assure you,' her companion insisted, giving Emmaline the kind of look that no man had ever given her before.

'A man and a woman, if they love each other, can be happy anywhere, or at least that is what I have always understood,' Emmaline told him.

'Indeed, you are right. A man and a woman can make a paradise out of very little, for that paradise is in their own minds, is it not?'

Emmaline found Mr Aubrey's look difficult to return. After all, they had only known each other for two dances, and a short walk. As she understood it, emotions . . . feelings . . . in particular those that led to a man's making a declaration to one, took longer than that to develop, could not mature in a moment or two. And yet . . .

'I have often wondered about the story of Adam and Eve, how it was that it all went so wrong, and why Eve was the reason that they were thrown from Paradise.'

'And you are right, Miss Nesbitt. Why, now I come to think of it, it is most unfair! Adam, if he had been any kind of gentleman, would have shouldered the blame. He would not let a lady take the full complement of God's wrath.'

Emmaline saw that he was amused by this fantasy that she had begun, and she continued on the theme with him, both of them finally agreeing that the first story in the Bible should be rewritten to show Adam in a better light.

'And it's hard on the snake too,' Aubrey continued. 'People have been hard on those gentle creatures ever since on account of that story.'

'Mary, our old nurse, who is now our maid, says that if you leave snakes alone they'll leave you alone, and I have never found any different. But then she is Irish, and there are no snakes in Ireland. She tells me Saint Patrick banished them.'

They laughed together, and then walked along in companionable silence, a silence which Emmaline finally broke.

'So when exactly is it that you sail, Mr Aubrey?' she asked.

'Early tomorrow morning, Miss Nesbitt. We sail from Boston on the flood, and let us only hope the return journey is considerably calmer than the outward one, where very few of the passengers ever saw the light of day – outside their cabins, that is. Gracious, the sea can be masterful, can it not?'

'I have never sailed the Atlantic,' Emmaline confessed, 'but I know from Mary that it can be as rough as anything.'

'It can indeed. And now I am being called to

brave it for a second time I have to tell you that I am feeling very cowardly. I wish you were coming on the journey to alleviate the tediousness. You have no idea how long a journey can be when everyone else is nowhere to be seen. Why, I didn't even have anyone to play cards with, or share a drink with. I spent the outward journey playing patience in my cabin and walking the deck like some poor spinster sent to America by her family to become a housekeeper!' He stopped, and began again, his voice light and persuasive. 'Miss Nesbitt, I have no wish to be forward, but I was wondering if you have the slightest curiosity as to why I should wish to see you again, after our dances together?'

Emmaline stared ahead of her. It was strange to be asked such a direct question, particularly since she had been brought up to consider direct questions discourteous. More than that, to answer a direct question from a gentleman, and a foreign gentleman at that, was not at all the thing. She frowned, still looking anywhere except at Mr Aubrey.

'I am sure you have your reasons, Mr Aubrey,' she finally replied with a nod, walking on one pace ahead of him, 'but as to what they might be, well, I am afraid I cannot guess. Yet I do realise that you must have your reasons.'

'Indeed I do have my reasons, as you call them, Miss Nesbitt, and they are fine ones, too, the most potent of them being a wish that I might see you once more, before setting sail. You yourself must be glad to see again someone who is so entranced with you, surely?'

'I see.' Emmaline could not help glancing quickly at him in order to gauge what his expression might be, and whether or not he was smiling, which he was.

'I wished most sincerely to see you again,' he repeated.

'That is very kind of you, Mr Aubrey, and indeed I am glad to see you before you set sail. Truly, I am glad.'

Her clear answer seemed to satisfy him.

'Thank you, Miss Nesbitt,' he said. 'You have made me more than a happy man, you have made me a gloriously happy man. But that is not the last of my reasons. I am here to tell you, now, if perhaps I might elaborate without causing you any—'

But further explanation was curtailed by the sound of a voice calling Emmaline. They turned to see one of the housemaids running as fast as she could in their direction from the house, skirts held to the side in one hand, while the other was on top of her head to prevent her cap from being blown away.

'Miss Emmaline! Miss Emmaline! Miss Emmaline, you're to come back to the house at once, please! You have to return to the house at once!'

'Forgive me.' Emmaline turned quickly to her companion. 'I am needed up at the house – my mother, you know. She suffers dreadfully from her nerves. Please forgive me. I will be back.'

As she hurried back towards the house in the company of the maid, Emmaline learned, as expected, that her valetudinarian mother had suffered another of her famous setbacks and was calling for her eldest daughter.

Another setback, Emmaline thought. *Mother always has a setback just when it matters. She always does. It is as if somehow, heaven only knows how, she knows that I am happy, and wishes to spoil it – as if she wants to punish me for Papa's being such a philanderer.*

Emmaline flung off her outdoor clothes, handing them to the maid, and hurried upstairs. She found her mother as always in her bedroom, her devoted if aged maid Jean in attendance. Jean was a woman who liked to make it clear that any and every setback her mistress suffered was entirely due to the indifference of her family, most particularly her eldest daughter.

Of course, as Emmaline and everyone else knew, it would inevitably turn out that there was nothing really wrong with Anthea Nesbitt, certainly nothing that poor Dr Hill could ascertain. But then, according to his patient, the good, kind and long-suffering doctor was useless, and when not useless, on holiday, and when not absent inept. No different from all the rest of the doctors, some of them specialists, that Onslow Nesbitt was always being asked to call in. Anthea Nesbitt had been ill ever since her marriage to Onslow, and possibly always would be, the reason being something to which no one in the household would ever dare to refer, although everyone knew that the faithful Jean guarded it jealously, administering the precious laudanum drops when she imagined no one else was around.

Mrs Nesbitt was not in fact in bed when Emmaline hurried into her room, but standing at the window overlooking the parkland. Emmaline realised immediately that her mother must have seen her walking with Mr Aubrey.

She turned as her eldest daughter came in, and smiled. It was a smile that Emmaline had seen all too often before. It was a smile that said, 'Ruined that for you, did I not?'

'Mother—'

'Emmaline, it is simply not suitable for you to be seen alone in the park with a gentleman, without your maid. Just not suitable.'

'Mother—'

'No, Emmaline – no. You may be desperate, we may all be desperate for you, but that is one way to become worse than an old maid. That is a way to get yourself a *reputation*.'

Emmaline's heart sank. She had left Mr Aubrey in such a hurry. He would surely not wait around for her. He would leave for England, and she would never see him again.

Chapter Two

The Atlantic Ocean was rougher than it had been in an age, according to all the experienced passengers, with winds so strong and seas so high that on the first day out from New York grab lines were put up in all the public rooms and the captain found himself forced to consider returning to the safety of the Hudson river rather than risk the lives of his passengers by continuing his journey.

By midday the gale had died down a little, sufficient for the captain to keep his ship headed east, but the momentary lull was followed by a full-scale blizzard that lasted all night and the following morning, coating the ship's decks with nearly a foot of snow, and keeping the seas rough enough for the next forty-eight hours to cause the great liner to pitch, roll, toss and shudder as violently as any of the crew could recall. Yet the seasoned captain stuck to his guns and continued on his course, his only concession being to change shipping lanes to find better waters before continuing to plough on through the still tempestuous seas.

Emmaline had never before left her home state of Massachusetts, her greatest distance of travel having been the hundred or so miles from where her family lived, on the edge of a small but prosperous town, to the great city of Boston. Now, however, she found herself crossing one of the largest oceans in the world on one of the greatest steamships in the world, RMS *Etruria*, the latest holder of the Blue Riband for the fastest Atlantic crossing, heading towards a country which her father had told her was smaller than most American states. Moreover, she was travelling alone, without even a maid, since none could be engaged in such a short space of time. Instead of a maid it had been suggested that Charity, the eldest of her younger sisters, should make the journey as her companion, but this only posed the problem of what was to be done with the girl on the return journey, since Charity too would be without a maid, and was two years younger than Emmaline. As a compromise it was decided to find a chaperon from the passenger manifest with the help of a reliable contact in the shipping offices, someone personally known to the family. Finally, a middle-aged New York widow was approached, and discovered to be only too happy to agree to act *in loco parentis* in return for joining Emmaline in a first-class cabin.

In the event her services were hardly needed,

since due to the violence of the crossing Emmaline spent most of her time in her cabin suffering from what her chaperon politely referred to as *mal de mer*, emerging for the first time only on the final day of the crossing when the sea subsided to a steady swell, allowing the great liner to regain its pomp and splendour and to steam all but undisturbed round the south coast of Ireland and on to Southampton, where she was due to dock mid-morning on the tide, the only time the waters of the port were able to accommodate such a vast ocean-going liner, and hardly more than seven days after the liner had been put astern and slowly edged out into the Hudson river by the cream of the shipping company's tug boats.

'As you know, my dear,' Mrs Winfield said to her charge as they sat in the train waiting for it to begin the journey to London, 'I am to accompany you only as far as the capital, where, as I understand it, you are to be met and escorted to your final resting place – I mean destination.'

'I sincerely hope that Bamford in Somerset is not going to be quite that, Mrs Winfield,' Emmaline smiled in return, happy to be on terra firma and not the violent, storm-tossed sea.

'Oh, I see!' Mrs Winfield laughed, putting one laced glove to her mouth. 'No, of course not. I meant the place that is to be your new home. Tell me, is it really so, what you told me over breakfast this morning? That you have only met this gallant gentleman once?'

'Twice, actually, Mrs Winfield. And yes, it does seem most unusual, I must agree.'

'I am not being critical, my dear,' her companion replied. 'Just somewhat . . . somewhat wondrous. Such things I thought only happened in novels – yet here we are, in real life, with such a story being shown to be true. Pretty American miss meets handsome Englishman at a dance – is quite swept off her feet – and the next thing she knows she is travelling to England to be wed! My – that such a thing should be true.'

'Yes, I know,' Emmaline agreed, not knowing quite what else to say. Instead, she looked out of the train window at the last of the passengers hurrying from the great liner sheds on the docks to board the waiting train, which from the sound of it was now working up a preparatory head of steam. 'It is all rather . . . rather unusual, I suppose.'

'I think it is *deeply* romantic,' Mrs Winfield sighed. 'My own fatal collision, as the Greeks so like to call the meeting of two souls, was considerably more mundane. We were both schoolteachers, in a small town near Conway, New Hampshire.'

'I am not very familiar with New Hampshire, Mrs Winfield.'

'No matter. I meant it only as a reference. But as I was saying, we both taught at the same school in a very small community, so small in fact that finally I was the only eligible young woman of suitable age really, and that was that.'

'I feel sure there is quite another side to the story. He had probably loved you for a very long time before he declared himself.'

'I do so wish,' Mrs Winfield sighed. 'But alas, until the day he died I would swear my husband did not even know the colour of my eyes.'

Mrs Winfield fell to silence, her hands clasped on her lap as she too turned to look out of her window, seeing not the scurry and hustle of the passengers but rather the day just over a year ago when she had buried her late husband, a white-bearded mathematician twenty-six years her senior.

'So,' she said, coming out of her reverie as the guard blew a shrill whistle. 'Off we go then, my dear, I to my valetudinarian sister in Greenwich, London, and you to your wonderful romance. And in case I fail to do so in the hustle and bustle of our arrival, I do wish you the very best luck in the world, and hope that you will enjoy a marriage as happy as the dreams from which it is so obviously spun.'

With the noise of the train's departure – the clanking of the coach couplings, the sudden vigorous exhalations of steam, the shouts of the officials, the slamming of the doors and yet more shrill whistling – conversation understandably ceased for a while, allowing Emmaline to sink into her own thoughts. The speed of events back home, the exhausting preparations for her sudden departure from the family, and finally the initial excitement and subsequent woes of her first sea journey, had left her little time for reflection until now.

It had, as everyone kept saying, been just like a dream – the ball, held on her twenty-fifth birthday, her fateful meeting with the handsome and debonair Julius Aubrey, his waiting for her after their walk in the park to tell her that she would be hearing from him as soon as he reached England; and six weeks later the extraordinary summons to her father's study, where she had been informed that Mr Aubrey had requested her hand in marriage and her father had been only too pleased to give his consent.

Emmaline had found herself briefly wondering why her father should be so pleased to give his consent when she herself had not even been consulted, but since her own feelings for Julius Aubrey were already apparent to her, and she was really very frightened of her powerful and influential father, she had not dared pose the question. Besides, the more she thought about the prospect of marrying a man of such elegance and urbanity, so blessed with good looks, the more absurd it seemed to her to question the proposal. After all, as everyone, most of all herself, was all too aware, Emmaline might be clever, but she was certainly no beauty. She might have a fine pair of green eyes and a slim figure, she might have a pretty enough mouth and a nose that was not over-large, but the whole put together was not so much beautiful as pleasing. She considered that her only real asset was her thick, dark brown hair, over which she took much trouble, brushing it and dressing it with as much care as the grooms in her father's stables bestowed on the Nesbitt horses.

Her unremarkable appearance was something that Emmaline had come to accept, telling herself, as she grew to maturity, that in place of looks she would just have to concentrate on cultivating beauty of character. Her sisters, on the other hand, were all beauties, and they knew it. The three younger Nesbitt sisters had only to look in the mirror to know that God had favoured them, because they were all as pretty as flowers.

'I cannot believe he *really* wants to marry you!' her second sister, Ambrosia, had kept saying, weeks earlier, as she followed Emmaline around their bedroom. 'I am sure it is some sort of practical joke that will end with you falling on your face. You will reach England and there will be no husband-to-be, no handsome Mr Aubrey, only an old man with nasty ways come to meet you in his place. After all, no one has ever been to his house, no one here knows him, he is not an American—'

'I do not think that a man of Mr Aubrey's standing would play such a practical joke, Ambrosia dear,' Emmaline had replied with as much conviction as she could muster, knowing that the wretched girl might well be right.

'Perhaps it is just a way for Mr Aubrey to become better acquainted with the family,'

Charity suggested. 'And once he does and once he grows bored with poor Emmaline—'

'Which he *very* soon will!' Ethel, the youngest of the four Nesbitt girls, exclaimed. 'How could any gentleman as dashing as Mr Aubrey not soon grow bored with our elderly sister?'

'Before he started dancing with Emmaline I am sure he only had eyes for me,' Charity continued blithely.

'And the only reason he was not dancing with any of us was because he knew all *our* cards were full!' Ethel laughed. 'Mine was full before I ever even set foot on the floor,' she added, smoothing down her dress.

'Mine too,' Ambrosia asserted. 'You were not the only one.'

'Well, that is neither here nor there,' Charity went on, staring at herself in a hand mirror, loving what she saw. 'Now, now, girls, we all know Mr Aubrey would rather have one of us, but Emmaline must marry, or *we* will all be left on the shelf, so we will *have* to let her marry Mr Aubrey!'

'I do declare Charity is right. But as soon as the dashing Mr Aubrey tires of Emmaline here, he will deny ever wishing to be married to her and instead he will send for one of us, I am sure,' Ambrosia announced.

The three sisters regarded each other un-smilingly. They knew that Emmaline must be married first, and yet the fact was that now the possibility of Emmaline's betrothal had actually become a reality, it posed the question of whether any of them would be able to find a husband. Not only that, but Charity would now have to be married before either of the other two could leave home. For once the mouths of the garrulous trio remained firmly shut, and only their eyes reflected their fears. The marriage market was such a lottery that even very pretty girls sometimes turned into sour old spinsters.

Emmaline turned away. She loved her younger sisters, as a good sister should, but now that she knew she would be leaving them – whatever happened after her journey to England – she knew that she would be forever grateful to Mr Aubrey for removing her from her home when she had quite given up all hope. She was only too aware that thanks to her mother's open despite for her eldest daughter, she had not really enjoyed any kind of life in the Nesbitt household, whether in Massachusetts or at their town house in New York. The truth was that in a prosperous family, with many servants, life held nothing for an unmarried young woman of twenty-five: so even if Mr Aubrey proved to be a cad or a bounder or even a bigamist – which she very well knew that he was not – Emmaline was quite certain that she would always be grateful to him for throwing her a lifeline. If it weren't for him she would not be journeying to a new life, but sitting at home waiting for her mother to ring for her, or sewing some useless welcome cushion for the coming baby of a happily married friend, or an evening purse for an elderly relative.

So, as she sat and considered her situation while the train drew well clear of the dockland station and gathered speed for London, Emmaline reckoned that with all things being equal – as her father was only too fond of saying – she most probably was facing no worse a prospect than she had faced back at home, and possibly a far, far better one. At the very least she would be getting married to a man with a flourishing business, whose personal and professional contacts were substantial. That at least was certain.

None the less, one thing concerned her, something about which she had been unable to seek advice before leaving the shores of her homeland, although it concerned so many young women with similar upbringings. While she was sure she could cope with the social side of marriage, however complicated the rules of class and behaviour in England might be, when it came to other aspects of intimacy she drew a complete blank. She could never ask her mother, and certainly not her father, what she knew she must learn about how to make a happy union, and she certainly could not ask any of her sisters, for they were just as ignorant as she was. True, the maids were often caught sniggering about the summary dismissal of one of their number, but the reason for the dismissal was never, ever disclosed to the Nesbitt sisters, despite the fact that hints were often given that nine months later the individual

41

concerned had been seen in the company of a baby, and, if she was lucky, its reluctant father.

When she eventually came back down to earth, and removed her gaze from the landscape beyond the window, Emmaline noticed that Mrs Winfield was staring at her. The moment Emmaline met her eye Mrs Winfield smiled, and at once looked away out of her window to study the countryside in her turn.

'That was the pretty village of Tintbury we have just passed through, my dear,' she said. 'And did you have a nice sleep? I find it very difficult to sleep on trains myself.'

'I wasn't really asleep, Mrs Winfield,' Emmaline replied. 'I was daydreaming, considering my situation, wondering about my future.'

'I find train journeys so very interesting,' her companion continued. 'And new train journeys particularly so. They allow you time to yourself while engaging your interest in new scenery, don't you think?'

Mrs Winfield gave a sudden and sad little sigh, which made Emmaline look away. It was as if the older woman was actually dreading the moment when she would reach her destination. Emmaline immediately felt an unusual sense of discomfort settling on her, and so with a polite excuse she produced a book from her handbag and began to read. She hoped that her travelling companion would take the hint and do the same, for not only was she disinclined to continue talking, she also needed some quiet in order to try to quell the strange fear she felt rising in her as the truth of her odd situation really began to dawn on her.

Happily, despite her recent assertion, Mrs Winfield fell fast asleep not ten minutes later and remained comatose until the train drew to a halt at the end of the line.

'My goodness,' she gasped as she was woken by the juddering of the braking train. 'Where are we? This must be – goodness, it can't be, surely? I must have dropped off for a moment—'

'I think we have reached the terminus, Mrs Winfield,' Emmaline replied, lowering the window to look out across the busy station. 'Yes indeed, we have reached Waterloo.'

'Waterloo? I really cannot believe it,' Mrs Winfield said, straightening her skirt and jacket before pinning her hat carefully back on her head. 'It must have been all that sea air, do you see. Do forgive me. I really never ever fall asleep on trains, Miss Nesbitt, truly I do not.'

'You have nothing to excuse yourself for, Mrs Winfield,' Emmaline assured her. 'I was quite tired myself and I too slept for a good deal of the journey.'

'I suppose this then is where we make our farewells,' Mrs Winfield said a little later as they stood under the large clock on the station concourse. 'You are quite sure someone is to meet you here? I think I must stand with you until I see—'

'I am quite sure, thank you, Mrs Winfield,' Emmaline said, thinking she saw a tall man in a black stovepipe hat with a white flower in the buttonhole of his overcoat coming towards her. 'And thank you for your companionship on this long journey. I am only sorry we could not spend more time together on board.'

'One thing I have always been blessed with, my dear,' Mrs Winfield said as she shook Emmaline's proffered hand, 'is good sea legs. I cannot imagine why, since there is no sea whatsoever in my family, but there it is. Now, the luggage? Where is that wretched fellow?'

On cue a porter arrived with a trolley bearing both the passengers' luggage, Mrs Winfield's steamer trunk and four large suitcases taking up most of the space, quite dwarfing Emmaline's small leather-strapped trunk and one medium-sized case.

'Miss Nesbitt?' the gentleman with the white flower in his lapel wondered, raising his tall hat. His expression showed no sign of having remarked on anything unusual. 'Henry Ralph at your service, miss – Mr Aubrey's works manager. Please leave all your luggage as it is and I shall see to it that it is taken to our carriage. I trust you had a good journey over?'

Once the niceties had been observed and final farewells exchanged with Mrs Winfield, Emmaline embarked on the third phase of what was turning into an exhausting journey, across London to Paddington under the protection of Mr Ralph.

*   *   *

In the privacy of a suite in a small hotel, two men were closeted in private conference, one standing by the window that looked out over gardens already blanketed in new snow, the other sitting behind a handsome partners' desk whose top was covered in fine black leather tooled in gold. There were papers in front of the man seated at the desk, papers which were being closely consulted even though practically every word and phrase was known to both the men present.

The one reading the documents rhythmically tapped the blunt end of his pen on the leather-topped desk while the man at the window slowly smoked an oval Turkish cigarette.

'I fail to understand the delay—'

'There is no delay,' the man at the desk replied slowly. 'I am simply checking that everything agreed is implemented by these documents.'

'I think you're simply delaying the moment, my dear fellow,' the one at the window sighed. 'You aren't going to fail me now, are you? Look on me as having done you a very good turn—'

'No, of course not,' came the weary response. 'How can I fail you now? If I fail you I fail everyone. No, no, what must be, must be.'

'It's all in order. You know that as well as I do. The beagles went over it with fine-tooth combs, as did you, as did I.'

'It is all in order, no question of that.' The man at the desk carefully cleaned the nib of his pen on a corner of blotting paper preparatory to signing. 'I think we may proceed to call a witness.' He rang a bell by the desk and sat back in his chair to wait for the summoned person to appear.

'Remind me when you intend to leave, will you?' he said, adjusting the immaculate white cuffs on his shirt. 'Is it still to be next week?'

'I sail for Australia next Friday, yes. By the end of next week I shall be out of your way for good, you will be pleased to hear. Finally out of your hair, think of that.'

'That it should come to this.' His companion shook his head, then looked up at the man still standing by the window and watched him as he lit a fresh cigarette. The smoker took no notice of the look, even though he could see from the reflection in the glass that he was being observed.

'It's all right, my dear fellow,' he said with a smile. 'I don't need reminding, and I don't need a lecture. I know what a bad boy I have been, and I know that without your help . . . But, my dear fellow, just think. You may well find that it turns out to be the best of all possible eventualities in this best of all possible worlds.'

They were interrupted by a knock on the door and the appearance of the hotel manager. The man at the desk thanked him for coming up and informed him that they needed him to witness their two signatures on the document that was lying ready on the desk. The manager nodded his assent, duly witnessing the signing.

'I trust everything is to your liking, gentlemen,' he said as he returned the pen.

'Perfectly satisfactory, thank you,' the man at

the window replied. 'And have them bring up a bottle of champagne, there's a good fellow.'

As the manager withdrew, the other man poured two large glasses of dry sherry from a heavy decanter standing on the sideboard and handed one of the glasses to his companion.

'So,' he said, taking up the other glass, having lit a cigarette from his own silver case. 'That, then, is that.'

'That then most certainly is that,' the other agreed. 'Or rather that then most certainly is the end of that bit of that. The rest of it – or that, depending entirely on how one sees it – the rest of it starts now. And with that in mind I drink to your good fortune, and your future happiness.'

'And I to your future in the Antipodes,' his companion replied. *'Bon voyage.'*

The other man smiled.

'Mm, quite. *Bon voyage* indeed.'

Chapter Three

The house was a painting of a winter landscape executed by a talented artist of some sensitivity. The air was as still as a summer day and the fresh fall of snow glistened under the January sunshine. Emmaline's carriage drove carefully up the long driveway, which was still being cleared by a small army of estate workers armed with shovels and brooms. Naturally the two coach horses were only allowed to walk, their feet clad in sacking to prevent snowballs from forming in their shoes and the wheels of the carriage studded with small spikes to prevent them from spinning or skidding.

From under her wrap of two heavy wool rugs Emmaline could not help but feel stirred at the sight of the ancient house and the fine parkland under its mantle of snow. The carriage passed by one of the great trees that lined the driveway, and as it did so a welt of snow slid from a thick branch, stripping off as quickly as an evening glove taken from a lady's arm by an impatient maid, while the horses walked slowly round the sweep to the front of the house and into the full beneficence of the sun, so that Emmaline found herself shielding her eyes against the brilliance of the reflected light.

From nowhere a servant, well muffled against the weather, appeared to open the carriage door with outstretched mittened hands. The end of a red nose was visible above his scarf, and a pair of half-shut dark eyes took due note of the slim and elegant young woman in her fur-trimmed velvet travelling clothes and fur muff, who was now being helped from the carriage by her travelling companion.

'Here we are, Miss Nesbitt,' Mr Ralph said, once he had got his charge safely to the ground. 'All in one piece, praise be. Still, be careful, mind – you might have come halfway round the world in a week but icy steps like these could still carry a person off.'

On his arm, Emmaline carefully climbed the flight of stone steps leading to the half-glassed double front doors, which were opened from within the moment she appeared before them. A man in liveried uniform bowed as they entered, then all but silently shut the doors. A vast fire of huge logs burned and crackled in the hallway grate, and yet the great house was so cold that any visitor would have had to stand very close to the blaze to feel any warmth. In spite of the comfort of her father's last gift to her – a thick fur cape to be thrown over her travelling clothes – Emmaline shivered as she stood in the echoing stone-flagged anteroom taking in the apparent vastness of the house, while Mr Ralph informed the butler of their identities.

'Miss Nesbitt and Mr Ralph,' she heard him say. 'For Mr Aubrey.'

Turning, Emmaline saw a look in the butler's eyes which she realised she was either too tired or too unversed to be able to read, although she was quite sure it was not a warm look of welcome. The grave-faced servant only made a half-bow before walking slowly across the hall and opening a polished wood door.

'If the young lady and your good self would like to wait in here, Mr Ralph,' the butler announced, 'I will try to locate Mr Aubrey and inform him of your arrival.'

Indicating to Emmaline that she should go before him, Mr Ralph followed her across the hall and into a book-lined morning room warmed by a coal fire burning in a small wrought-iron basket. Thankfully the room, being smaller, and of a more informal shape, was considerably warmer than the vast hallway, and Emmaline at once took herself to the fireside, where she sat as close to the burning coals as she safely could.

'I would have to say that when we first came inside, why, it was even colder than it was outside in the driveway,' Emmaline remarked with a smile. 'That hall is positively *arctic.*'

'Often the way with these great houses, Miss Nesbitt,' Mr Ralph replied. 'They are a mixed blessing indeed. Few owners of such places are much envied nowadays, I think you will find.'

Emmaline glanced up, for some reason finding herself slightly disconcerted by the remark yet not knowing quite why.

'It's a very – a very *fine* house, Mr Ralph.'

'Fine as maybe, Miss Nesbitt. But fine is as fine does when it actually comes to living in these places. They are inclined to make the visitor unwelcome. Now, if you will excuse me, I have to return to our offices – and given the prevailing conditions I should leave now if I am to be there before dark.'

'Of course. I quite understand, Mr Ralph,' Emmaline said, standing to make her farewell. 'Thank you for all your kindness.'

'It has been my great pleasure, Miss Nesbitt, I do assure you,' Mr Ralph replied, shaking her hand so carefully, it was as if he thought it might otherwise break. 'And please, please remember if you ever need any help or – or anything at all, for that matter – you must get in touch with yours truly. This is a strange and foreign country for someone like yourself, so if any help is needed, just let me know.'

'Help?' Emmaline frowned. 'Heavens, why might I need help, pray, Mr Ralph?'

'You never know, Miss Nesbitt,' Mr Ralph replied, after a moment. 'Strange town. Strange place. Strange country. You can always find me through the company offices.'

'Thank you again, Mr Ralph,' Emmaline said. 'You really have been most kind.'

When he had gone, Emmaline found she could not move from the fire, such was the cold elsewhere in the room. And she was more than a little curious about Mr Ralph's remarks regarding the great house. Was it as difficult and uncomfortable to live in as he had implied? If so, what would happen to her? After all, this was going to be her future home. Could living here in England really be as daunting as Mr Ralph had hinted? Cold certainly it might be, but also, surely, quite splendid?

She turned to look around the room in which she was standing, and became aware of large damp patches on one of the walls by a bookcase. Closer examination revealed a section of the wallpaper to be coming away, and when she went to look out over the snow-covered park she had to pull her coat about her against a freezing draught caused by the ill-fitting window, and quickly returned to the fire. It was now starting to sink, and Emmaline found herself searching the grate for wood or coal, anything to rekindle the flames. Finding nothing, she went out into the hallway hoping to discover a servant in attendance, but there was no one in view, and no sight of anyone down the long dark corridors that led off the anteroom. She went over to the great hall fireplace to see if any small logs might have been left there, but that too yielded no comfort, only vast cuts of wood designed for the larger fireplaces, so, pulling her fur cape even more tightly around her, Emmaline returned to the morning room to make the best of the dying coals.

One hour and twenty minutes later the door opened and a figure appeared, a tall elegant man with a head of thick dark hair, the unmistakable outline of her future husband.

'Mr Aubrey!' Emmaline said through chattering teeth, getting quickly to her feet. 'How much I have been looking forward to this!'

She hurried towards him, relief and happiness mingling in her chest as she realised that she remembered him perfectly. It was so long since they had seen each other that she had wondered whether, in fact, her recollection bore any resemblance to the reality, but now here he was, and he was just as handsome as ever.

For a moment he stood with his arms by his side, staring at her as if he had never seen her before, but then he smiled.

'Miss Nesbitt?' He stopped. 'Why, you are even prettier than I remembered,' he said shyly, and now he did take her by the arms and hold her from him.

'I am a great deal more purple and blue than when you last saw me, Mr Aubrey,' Emmaline laughed, her teeth still chattering.

'Forgive my being so dilatory in greeting you. Where is Ralph?' He looked round, perplexed. 'Has he gone already? That is too bad.' He shook his head. 'He knew there was something I had to finish, and he should have stayed with you while

I did so. I will give him a scolding when I see him tomorrow, leaving you alone like this. It is simply not the thing at all.'

'I confess I had all but given up hope of seeing another human being when the door opened, and there you were at last,' Emmaline admitted, as lightly as she could, because she could not deny feeling disappointment at the manner of her arrival. However, she quickly put it down to English ways, to which she must grow used.

'I see the fire has gone out, Miss Nesbitt. Please accept my apologies. The servants here are a slovenly lot, and it is hard to make them do anything without giving them a sovereign!'

'It most certainly has gone out, but I promise you I did not just sit here waiting for it to light again of its own accord. I went in search of someone, but I couldn't find anyone to help me—'

'That would not be uncommon. They all plunge down to the kitchens when the weather is bad, like mice in search of warmth.' Aubrey stood aside in the doorway. 'Please come with me. I shall find someone to show you to your room.'

'Oh,' Emmaline said, hesitating. 'Would it be possible to have some refreshment first? It has been something of a long journey – added to which the cold, as you observed, has been quite considerable.'

Aubrey consulted a fob watch which he pulled from his waistcoat and raised his eyebrows.

'I shall see what can be managed. But first I feel sure you would wish to be shown your room. After all, you have come a long way.'

Since it sounded a little more like an order than a suggestion, and since Emmaline was well used to being given orders by her parents, she dutifully followed her fiancé into the hall.

'This is a very large house,' she observed, as they clattered across the stone floor. There was still no servant in sight.

'It is, I am sorry to say, far too large and in a quite deplorable state,' came the even reply. 'The sensible thing would be to knock it down. Excuse me?'

A maid had come scurrying into the hall, blowing into her cupped hands in an attempt to keep them warm.

'Sir?'

'I wish you to show Miss Nesbitt to her room,' he said. 'In the East Wing. The Pink Room? At the end of the passageway.'

'I don't know, sir,' the maid replied, wiping the end of her nose on the back of her hand. 'I'm still new here. I keep getting lost, really I do, been lost all morning, really I have, I need a ball of string, really I do, just so's I can follow it, you know, there an' back, make everything much easier, and that's a fact.'

He opened a door at the side of the hall.

'Down this corridor to the end. Up the stairs. Down the landing on the right to the door at the end, where you will find another corridor. Down it, through the door, up the stairs in front of you, down to the end of the passageway – you will come to the Pink Room.'

'Yes, sir.'

'Miss Nesbitt,' he turned back to Emmaline, 'I shall do what I can to arrange some refreshment for you.'

'Thank you, Mr Aubrey,' Emmaline replied, and then lowered her voice. 'I wonder, given our circumstances, if it would be possible for you to call me by my Christian name?'

Her handsome husband-to-be looked at her without expression, but after obviously carefully considering her question he nodded.

'Very well.'

'And you wish me to call you . . . ?'

Again he regarded her silently for a while before replying.

'You may call me by my first name, despite the fact that we are not yet married, and it is not the way we behave in England. It is not the custom, but even so, you may call me, yes, you may call me . . .' He paused. 'You may call me Julius, but not in front of the servants, if you wouldn't mind, gives the wrong impression in front of the servants. First-naming in front of servants leads to all sorts of trouble.'

'Thank you.' Emmaline nodded. 'I would like that.'

'Yes, you may call me Julius, rather than Mr Aubrey, when we are alone.'

'Thank you, that will be so much nicer. And

you will call me Emmaline, not in front of the servants, if you would?'

The young maid looked away, trying to pretend that she wasn't listening, and Emmaline, realising this, smiled at her half apologetically, hoping that she hadn't been offended by her fiancé's observations.

'Now I will leave you. The girl will take you the rest of the way,' Julius announced, as if Emmaline was a guest rather than a young woman whom he had promised to marry.

As she and the poor little maid, whose name was Enid, became more and more lost in their efforts to find the East Wing, let alone the Pink Room, Emmaline kept wondering about the conversation she had just had with her fiancé. She had expected a warmer welcome, particularly given the tone of the note he had written on the eve of his departure, not to mention the letter he had sent her once the terms of their marriage had been agreed. Yet he had received her just now as if they had never met before – as if she were someone coming to him seeking employment rather than about to make a union for life. Had he perhaps changed his mind? Such things happened, she had read about them, hasty decisions regretted at a later date, confusions resulting from everyone's acting for the best and making things worse. Perhaps the reality of a young American girl arriving in his house without a maid, with nothing but a valise and a trunk, had been too much for him? Perhaps he felt disappointed in her appearance in some way? Perhaps seeing her again was a severe shock, instead of a delight?

But all such fevered thoughts were soon dismissed as they came at last to the end of a likely passageway.

'This must be the Pink Room, don't you think?' Emmaline asked.

Enid, blue-lipped, and hardly able to speak clearly for the cold, nodded, and for a moment the only sound they could hear in the silence of the old, damp house was the noise of their chattering teeth.

'I dare say it is, miss, given the instructions what was said to us, I dare say it is,' Enid replied at last, her breath making small circles in the freezing air.

Emmaline stared round at the walls bulging with damp, at the cracked plaster above them, at the grey-green film on the furniture, and for a full minute she was filled with unaccustomed despair. So this was the land of summer where the Romans built graceful villas, and grew vines, and the days were far longer than the nights?

'I see,' she said. 'Now I wonder if I might be shown the bathroom – and perhaps you might bring me a tray of something, with a hot drink?'

'Yes, miss. I'll do my best, really I will, but I am only new, and finding my way around is wuss than the maze in the garden, I tell you it is.'

The day was now turning fast to dusk and the wretched maid, having finished her short speech, had run off, perhaps to lose herself somewhere else in this unfriendly mansion, leaving Emmaline without so much as a bedstick, or matches with which to light it. Emmaline stared around her, realising that she was hungry, cold and thirsty and not a little frightened too. At last she found a candle, but no matches. Feeling more than a little faint, she took up the unlit candle and ventured cautiously out into the corridor in search of some form of illumination. At last a light appeared at the end of another corridor and she hurried forward, finding when she reached her destination, to her great relief, a pair of illuminated candle-powered wall brackets. Once she had lit her own candle it seemed to her she could hear voices. Her spirits rose as she walked quietly over to the banisters on the landing and looked down. Below her she saw a small group of servants standing by a half-open doorway, talking in low voices. They were also drinking, as a bottle of what was obviously alcohol was passed around between two young men and a group of housemaids, one of whom was the delighted Enid.

Emmaline was about to call down to them when something stopped her, some feeling that to do so would be wrong, would break up what was obviously an impromptu party. Instead she stepped back into the semi-darkness, at which point she suddenly became aware of someone standing immediately behind her.

'May I perhaps be of some assistance, madam?'

a deep, although definitely female, voice enquired, causing the startled Emmaline to turn quickly about, the sudden movement dislodging her candle from its holder. She found herself face to face with a tall, raven-haired woman dressed from head to toe in black, with a set of housekeeper's keys hanging from the belt around her waist.

'Permit me,' the woman said, after a moment, when it had become obvious that Emmaline was not going to pick up the fallen candle. She handed it back to Emmaline, who somewhat pointlessly replaced it in its holder. 'As I was saying, miss, could I perhaps be of some assistance?'

'And you are, please? My apologies, but I have only just arrived and no introductions have been effected.'

'Mrs O'Clee,' the housekeeper replied in a voice smoked by peat fires. 'You seem, if I might say so, a little off course.'

'I had no light in my room,' Emmaline explained. 'No fire either, as a matter of fact.'

'Now, that is a great and terrible pity, but could you not have called someone?'

'I would have done, had there been anyone to call. And since you ask whether there might be something you could do for me, I should be grateful for some refreshment. I have eaten nothing, nor drunk anything, since my arrival here.'

'Mr Aubrey has not told anyone to attend to your needs?' the housekeeper wondered, relighting Emmaline's candle. 'Then I shall see that something is sent up to your room.'

'And what time will dinner be served, please?'

Mrs O'Clee frowned. 'Dinner, you say?'

'That is correct, yes. I should like to know what time dinner is, and furthermore I should like my luggage sent up to my room, and finally I shall need a maid to help me change.'

'Forgive me, miss,' Mrs O'Clee replied after a moment. 'I was not aware you had been invited to dinner. If you would like to return to your room, I shall at once make the necessary arrangements.'

As quietly and mysteriously as she had arrived, the housekeeper vanished into the darkness, leaving Emmaline to find her way back to the Pink Room.

After several abortive attempts, she at last identified the correct corridor and finally her nominated bedroom, which was sadly unchanged, still dark and freezing cold. Thanks to now having a lit candle, whose life she had nursed most carefully on her trek back through the draughty passages and corridors, she managed to get the fire alight, and, after a quarter of an hour of attending to it with a small pair of bellows, was sufficiently hopeful to sit and warm herself by it, albeit still wearing her fur cape, fur hat and fur-lined gloves. Ten minutes later the fire was smoking so badly she was forced to open the window to the night air.

'Alas me no,' a tired voice said from the semi-darkness of the corridor. 'Who was fool enough to light that fire now?'

Peering into the smoke-filled gloom, Emmaline made out the figure of an elderly male servant bearing her luggage, followed by Enid carrying a tray with the rudiments of refreshments on it.

'Whoever did that should have known better,' the old man continued. 'That fire is not to be lit for this very reason. This fire is a known smoker.'

'I'm afraid that I lit it,' Emmaline replied, earning herself a look of undisguised reproach followed by much clucking of what sounded like very loose teeth. 'I fear had I not you would have come upon a human stalactite. Or do I perhaps mean a stalagmite?'

'You shouldn't have been given this room in the first place,' the servant said severely. 'Not that it's my place to say, but there you have it. It's beyond my fast disappearing memory to recall the last time anyone stayed in this room. So if I may suggest, miss, we put you in the room across the corridor from here, which is altogether more salubrious? Enid? About turn, girl, and follow after me.'

The ancient retainer led the way, stooped by the weight of Emmaline's luggage, her case in one hand and her trunk dragged along by the other, with Emmaline in second place followed by the maid bearing the tray. He showed Emmaline to a room which was indeed generally decorated in pink and in whose fireplace a healthy fire still burned. Having set the luggage down, the manservant placed some more coal and then a couple of small logs on the fire to stoke it up, drew the curtains, lit the rest of the candles and prepared to take his leave.

'Enid has some refreshment for you, miss, as requested, and she will also help you in your toilet,' he informed Emmaline from the doorway. 'Dinner will be served in thirty-three minutes precisely. Thank you, miss.'

'Thank you, um . . .'

'Roderick, miss. If you need anything more, at any time, Roderick will see to it for you.'

With half an hour to prepare Emmaline barely had time to eat more than half a fish-paste sandwich and a mouthful of seed cake while trying to instruct her appointed maid in helping her to dress for dinner.

'I should like to have changed my stays,' she said as she raised her arms ready for her evening gown to be slipped on, 'but I am afraid time is against us.'

'I carned reach,' the maid muttered in a thick and, to Emmaline, all but indecipherable accent. 'I carned possibly poot this on yer wi' yer arms all stook oop like thart.'

'Have you not dressed a lady before, Enid?' Emmaline wondered, still with her arms in the air.

'Nevaire the wonce, miss. Arm scull'ry.'

'Scull'ry?'

'Arm a scull'ry maid, miss. All at cud be spared at this time.'

Eyeing the girl, who stood possibly no more than four and a half feet tall, a diminutive figure now largely swathed in one of Emmaline's evening gowns, Emmaline shook her head and reflected on the chaotic organisation of this outwardly grand house. She remembered with deepening nostalgia how well-trained and skilled every member of her father's household was required to be. No one who stayed at any of the Nesbitt residences could fail to be impressed by the attendant domestic service as well as the high standard of the cuisine. Still, Emmaline sighed to herself, having instructed the maid to stand on a chair in order to gain the height necessary to lower her gown over her head, given her own domestic experience it would not be long before she managed to instil some sort of sense and order into this chaotic household. It certainly was in need of it.

By some miracle Emmaline arrived in thirty-four minutes precisely at the library doors, escorted by Roderick, and only seconds after a gong had been sounded in the great hall, summoning everyone to dinner. Not that it seemed to be a party of any size, Emmaline noted, as she followed the five people she imagined to be the last guests leaving the elegant book-lined room on their way to table. However, when she arrived in the enormous dining room, whose walls were heavily hung with dark wallpaper, it became clear that the total head count was only five, six including herself, a half-dozen that did not, for some strange reason, include Julius Aubrey, Esquire.

As she stood waiting to be assigned a place at the table, Emmaline took stock of the dinner party, which consisted of a short stout bucolic-looking elderly gentleman with a monocle, an extremely tall and thin woman wearing a considerable amount of diamond jewellery, two indifferently dressed middle-aged ladies with large feathers in their hair, and a Roman-nosed cleric with a large, over-red moist mouth and bushy eyebrows who for some reason was clutching a Bible closely to his chest. With no one paying her the slightest attention, Emmaline remained standing until everyone else was seated, whereupon she took one of the two remaining places, the monocled gentleman to her right and the Roman-nosed clergyman on her left. When everyone was finally seated the clergyman immediately arose, whereupon everyone else stood up again except for the monocled gentleman, who ignored the reverend guest, proceeding instead to tuck a highly starched table napkin under his chin and spread it carefully over his chest.

'Grace,' the vicar announced.

'Stuff and nonsense,' the monocled gentleman said, still attending to the set of his bib. Then he took hold of his soup spoon in his right hand and a fish fork in his left and held them in the vertical position, in the manner of a badly mannered child in the nursery, throughout the longest grace Emmaline thought she had ever heard. While she stood with her head suitably bowed she noticed a silver animal set at the top of her place bearing her name card. There was no name on the card, just a question mark.

'No soup! No fish! Just entrée!' the monocled gentleman bawled, still with spoon and fork at the ready. 'And wine, Wilkins! Wine, man! And at the double!'

It seemed little notice was taken of the outburst as butler and staff set about the business of slowly serving dinner, giving both soup and fish to the monocled gentleman, who ate both courses rapidly before attacking the entrée with the same spoon and fork he had raised in the first instance. During all this time no one made any conversation, simply following the example of the monocled gentleman and eating as much and as fast as they could. Despite feeling desperately hungry Emmaline only slowly followed suit, for the food was not just strange to her, it was unpleasant too, being less than hot and greasy with it.

Finally, after consuming his entrée, the monocled gentleman turned to stare at Emmaline in silence for a good while before shaking his head from side to side several times, as if being annoyed by a fly or a wasp.

'You are?' he shouted suddenly. 'You are? Who the devil are you? You are? You are?'

'I am Emmaline Nesbitt, sir, here at the invitation of Mr Aubrey.'

'The devil you are,' the gentleman retorted, his monocle dropping out of his eye. 'The devil she is!' he bellowed down the table at the gaunt, heavily bejewelled woman.

'I was wondering where Mr Aubrey might be, as it happens,' Emmaline ventured, beginning to ask herself quite where she had landed up. 'I have not seen him since my arrival.'

'Where he should be, of course,' the gentleman snapped, indicating to the butler for more wine for himself. 'At his work. Where he should be, of course.'

Dessert was taken in silence, and then the tall, gaunt woman nodded for a maid to pull back her chair and rose.

'Shall we?' she said generally, and led the ladies from the room, leaving the monocled gentleman and the Reverend to their port, which no doubt they would proceed to drink in silence, Emmaline reflected as she followed the others in their trailing faded gowns into the library.

'We have met before of course, have we not?' one of the two feathered ladies asked her.

'Of course we have,' her companion agreed, nodding at the gaunt lady.

'I think not, ladies,' Emmaline replied as politely as possible. 'After all, I have only just arrived—'

'At the Faynes', one would imagine,' the first lady said vaguely, patting her grey hair back into some sort of shape. 'It generally is.'

'Or it could have been the Cuthbertsons',' the second lady ventured. 'They do hold some excellent soirées.'

'Perhaps you failed to understand me,' Emmaline persisted. 'As I just said, I have only just arrived here.'

'No, no,' the first lady corrected her. 'I am absolutely sure we have met before.'

'Everyone one meets here one has met somewhere before,' the second lady insisted, nodding her feathered head at Emmaline. 'That is simply the way it goes.'

'This is my first time in England,' Emmaline tried.

'Charming,' the first lady remarked in a vague voice, beginning to drift away. 'I do so hope we shall meet again one of these fine days.'

'Goodnight,' the tall, gaunt lady suddenly said out of the blue, waving one dismissive hand. 'Goodnight, goodnight, goodnight, all and sundry.'

She rose and swept out of the library, her exit marred only by the fact that the attendant servant failed to get the doors open in time and had to raise and press a silver-buckled shoe against one of them while forcing the stuck one open. To show her displeasure at the delay, the gaunt lady cracked him on the back of his head with her folded fan before disappearing into the faintly illuminated depths of the house. She was followed almost at once by the other two, leaving Emmaline alone in the library, until the faithful if ancient Roderick appeared at the doors to give a significant nod to his charge.

'I wonder if you could help me?' Emmaline asked, as she followed him out of the room.

'If it is in my power to do so, then most certainly I shall, miss,' Roderick replied, lighting the way

68

up the creaking grand staircase with a hand-held candle.

'I was expecting to see Mr Aubrey at dinner, Mr Julius Aubrey, but he did not appear.'

'Ah.'

Roderick paused, not to consider the remark and provide a solution, but simply to allow Emmaline to pass through a door he was holding open.

'Beware,' he said. 'There is a step on the other side.'

'As I said,' Emmaline continued, following the servant down a long, dark corridor, her skirts whipped up by a sudden draught, 'I was expecting to see Mr Aubrey at dinner.'

'So I understand, miss,' Roderick agreed. 'From your previous remark.'

'Exactly,' Emmaline continued. 'So I was taken aback somewhat by his absence.'

'Indeed.' Roderick paused to open another door for them both to pass through. 'That is perfectly understandable.'

'Forgive me. What is?'

'Your concern at his absence, miss. Since you were expecting the very contrary. Your room, miss.'

Roderick held the door to Emmaline's bedroom open, waiting for her to enter.

'I wonder . . .' Emmaline began, looking into the dark room, 'I wonder if you would know the whereabouts of Mr Aubrey, Roderick? As also my maid, the very small maid who helped me dress? Enid, who helped me dress?'

'Alas no, miss,' Roderick replied, following Emmaline into the room and lighting two small bedside candles from the one in his hand. 'It is all but impossible to find even those whose location one assumes one knows in this house. People are rarely where you expect them to be. If that will be all?'

'Yes, thank you, Roderick. That will be all – except,' Emmaline said, raising her voice to prevent the servant from finally taking his leave, 'except if you do happen to learn of Mr Aubrey's whereabouts, I should be most grateful if you could either tell me or pass a message to Mr Aubrey to say I – to say I would very much like to see him.'

'Yes, miss,' Roderick replied, with a sigh and a shake of his head, before closing the door and going, leaving Emmaline alone.

Other than the servants, there was no one at breakfast when Emmaline came downstairs the following morning. Helping herself to some luke-warm over-scrambled eggs from under a cover, she sat down alone at the vast dining table and forced herself to eat. When she had finished and was rising to leave she suddenly caught sight of Julius hurrying past the open door. Still holding her napkin, she ran after him.

'Mr Aubrey?' she called down the corridor. 'Mr Aubrey? Julius? Mr Aubrey!'

In response to the final and loudest summons Julius stopped and turned to stare at her. Seeing

Emmaline he frowned and waited, tapping one foot on the floor until she caught him up.

'Something the matter, Miss Nesbitt?' he wondered. 'Because I am, as you see, somewhat busy.'

'Yes, something is the matter as it happens,' Emmaline replied calmly, which was not at all how she was feeling. 'I wonder if we might speak?'

'I am in rather a hurry, Miss Nesbitt.'

Emmaline looked round, and since there were no servants in sight she lowered her voice and said, 'Emmaline.'

'I am particularly busy.'

'It will not take long, Julius.' Emmaline opened the door to a room behind her. 'Perhaps we could talk in here.'

She waited, and Julius quickly followed her into a small sitting room where the curtains were still drawn.

'What exactly is troubling you, I wonder,' Julius asked in a suddenly concerned voice as Emmaline pulled the curtains back, letting in some wintry sunshine. 'Are you not comfortable?'

'No, I am not comfortable, Julius, but that is not my entire point, if I may say so,' Emmaline said, as Julius leaned down to light the fire with a long taper from the spills jar.

'It does not surprise me that you are not comfortable,' he said, still trying to light the fire. 'There is really very little that can be said in favour of this place, except that it is so uncomfortable that no guests linger here for long, which has to

71

be something of an asset, you must agree?'

'Where were you last evening, Julius?' Emmaline demanded. 'I came down to dinner with a room full of complete strangers, and I have to tell you distinctly odd strangers.' Julius stopped tending the fire for a moment and looked round at Emmaline, smiling slightly, before continuing with his task. 'First of all, when I arrived you were not here to greet me. I was left to shiver and all but freeze to death for simply an age, and then after – after we were reacquainted you vanished again, and for the entire evening I may say, the whole and entire evening.'

'My apologies, Miss Nesbitt – Emmaline,' Julius muttered with his back to her. 'I had a great deal to do. As a matter of fact, I was wondering, may I call you Emma from now on, when we are alone? I should like that very much.'

'Yes, of course,' Emmaline agreed, distracted for a second. 'But where was I? Oh, yes. As I was saying, Julius, I didn't even see you at dinner. You didn't even come down to dinner. Were you not feeling well?'

'I am perfectly sure I did not miss very much, did I?' Julius replied, standing back up now the fire was alight and admiring his handiwork. 'The food is execrable. And the company little better.'

'I was not even *introduced*, Julius. No one seemed to have an idea as to who I might be.'

'Personally I would not let that concern you, truly. To my mind they are all as mad as hawks, as Mrs O'Clee keeps observing.'

'Yes, you may well be right, but put yourself in my position. I had no idea who these people were. They were most unattractive, a most unattractive group of people, not the kind of people whose company I am accustomed to keeping, truly they weren't. Why, one of them even hit a servant with her fan!'

'If you have to know,' Julius said with a shrug, fixing her with a pair of bright blue eyes somehow made bluer by their dark, sad surroundings, 'your host and hostess are the Earl and Countess of Parham, the two older ladies are second cousins, and as for their friend the Reverend Archibald Welton, well, he is the dullest ditch I ever came across, and you will ever come across too, I hope. I am only sorry I was not there to introduce you, but frankly I couldn't stand another dinner in their company. I find them intolerable.'

'I don't understand, Julius,' Emmaline replied, puzzled. 'Why do you have these people here, if you don't like them?' She paused, frowning. 'Except you said these people – these people were the host and hostess?'

'Which is perfectly correct – that is most precisely what and who they are.'

'How can they be? Unless they were acting as such in – in your absence?'

Julius blinked as if quite unable to understand what Emmaline had just said, frowned, and then folded his hands behind his back, bending his tall frame forward towards her.

'You believe this to be *my* house?' he asked,

his eyes widening. 'You thought . . .' He paused to shake his head slowly. 'You thought this was where *I* lived. Where – where *we* were to live. You imagine I would live like this?'

'You seem affronted, Julius—'

'No, no, not in the least affronted, Emma. No, you misunderstand me, I am *horrified* that you should have been so mistaken.'

'There is no cause to be. It was a natural mistake. No one made me any the wiser, do you not see? Mr Ralph brought me here, and never once did he mention that this was not your residence. I was never told anything to the contrary, and even you, Julius – even when you and I were finally reacquainted—'

'Yes, *reacquainted*, we were reacquainted, yes.'

'You never explained to me that this was not your house,' Emmaline concluded. 'You simply abandoned me and – and disappeared.'

'I know, I realise now I was most remiss to abandon you in that way, but there is so much to do – there still is, alas – and the Parhams are full of the joys of spring, except when it comes to making decisions, at which point they chew the cud like so many beasts in the field.'

'Perhaps if you could explain to me what exactly this work is that you do here, Julius . . .'

'I am here to try to restore and redesign the interior of the entire house and to supervise the works. The plumbing is non-existent, the walls bulge with damp, and yet all must be made good within the year. It is an impossible task. And by the way, you might do well to remain in here until lunch time. At least you will keep warm, and there is quite an interesting small library for guests behind that glass that you might enjoy.'

Having indicated a glass-fronted bookcase Julius went, leaving Emmaline to examine the contents of the shelves. Most of the books seemed to concern the history of minor military regiments or extended journeys across obscure parts of the world, which could be of little interest to anyone except the most dedicated of travellers. Finally, and more or less out of desperation, she settled on *An History of the Peloponnese* because it was at least illustrated with some fine line drawings, but thanks to the dullness of the text and the warmth now generated by the fire in the little sitting room she was soon fast asleep, so fast asleep in fact that she missed hearing the gong for lunch and consequently the entire meal itself, which could only have been a blessing.

Having now identified the situation in which she found herself placed by Julius, Emmaline was discovered at last by Roderick, albeit a little too late for any lunch. With the old servant's help Emmaline once more went in search of her errant fiancé, whom they finally found in what her escort informed her was the State Drawing Room.

Julius was sitting looking handsome, elegant but disconsolate on the top of a small ladder surrounded by a sea of furniture covered with vast dust sheets. He was holding a palette of colours in one hand, and a cigarette in the other.

He took no notice of Emmaline when she arrived in tandem with Roderick, continuing to sit and smoke and stare, first at the wall in front of him and then down at the small palette in his hand, until Emmaline dismissed the manservant and walked over towards the ladder.

'Good afternoon, Emma,' Julius called down to her. 'I trust you enjoyed your morning, and all the rest of it? I apologise if I seem preoccupied but I am having a great deal of trouble mixing this particular colour. May we converse later, perhaps?'

'When might be a good time?' Emmaline wondered in return. 'If you could just tell me when you might be free.'

'I would imagine the answer to that would be never, would not you?'

Realising that silence and tact were her only possible weapons, Emmaline moved away from the ladder and looked around the vast apartment. She had thought the rooms in her own home were ample enough, yet never in her life had she seen a reception room as enormous as the one in which she was now standing, nor had she ever seen furniture so massive. Even under the dust sheets it was obvious that the two grand sofas lined up along one wall could seat ten or twelve people in a row, and the room itself could accommodate well over a hundred guests with ease. The salon was unutterably grand in conception, set with four enormous marble pillars that supported a domed roof decorated with a faded mural depicting the Creation, and its walls hung with immense formal portraits of crowned and robed men and heavily bejewelled women that from the way they had been framed appeared to have been painted directly on to the walls. Yet like every other room she had seen in the house it was in a bad state of repair, the paint peeling or in some places practically non-existent, the drapes badly frayed and moth-eaten, and the plaster cracked and broken, or at the very least discoloured.

'I certainly do not envy you your task, Julius,' she could not resist calling up to him after she had walked round and inspected the entire room. 'Where would a person start?'

'This is hardly a task,' Julius replied from on high. 'It could be more readily compared to one of the labours of Hercules.'

'Are you thinking of restoring the paintwork to the original colour, perhaps?'

'I might be, and there again I might not.'

'Might I perhaps make a suggestion?'

'And what might your suggestion be based on?'

'If you remember the ballroom, our ballroom at home?' As soon as she said 'home', Emmaline felt a stab of homesickness. 'The ballroom at home – yes – and how at one point you admired the colour with which the walls had been painted?'

For the first time since she had entered the room Emmaline found Julius looking down at her with some interest.

'I did, did I?' he asked, a little uncertainly.

'Yes,' Emmaline replied, made vaguely uncomfortable by the concentration in his gaze.

'If you say so, then it must be so,' Julius murmured, once again staring at his palette. 'The point being, your point being?'

'I chose that colour,' Emmaline informed him, careful to keep the pride out of her voice. 'We had the ballroom repainted only last year, and because I – well, because Papa thinks I have a good eye for colour, and because Mama was not happy with the previous selections, I ended up choosing the colour.'

'Now, let me see.' Julius now held up his palette as if to try out the shade he had in mind against the remains of the existing colour. 'Are you suggesting you might do the same here, with the same degree of success? Make a suggestion as to the correct colour?'

'Only if you would welcome such a suggestion, and were unable to decide yourself, Julius,' Emmaline replied. 'Or if you were in two minds about one shade or another.'

Julius shook his head, but said nothing. He continued to sit staring at the wall, and then at his palette, then back at the wall.

'Here!' he said suddenly after some minutes. 'Catch!'

Emmaline found the small wooden palette

flying down her way and just managed to catch it before it fell to the floor.

'None of those colours are right,' he said, sliding down the ladder to walk over to the fireplace, where, mercifully, a large log fire burned. He lit a fresh cigarette, blew some smoke upwards in a plume, watched it disperse, and then took another deep pull. 'And it has to be plain painted paper – anything else would be completely wrong. We need a clean, firm line. Patterned paper would just be so entirely wrong in a room this size.'

'What do you mean?' Emmaline asked, looking at the palette. 'When you say a clean line, do you perhaps mean to lighten the colour, and make the room somewhat less – less daunting? Because if so I think you may be right. The room does need warming up.'

'The whole place needs warming up,' Julius interrupted from the fireplace, his back to her. 'I have never been in such a cold, unwelcoming house.'

'Then blue – all of these blues – you are quite right to reject them. Blue is such a cold colour for a room, particularly a room this size.' She knew Julius was looking at her now, but she refused to meet his eye. 'Perhaps what the room needs is a warmer paint altogether – may I?'

She was standing by a worktable where Julius had placed his pots and brushes among samples of various papers and fabrics, and she gestured to it as if seeking permission to try mixing up some colours.

'What?' he asked with a look of disbelief. 'You want to—'

'It's all right, Julius,' Emmaline assured him, interrupting him deliberately to stem any immediate objection. 'I won't make a mess.'

'Oh.' Seemingly at a loss for words, Julius hesitated. 'Oh, very well,' he muttered, returning to the fireplace, where he lit another cigarette. '*Very* well.'

When she had finished preparing her mixes Emmaline put samples of those she considered the most suitable on a clean wooden palette and took them over to Julius, who now sat stretched out in a large dust-sheeted chair.

'They're only suggestions, but they might be something to work on,' she said, offering Julius the palette. 'This kind of peachy mix has warmth.'

Julius stared at the samples in the silence which seemed habitual to him when working, yet Emmaline noticed that he kept hold of the palette, not discarding it or consigning it to the fire as Emmaline had half expected him to do, just tapping it slowly on one knee as he continued to consider her work.

'This is what you would choose?' He stared around. 'I see. In that case, you should know how to achieve this effect.' He smiled at her suddenly. 'Which of course you don't, because the light in your ballroom at home was quite different from the light here. If we applied this colour to these walls, because of the way the light plays you would find that it would come out a baby pink, not an apricot. To achieve your colour,' he leaned forward and pointed, 'we will have to use *this* one.'

Emmaline stared first at his choice of colour, and then at him.

'But – but that looks brown.'

'Precisely. Until we put it up on the walls, when the light will turn it into a beautiful apricot. You will see. But first we must apply two coats of white distemper, and then probably two or three coats of this brown, and go on building on and on until this lovely colour you have chosen is reached.'

'I can't quite believe this—'

'No, of course you can't, because you have not studied the light in here. But you are right – it will be a lovely colour on which to work.'

Emmaline spun round, half pleased that he had approved her choice and half disbelieving that he was right about the method that must be used to achieve it.

She turned back. 'There is something else that I wanted to ask you, if you don't mind?'

'Of course. Please ask me anything you wish.'

'You seem very different from the person I met in America. Is it because I – well, is it because I disappointed you, once I was here? Because if this is so I will quite understand.'

Julius stared at her, astounded.

'Disappointed? Gracious, no, and I am only sorry that I could have in some way given you that idea.'

'I was wondering whether or not you might wish to discuss the reasons – the reasons for my being here at all,' Emmaline replied, staring at the top of Julius's head of luxuriant hair. 'In England, in my being in England, here.'

'Well, I thought it might be obvious,' Julius said, looking away. 'It is because I was so taken by you that I—'

'I am here at your express invitation,' Emmaline persisted, clasping her hands tightly in front of her. 'To fulfil a specific wish. Perhaps proposal might be better.'

'There is no need to be too frank – an understanding is what we have, I will agree. An understanding of a certain nature.'

'Julius,' Emmaline went on, taking her courage now firmly in both hands. 'We are engaged to be married.'

'That is a fact I had not forgotten, Miss Nesbitt.'

'Until such a time as we are duly married, *Mr Aubrey*,' Emmaline said quietly, 'I need to know where and how I am to live. I trust I shall not be expected to spend the rest of my days here, as that would not be in the least satisfactory.'

'I see.' Julius raised his eyebrows, then sat back in his chair. 'As it happens I shall be returning to my house shortly, once I have finalised my intended designs for this place and had them approved, and when I do you can rest assured you will be provided with suitable accommodation locally until – until you take up residence at Park House – with me. Now, if that will be all?'

'I should be grateful for a little more detail, Mr Aubrey.'

'Perhaps, but that is all the information and *detail* that you require.'

'I need a personal maid, Mr Aubrey.'

'You will have everything you want when we return to Bamford, Miss Nesbitt.'

'But until that time, sir—'

'Until that time, madam,' Julius told her, looking at her with sudden sympathy, 'I suggest you try to manage. If you must know, I intend to leave here in the morning. And now I should continue with my endeavours. Thank you.'

'Very well, Mr Aubrey,' Emmaline replied, as she saw the far door opening and a servant hovering. 'Thank you. Perhaps I shall see you at dinner tonight with all the other strangers?'

'Perhaps you will,' Julius agreed, but then he smiled suddenly, and leaning down he touched her cheek with a suddenly tender hand. 'Perhaps you will, *Emma.*'

Chapter Four

She had always wondered about the beautiful little hand mirror he had made her a gift of, which Emmaline had appreciated not just for its delicate inlay and the warmth that the old silver-backed glass gave to her image in it, but also for the note that had come with it, written in a sloping artistic hand.

You are infinitely more beautiful than you think yourself to be. JA.

After another distinctly uncomfortable evening in the company of the same unpleasant group, although this time with Julius among their number, Emmaline remembered the note with gratitude as she sat alone in the carriage the following morning on her way to her new life in Bamford. She straightened her change of travelling clothes. The pale grey paletot, the yellow-lined sash of her travelling coat, and the hat with the mixed feathers, had given her the confidence to realise that she could look stylish, that she was not just a drab female from across the Atlantic. She was the future Mrs Julius Aubrey, and never would she allow herself to look as the company at dinner the previous evening had looked, eccentric and strange, worn and careless.

Nevertheless, despite the fact that she had formed a resolve not to accept without reservation whatever was given to her, now she was finally travelling towards her new home she fell back to wondering where she had actually landed herself.

The more she thought about it the more she became convinced that Julius's odd behaviour over the previous days was due to the magnitude of the task he had undertaken at Hartley Abbey, on behalf of his business. It had to be this that had made him seem so aloof, when in fact he was obviously merely preoccupied. She imagined the responsibility and weight of the work was distressing in the extreme, with the result that he was unable to concentrate on his own life and the fact that he had promised to marry her. There could be no other explanation for his erratic behaviour, for his seeming neglect, for a more different man from the one she had danced with that first night could not, surely, be found. Once she had accepted this idea she found she could relax a little, and she tried to enjoy her carriage ride through the quiet countryside. The sky, she noticed, was a soft mix of blue and grey – a mix that someone like Julius would do well to emulate. Everything was so small compared to America, as if England had been shrunk by some unseen process. She tried to imagine the Romans in their chariots coming out to their villas, making their way along the long straight roads they had so stylishly hewed – the very roads along which her own carriage was now travelling. She tried to imagine the sound of the horses' harnesses clinking, the sight of the morning sunlight catching the tops of the Romans' helmets, their eyes perhaps watching out for the fierce island people whose land they had invaded, who they knew might still be waiting in the forests to attack them.

The beauty of the scene, however, proved to be ephemeral, for she had hardly begun her long journey when the sun came out and a thaw started to set in, turning the countryside that had only an hour before been so picturesquely whitened into a damp and saddened sight, so that all too soon the view on either side of the carriage was only of dripping hedgerows and flooding roads. With this turn in the weather, Emmaline's previously buoyed-up spirits started to sink. Supposing, despite his attempts to reassure her, Julius's house was as damp and unwelcoming as the house that she had just left behind? The all too possible prospect did little to raise the morale of the young woman whose driver was even now being forced to slow his two horses down to a walk in order to try to negotiate the increasingly bad conditions.

Eventually, after what seemed like days, not just hours, Emmaline arrived safely at her destination late in the afternoon. The light had already begun to fade and the lamplighter was at work on streets ankle-deep in melted snow, where passers-by picked their way through the lumps of half-frozen slush that lay on the pavements while trying to avoid the mire thrown up by the passing traffic. From what Emmaline could see from the window of her carriage the part of town they were passing through had some fine stone-built houses, albeit lining steep streets, but of course they seemed too close to each other and surprisingly narrow after her own home town with its broad and generous thoroughfares.

She peered out into the increasing gloom as her carriage slowed at a road junction, and her eye was caught by a large sign above what was obviously a works entrance. Immediately above the main doorway, lit by a large lamp, she could make out the words *Julius Aubrey Ltd*. It seemed the board had been newly painted, for a sign writer was just descending his ladder, while the smaller plate at eye level in contradiction read *Aubrey & Aubrey Ltd*.

Staring at the signs, Emmaline called to the driver to stop. Had there been a death in Julius's family? He had not worn any sign of mourning, no black band, nothing to denote the death of a close relative.

'Carry on, driver, thank you!'

Shortly afterwards, the carriage stopped in a quiet street and the driver jumped down from his box to help Emmaline alight. As she stood with her skirts gathered up in her hands to protect them from the puddles formed by the thaw the driver knocked at the door of the building outside which he had drawn up his horses, and moments later Emmaline found herself inside a warm and welcoming lodging house, where fires were lit in every visible room, heavy curtains hung closed at the windows to keep out draughts, and gas lamps burned brightly everywhere.

The woman who showed Emmaline into the drawing room and served her with tea and cakes introduced herself as her landlady, Mrs Shannon.

'I understand that you have entered into an arrangement with Mr Julius Aubrey, a gentleman to whom I am enormously grateful, since he has promised me more business in light of his plans. People will be coming here to see him concerning their homes, to inspect materials and suchlike. Bamford should be most grateful for him, for I understand from his manager Mr Ralph that many of the fine fabrics which were formerly made in Lyons will now be made up here, and will be used by Mr Julius Aubrey in his work, travelling as he does all over England, helping in the restoration of many fine houses.'

'Yes, I understand that Mr Aubrey is more than brilliant at his line of work. He is even now restoring Hartley Abbey for Lord and Lady Parham.'

'I would think that would be a task that will take until kingdom come.' Mrs Shannon laughed. 'The Parhams have not been noted for anything except eccentricity for many a century, although they are held in great respect, I believe.'

She stopped talking suddenly, and leaning forward she touched Emmaline lightly on the arm.

'Are you feeling all right, my dear? You look a little pale.'

'I am in perfect health, thank you,' Emmaline told her even as a sudden wave of such homesickness swept over her as to make her feel almost faint. 'Perfect health,' she repeated, thinking that never had her mother, or her sisters, or Mary, or anyone back home, seemed more dear or more distant.

'You are looking a little peaky after your journey, Miss Nesbitt, if you don't mind me saying. I would say that you need a little bit of Mrs Shannon's best looking-after comforts, really you do.' Mrs Shannon leaned forward once more, and this time put a still motherly but more insistent hand on Emmaline's arm. 'Do not fret yourself at all, young lady. You will soon find your land legs in Bamford, really you will. My father was a seagoing sailor, never liked being on land, but even he found his land legs when he settled here. The town is steeply built, that I will grant you, and there is much to be done for the poorer section lower down by the river, but it is a pretty place, most of it built in the early eighteenth century when folk knew how to build elegant houses, not these grand places with every high-falutin' inconvenience possible. No, the folk in the last century knew what was what. No grandeur, no splendour, just an elegant sufficiency.'

'And Mr Aubrey's own house?' Emmaline enquired, as she accepted another slice of her landlady's delicious sponge cake, more to please her than because she felt in the least bit hungry.

'Of course, you'll not have seen that yet,' Mrs Shannon replied, 'this being your very first visit. It's in Park Walk, the very best of the avenues in Bamford. There are some exceedingly fine houses there, Miss Nesbitt, Mr Aubrey's being perhaps the most notable. But no doubt you'll be seeing it for yourself tomorrow, when Mr Aubrey calls on you here. I should imagine the very first place he'll be taking you to will be your future home, and about time too, I expect you will be feeling by then!'

In fact, true to form, Julius did not put in an appearance the following day, nor indeed the day after, finally showing his face after dinner on the Saturday evening. During the intervening period, however, on the advice of the good Mrs Shannon, Emmaline made splendid use of his lack of attention by walking about Bamford and getting to appreciate the feel of it, before returning to the comfort of Mrs Shannon's lodging house, not to mention her splendid home cooking.

'It is the way of men, you know, dear,' Mrs Shannon told her at one point. 'Before they marry they can't see any reason to think of the feelings of others, let alone the girl they are to wed. Mr Shannon did at least turn up at the church, but I always think my father had something to do with that.' She gave a rich laugh. 'There's nothing like having a father who is a gunsmith to get a man to the church on time!'

At last there was Julius, looking tall and handsome, and beautifully dressed, reminding Emmaline exactly why she had consented to come to England to marry him. And yet, divine-looking though he might be, and fine though his manners undoubtedly were, nevertheless, deep down inside, she could not help feeling bewildered.

'Was there no way of getting word to me that you had perhaps been delayed?' Emmaline quietly enquired when they sat on either side of the fire in Mrs Shannon's drawing room after Julius's unannounced arrival, with Mrs Shannon placed discreetly at a table in the bay of the window playing a hand of cards with another of her guests. 'It really is so strange not to know from one moment to the next what I may or may not be doing.'

'Is that so? I am most apologetic,' Julius replied, staring at the toes of his highly polished shoes. 'Does this place not suit you, Emma?'

'It suits me admirably, truly it does. But its suitability has nothing to do with your manners, Julius.' Emmaline looked round discreetly to make sure her landlady was not visibly eavesdropping. 'This is a very comfortable establishment and I am more than perfectly suited here, thank you.'

'Then what is the cause of your unease, I wonder?'

'The cause of my unease is that I am seemingly without purpose, Julius. As far as I can see I could well be sitting here waiting for you to arrive or not to arrive indefinitely, until the end of the world, until God himself appears on a cloud.'

'I see.' Julius nodded, tightened his mouth and breathed in slowly and deeply, before rising from his chair. 'Perhaps your mind may become easier tomorrow when we attend church and the banns are read. I shall be here to collect you in plenty of time, have no fear. So until then, Emma, I bid you farewell.'

He leaned forward to take her hand and shake it, but then, with a quick look at the window, he raised his fingers and once again touched her cheek, a look of sudden longing coming into his eyes.

They walked to the church in company with what appeared to Emmaline to be the entire population of the town, all dressed in their Sunday best. On arrival, Julius and Emmaline were shown to the Aubrey family pew, one of a select number of box pews set to one side of the nave at right angles to the rest of the congregation, who were taking their places under the supervision of the churchwardens. Every seat in the large building was filled, the overspill having to stand at the back. To Emmaline's surprise, and somewhat to her dismay, Matins was celebrated by the Reverend Archibald Welton, who, it transpired, had been invited to Hartley Abbey by the

Earl and Countess of Parham in the mistaken belief that, coming from the same town, Julius must find their old friend as congenial as they did. Emmaline noticed that he adopted a completely different voice from the one he had used – albeit sparingly – over dinner at Hartley Abbey, conducting the service in a slow, high, monotonous quaver, a tone he sustained from start to finish of the service, including a twenty-five-minute sermon on the proper meaning and understanding of the Trinity. Emmaline did her best to follow the service, but due perhaps to the curious intonation of the rector she found it more than difficult, and of course her feelings of piety were somewhat distracted by Julius, who sat quietly sketching the church pillars in a small pocket book held low in the pew.

'I hope you heard more than I did,' he said cheerfully as they walked away from the church with the rest of the congregation, having shaken the hand of the rector as they left the building.

'And I only hope, Julius, that you did not attract any attention to yourself,' Emmaline told him in a low voice. 'I am quite sure that you did, however, and now everyone will think that the banns, the reading of our banns, that is, is about as important to you as the poor rector's sermon.'

'Forgive me, Emma, but I have been subjected to that wretched man's interminable homilies for longer than I care to remember. I attend morning service regularly, I give money to the church, I have – I hope now to have done well by requesting that our banns of marriage be read in that same church, but having done all that there is nothing to say, absolutely nothing to say, either in the ten commandments or anywhere else, that I may not sketch those columns. After all, the church was built to the greater glory of God, was it not?'

'It must indeed have been since it is so beautiful, but you must know that to my ears it sounded as if Mr Welton might have muddled me up with someone else, so you may well be about to be married to quite a different lady.' She laughed with sudden gaiety as Julius stared at her.

'How do you mean?'

'Only that it sounded as if he might have got my name wrong. Rather than Nesbitt it sounded as if he called me *Norbutt* – but at least he did get *your* name right, at least I think he did. I was so nervous that someone would stand up and object to the marriage that I hardly heard anything more than my own mispronounced name.'

'I would not put it past the Reverend Archibald for one moment,' Julius sighed, accelerating the pace of his walk as they turned away from the centre of town. 'One year he preached an Easter sermon on Christmas Day, talking of crucifixion and death and rising from the dead rather than the birth in the stable and the ox and the ass. This upset a large number of the more sensitive members of the congregation, those who had the misfortune to still be awake, that is, so much that they refused to make any Christmas offerings.'

Emmaline started to laugh at this, but then, unsure whether Julius was fully intending to be comical, she settled for smiling instead. As they walked on she took the opportunity to look around with growing appreciation. It was a fine sunny morning, and they were walking through the town in which she was hoping to start building a life, a life that she hoped would be like that of every other well-dressed, happy-seeming couple they passed.

Now and then gentlemen known to Julius would doff their hats as they walked by, Julius acknowledging their salutes with a brief wave of his ebony walking stick rather than a touch of his own hat, although to several of the more beautiful women who passed them by he raised his top hat most elegantly.

'We shall be eating luncheon at my house,' Julius announced as Emmaline hurried along beside him, doing her best to keep up with his long, loping stride. 'Did I say earlier that we would be taking luncheon at Park House?'

'No, you did not, Julius,' Emmaline told him breathlessly as she at last managed to draw alongside. 'But no matter. Except of course I should like to have mentioned it to Mrs Shannon. It would only have been polite.'

'No need to concern yourself there,' Julius said, suddenly twirling his cane expertly round his fingers like the leader of a military band. 'I mentioned it to her when I was waiting for you.'

'But not to *me*. You did not think to mention

it to me,' Emmaline replied, careful to adopt a politely cold tone.

'Did I not?' Julius looked vaguely guilty. 'Never mind. Mrs Shannon is the one concerned with numbers. And by the by, may I say that you have a great sense of elegance in your dress, which is very pleasing.'

Just as Emmaline had begun to feel out of sorts again at Julius's lack of manners, just as the memory of his drawing the interior of the church rather than attending to the service and in particular the reading of the banns was coming back to her, his suddenly appreciative words allowed a little sunlight to enter her soul.

As for Julius, his latest remark seemed to cheer him up too, for he strode ahead twirling his cane in one hand and once again doffing his hat to each pretty young woman who passed him smilingly by.

Park House was built well back from the roadway to the front, set behind a high stone wall hung with a pair of fine wrought-iron gates. Passing through them and past a small gatehouse, visitors found themselves faced with a short but impressive driveway, particularly for a town house, a broad stretch of gravel lined with mature chestnut trees and flanked by cultivated lawns enclosed with traditional park fencing.

There was a curved carriage sweep in front of the house which enhanced its graceful proportions, emphasising its gentle air of domestic history. The house itself was built of mellowed stone on three floors, the façade greatly enlightened by the fitting of large sash windows that on the lower floor reached to within a few inches of the ground. Above the fine doorway was a lead-roofed portico supported by un-decorated pillars, while the slate-tiled roof was fixed with generous eaves projecting two feet or more, giving the house an elevation that was both handsome and balanced. Emmaline approved of it at once. Different though it was from the large houses of her home town, it nevertheless appealed to her untutored eye as being the very epitome of an English gentleman's residence. To add to its air of quiet elegance, the house was surrounded by beautiful gardens, gently sloping lawns to the front and flower beds to the side.

Stepping inside, Emmaline found more domestic perfection. From the moment she walked into the hall with its simple flagstoned floor and marble bust on a plinth, its vast glass vase of winter leaves and hothouse flowers, she realised that she was in the presence of carefully designed and quite exquisite taste, neither over-furnished nor over-ornate. The rooms, she sensed at once, would be set with elegant furniture, the whole decorated with light colours and pale silk wallpapers. And so it proved to be.

As she entered the double drawing room Emmaline observed not just beautifully placed delicate pieces of furniture inlaid with pale honey-coloured woods, not just a careful use of damask and other fabrics, but walls hung with paintings of landscapes rich in colour, some painted as though seen through a gauze and some with bold thick applications of oils, full of movement, light and warmth. And, too, she observed other smaller paintings that she imagined must be from a completely different school, landscapes more sombre in colour depicting rural scenes with windmills and canals, peasant women in white pointed bonnets and barges with large flaxen-looking sails, and interiors with their subjects formally posed and dressed in clothes of luxurious textures in which it was apparent the artists had gloried. Used to the sorts of paintings that were hung in neighbours' houses back home, most typically ancestral portraits of illustrious forebears, or illustrations of epic battles fought and won in the War of Independence, Emmaline was quietly astounded by the vibrancy and originality of the paintings she saw as she was led from room to room by Julius, who seemed to be suddenly at his ease, pointing out to her his particular favourites among the objects that met her gaze.

She also admired the elegance of the actual furnishings of the room, the way that the drapes had been arranged at the windows, the disposition of the sofas and chairs, everything adding up to an elegant whole totally lacking in any feeling of pomposity or anxiety to show off the wealth or importance of the owner of the house. Nor was it fashionably overcrowded, no chimneypieces covered in heavily fringed cloths or vastly ornate swags.

'So,' Julius said, drawing to a halt in front of a fine fireplace in which was burning an equally fine fire. 'I think, now we have recovered from church, we may indulge in a glass of sherry before we go in to luncheon. We shall be eating promptly at one of the clock, because my cook, unlike that of Lord and Lady Parham, is most exacting.'

'This is a most beautiful house, Julius,' Emmaline remarked, coming to stand beside him and looking around the lovely light-filled room. 'It is really very fine indeed. And what beautiful paintings you have collected. You have the most exquisite taste.'

'In the main they are French and Dutch,' Julius said with a suddenly shy look at her. 'Now, before luncheon I like a particularly good medium dry wine, unless of course you prefer something sweet?'

'The medium dry will suit me perfectly, thank you.' Emmaline smiled happily at the maid who had advanced into the room to offer her a glass on a silver tray. 'Is there a painting missing here by any chance?' she went on, noticing a blank on the wall to one side of the display case where to judge from the marks on the silk wallpaper a painting must once have been hung. 'Is it perhaps being cleaned? My father is always having some of the older paintings cleaned, and then they return *too* clean, Mother says.'

Julius looked briefly at the marks on the wall, and then walked over to a table where some drink decanters stood, still followed by the obedient maid with the tray.

'It is away,' he replied, after a short silence. 'It is away. Now, it is surely time for you to meet the servants. This is Dolly.' He raised his voice a little as if Dolly might be foreign and not understand him. 'This is my fiancée Miss Nesbitt, soon to become Mrs Aubrey, after which event you will be answerable to her for everything and anything she wants.'

He pressed a bell set by the fireplace and strolled to the French windows to stare out over his gardens, leaving Emmaline to drink her sherry by the fireplace. Only a moment later, as if they had all been waiting for their cue, there was a knock on the door and a line of servants entered, variously attired.

'Introduce everyone to Miss Nesbitt, Wilkinson,' Julius commanded. 'Miss Nesbitt who is soon to be Mrs Aubrey.'

'As indeed we understand, sir,' the man Emmaline took to be Julius's butler replied, stepping forward. 'May I say on behalf of the household how much we are looking forward to welcoming you here, madam, and to serving you as mistress of Park House.' Wilkinson half bowed to Emmaline before introducing each of the servants to her. 'Mrs Graham, our housekeeper, Mrs Field, our cook, Alan, footman, George, under footman, Helen and Dolly, housemaids, and young Agnes here from the works, who I understand is to be your personal maid from now on.'

'Mrs Graham, Mrs Field, Alan, and George,' Emmaline repeated, marrying names and faces and locking them into her memory, and nodding as she did so to each individual. 'Helen, Dolly, and Agnes. Thank you, Wilkinson.'

'My pleasure, madam,' the butler replied, nodding to the line of servants to indicate that they could now leave the room. 'Luncheon will be served in five minutes, sir.'

'Are you expecting guests, Julius?' Emmaline wondered, imagining that a house such as this would always be, like the Nesbitt houses, full to overflowing with friends and acquaintances.

'Good gracious, no,' Julius replied, finishing his sherry, and looking away from her. 'There will be just the two of us. We shall go in now. And by the by, for your future reference, although in your case it is forgivable, and indeed understandable, to comment on my house and its furnishing, since you will soon be,' he stopped, clearing his throat, 'er, you will soon be mistress of it, it is simply not proper to mention a person's possessions when you are in their house.'

'I beg your pardon?'

'I know, I know, it does sound somewhat strange, I will admit, and I believe it is different in America, but here people will take great offence if you look at their paintings and tell them how beautiful you think they are, or even their houses. It is considered vulgar and offensive, and Lord Parham has been known to ask the unfortunates who do so to leave his house.'

'How very strange! I should have thought that most people would like their guests to show their appreciation.'

'I am afraid it might stem from English hypocrisy, everyone pretending not to know what they have, or how rich they are, or anything else, but it is a fact. And the same of course goes for the mention of money. That is absolutely not done, nor is talk of your or anyone else's health, beyond saying, in a general way, that you hope they are well.'

Emmaline took a deep breath, part of her wanting to laugh, and part of her feeling indignant.

'May I mention the flowers in the garden?' she asked finally.

'Strangely enough,' Julius held up one hand as if he was stopping something advancing towards him, 'strangely enough I actually think flowers and gardens are generally perfectly acceptable. "What a delicious scent, what a perfect rose, what a beautiful garden." Yes, I do think that is perfectly acceptable,' he said, smiling.

He waited for Emmaline to go in front of him, and as he did so his eyes ran shyly but appreciatively over her fashionable dark blue tight bodice with its matching flounced skirt, and lingered on her beautiful dark brown hair, which was presently caught up in a thick piece of lace tied at the nape of her neck.

Lunch began with a soup laid at one end of the table, followed by excellent patties served with a sauce, and fish. Once this was removed, roast beef with a side serving of mixed vegetables and two sorts of potatoes, duchesse and roast, made its appearance, together with a selection of sauces. A large choice of puddings followed, and lastly a cheese fondu.

It was far and away the best food Emmaline had tasted since she came to England, and with Julius seated at the head of the long dining table and she herself some twelve feet distant at the other end, she thought they must make a pretty enough picture. As they enjoyed their first course she found herself diligently searching for something to talk to Julius about, but every subject upon which she embarked was dismissed out of hand by Julius's seeming lack of interest. By the time the beef had been served, Emmaline considered that perhaps a conversation about his work might be safe, since Julius was obviously a man of great talent as well as taste, and, as Emmaline well knew, men loved nothing better than to be flattered, and nothing flattered them more than being allowed to talk about themselves.

Her approach, however, proved to be a little too direct for Julius's liking.

'I noticed the other day, when I was passing through Bamford in your carriage, that a very pretty sign had just been painted, or, rather, re-painted, bearing your name.'

'That was of interest to you?'

'Yes, it was of interest to me, Julius,' Emmaline retorted. 'Perhaps because the smaller sign said

Aubrey & Aubrey Limited while the new sign – the one above the main doors—'

'Yes, yes, I know. The other sign reads something quite different. The company has gone through some changes of late, and with the changes came a change of name.'

Julius laid his knife and fork together neatly, so neatly that Emmaline could only feel relieved that she had finished first, since the idea that Julius might watch her eating was disconcerting, particularly in view of his instructions about the dos and don'ts of English behaviour.

'It was just interesting to me that one sign said – well, one sign said one thing,' Emmaline continued, all too aware that she must sound uncertain to the point of lameness, 'and the other said another. That was all.'

'Very interesting, I am sure,' Julius agreed, sounding to both of them as if he were meaning the very opposite. 'You are very observant, are you not?'

'No more surely than the next person? It was only that, having noticed the difference in the signs, I just now found myself wondering, one way or another, whether the missing painting in the drawing room – whether the painting being cleaned might be, could be, perhaps, of Mr Aubrey senior? I would so like to have known Mr Aubrey senior—'

'And if it was of him? What has that to do with anything? If it was a painting of my recently deceased father it is my affair, and no one else's,'

Julius interrupted shortly. 'It is no concern of yours, my dear Miss Nesbitt. Your concern should be with your future here, with the running of the house, getting on terms with the servants, and so on, and so forth.'

Emmaline decided to ignore this sudden display of impatience. Not caring what he or any of the servants present thought, she ploughed on.

'Seeing the signs I deduced that there had been a loss, that is all, Mr Aubrey,' she said, her mood now changed to one of stubborn determination. 'At least, I thought that there might have been, and if there had then I considered that you might perhaps be in need of my sympathy. I thought it might explain—'

Emmaline stopped mid-sentence, realising she might have already gone too far.

'It might explain?' Julius wondered after a significant pause, during which he stared down the length of the table at Emmaline. 'It might explain what, Miss Nesbitt?'

'Never mind indeed, truly. I am afraid you are displeased enough already, Mr Aubrey.'

'It might explain?' Julius persisted. 'I am most interested in what it *might explain*, Miss Nesbitt.'

'Please, Mr Aubrey—'

'What, please, Miss Nesbitt?'

Emmaline dabbed her napkin against her lips, buying time, trying not to sound or look distressed. 'Very well, Mr Aubrey. I have to tell you that I really am finding it most upsetting – the variance in the way you address me.'

'Please, let us continue with the same line of conversation, Miss Nesbitt. What exactly might it explain?' Julius repeated.

Emmaline felt chilled. As old Mary back at home would have said, 'Someone's walking over your grave, Miss Emmaline.'

'It might, it seemed to me, explain your – your reticence towards me since I arrived in England, that is all,' she said, bowing her head to stare down at her plate. 'As well as your somewhat unusual behaviour. I imagined you might have suffered a very recent loss, prior to my arrival.'

'I see.' Julius pushed his plate to one side and rang the bell on the table to call the maids to remove the dishes. 'Do you know, I was really rather enjoying my luncheon up until this moment.'

'I'm sorry, Mr Aubrey. I truly didn't wish to upset you.'

'Very well, since you obviously will not be satisfied until you have an answer,' Julius continued, 'you shall have one. Yes, as you surmised, Miss Nesbitt, there has been a loss, but in England we do not talk about our losses. We carry on. That is what we do.'

'I am so sorry, Julius,' Emmaline said. 'I thought it might be so.'

'These things happen, as you may have noticed, in life,' Julius went on. 'It is the way of the world and of the life we have been given in this world.'

Wilkinson reappeared with two of the maids.

As the maids cleared the table, the butler took the dishes off the sideboard and disappeared once more through the service door.

'Where were we?' Julius wondered, folding his table napkin carefully into a square before unfolding it again. 'I simply have no idea.'

'We were discussing the matter of your loss,' Emmaline prompted him. 'Was it – was it perhaps your father?'

'Yes, perhaps it was my father.' Julius folded his napkin back into a square once more, smoothing it down with one hand. 'Yes, my father is indeed dead and gone.'

'I see,' Emmaline replied with a thoughtful frown. 'And only recently.'

'So it would seem – but what is recent when it comes to death, Miss Nesbitt?'

'What is past is past is what you are saying?' Emmaline stared at him, wondering suddenly at his lack of mourning bands. 'To have lost someone so close to you, someone with whom you were in business, must indeed be a tragedy.'

'Yes, yes,' Julius sighed. 'My father began life as an artist, before starting the business that I now run. Anything else you would like to know, Miss Nesbitt?'

Emmaline at last felt brave enough to look down the table at her fiancé, who she found was looking steadily back at her, without expression.

'Forgive me, Julius,' she said slowly. 'But you see I really know very little about you – about you or your family. Coming into such an interesting family, it is only natural to want to know more, surely?'

'I have no family that could be of any possible interest to you,' Julius interrupted quickly. 'So it follows that there really is very little to know, wouldn't you say?'

'You have no brothers or sisters?'

Julius glanced down the table at her before returning to the folding of his napkin. 'I have a sister who is married and now lives in Canada.'

'And she is called . . .'

'Does it matter? You're not going to meet her. She never comes to England.'

'I should still like to know her name.'

'Her name is Eleanor, if it is of any interest.'

'Does she have any children?'

'Yes, she has a boy and a girl and they're called William and Margaret. Is there anything else you wish to know?'

'Yes, since you ask, I would so like to visit your business with you,' Emmaline replied with utter sincerity. 'I really would very much enjoy—'

'No,' Julius interrupted firmly.

'No? No as to quite what, Mr Aubrey? No that I would not enjoy seeing your company at work? Or no—'

'No you may not visit the works,' Julius finished for her. 'That is not possible. The works is a place of trade, only tradespeople go there. Is that understood?'

'No.' Emmaline clasped her hands tightly together, well out of sight below the line of the table as the maids continued to remove all the condiments and plates and other items. 'I am afraid it is not understood at all. Why am I never to visit the business? It is something in which I really am interested.'

'Because it is not your place, Emmaline, that is why. It is not – your place.'

'I see.' If it had not been for the presence of the maids Emmaline felt she would have given way to shaming tears. 'My place, as I understand it, therefore, is here, I imagine that is what you are saying?'

'You imagine quite correctly, I am happy to say. I think I am done here now. Tell Cook, thank you, but we need no more removes. I will forgo the rest of luncheon,' he added as he rose. 'I will, instead, go for a walk.'

Emmaline did not rise from her place. 'You wish to go alone?'

'Yes, thank you,' Julius replied, leaving the room. 'Quite alone,' he announced, seemingly to no one in particular. 'Quite, quite alone.'

Going upstairs to dress for dinner at her lodgings before returning to Park House, Emmaline discovered that Agnes, the young girl who had been assigned to her as her personal maid, was already waiting for her in her room, but that nothing was laid out in readiness on the bed or in the bathroom, or indeed anywhere else. It was most puzzling.

'Have you not done anything like this before,

Agnes?' Emmaline asked, as she looked round the room.

'No, miss,' the sad-eyed girl replied. 'Or should that be madam, miss?'

'Madam only once I am married, Agnes, and I am not married, and perhaps may never be,' she said, attempting a joke.

Agnes looked horrified. 'But you've come all this way, Miss Nesbitt. You gotta marry now, or you'll have an awful long journey back.'

'Yes, I will, won't I?' Emmaline agreed. 'Now, are you telling me that you have no idea how to help a lady dress or undress?'

'No, miss, I have no idea at all,' Agnes answered with utter truth. 'But I am willing to learn, and I learns quick, you'll find, 'cos I want to learn, and that's half the battle, i'n't it, madam, if you want to learn quick?'

But Emmaline was hardly listening; wondering instead at the strange ways of the English, what with maids who weren't maids, and husbands-to-be who disappeared for hours if not days at a time.

'Gracious, does no one ever train maids in the way of doing their work in England, Agnes? You are the second girl assigned to me since my arrival who has had no previous experience in being a personal maid. It is so hard on you all, truly it is. Ah well, never mind that now. I will train you, and we will then work together in happy unison, or else I shall have to return you double quick to the works, shan't I?'

Emmaline smiled encouragingly at Agnes, hoping to cheer her up, and guessing that she could only be in her early teens, so childlike were her features, and so undeveloped her body. To her horror, she saw almost at once that tears were threatening to form in Agnes's large eyes.

'I'm a good girl at the works, miss, or is it madam, or should it be miss? Truth is I've never been employed outside the works, truly I haven't, and I am ignorant, so I am, I admit it. I think it should be madam, my ma said it should be, she was sure of it, but you said . . . Oh dear, never tell no one I don't even know how to address you, madam. I'm a London girl only recently come to Somerset and they will laugh at me if they hear I was that ignorant.'

'Calm yourself, Agnes, please. It doesn't matter, truly it doesn't, particularly since we are alone, but since you ask, and since Mr Aubrey and I are not yet married, please call me Miss Emmaline. That is how I was always addressed by our maids at home. So, now, let us start again. I gather you have never dressed a lady before?'

'No, Miss Emmaline,' Agnes replied, looking dejectedly at the floor. 'Until I came here I was cutting fabrics at the works.'

'I see.' Emmaline nodded gravely, trying not to laugh at the idea that you could take a young girl who had been cutting fabrics one day and assign her to be a personal maid the next. Only a man, and a bachelor at that, could ever think that such a thing was possible. 'And how long have you been in service at Park House?'

'Just over a week, miss. Same as everyone else.'

'I *beg* your pardon?'

The force of what Emmaline had just said surprised even her.

'You have only been there a week, and the rest of the servants too?'

'Yes. I'm just the same as everyone else, miss. I ain't no different, truly I ain't.' Agnes looked as though she was once more about to burst into tears at any moment.

'The entire staff, you mean?' Emmaline stared at the girl in disbelief. 'Are you saying that none of the servants at Park House – that everyone has only been working there for a week?'

'Yes, Miss Emmaline. The last staff, they were all – well, they all left just before we come, miss. We're all new, though course most of them's been in service before, unlike what I have been. I mean Cook, and Mrs Graham, and of course Mr Wilkinson and George and Alan, like. But Dolly and Helen and me, we was in the factory cutting fabrics a week ago. But all the rest of them they've come from all over England, quite new to here, and quite new to the house and the master too.'

'So you have no idea of what is expected of you?'

Agnes shrugged her shoulders, and then shook her head.

'Mrs Graham said she'd soon lick us into shape. Said there was nothing to it really. Said she was trained herself, like, in two days, and now look at her, she said. Head of the household with charge of the keys, and all.'

'Why?' Emmaline wondered as she turned her back on Agnes preparatory to being undressed.

'Beg your pardon, miss, but why what exactly?'

'I was just wondering why the entire staff had to be changed all at once, Agnes. It just seems a little odd, that's all. More than a little odd, in fact.'

'I don't know, miss. No one said anything to me and Helen and Dolly. We were just told to report up to Park House to start work as domestics beginning of last week. And Mother she was pleased because she said it was a leg-up for me, and less dangerous than the fabric cutting 'cos a lot of fabric cutters end up blind, what with bits in the eyes an' all, worse than bookkeepers and clerks, she said, because all of them go blind.'

'Very well, Agnes.' Emmaline held up one hand, and after a moment of thought she continued, 'We had best start from the beginning, then. First you must learn how to take a lady's dress off, how to do up and undo stays properly, how to fix stockings and garters, and how to hold out the bodice of a day dress and fix the skirt. Most of all, how to be of assistance when helping me on with an evening gown. Over the head – always over the head, and preferably on hooks so we do not, I repeat do not, get any dirty finger or hand marks on fine materials. We are going to have to spend a great deal of time together, and I mean a great deal, so first we have to get it right, and then we have to get along. That is all-important. Is that understood?'

'Yes, Miss Emmaline,' Agnes whispered, looking as though she were just about to evaporate.

'Oh, don't look *quite* so abject, child!' Emmaline laughed. 'I'm not going to eat you, only teach you!'

And as they stood there regarding each other, Agnes fearfully, Emmaline affectionately, Emmaline realised with surprise that this was the first time she had really smiled, let alone laughed, since she had set foot aboard the RMS *Etruria*. It was a shocking fact, but a true one.

Chapter Five

Julius and Emmaline were finally married six weeks later at a private service in St Mark's Church, Bamford, conducted by the Reverend Archibald Welton. Henry Ralph acted as Julius's best man, while in the glaring absence of any male relation, Emmaline was given away by Wilkinson, Julius's butler, with Agnes in attendance. Her marriage was so unlike anything Emmaline had ever dreamed or imagined for her wedding day that the chief memory she took away from it was one of sheer originality, as she doubted that many young women of her upbringing and background were married with so little ceremony, let alone so few displays of affection, be it familial or marital. Whenever Emmaline had stolen a look at Julius from beneath her veil during the ceremony she had seen that his eyes were closed, and his mouth – normally one of his most attractive attributes – was pursed like that of a small boy. He stared ahead of him, past the rector, at the altar, as if he could see someone there, someone that no one but himself could see. Even as he took up the

115

ring, and his gaze shifted from that far distance to Emmaline's small elegant hand, even as he slipped the ring on her finger, and the words of the blessing rang out round the church, he did not look at Emmaline, they did not meet each other's eyes. He could have been a ghost, she could have been a ghost, so little did they seem to register each other's presence at the foot of the altar, so much did they appear as two people going through a ceremony of which they were barely aware.

There were no more than half a dozen witnesses in the congregation, the only faces familiar to Emmaline being those of their housekeeper and Mrs Shannon, the kindly landlady from her lodging house. No arrangements for the wedding had been discussed by Julius with his bride-to-be, his only announcement being the date, upon which it seemed he had decided without consultation. As soon as Emmaline touched on the matter of guests, hoping for at least a small celebration afterwards, Julius had made his excuses and left the room. Emmaline was not even invited to choose her own wedding gown. Instead, once the date had been fixed, Agnes had simply arrived in Emmaline's lodgings with a large cardboard box containing a bridal dress which was pretty enough, but since the box bore no sign of a shop name, both Emmaline and Agnes suspected was not new.

'Do you think as I do, Agnes, that this gown has belonged to someone else?'

Agnes had turned away, looking embarrassed.

'I dunno, Miss Emmaline. I was just told by Mrs Graham to come round to your lodgings and bring this with me, that's all I know.'

'I think I will have to speak to Mr Aubrey in person about this,' Emmaline told her. 'I am not going to wear a dress of his choosing, and he must know that. He *will* know that.'

Emmaline confronted Julius that evening when he called round to her lodgings, determined that if she were asked to wear a second-hand dress there would not only be no wearing of the dress, there would be no wedding.

Julius shook his head, turning away. 'I just thought – I just thought . . .'

'No, Julius, this is not something with which you should concern yourself, just as you told me that I should not concern myself with your work. You may not know it, but I do know it. It is the custom for a bride . . .' She took a deep breath and began again. 'It is the custom not only for the bride to choose her own wedding gown, but also for the bridegroom not to see it until their wedding day.'

'How quaint,' Julius returned. 'Almost medieval, I would say.'

'You must be aware of such traditions, even you,' Emmaline had replied, doing her best to control her temper. 'And it is not *medieval*, as you call it. It is the way with weddings and wedding days, that most special of days for a young woman, the only day when she can guarantee that all eyes will be on her.'

117

'Perhaps so, Miss Nesbitt—'

'And *please* do not start your mock formality again, Julius. I really would rather not get married not only in a dress of someone else's choosing, but in a dress in which someone else has perhaps already been married.'

'Do you not like the dress, I wonder?'

'Now who is sounding quaint, *I wonder*? It is neither here nor there whether or not I like the dress. I wish to get married in a dress that I have chosen myself.'

'And that I have not seen?' Julius had looked at her, frowning. 'I must apologise. I see there are things which are definitely not the subject for men.'

'I shall see what can be done at such short notice. Mrs Shannon has already indicated that she will help me. Might we now discuss the day itself – and perhaps whom we may invite?'

'There is nothing to discuss,' Julius had replied, turning hurriedly to the door. 'As far as I am concerned, the ceremony is a pure necessity to legalise our union. It is not a reason for an inordinate amount of money to be frittered away on a lot of people one hardly knows, if at all, most of whom one will never see again.'

'It will not be your money being frittered away, as you so cruelly call it, Julius,' Emmaline had argued, following Julius out into the hallway. 'If you recall, it is the obligation of the bride's parents to pay for the wedding, so perhaps you, or indeed we, ought to take that into some account.'

'I have done so, Miss Nesbitt,' Julius told her in a low voice, collecting his hat and coat. 'Your father and I have corresponded on this matter, and since he will not be travelling over for your wedding he is only too happy to leave all the arrangements to me, and even happier to learn that it is to cost him nothing. Now, if you will perhaps excuse me?'

'My father gave me money before I left America, and with some of it I shall at least purchase my own dress.'

The following day, with Mrs Shannon and Agnes accompanying her, Emmaline found a beautiful cream dress and a Brussels lace veil which entirely filled the ideal of what a wedding dress should be, and in the opinion of her companions Emmaline also filled the ideal of what a bride should look like on her wedding day, slim, beautiful, and for that moment at least, standing in the shop in front of the dressing mirror with all eyes on her, happy.

After the wedding service had been concluded, their carriage took the bride and groom back to Park House where they were received by Wilkinson and Mrs Graham, who had hurried back from the church ahead of the others. The rest of the staff lined up in the hallway to applaud the couple as they entered the house, earning themselves a grateful smile from Emmaline, although her bridegroom looked as if he found it faintly absurd to be greeted by his own servants.

In the drawing room an open bottle of

champagne on ice awaited them. Julius poured himself a glass, having dismissed not only his best man but also for some reason the attendant Wilkinson with a vague wave of one hand, and held the bottle up significantly in Emmaline's direction to see if she might like a glass as well.

'Thank you, Julius,' Emmaline replied, dismally surveying the large empty room. She had nursed a secret hope that, even though the church ceremony had been attended by so few, her new husband might have arranged a surprise reception back at Park House to celebrate their union.

'So,' Julius said, as was his wont, having handed his new wife her drink.

'So?' Emmaline wondered. 'So this is all we must expect by way of a celebration, is it, Julius?'

'This is your home, Emma.' Julius stared back at her with what seemed to be genuine bewilderment. 'This is where we are to live, together. Did you expect more?'

'I am very much afraid I did expect more, Mr Aubrey,' Emmaline responded as calmly as she could. 'This is all there is? For our wedding celebration?' She looked round the drawing room empty of anyone but themselves.

'So it would seem, Emma, but you must be happy now that you are married, surely? Are you not happy?' Julius replied, as if still puzzling out a riddle. 'You are married. You were able to purchase your wedding dress. What else should there be?'

'What else should there be? A reception, at the very least. Something, Julius, more than just a handful of people in a church. Are you not even going to kiss the bride?' She looked challengingly at him, but did not move any closer.

'Very well, Emma, yes, of course I will kiss the bride.'

He leaned forward and kissed her briefly on the lips, but before Emmaline could respond he quickly turned away.

'May we not embrace a little longer?' she asked him in a low voice.

'Most certainly not. It would not do at all. One of the servants might come in, and it would be a very bad example. Your good health.' He raised his glass and emptied it quickly, before moving back towards the champagne in its wine cooler.

'Julius?'

Surprised by the tone of her voice, Julius turned.

'Oh, Julius!' Emmaline threw aside the small bridal bouquet she was holding and hurried over to the French doors so that Julius could not see her expression.

'Not there, Emma, if you don't mind,' she heard him complain from behind her. 'Not on that chair. If there is any water in those flowers—'

'Oh, *Julius*,' Emmaline sighed hopelessly.

'If there is the slightest bit of water it will mark the silk.'

'Julius.' Emmaline turned back to him as he crouched over his precious chair to check for any possible damage. 'Julius – are we not even going to go away somewhere?'

Julius stood back up to look at her, clutching the bridal flowers and looking more than faintly absurd.

'Go away somewhere?' he echoed. 'Why?'

'I don't believe you can be so ignorant of wedding arrangements,' Emmaline said. 'I just do not believe any of this, I really do not.'

'And I fail to understand your distress,' Julius replied, belatedly pouring himself a second glass of champagne. 'If your desire was to *go away somewhere*, Mrs Aubrey—'

'I see,' Emmaline interrupted. 'It's to be Mrs Aubrey now, is it?'

'That is what you have become, is it not?'

'That does not mean you have to call me by that name, Julius. Unless you deliberately wish to be hurtful?'

'No, no, of course not.' Julius looked genuinely appalled. 'I would not hurt you for the world, but I am not versed in these matters. If you wished to go away you should really have mentioned it before, and then I could have arranged something to your liking.'

'And what chance did I have? Every time I wished to discuss the arrangements for our marriage, you found an excuse to leave the room.'

'I am a very busy man, Mrs Aubrey. There is much to which I have to attend at my works, the company is in need of fresh direction—'

'Stop it, Julius. I mean it. Please stop it.'

'Stop what, please?'

'Please stop calling me Mrs Aubrey. I am your wife now. And my name is Emmaline, or Emma, as you seem to prefer it.'

'Very well, Emma,' Julius nodded. 'But, to return to our subject, as for this business of going away – by that am I to take it you wish for a . . . a honeymoon?'

The way he pronounced the word *honeymoon* and the expression on his face suggested to Emmaline that Julius found something appalling either about the word or perhaps even in the notion. She thought carefully before continuing, finally concluding that perhaps Julius was nothing more than shy, possibly even shyer than she was herself, and that all his odd behaviour, such as his disappearances, the verbal dismissals, his calling her formal names and his constant state of apparent bewilderment, could be put down to diffidence. Having decided that such a thing was entirely possible, Emmaline determined to try quite a different approach.

'It's all right, Julius,' she said with a smile, even though she did not feel in the least like smiling. 'I think – I think this reaction of mine is possibly due to nerves. After all, it isn't every day a young woman gets married – and the last thing, the very last thing, I would want is to upset you on this matter, which after all is your wedding as well as mine. I was just being thoughtless. Selfish, in fact, so please forgive me.'

Julius frowned again, giving Emmaline a fleeting impression that she might have been speaking to him in a foreign language, and nodded.

'I was going to say that if you wanted—' he began, but Emmaline stopped him, managing to get closer to him now and looking up at him.

'It really doesn't matter, Julius,' she said quietly. 'I am perfectly content. Really I am. And you are right – it isn't the ceremony that matters, it is what happens between us now, in our lives, in the rest of our lives. That is what Mr Welton was saying in his address.'

'I'm sure,' Julius agreed, unable to look her in the eyes. 'I just wish he wasn't quite so prolix.'

'Prolix?'

'Long-winded.' Julius quickly moved away from Emmaline and poured himself more champagne. Once more he held up the bottle in offer to Emmaline but this time she shook her head, putting her hand over her glass. She could already feel the wine going to her head and the last thing she wished for now was to get intoxicated. 'So,' Julius said once more, after sipping his drink. 'Time for lunch, I would say.'

'I would prefer it if I could change before we sat down to lunch, Julius.'

'Yes.' Julius stared past her, frowning as he gave the matter his consideration. 'The trouble is I doubt if Cook will have taken that into account, Emmaline. This is the way it is with servants, do you see? One always has to take them into

124

consideration. You see? Even as we speak,' he held out a hand in illustration, 'there is the gong.'

So it was that on her wedding day Emmaline sat down to lunch with just Julius for company, both of them in their bridal attire; had there been others present it would not have seemed the slightest bit unusual, but since they were entirely alone except for their servants Emmaline felt as though she were playing a part in some drama which she had just finished rehearsing, and was now taking refreshment in full costume.

Glancing down the table at her new husband as he ate and drank she could sense that he too felt discomforted, and at a loss as to what to say. To break the silence Emmaline was just about to ask what they should do that afternoon when she realised it might sound a little forward, although she was not quite sure why. Certainly she felt embarrassed for her near lack of tact, sensing that whatever was to happen next had to be instigated by the man to whom she had just been joined in holy matrimony, the tall, handsome, elegant gentleman sitting opposite her.

What happened next was that Emmaline left Julius at the dining table to enjoy a glass of port and a smoke, and when she came back down-stairs he was nowhere to be seen.

'Mr Aubrey has taken himself off for a consti-tutional, madam,' Wilkinson informed her when she enquired as to her husband's whereabouts. 'Will there be anything else now?'

'Yes,' Emmaline replied, feeling herself colour.

'Please send Agnes to me. I wish to change my clothes.'

It was far too early to dress for dinner so Agnes put out an afternoon dress, and they both began to reset her hair, Emmaline instructing Agnes as they went along.

'If you don't mind me saying, madam,' Agnes said as she carefully began to brush out her mistress's long tresses, 'we all thought you looked absolutely beautiful in your wedding gown. I never seen no one look so lovely.'

'I'm quite sure you have, Agnes,' Emmaline said, smiling at the serious-faced young girl in her looking glass. 'The dress was certainly pretty.'

'Yes, your dress was lovely, madam,' Agnes agreed. 'But I thought you yourself looked really beautiful. Like something – like something from a fairy story.'

'I think possibly all brides look a little special, Agnes. As I'm sure you will when you get married.'

'Me, madam?' Agnes stared at her in astonishment. 'I won't never get married, madam. Likes of me? I won't never get married. My mum says I'm as plain as a poker.'

'My mother thinks the same of me, Agnes.'

'Never. She never could have. You, madam?'

'I assure you she does, Agnes. She is forever telling me how plain and how commonplace is my appearance. My sisters are the pretty ones. I have three sisters and they are all considered to be beauties.'

126

'Perhaps so, madam,' Agnes muttered. 'But I still don't know why anyone thinks that of you. Everyone downstairs, everyone below stairs that is, Dolly and Helen and me, George and Alan – even old Mr Wilkinson – we was all saying how beautiful you are and what a lucky gentleman Mr Aubrey is.'

'That's very kind of you, Agnes.'

'We were not being kind, madam, with respect. That's what us all thought when we first saw you. And again now, when we seen you in your wedding gown.'

'You are flattering me, Agnes,' Emmaline said, smiling and getting up from her dressing table now that Agnes had finished helping to put up her hair again. 'But I don't mind.'

'I'm not flattering you, madam,' Agnes insisted, now quite readily. 'We all think so.'

'Then you are all very kind. Thank you.'

'You got a lovely silhouette as well, madam,' Agnes added. 'Sure I shouldn't be saying as much—'

'You can say what you like, Agnes.' Emmaline laughed. 'As long as it continues in this vein.'

'Well, so you has, madam,' Agnes continued, carefully doing up the back of her mistress's dress. 'I'd die to have a figure like you – and hair like you – and as for complexion—'

Instinctively Emmaline raised a hand to her face and stopped smiling, realising that everything her maid had said, the feelings she had attributed to her colleagues, must have been

127

rooted in sympathy for her as a lonely young woman from another country with not even a father to give her away, only her fiancé's butler, who had slipped back into servant mode as soon as the service was over.

'Thank you, Agnes,' she said, giving one last longing look to the beautiful cream gown that would doubtless never be worn again. 'That will be all for now, thank you, Agnes.'

Agnes hesitated, standing scratching the back of her neck as she stared at Emmaline, worried by her mistress's sudden change of tone.

'Madam,' she said anxiously, 'I haven't said nothing improper, have I? I mean, what I said—'

'No, Agnes.' Emmaline smiled at her maid and put a hand on one of hers. 'You have been very sweet and very kind. I just want a little time to myself now, that is all.'

'I meant what I said, madam.'

'I'm sure you did, Agnes. But really, that will be all now.'

'You really looked so beautiful today, madam.'

'Thank you, Agnes.' Emmaline smiled again, but Agnes still showed no sign of leaving. 'Thank you, Agnes?' she repeated a little more firmly, and finally with a bob the maid was gone.

When she had left, Emmaline went and stood in front of her cheval glass, regarding herself. There was no doubt that she did indeed have an exemplary figure, whose natural grace and shape hardly needed corseting, so that she was able to get away with only the lightest of stays and the minimum of tightening, and there was also no doubt that she was well proportioned as far as the length of her limbs and the set of her head went. She had a smooth and creamy complexion, made even more so by the contrast with her lovely dark brown hair and pale green eyes. Yet how could she be beautiful, when she did not think of herself as being even pretty? But now she was married, she must force herself to outgrow her lack of self-confidence. After all, looked at from the outside, Emmaline had to all intents and purposes married well, wedding a rich and successful man with his own business. Julius must be considered by everyone as a man of taste and elegance, although perhaps a little eccentric, and he was certainly very well connected in English society.

As she prepared to take herself back downstairs to the drawing room, to read while she sat and waited dutifully for her new husband's return, Emmaline determined on keeping calm, on making the most of her position. She was married. Her marriage mattered a great deal more than any wedding reception crammed with cheering guests. She was *married*.

She kept repeating the words in her head all the way down the stairs to the drawing room, because it seemed to her that if she didn't she might start to forget that she was indeed married, and only remember that she had been to church, and then had lunch, which, looked at bleakly, was all it felt as if she had done. Still, as she entered the drawing room and remembered all the fine paintings and the beautiful furniture, it was good to remind herself that she had at least married a man of erudition and learning, a man of education who was consulted by important people who thought a great deal of him. And she was now living in their house, her home, and she had a wedding ring on her finger. And certainly, given all the misgivings about herself with which she had grown up, she had never expected to find herself in such a position. So all she had to do was be patient, as indeed she had been brought up to be. *Good things come to those who wait,* her governess had always instructed her. *Patience is one of the great virtues and must be practised wherever possible.* So if she was right in thinking that Julius was just a little introverted, even shy, and perhaps even timid about the union that had just been blessed by the Church, then if ever there was a time to practise the art of patience, this must surely be it?

With that in mind, and confident that her appearance was everything that it should be on the afternoon of her marriage, Emmaline sat herself down by the fire that Dolly had laid and lit in the drawing room, and it was there that she took tea, alone, while forcing herself to start reading a book about the latest movements in French painting which had been left out on the side table, perhaps for her edification.

*   *   *

Since Julius did not return that afternoon Emmaline sat and read until finally she could read no more, and with time still to kill before she needed to dress for dinner, greatly daring, she sat herself down at Julius's grand piano and played for the best part of an hour. During that time Dolly came in to see to the fire, and Wilkinson arrived with consummate timing just as Emmaline finished playing a Chopin *étude*, one of several pieces to which even her father had always considered she did justice.

Wilkinson waited for her to recover from the emotion she had put into the piece before politely informing her that dinner would be served in one hour. Emmaline repaired upstairs with Agnes to change for dinner.

When the gong sounded Julius had still not returned.

'Do you not think perhaps we should wait for Mr Aubrey?' Emmaline, who was beginning to feel understandably desperate, enquired when Wilkinson appeared at the drawing-room doors.

'I quite understand, madam,' Wilkinson replied with great courtesy, 'but Mr Aubrey's strict instructions are that all meals are to be served at the given times whatever the circumstances.'

'Even when Mr Aubrey himself is not yet returned?'

'Indeed, madam,' Wilkinson assured her. 'Your husband was quite adamant on the matter.'

And so on her wedding night Emmaline found herself sitting down to dinner alone, a dinner served by Wilkinson and Dolly and supervised by Mrs Graham, who looked in after every course to make sure everything was satisfactory, a five-course dinner which Emmaline felt she could barely even begin to eat, but to which she tried to do full justice, if only to please the servants, who somehow made sure that full and due ceremony was observed, as if there was nothing untoward in the sight of a bride dining alone on her wedding night. Nor was any comment of a forward or untoward nature made; far from it. The faces and manners of the servants were nothing if not caring and concerned.

Afterwards, Emmaline sat alone by the fire, waiting. She did so in vain, because by the time the clock chimed eleven and the fire had begun to die down there was still no sign of her husband. However, she was determined to play her part in this particular pantomime with as much dignity as her quite obviously dedicated set of servants had demonstrated at dinner time, so she rang for her maid and announced she was retiring for the night.

She was uncertain at first where she was to sleep, but Agnes was not. Once her mistress was attired for the night, Agnes opened the door from Emmaline's dressing room to what Emmaline now saw was the main bedroom, Julius's bedroom. A fire was lit in the grate, there were bowls of sweet-smelling early spring flowers set about the room, and the bedding on the large four-poster bed had been turned back on both sides. Having

132

made sure that her mistress had everything she required, Agnes wished her goodnight and went, leaving Emmaline alone and more than a little fearful in her wedding bed.

Still Julius did not return. Even when the clock in the hall struck midnight there was no sign of the errant bridegroom. Half an hour later, in spite of her best efforts to stay awake, Emmaline was finally fast asleep, only to be woken almost at once by the sound of what appeared to be someone falling upstairs, if such a thing were possible. Sitting bolt upright in bed and grabbing the bedclothes around her, Emmaline waited, her whole being turned to gooseflesh as the person making all the noise proceeded to do so along the landing outside the bedroom. Finally the door opened and an extremely dishevelled Julius appeared.

Although Emmaline had only read about people being drunk before, she recognised her husband's state at once, even before she became aware of the fumes of alcohol overpowering the scent of the flowers. She knew it from his unsteadiness as he leaned against the doorpost but most of all from the tragi-comic expression on his face.

'What have I done?' he muttered, before throwing back his head and shouting aloud. *'What have I done? What have I done!'*

'Julius?' Emmaline asked anxiously, not knowing whether to stay in bed and see out the nightmare of the scene in front of her, to go and try to help him, or to get out of bed and for her own safety's sake try to shut him out of the room. 'Julius – what's happened? What is the matter?'

Julius focused on her and to her horror she saw his eyes slowly filling with tears.

'How could I do this?' he mumbled, swaying dangerously as he stood away from the doorpost. 'How could I do such a thing? A terrible thing.'

'I don't understand, Julius,' Emmaline said, keeping her voice as calm as she could while deciding it was safer to stay where she was. 'What have you done? What is this terrible thing—'

'How could I *do* it?' he interrupted, shaking his fuddled head slowly from side to side, the tears now running down his face. 'How could I *do* such a thing?'

'Julius—'

'How *could* I? *How could I!*'

'Julius, hush! You'll wake the whole household.'

'So what?' Julius replied, switching moods suddenly. 'So what! It's my damned house and I'll damned well wake who I damned well like!'

'Julius—'

'I'll wake who I like, I tell you! And then everyone can hear what a terrible thing I have done! What a terrible, *terrible* thing.'

'I think you ought to go to bed, Julius,' Emmaline told him feebly, all too aware that she was quite unable to think of anything else to say. 'I don't think you're very . . . well.'

'I think I shall go to hell, that's where I think I shall go,' Julius muttered darkly. 'I shall go to hell, that's where *I* shall go. For doing such a terrible, *terrible* thing.'

'I really think you ought to go to bed rather than to Hades,' Emmaline repeated fearfully, frightened now and preparing to grab the gown that was lying on the chair near her side of the bed and to do a bolt into the sanctuary of her dressing room.

'May God forgive me,' Julius whispered. 'May God forgive me because you never will.'

And with that, he slowly slipped down the doorway to collapse in an unconscious heap on the floor.

For a moment Emmaline stared down at him, horrified, while a feeling of utter helplessness filled her. Then she jumped out of bed, grabbed her dressing gown and threw it on. Just as she was tying the cord round her slender waist another figure appeared at the door: Wilkinson in a tartan wool dressing gown, flannel pyjamas and a pair of beige felt slippers.

'Wilkinson? Is that you?' Emmaline said in amazement, although it clearly was.

'It is indeed, Mrs Aubrey. Now, if you will, please leave this to me, madam, if you would,' Wilkinson replied, bending down and beginning to try to sort out the crumpled form at his feet. 'I think this will be much the best left to me.'

'How, Wilkinson?' Emmaline enquired. 'I can't see how you can possibly cope with this by yourself.'

'I am not by myself, madam,' Wilkinson replied

135

quietly, indicating with one hand for someone to come out of the shadows behind him. 'I was waiting up, you see, madam, for the master,' he continued as the sturdy figure of George appeared by his side. 'I had to wait up because he had gone out without his keys and we couldn't have the house left open all night, do you see.'

Emmaline stepped back. 'Of course.'

'And so then when I saw the master returning, I thought it best to get George here up as well,' Wilkinson continued. 'Just in case, do you see.'

'Of course,' Emmaline said again. 'Very thoughtful of you.'

'So if you take yourself back to bed, madam,' Wilkinson suggested, 'young George and I will make sure the master here gets safely to his dressing room. A man in his state ought to be in his bed. A man in his state is heavy too, madam, very heavy.'

By now they had the comatose Julius back on his feet, holding him up under his arms on both sides, and were beginning the unenviable task of guiding their dead weight along the corridor.

'Thank you, Wilkinson, and thank you, George,' Emmaline said, preparing to shut herself back in the bedroom, this time making sure to lock the door.

'That's perfectly all right, madam,' George said.

'Goodnight, madam,' Wilkinson added. 'You just leave this to us.'

'Oh – and Wilkinson?' Emmaline added, as a

seeming afterthought. 'If it is all the same to you, Wilkinson . . .'

'Rest assured, madam,' Wilkinson called back over his shoulder, 'this shall go no further. Good-night, now.'

Emmaline climbed quickly back into bed, pulling the covers over her head and trying to make some sense of the mayhem that had been her wedding day before falling into a deep and tear-filled sleep.

Nothing was said the next morning, and when Julius finally reappeared at midday he looked and acted as though he had witnessed some sort of dreadful accident.

Emmaline, having risen and breakfasted alone, was waiting in the drawing room when Julius walked in, very slowly and carefully, as if every bone and sinew in his body was hurting him severely.

'Good morning, Julius,' she called from where she was sitting by the fireside.

'What?' Julius started, the sudden movement making him clutch at his head as he stared round at Emmaline. 'Oh, yes. Right. Yes. Good morning.'

They eyed each other before Julius continued on his way, a short slow walk that was leading him inexorably to where the drink decanters stood.

'Do you think that is wise, Julius?' Emmaline wondered as he poured himself a drink. 'I would not have said that that was at all advisable.'

'No, you are right, it is most unwise, Mrs Aubrey,' Julius muttered, obviously determined to get straight back to his traditional irritable form. 'But I very much fear that it is being unwise after the event.'

There was a short silence.

'What happened to you yesterday evening, Julius?' Emmaline finally continued. 'But perhaps it is too much to ask, since I have only been married to you for a day.'

'It is a little too much to ask, at present,' Julius admitted. 'But, if you must know, I went for a walk, I became lost, and then I found my way back here, but I was too late for dinner.'

'We are not just talking about your missing dinner, Julius. If you remember, and, if you don't, let me remind you, you left the lunch table while I was upstairs, disappeared for a so-called constitutional and did not return until well after midnight.'

'Is that so?' Julius muttered, looking mortified. 'I am afraid I was not aware of the time.'

'You were out for over ten hours, Julius, and you say you were not aware of the time?'

'I was . . . preoccupied.'

'I would suggest that in future, when you intend to be *preoccupied*, Julius,' Emmaline told him quietly, 'I would suggest that you at least tell me where exactly you are going to be while you are preoccupied, and exactly how long you are going to be preoccupied for.'

'I do not think that will be necessary, Emma. That is not—' Julius stopped to draw breath, wishing the terrible throbbing in his head would ease. 'That will not be necessary, truly it won't. You will find that is not how things are done here.'

'I have to tell you that as far as matters such as this are concerned, Julius, I am not particularly interested in how things are done or not done,' Emmaline informed him. 'I think that now we are man and wife I have the right to know where you are going, if only in case something should happen to you.'

'And that would matter to you, would it?'

'Of course it would. What else would you imagine?'

'I really don't know, Emma. I would perhaps have imagined that you would not care.'

'Then you would be wrong, Julius,' Emmaline replied. 'Quite, quite wrong.'

Julius turned and looked at her. Emmaline matched his look and held it.

'I was at my club, if you're still interested.'

'Thank you.'

'And I was not aware of the time.'

'I understand,' Emmaline replied, not wishing to push her advantage.

'I – I don't really remember very much, as it happens,' Julius added, staring up at the ceiling, as if he was no longer able to meet his wife's steady gaze. 'I think I must have mixed my drinks. I must have. Because I simply do not remember one thing about – about most of yesterday.'

'I see,' Emmaline said, giving a little sigh. 'Since about what time yesterday is your mind a blank, Julius?'

'The last thing I remember with any accuracy was arriving at my club,' Julius replied. 'It really is most extraordinary. I must definitely have mixed my drinks because after that my mind is a blank.'

'You remember nothing at all?' Emmaline was puzzled. 'Are you not entirely well, Julius?'

Julius frowned at her, realising that she might be supposing something was wrong with his mental health.

'I am perfectly well, thank you, Emma,' he replied firmly. 'As I say, I just perhaps mixed my drinks somewhat indiscriminately, that is all.'

'And that is what happens if someone mixes their drinks?' Emmaline asked with genuine interest, such things being beyond her experience. 'They lose their memory?'

'There can be no other explanation for my behaviour,' Julius assured her, relieved to have escaped any accusation of deliberate drunkenness. 'Such a thing has never happened to me before.'

'Then in case you are still unwell,' Emmaline said, going over to him and confiscating his glass, 'I think it only sensible not to have anything more to drink. My father always takes a stomach powder when drink has *disagreed* with him. So perhaps I could ask Wilkinson to bring you something similar?'

'I have already taken a powder,' Julius returned

140

a little too readily, suggesting to Emmaline that this was not the first time he had supposedly mixed his drinks. 'Thank you. All the same, thank you.'

The gong sounded for luncheon, saving Julius from any further embarrassment. He showed little appetite for his food, and after they had eaten he retired to his study on the pretext of catching up on some important business, leaving Emmaline to spend the rest of what was now a rainy and windy afternoon sitting reading by the fire.

When Julius failed to appear at tea time, Emmaline suggested to Wilkinson that he might go and summon her husband from his study. Julius emerged with every appearance of a man who had been dead to the world, suggesting to his new wife that far from catching up on business Julius had yet again been indulging in liquid refreshment, or at the very least endeavouring to sleep off the effect of too many so-called mixed drinks.

Emmaline stared at him, her feelings going from inner rage to total despair. Later, when Agnes came to help her dress for dinner, Emmaline sent her back downstairs to tell Mr Aubrey that Mrs Aubrey had a sick headache and would not be down that evening. Then she sat propped up on the bed in her dressing room staring ahead of her and wondering if it was time to leave Park House, England, and most of all Julius Aubrey.

Chapter Six

After much soul-searching Emmaline finally decided to give herself and her marriage a little more time. It was not just that she could not face the idea of returning home to be humiliated by her family. The daunting length of the frightening sea journey, and the fact that she still cared for Julius, combined to delay any precipitous decision. But despite adopting this sensibly cautious approach to her bewildering situation, she found that time passed ever more slowly – so slowly, in fact, that she began to feel that she was frozen in time, that the clocks about the house were moving on while Emmaline Aubrey née Nesbitt had turned to stone.

Julius might have given up his disappearing acts, but it seemed to Emmaline that now that the actual marriage had been celebrated – for want of a better word – Julius had returned to exactly the same sort of routine that he had enjoyed before their fateful wedding day. He breakfasted early after taking a short walk on rising, departed for his office as soon as he had finished his meal, and remained there all day, returning in time to change for dinner, which they ate alone. After dinner he always had a nightcap and a smoke, while Emmaline read or played the piano until it was time for bed.

When Julius's behaviour on his wedding night was not repeated, Emmaline began to look forward to bedtime, believing that now that their life had become regularised, whatever it was that was meant to happen between a new husband and his bride would surely happen sooner or later.

She hoped so much for this that she would be first into the double bed, with her hair beautifully brushed and in her most attractive nightdress. She would sit in bed in the exact pose she had observed in an illustration in a novel she had recently finished, her hands folded demurely in front of her and her beautiful brown hair lying loose but carefully arranged on the pillow behind her head. Julius would then enter the bedroom in his quilted dressing gown, carrying his book. He would stand by the door looking appreciatively at his wife.

'I have come to say goodnight, Emma, and to wish you a good night's rest in your new home.'

After which he would lean forward and kiss her on the forehead, as if she was his daughter, and with a kind smile leave the room, quietly closing the door behind him.

And because she was too shy to voice her thoughts, he was always gone before Emmaline could even begin to pluck up the courage to ask him why he was not staying.

As if Julius's bedtime behaviour was not enough, his strange words on the night he had so infamously mixed his drinks began to haunt Emmaline.

What have I done, what have I done?

What *had* he done, Emmaline could not help asking herself. What sort of terrible thing could it have possibly been – and how could he do any terrible thing without her being aware of it? He had certainly been thoughtless, heartless even. He could even have been said to have been deliberately cruel to her in the earliest part of their relationship with his many unexplained absences. Yet Emmaline had been able to ascribe everything to shyness, or to his emotional immaturity. After all, maturity of years did not necessarily mean maturity of mind, and while she did not doubt that he cared for her, the precipitate way in which he had courted and proposed marriage to her did not argue that he was in any way an experienced suitor.

So day after day, as she walked or read, or played the piano, with only the occasional servant to whom she could talk, Emmaline's thoughts were necessarily preoccupied with the terrible thing to which Julius had kept referring on their wedding night.

It had to be something of which she was as yet unaware, some unnoticed slight perhaps, or even some indiscretion on his part too trivial to have come to her notice, and if that were the case she was quite certain she would readily forgive him for whatever it was. In fact, were Julius to seek her forgiveness she knew that she would not only forgive him, but do so without demanding that he tell her what it was that he was meant to have done.

On the other hand, she could not but take the fact that he had not yet shared their marriage bed as an unspoken insult. Day after day, night after night, she had to face the embarrassment in the servants' eyes as they pretended that they had not noticed that the newly-weds occupied different bedrooms. She longed with all her heart for someone in whom she could confide, but thanks to Julius's aversion to visitors she had not had the opportunity to make friends with anyone of her own standing. This was something else that was beginning to worry her, since she knew from what she had read that when someone new arrived in an English town there were certain procedures to be followed, certain protocols to do with the placing of calling cards. She had understood, and Mrs Graham had confirmed, that it was the custom for the ladies in society to call upon any newcomer and leave their cards by way of introduction.

Emmaline had received no such cards, although on several occasions she had thought she heard various comings and goings at the front door. However, since no cards were left Emmaline assumed that whoever it was had not come to call on *her*, or was merely one of the many postmen who came, sometimes hourly, with letters for her husband. Occasionally there would be a letter from one of Emmaline's own family, telling her of the parties and dances they were all enjoying, or how they were all looking forward to going to Newport for August, how Ambrosia and Charity both had adoring beaux, and how pleased their father was with the men of their choice, who were wealthy and of good families, all of which news only increased Emmaline's homesickness.

And even what she understood to be the newly installed telephone never rang, either for her or for Julius. It sat in solitary splendour asking to be used, and Emmaline longed to telephone to someone, but to whom?

Then one morning, although the telephone remained resolutely silent, and the doorbell seemed to be as uncommunicative as her husband at mealtimes, Emmaline happened to enter the hall just after someone had actually called. She saw Wilkinson closing the door on a well-dressed young woman whose carriage was waiting for her in the driveway, a visiting card in his hand. Emmaline remained where she was by the foot of the stairs as Wilkinson placed the card on a tray.

'Excuse me, Wilkinson,' she said. 'That young lady. Was she calling to leave her card on Mrs Julius Aubrey – is that card perhaps for me?'

'I am not at liberty to say, madam,' Wilkinson replied. 'If you will excuse me . . .'

'No, Wilkinson, wait,' Emmaline demanded. 'Why can you not say? I don't understand. Surely you must know what the caller said?'

'Indeed I do, madam. But my instructions are to relay all calling cards straight to the master.'

The butler made for Julius's study, followed closely by Emmaline. Julius was at work at his desk when Wilkinson entered with the silver salver, and he did not see Emmaline. When Wilkinson would have closed the door Emmaline prevented him by taking hold of the handle and nodding for the butler to leave. With what seemed like perfect understanding Wilkinson nodded silently to Emmaline and went, leaving her standing in the doorway with the door sufficiently ajar for her to be able to see Julius, who still had his back to her. She watched him read the card and then, having torn it in two, consign it to his waste-paper basket.

Half an hour later, with Julius safely out of the house on his way to the works, Emmaline went straight to retrieve the torn card from her husband's waste-paper basket and returned to the drawing room without anyone's observing her.

'Did anyone call for me today, Julius?' she wondered at dinner time, asking her question quite deliberately as Wilkinson was serving his master with wine.

'Not to my knowledge,' Julius muttered, staring at the decanter in the butler's hand.

'I'm sorry, Julius, I didn't quite hear what you said. Did anyone call for me?'

'I heard you the first time,' Julius grumbled.

'Yes, I'm sure,' Emmaline replied firmly. 'But I did not catch your answer. Well?'

'Well what?' Julius stalled, hoping he could get away with not replying until Wilkinson was out of the way.

'Did anyone call for me today?' Emmaline repeated, this time with a carefully sweet smile. 'Or any other day for that matter?'

'Thank you, Wilkinson,' Julius said, eyeing the butler edgily. 'That will be all for the moment.'

'Perhaps I should ask Wilkinson before he leaves,' Emmaline suggested, 'since it is he who opens the door.'

'That will not be necessary. Thank you, Wilkinson.'

'Wilkinson—' Emmaline began.

'That will be all, Wilkinson,' Julius said, raising his voice. 'Thank you.'

As he left with his usual half-bow, Wilkinson caught Emmaline's eye, and for a second it seemed to her that in his she could see a mischievous complicity.

'I do not much care for this dish, whatever it is meant to be,' Julius announced, hoping to change tack. 'I suggest you have a word with Cook.'

'It's one of your favourites, Julius,' Emmaline replied. 'According both to Cook and to you.'

'I don't care, Emma. It isn't good tonight. Convey my feelings to Cook, please. There's too much something or other in it.'

'I shall tell Cook you didn't care for it. That there is too much something or other in it.'

'You do not have to say quite that, Emma.'

'Forgive me,' Emmaline replied with a small sigh. 'I thought that is what you wished me to say, Julius.'

Julius said nothing, knowing he was bested and feeling that, as always on such occasions, silence was by far and away the safest thing.

'So as far as you know, Julius,' Emmaline continued, about to play her trump card, 'there were no callers for me today. Or any other day come to that.'

'If there had been, Emma, no doubt you would have been informed.'

'By?'

'By?' Julius frowned as Emmaline smiled.

'By whom would I have been informed, Julius? Wilkinson, perhaps? Or your good self?'

'I have no idea what you are talking about, Emma.'

'Mrs Algernon Thackeray, for example,' Emmaline said deliberately. 'Just a name out of the blue, you understand, Julius. Let us say a Mrs Algernon Thackeray had called on me this very morning, by whom would I have been informed?'

'Can we please talk about something else?' Julius begged, looking embarrassed. 'This really is most uninteresting. There were no callers for you today or any other day, will that suffice?'

'No, Julius, I am afraid it won't.' Emmaline produced the torn calling card, waved the two pieces at Julius, then put them carefully together on the table beside her.

'Mrs Algernon Thackeray.' She turned the two pieces over. '*Mrs Algernon Thackeray of The Little Manor, Bamford,*' she read. Looking up, she smiled down the table at her now tight-lipped husband.

'So?' he muttered. 'I must have forgotten. It must have quite slipped my mind.'

'I suppose it must have done,' Emmaline agreed. 'Possibly like all the others.'

'Where did you get that?'

'Mrs Algernon Thackeray left it for me.'

'Where did you get it, Emma?'

'Perhaps more to the point, Julius, where did *you* get it?'

There was a silence, while Julius examined the possibilities of escape.

'I do not have it, Emma,' he replied finally. 'You have it. So rather than where *I* got it from, surely the point is where did *you* get it from?'

'I take your point, Julius, but I'm afraid I find that a rather childish riposte,' Emmaline told him. 'That is rather the sort of argument one has around the nursery table. The real point is – and it is an inescapable one – this card was left for me, according to the message written on it, and I did not receive it – and so I must wonder why.'

Wilkinson's reappearance through the service door prevented Julius from replying. He breathed in deeply, took the last forkful of his by now cold food and nodded to the butler to remove it.

'Well, Julius,' Emmaline continued, deliberately

blithe. 'I would like to know not just the whys, but also the wherefores.'

'*Pas devant,*' Julius warned quietly, with a glance towards Wilkinson and Dolly, who had arrived to help.

'Julius,' Emmaline scolded lightly. '*S'il vous plaît, ils comprennent "pas devant".* Truly, they do.'

Julius's eyes widened a little at that, and Emmaline guessed at once that he had never realised before that she could understand French. He stared at her in surprise. '*Merci, madame. Nous parlerons dans un moment, n'est-ce pas?*'

After the main course had been removed, while they waited for the puddings to be brought in, Emmaline determined on continuing her line of questioning. She would not give up, no matter what.

'So perhaps now you will be good enough to tell me, Julius, why you saw fit not to allow me sight of Mrs Thackeray's calling cards? I am sure she is a lady with whom I should do well to become acquainted.'

'I do not happen to like the Thackerays, that is why,' Julius growled, having had sufficient time to come up with an excuse. 'So if we could now leave this matter to one side, please?'

'Do you not then like anyone else who has called on Mrs Julius Aubrey, Mr Aubrey? Are you saying that I am to become acquainted with no one in Bamford?'

Emmaline was glad to see that Julius was silenced, quite obviously left high and dry, with no answer at the ready. He sat, as always at such moments, folding and refolding his napkin into neat shapes.

'Wilkinson informed me that all visiting cards were to be taken directly to you, Julius,' Emmaline continued, watching him. 'Is this correct?'

'Perfectly,' Julius agreed, unable to meet her eye.

'I didn't hear what you said, Julius.'

'I said perfectly, Emma.'

'There is no need to drop your voice, Julius.'

'I told Wilkinson to bring me every calling card in case – in case anyone undesirable might come calling on you. You are a stranger here, and need to be protected at all times. You have no idea of how tiresome some of these people can be, the local people, tiresome and interfering—'

Julius stopped speaking the moment the service door opened and Wilkinson reappeared with Dolly to serve dessert. While the dishes were put in front of them Julius stared down at his hands and Emmaline watched him with something approaching detachment, feeling more like a nurse watching a patient than a newly married woman watching her husband.

'You were saying, Julius?' Emmaline wondered. 'Something about my being a stranger here and in need of protection, was it?'

'Yes,' Julius said, eyeing the servants and then Emmaline in swift succession.

'You said all cards were brought to you for inspection, in case anyone undesirable might come calling on me,' Emmaline continued. 'Is that right?'

'It can wait.'

'Very well,' Emmaline agreed. 'If you say so. But not for long, I think, not for long. After all, I cannot be expected to stay alone in this house for the rest of the century, can I?'

Wilkinson was giving her a carefully guarded look which could have held more than a hint of warning in it, but Emmaline was feeling almost gleefully brave, although she did have the grace to wait until Wilkinson had left the room once more, with Dolly in tow, before continuing, 'As I was saying, Julius—'

'No,' Julius warned her. 'That is enough. Yes, you are quite right. I ordered Wilkinson to bring all calling cards directly to me for the reason I have just given you – so that I could vet all callers to this house – please, if you don't mind, let me finish.' He held up one hand to forestall any interruption from Emmaline, who was in fact perfectly content to stay silent in order to hear her husband's explanation of his social censorship. 'I wished to make sure that everyone who came to this house was suitable for you to know, because the last thing I want is to have my house, my drawing room and finally my dinner table peopled by those with whom I would prefer not to exchange the time of day. I wanted to spare you time and trouble. I trust I have made myself clear.'

'You have made yourself perfectly clear, Julius.

You wish to choose my friends for me, the way you choose everything else.'

'That is a husband's prerogative, Emma. You are living in England now, and that is the way we are in England.'

'And what else is a husband's prerogative, please? To sleep alone in his dressing room, perhaps?'

'You go too far, Emma,' Julius warned, his handsome countenance darkening. 'Beware lest you stray a little *too* far.'

'I am simply curious, Julius, as to the exact measure of an English husband's prerogatives, that is all. In America, as you know, marriage frees a woman. Here, on the other hand, it seems that it constrains her, until she becomes much like a Chinee, walking several yards behind her husband, on feet that might as well be bound.'

'I perfectly understand, Emma, that it is very difficult for you, of course it is. I am sure I should find it hard to live in America, as an American husband. But there is little I can do about our situation except try to sympathise with you, as all good husbands must, surely?' He stared down at his place, looking suddenly miserable.

It was clear that he had nothing further to say at the moment, and Emmaline sat back in her chair, her back straight, her eyes on the dessert served in front of her. As it happened, she was happy to remain silent, if only because she now knew that she had all too much to think about. She was even happy to finally rise and leave Julius to enjoy his port and cigar by himself, as usual, while she took herself off to the drawing room, where she sat playing the piano and waiting for Julius to reappear. But tonight, for whatever reason, he did not reappear, nor did he come to the bedroom door to wish her goodnight. She heard his dressing-room door closing half an hour after she herself had gone to bed, and it did not open again before she blew out her candle, and lay patiently waiting to go to sleep.

Since sleep did not come, she lay staring into the darkness, turning over in her mind what she might do to try not just to bring some warmth into her marriage, but simply to bring it to life. It was almost impossible for her to believe, but in the weeks she had been in England, Julius had not even kissed her. In fact the only physical contact they had was when they were out walking, a rare enough occasion heaven only knew, and even then, it seemed to her, Julius only offered her his arm when he had seen someone he knew coming towards them. It was as if he wished to make a show of affection in front of his acquaintances outside the house, walking arm in arm with his new wife, smiling, happy, quite unlike the real man who lived at Park House.

'He leaves his smile at the gate.'

That was an expression often used by the older women in the Nesbitt household of some seemingly charming husband who was well known to be a coldheart at home.

As it was, Emmaline knew enough to understand,

if only from the novels she had read, that men and women embraced, they kissed, they held hands not just arms, and these shows of affection, in time, led to passion, which sometimes but not always produced children. Her own mother had once said to her, in one of her more lucid moments, *Do not worry yourself about such matters, Emmaline. When the time comes, all will be made clear.*

Yet nothing had been made clear to Emmaline, certainly not since she arrived in England.

As she lay alone in the big double bed she struggled with the idea that there must be something she could do to ignite the spark that seemed so tragically missing from her and Julius's marriage. Yet the more she thought about the problem the more helpless she felt as she realised that it was not just her bewilderment at Julius's behaviour, but her own sheer ignorance, that was holding her back.

The thought occurred to her that if she only knew more about the intimacies of marital life she would know what to do to help her own marriage. Was there something physical she should be doing, or at least know about, that was the key to all that was missing in what was now so patently a truly wretched alliance? And if so, what *was* this physical thing? The truth was that she had simply no idea, and the more she wondered the more she tossed restlessly in the bed, unable to sleep, worrying endlessly about which way to turn.

In desperation she lit her bedstick and in its

flickering light began to walk the bedroom floor, backwards and forwards, round and round, until finally she found herself sitting on the edge of the bed with her head in her hands, her long brown hair falling on either side of her face, her cheeks wet with the tears she had been crying for longer than she cared to realise. The truth was that she had no idea what to do, and she had no one to whom she could turn to ask for help.

Eventually, drawing the curtains back and seeing the faintest light of dawn in the sky, Emmaline sat herself down in front of her dressing-table mirror and began to brush her hair, as she had been taught to do as a little girl, while she wondered for perhaps the thousandth time what she could do.

If only I had someone to talk to. If only I had a friend, or a relative, or anyone – just someone who would help me, who would show me where I am going wrong and how.

But she had no one, no one at all, and so desperate had she become that as dawn began to break over Bamford, and trade carts could be heard in the distance, she wondered if she could at least make a friend of Mrs Graham.

All of a sudden it seemed that this could be a solution. If she made a friend of Mrs Graham, she would have an ally in her own household. It would be a way out of her loneliness, her homesickness. After all, Mrs Graham was her housekeeper, and better than that she was a married woman. She might be able to help

Emmaline understand not just English life, but married life. Besides, she seemed such a kindly soul, always smiling and happy, with an encouraging word for everyone.

Emmaline climbed back into bed and snuffed out her candle. It was a solution. More than that, it was a happy solution. She was dropping off into a thankful sleep, convinced that she had at last stumbled on an answer to her problems, when a thought struck her. She remembered reading in an English novel that housekeepers always assumed the title of *Mrs* in order to give themselves some authority over the rest of the servants, but that generally speaking they were, like cooks, nearly always single women who had worked their way up through the household ranks until they had enough experience to seek a superior position elsewhere.

Which means I can't possibly ask her for advice about marriage. If she knew how to help me she would gain a bad reputation for herself, and if she did not know it would be sure to get out that I had asked her and I would become a figure of fun, and, what is worse, remain as ignorant as ever.

Emmaline turned on to her front and groaned into her pillow, realising just how foolish her tortured thoughts had been, up what a blind alleyway they had led her. She would have to give up the battle and return home. Never mind that she would become an object of pity, never mind that her three sisters would hate her for the rest of her life for throwing their chances of

158

marriage into disarray, she could not, would not, go on as she had.

She sat up and yet again lit the bedstick beside her, but as she did so a new thought came to her, and the moment she realised its potential she was able to blow out the candle, and finally, at last, fall asleep.

Chapter Seven

When Emmaline went into the town she always took Agnes along with her, more for companionship than anything else. She had quickly grown fond of her awkward young maid – whom she now called Aggie – for in the warmth of Emmaline's kindness and good humour the girl had soon become much more confident, eager to learn and to help, so that she now served her mistress well. However, on this particular day, having planned her visit some days in advance, Emmaline knew her task would be made much easier if she went alone.

Agnes looked aghast.

'You can't go into town on your own, Mrs Aubrey, truly you can't. It's more than my life's worth to let you even think of doing so, truly it is. Why, Mrs Graham would dismiss me on the spot if she ever caught wind of it, and as for Mr Aubrey, he would cut off my head, so he would. Besides, what about my reputation? You go parading about without your maid, without your Aggie, my reputation as a lady's maid is going to end up in rags and tatters, so it is. You won't be going into town on your own, so you won't, begging your pardon, Miss Emmaline, sorry, Mrs Aubrey, you will stay here, or else we will go together.'

Agnes stopped, her face quite flushed with the effort of trying to get across to her young mistress just how disastrous her plan could turn out to be.

Emmaline smiled. 'Why, Aggie, I do believe you are cross with me. Very well, you and I will go into town together, but there are some things that I must accomplish, even so, on my own. I will leave you in the carriage for a few minutes, somewhere quite central, and then re-join you, after which we will return to the house.'

Agnes knew better than to enquire into the nature of her mistress's business, and although she considered Mrs Aubrey to be above suspicion she was none the less curious as to the reason for the change in their routine. Nothing was said on their carriage ride into town to indicate that this outing was any different from any previous one, until they had finished some light shopping. After a call at the dressmaker's, Emmaline instructed Agnes to get back into the carriage to wait for her, then turned away and walked quickly up the High Street.

From the window in the carriage Agnes watched her mistress for as along as she was able, until eventually Emmaline turned down a side street and disappeared from view.

For a moment Agnes was tempted to step down

out of the carriage and follow her, not because she was worried but because she was curious, having already guessed from Emmaline's demeanour on the ride into town that whatever it was she had chosen to do was making her unusually fretful, or perhaps excited. But she knew she had to resist the temptation. It was none of her business, and prying would get her nowhere. She would just have to possess her soul in patience and wait in the carriage, watching what seemed like the whole of Bamford on their way to the shops.

Besides, as George the under footman was forever reminding them, as they sat eating their meal round the table below stairs, *You may make what you like of 'em, but in the end there's no telling. They're them, and we's us, and there's a world of difference between being them and being us, but sometimes we have to draw a line, especially when they forget that they are them and try to become like us.*

So Agnes remained sitting, more than somewhat impatiently, in the carriage while Emmaline hurried to her destination, namely the shop owned by Mr Arthur Hunt, bookseller.

When she arrived outside the tidy, freshly painted frontage of the bookseller's premises, she found that there was a cluster of carriages waiting nearby, and a general air of something that was more than just a shop, more of a meeting place, perhaps, where like minds, and like souls, congregated.

And so it proved when she pushed in through the door to the interior. There were even more people in the shop than could have been anticipated from the horses and carriages standing outside. Emmaline had never had the pleasure of visiting the bookshop before, but since it was still early in the day, not to mention the beginning of the week, she had hoped for fewer people, with luck no more than two or three other customers. But she soon came to realise that a crowd could be in her favour, since the staff would be preoccupied and most likely would hardly notice her, or pay much attention to her request.

'Might I help you?' a soft male voice with a distinct Scottish accent said from behind her, startling Emmaline, who had, with a purposefully casual air, begun to browse through the shelves in the hope of being able to find what she wanted without actually having to seek any advice.

The owner of the voice held out his hand – a slim, elegant hand used more to turning pages than to smoking cigars or riding horses.

'I am Arthur Hunt, and I don't think I recall seeing you in here before, madam.'

Emmaline looked at the owner of the voice, who must also be, she imagined, the owner of the shop. Mr Hunt was a tall, well-built and hand-some, if red-faced, man, already in late middle age, who looked to all intents and purposes to be both very prosperous and very serious, until you noticed his twinkling blue eyes, which betrayed a good deal of humour.

'Is it fiction you might be after, madam?' Mr

Hunt enquired. 'Some poetry, maybe? Or perhaps something a wee bit more – more *earnest*?'

'Oddly enough, sir . . .' Emmaline began, only to be promptly interrupted.

'Oddly enough?'

'Yes, oddly enough,' Emmaline said, stalling.

'I am at a loss, an embarrassing loss, madam. May I know who you are?'

'Mrs Swallow,' Emmaline announced, her head on one side.

'Mrs Swallow.' Mr Hunt smiled and nodded. 'Well, let us hope you do not take your custom elsewhere in wintertime.'

Emmaline stared at him, not picking up on the rather laboured joke until he began to explain it, when she held up a hand, laughing.

'Of course, of course, I do see, yes. English swallows do not stay here in wintertime. Yes, I do see.'

'Forgive me, Mrs Swallow,' Mr Hunt said, cleaning his spectacles carefully on a spotless white handkerchief. 'A weakness of mine, alas – the making of dreadful jokes. So what guidance might I give you, Mrs Swallow?'

'Do you have a – a . . . ? What I am looking for is something – something scientific.'

'The scientific books are over here,' Mr Hunt said, leading Emmaline round several large shelves towards the back of the shop. 'In what particular field of science might your interest lie, Mrs Swallow?'

Behind Mr Hunt's back Emmaline hesitated,

despite knowing that to do so might mean she was lost.

'Biology,' she said in what she hoped was a firm voice but soon realised was coming out as a whisper.

'I beg your pardon, Mrs Swallow?'

'Biology,' she repeated, this time too loudly as several customers, both men and women, glanced sharply at her when she spoke. 'I am interested in books written on biological subjects.'

'Biological,' Mr Hunt repeated calmly. 'You do mean biological and not botanical, now?'

'Biological is what I mean, Mr Hunt.'

'Good. Then we must look along this shelf here. Would it be physical biology, I wonder? Anatomical biology perhaps? Natural biology – or simply general biology?'

'If I might have time to peruse your shelves, Mr Hunt,' Emmaline replied, making a great effort to sound calm, 'I think I shall find what I'm looking for.'

'Of course, Mrs Swallow,' Mr Hunt said with a nod. 'But if you need any further guidance, please do not hesitate to seek me out. I shall be behind my desk over there. In the meantime, if I might suggest this volume?' He took a book from the shelf and handed it to Emmaline. 'We find it to be particularly well written and most educative.'

The book was titled *Haynes General Biology – a basic textbook, fully illustrated*. Emmaline was about to open it when she became aware of someone standing at her shoulder, so at once she shut the book and pretended to survey the shelves in front of her.

'What are you doing here, Emma?'

'Julius!' Emmaline jumped, trying her best to look pleasantly surprised. 'What brings you here?' Once again she strove to keep her voice normal, even as she realised that the colour was draining from her face.

'Nothing.' Julius shrugged, trying to see what Emmaline was holding. 'I saw the carriage in the main street, with your maid sitting in it alone—'

'I told her to wait for me,' Emmaline interrupted, anxious to establish an alibi of sorts. 'She had an errand to run so I told her to wait in the carriage. Besides, I didn't want Mr Hunt's shop to be crowded out with people who were not customers. It is perfectly safe to be alone in a bookshop.'

'Yes, of course. I only called in, not knowing you would be here. I was on my way back to the offices, which as you know lie at the end of this street.'

'Of course.' Emmaline smiled fixedly, having quite forgotten the proximity of Julius Aubrey Ltd. 'It's all right, Julius. I wasn't going to call on you, you need not be concerned.'

'So, what is the reason for your being here, Emma? I would imagine you still have plenty to read at home, surely?'

'I . . .' Emmaline began, trying to think as quickly as she could. 'I read in your newspaper about a – about a new anthology of Alfred Lord Tennyson's poems—'

'You will hardly find them on the scientific shelves, I would have thought,' Julius cut in, staring at the titles in front of him. 'Might I see what you have selected?'

He put out his hand for the volume that Emmaline was still hugging to her chest just as Mr Hunt arrived back on the scene with an armful of books. If he had been the Archangel Gabriel himself he could not have been more welcome.

'Ah, good morning, sir,' he said to Julius, giving him a warm smile. 'How delightful to see you here, and in such pretty company!'

'Mr Hunt. Good day to you.'

'Ah, I gather you two know each other, Mr Aubrey,' Mr Hunt continued with a nod in Emmaline's direction.

'Yes, we have met,' his handsome customer replied, laughing. 'We are indeed known to each other, since this lady is my wife!'

'Then you will be aware that she is a lady of impeccable taste,' Mr Hunt said, a little too slowly, as Emmaline gave him a look that reminded him of a frightened animal caught in some hideous trap. 'I have been helping her with a selection of books. Allow me, madam – that volume you are holding is not the anthology you were after at all. How silly of me. Here . . .'

The bookseller, having deftly removed the biology text book from Emmaline's hands, tucked it under one of his arms and handed her a red and gold leather-bound volume in its stead. 'I will fetch you the Tennyson anthology as well,' he added, having obviously overheard the end of their conversation. 'But if you have not read Robert Browning, I would very much recommend this volume.'

'Thank you, Mr Hunt, you are too kind,' Emmaline said, doing her best to hold out a steady gloved hand to take the book and giving him a tremulous smile. 'I am sure everything will be much easier once I know my way around your fine shop.'

'I too am sure it will be.' Mr Hunt smiled back at her. 'But just remember, if you need anything, I am at your service – Mr Aubrey?'

He bowed at Julius, who returned the compliment. 'Mr Hunt.'

The bookseller departed, leaving Julius alone with Emmaline. He took the slim volume out of her hand and examined the spine. '*The Ring and the Book*. Good. That is one I have not read so far either, so if I may? After you have finished, of course.'

'Of course you may, Julius,' Emmaline replied. 'I had not realised you were an admirer of Mr Browning.'

'I vastly prefer him to Tennyson, I assure you. Tennyson is a fine epic poet, no doubt about that. But Robert Browning has much greater profundity. Have you finished here now?'

'I have, thank you,' Emmaline replied, with a small look backwards at the science shelves as they started to leave. 'Yes, I have for the moment, thank you. Now I dare say you wish to return to your business, Julius?'

She gave him a pointed look, a look that said, 'If I may not come to your offices, then you may not chaperon me in a bookshop.'

The look worked its own stern magic. Julius made her a little bow and left the shop, and Emmaline went in search of the owner.

'Mr Hunt.'

'Mrs *Aubrey.*' Mr Hunt gave Emmaline a calm, avuncular look, the sort of look that could as well have been a reassuring hand on her arm. 'One of the grand aspects about owning a bookshop,' he continued, 'is that one gets to know the most interesting people, and sometimes those people have need of discretion. All my customers know they can rely upon my complete discretion, Mrs Aubrey. Now, this volume I was recommending to you ...'

After her narrow escape Emmaline made no immediate attempt to return to the shop, not only afraid that Julius might bump into her again and this time catch her red-handed with a volume that he would consider to be completely unsuitable for a well-brought-up young lady, but worried too that despite Mr Hunt's undoubted kindness (why else would he have rescued her from her dire situation?) she might be trespassing upon his good nature if she reappeared in his shop demanding to buy some sort of educational textbook on that most sensitive of all subjects – biology.

The real problem for Emmaline was that Mr Hunt's very kindness might set up some sort of conspiratorial relationship between them, and if Julius, who would not even countenance her receiving ladies' calls, chanced upon his wife and Arthur Hunt together a second time, he might well jump to an entirely wrong conclusion.

Despite realising that she might be making dramas where there were none, Emmaline decided it was better to play safe and eschew the bookshop until some time had passed. Besides, she had a feeling that she might have come up with a better idea, for while they had been in the bookshop together she had become aware that they shared an interest in poetry, a rapport out of which perhaps some sort of emotional contact might be made. It was of course possible that she was clutching at all too famous straws, but she decided to try to continue their poetry discussion at home, knowing that the more interests they found in common, the greater chance she had of founding a true relationship with Julius, of the tall figure and the thick dark hair, of the sudden bright gaze, and the elusive ways.

So while Julius was away on business, planning the redecoration and refurnishing of some neglected castle on the Scottish borders, Emmaline plunged herself into reading everything by Browning and as much as she could about Browning, starting with *The Ring and the Book*. She soon discovered that it seemed to be a sort of epic poem, not at all the kind of verse that she had somehow expected.

Confused, and feeling foolish, no matter which way she approached the work Emmaline could find no easy way into understanding it. She tried reading it aloud, she tried copying out passages – an old device much used by her governess when she was trying to get across some point – but still the meaning remained all too obscure.

It was a great disappointment to her. She longed to find that elusive key to Julius's personality, a key that she knew once found must open the door to his heart. Browning was a poet he obviously admired, but who was very new to her. The page was a blank to her, just as her lack of knowledge of fundamental biology was also a blank. Yet again she had to bring herself to realise that she needed help, and where better to seek assistance in deciphering Robert Browning than the place where she bought her very first volume of the poet's verses, Mr Hunt's bookshop in True Street? At last she determined to put aside any trepidation she might feel about returning there. The matter was too important. At least, since Julius was away, she would not be running the risk of his suddenly reappearing, even though this time she would be clutching the right kind of volume, and not a book of biology, with illustrations.

'Of course I would like to help you, Mrs Aubrey,' Mr Hunt assured her when she reappeared in his busy bookshop. 'The trouble is I am not quite as well versed as I pretend to be, my main concern being the recommendation and selling of books rather than their finer innermost meanings. However, do not despair – I can see from that pretty young face of yours that you are beginning to imagine your quest is hopeless, but it is not. For here within my own portals I have a young assistant, a graduate of Oxford no less, who is really quite brilliant when it comes to the illumination of modern poetry. Of all poetry in fact – it was and of course still is his subject. Naturally, a young man of such brilliance is only working here to pay his way while he tries to make his own name as a poet. If you like I can call him across and he will enlighten you about Robert Browning, and any other poets you might choose to try.'

'That would be very kind of you, Mr Hunt,' Emmaline replied. 'But are you sure he would not find it a burden? On top of all the work he has to do? I could perhaps pay him, of course—'

'Mrs Aubrey,' Mr Hunt cut in, holding up a hand to stop her. 'I shall introduce you to the young man and you may ask him whatever questions you need to ask about the poet and the verse. After all, that is what he is here for, that is what *I* pay him for. When a book is purchased here in my shop, I like to think that I and my assistants give our customers the very best attention, not only while they are thinking of buying it, but after they have done so. I make this a boast of mine, that my bookshop provides a unique service in this way. I doubt if you will find many other booksellers, if in fact *any* others, who adopt this philosophy.'

Leaving the acquiescent Emmaline by his desk, the courtly Mr Hunt went to find the person for whom he was looking, returning shortly afterwards with a fresh-faced young man, good-looking in a traditional Anglo-Saxon way, with curly flaxen hair and large inquisitive hazel eyes. He was tall and well proportioned, although not as tall as Julius, and Emmaline's first impression as she shook one strong hand was that his looks were more akin to those of a sportsman than a poet.

'May I present Mr Bray Ashcombe to you, Mrs Aubrey,' Mr Hunt was saying as Emmaline shook his hand, already aware of the bright hazel eyes trying to sum her up. 'Mr Ashcombe, this is Mrs Aubrey, and she is most anxious to learn to appreciate Mr Robert Browning's poetry.'

Bray Ashcombe looked at the pretty face staring up at him with such innocence of expression, and wondered at it.

'Are you a native of Bamford, Mr Ashcombe?' Emmaline enquired, much taken by the young man's open expression as well as the definite touch of mischief about his eyes.

'Most certainly, madam,' Bray replied. 'While I would guess that you are a long way from your home, which I think might be . . . in or near Boston.'

'Why, Mr Ashcombe!' Emmaline exclaimed, in mock surprise. 'How very clever of you. Have you been to America?'

'Sadly, no, Mrs Aubrey.' Bray smiled. 'I had a great friend at Oxford who was – well, he still is, actually, an American and a very fine mimic of accents from all parts of the world, especially his native country. We'd often pass the time doing accents. I taught him some English regional ones and he taught me to recognise various American ones. It's a bit of a party trick.'

'Yes, now, well, this is all very sociable, I'm sure.' Mr Hunt laughed. 'But our customer is here on a mission, young man. She wants a tutorial on Robert Browning. One of your own personal favourites, is he not?'

'Indeed he is, sir,' Bray replied, his eyes still on Emmaline. 'What in particular do you need to know, madam? How may I help you? Are you reading anything in particular?'

'*The Ring and the Book*, as it happens,' Emmaline replied. 'I purchased it here only the other day.'

'Yes, of course, I remember seeing you come in. You were wearing a dark red coat, and a fur hat. You reminded me of a painting I had just seen in London, by Mr Sargent, also an American.'

'I did? Are you sure?' Emmaline asked in some surprise, and she coloured a little at the idea that anyone could have noticed her at all.

'Indeed I do. Although my recollection is of the lady in dark red browsing in the science section rather than the poetry shelves.'

'I was looking for all sorts of books,' Emmaline said quickly. 'I like to read on many different subjects. I have a catholic attitude to knowledge.'

'As do I,' Bray agreed. 'I just don't have the time I need at my disposal.' He smiled at her, as if expecting her to say something, but Emmaline stayed silent, not wanting to seem too forward, while at the same time becoming all too aware that Mr Ashcombe's bright eyes were the twin beacons of perhaps a truly fine intelligence, and his attractive appearance was somehow the more startling for his standing in a bookshop discussing poetry.

'Very well,' Bray said, pulling a chair out for Emmaline to sit at one side of the desk. 'Please allow me. Nothing will give me greater pleasure than to help you to an understanding of Robert Browning. The distinguishing feature of Browning's poetry, the way he differs from his peers and predecessors, Mrs Aubrey, is that his style is to write mainly in monologues, not only so that he may best convey the setting and the dramatic action, but also to demonstrate the protagonist's character.'

'It is, I confess, not at all the sort of style I have been used to reading, Mr Ashcombe,' Emmaline told him, looking at him a little apologetically. 'I suppose I'm more accustomed to epic and narrative poetry, and this is where my difficulty seems to lie. I am trying to see him in a particular way and failing, and I know that, and yet I still founder, truly I do.'

'There's no need to founder, truly there is no need,' Bray assured her. 'We must still think of Browning as a Romantic poet, even though his style seems quite at odds with what we have become accustomed to see as Romantic poetry. If I may go on a little?' Emmaline nodded her consent, attending closely, loving as always to listen and learn. 'Many of these poems, not particularly the one before us, but much of Browning's verse, seem like soliloquies but this is just not so, believe me, and the deeper you journey into Browning the more you will understand this. Unlike normal soliloquies, the meaning of what Browning says in his *dramatic monologues* – which is how I like to describe them – is not what his protagonist actually seems to be saying, but often lies in what his subject reveals *involuntarily* – sometimes when trying to explain away something in the past, or to justify what he believes is the rightness of his actions. It's rather like sitting and listening in a court of law, which is where we come to the poem you are reading now – we hear Browning's character composing his defence, which we as his readers are challenged to accept or throw out of court, if you like. You'll find he chooses some pretty odd characters as his protagonists, Mrs Aubrey. No easy path for Browning – no handsome, heartbroken, dashing heroes in these pages. No, in his poems you will find some very debased characters, debauchees, perhaps even those who seem to be murderers.' Emmaline put a hand to her mouth and widened her eyes at the thought of reading about such characters in verse, the form of writing she had always taken to be the most romantic of all.

Seeing this Bray smiled, and nodded before continuing in his rich, light baritone. 'Have you read "My Last Duchess" for example, Mrs Aubrey?' When Emmaline shook her head, he went on, 'Then you will be in for a great surprise when you do, I promise you. It is written in a very sophisticated and cultivated rhetoric to suit the Duke, who is narrating it, yet it contains passages of sheer unadulterated horror, a depiction of someone losing their mind entirely, even though the lunacy is so eloquently expressed. Within the verses we learn that the duchess, the eponymous "last duchess", was murdered not because she was unfaithful or because she had no respect for her position, but merely because she enjoyed simple everyday things and habits and customs, which did not fit in with the mad Duke's scheme of things at all – while in the poem you are endeavouring to fathom Browning has written what may be described as a modern epic in which he tries to justify the ways of God to us, the readers, the jurors if you like, through twelve long monologues written in blank verse, all of them uttered by a group of people who are standing trial for murder. So you can see, if you will, that Browning is asking questions of his readers. He wants us to take an entirely different journey in poetry from the ones we have taken previously, and if we can learn his ways and accept his forms, then we shall see things in an entirely new light.'

'Thank you, Mr Ashcombe,' Emmaline said, after the short silence that followed when he had finished. 'I know that I could never, ever have arrived at such an erudite explanation.' She shook her head. 'He is obviously very demanding, is he not? Mr Robert Browning, a very demanding poet, possibly even a very demanding man, but then a man of genius, which justifies his poetic stance, does it not? Thank you so much for your exposition.'

'No need, no need at all, and you must remember, however much one is brought to *appreciate* verse, one can't be made to *like* it,' he said. 'Nothing and no one can make you like the poem other than yourself. We can admire the structure, the conception, the skill – but finally it has to involve us emotionally or intellectually. So if you are asking me to help you *like* this poet because you think you ought to, then there is no point, because that will not be the result. As is the way with so many wretched schoolchildren, who end up hating Shakespeare precisely because they have been taught to like him, instead of being taught to *understand* him while being allowed to form their own opinion.'

Bray's expression was so intense, his emotion so honest and so real, that Emmaline felt herself unusually affected. It was as if by sitting beside him she had drawn a chair up to a warm fire. His personality seemed to be radiating an impetuous vigour, a delightful determination to engage.

'Mr Ashcombe,' she said, rising and picking up her fur muff from the desk, 'I have taken up far too much of your time, but if you don't think it impolite of me I must say I have absolutely no regrets for my selfishness. You have been so very helpful with the brilliance of your explanation, and I leave this place with an altogether different and much enriched understanding of the work I am trying to read. Thank you, Mr Ashcombe. Thank you most sincerely.'

'Please, Mrs Aubrey.' Bray longed to catch at her arm, to stop her leaving, but refrained, determining instead to try to remember the exact line of her cheek, the way her eyelashes cast their shadow on that same cheek, and the delicate nature of her fragile personality. 'I assure you the pleasure has been mine. And if at any time you feel you might need any more guidance, I should be only too happy to help you.'

He felt suddenly overwhelmed by her femininity. She was not just a young woman, she was a whole essence, an aura, something come to life that he had never thought to meet.

'Thank you again, Mr Ashcombe,' Emmaline said, and turned for the door. Looking back, smiling, she called, 'Good day to you, and forgive the intrusion.'

'Good day, Mrs Aubrey,' Mr Hunt said as he showed his customer out, before glancing back to where Bray Ashcombe stood gazing after Emmaline as if he could not believe the vision that had come into the shop, that had seated itself beside him, that had listened to him with such reverence.

Arthur Hunt watched as Bray stooped to pick

up a lace-edged handkerchief which his auditor had inadvertently dropped from the confines of her furs. First he gazed at its delicate fabric, and then he held it to his nose, inhaling its scent, before slipping it into his coat pocket.

The bookseller turned away, knowing all too well what trouble that particular action could spell.

From then on Emmaline, in between setting herself to study, determined that she would also learn the rudiments of managing her household. While she was expected in the main to leave the running of the house to Mrs Graham, Emmaline, who had always liked to be involved in what was going on, decided that she was going to play a more active part in the domestic administration, so long as she did not upset any apple carts. She began by trying to find out more about the house itself.

'Is it not strange, Mrs Graham,' she asked her housekeeper one day, 'is it not passing strange that at Park House we have a newly installed telephone room—'

'Many of the larger houses in Bamford have telephones installed, madam.'

'Perhaps so, but we have electricity running everywhere downstairs, and upstairs – candles! It is as if part of the house is still living in the last century, another part in this century, and a third part, in other words the telephone room, looking towards the next!'

'I would agree entirely with you, Mrs Aubrey. The reason for it, I have been told, is that Mr Aubrey senior, whose house this was for so many years, would not compromise the plasterwork upstairs in any degree, and some of it is very old indeed, whereas downstairs it seems that it had already been altered, and could be replicated at a lesser cost.'

'You don't mind my mentioning this, Mrs Graham?'

'Certainly not, Mrs Aubrey. Mr Wilkinson and myself were talking about it only the other day.'

'Perhaps one day the upstairs will be brought into the present, Mrs Graham?'

'That would certainly be a delight. Candlelight causes so many accidents, and the marks on the ceilings, and the mess by the beds from the drips, are all too irritating, as you may imagine, Mrs Aubrey.'

'I will bear that in mind, Mrs Graham.'

Emmaline did bear it in mind, thinking as she did that it was positively dangerous to go to bed by candlelight just as if the nineteenth century had not happened. Her next project was more practical, however. She was determined to take a hand in the running of the house as far as the menus and the flower arrangements were concerned. Accordingly, she eased herself into the daily routine of talking to Mrs Graham and Cook, carefully consulting them about all the forthcoming menus, always suggesting rather than giving orders to either woman.

Before long Emmaline found not only that she was readily accepted by the servants, but that her active interest and even her contributions were actually appreciated. With Julius away once again on his business travels, Emmaline had plenty of time to get to know the people who worked for her, and due to her considerable diplomatic skills, as well as her innate good humour and charm, the atmosphere in what had previously been an eerily perfect house was now positively cheerful, on either side of the green baize door that led to the servants' quarters.

As it transpired, Emmaline's very real interest in domesticity proved to be a salvation for her, since instead of finding herself every morning and afternoon reading either in front of the fire or, now the weather had turned warmer, outside in the garden or in the conservatory, she was busy helping to organise anything with which she thought she could genuinely be of assistance. The result was an altogether better run and happier house, and an increasingly fulfilled mistress.

'One thing that concerns me, and I'm sure you will be able to help me with this, Mrs Graham,' Emmaline announced one morning as the two women were finishing their lists for the week, 'Mr Aubrey doesn't seem to entertain much, and I was wondering whether this was perhaps something in which I could take a hand? After all, it is normally the part of the wife to arrange the social calendar, as I understand it, and because of

Mr Aubrey's preoccupation with his business it might be an altogether useful and good thing if I were to pick up the reins, perhaps? What do you think, Mrs Graham?'

'It might and it might not be, madam,' Mrs Graham answered carefully. 'As you have just said, Mr Aubrey does not entertain very much, and I understand that before his marriage, when he took over the house, although none of us were here at the time, it was never his custom to entertain, except perhaps at his club. At least, that was my understanding from reading the accounts books of my predecessor. She had been at Park House for many years, do you see, so she must have known exactly how the place was run. I understand from the many and varied menus for many and varied guests – all carefully annotated, I am happy to tell you – that Mr Aubrey senior was a genial soul, and enjoyed a busy social life, but it seems his son does not take after him.'

'Well, quite; that is something I have noticed, Mrs Graham. My husband, for whatever reason, prefers solitude at home, perhaps because his work entails so much travelling.'

'Yes, indeed, madam. However, I have it noted in the household diary that it is Mr Aubrey's birthday at the end of next month, the twenty-third to be precise. So perhaps that might be a good time for you to start to entertain, madam? With a dinner in honour of Mr Aubrey's birthday, perhaps?'

'What a perfectly splendid idea, Mrs Graham.

Thank you so much.' Emmaline was about to continue with a question that had come into her mind, but the housekeeper was clearly keen to carry on talking.

'I have a list of the people who have called, something of which I always make a note,' Mrs Graham told her with growing enthusiasm. 'Sorry, Mrs Aubrey, begging your pardon – you were about to say something.'

'No, no – we must finish this piece of business first, Mrs Graham. If you would be kind enough to bring the list with you to our meeting tomorrow we could begin to draw up a guest list then, perhaps?'

'Very well, madam. Now, you were going to ask me something, Mrs Aubrey?'

'Yes,' Emmaline said, with a slight frown. 'Yes, I was. You were saying that Mr Aubrey senior enjoyed a full social life and that his son does not. Surely this might be because he is perhaps still in mourning for his father? As I understand it, the loss of a father can be particularly hard on an only son, very hard.'

'Hardly, madam,' Mrs Graham said, with a look of some surprise. 'From the records of the house which I have studied, I understand Mr Aubrey senior passed away some time ago now. Over four years ago, I think I am correct in saying. It would be surprising if Mr Julius Aubrey was still in mourning for him, unless he takes mourning to the same lengths as our dear Queen.'

'Four years ago?' Emmaline echoed, trying to

keep the dismay out of her voice. 'Are you sure, Mrs Graham?'

'Quite sure, madam,' Mrs Graham replied. 'As I say, it is all recorded in the previous house-keeper's day-to-day house diary. There is a longhand entry as well as a set of press cuttings from the local newspapers. Mr Aubrey senior was a very notable gentleman, it would seem, for apparently his funeral brought the town to a standstill, and was attended not just by the mayor of Bamford, but also by members of the aristocracy, and so on.' Mrs Graham stared at Emmaline. 'Do you find that surprising, madam?'

'No, no, of course not. My husband after all is treated as an artist by just such, so of course it would be quite natural for his father to have the same standing.'

Emmaline turned away, careful to keep her face composed while she wondered at the extent to which she was being misled, perhaps even by her housekeeper. Whom could she now believe? For some reason Julius had allowed her to presume not only that the missing portrait from the wall in the drawing room had been that of his late father, but that his father had only recently passed away, thus giving his young wife good reason to excuse her new husband's erratic behaviour on the grounds of a recent grief. Now it seemed that it must be far from being so, unless of course his love for his father had been quite extraordinary?

At all events, Emmaline was now aware that she was trying to organise a secret birthday celebration for a man who not only seemed determined on deceiving her – or encouraging her to deceive herself – but might very well, if he came to know about it, immediately forbid it.

Caught up in this new, warm-hearted conspiracy, she was obliged to leave aside her curiosity as to why Julius should have misled her about his father's death in order to concentrate on the arrangements for the first dinner she was to hold for him at Park House. It was a daunting prospect, but also, necessarily, exciting.

First of all there was the question of how many guests to invite, and then the menu to be settled, as well as the undoubted need for some kind of entertainment, musical or otherwise, after dinner.

Mrs Graham was, as always, most helpful over the choice of dinner dishes, but when it came to the baking of a birthday cake she was obliged to ask Emmaline just how many candles she should instruct Cook to put on it.

There was a short silence which turned into a long silence as Emmaline, and, she feared, Mrs Graham, realised that she had no idea how old her husband might be.

'Perhaps we should forgo the cake, Mrs Graham, in case my husband should find it an embarrassment. He might not wish anyone to know how old he was, might he?' she asked, trying to keep the hope out of her voice.

Mrs Graham considered this judiciously. It was true. Mr Aubrey, along with many other gentlemen, might indeed become irritated, a condition not unknown to gentlemen, if his age became public knowledge. She looked at her young mistress appreciatively. She was bright, but more than that she was good. Only a good person would have hesitated at such a moment in the planning, thinking of the subject of the celebration rather than her own personal feelings.

'Now, my main difficulty as hostess, Mrs Graham, as you must be well aware, is that I have had no visitors, no returning of cards, nothing that could bring about a situation where *Mrs* Julius Aubrey can make the acquaintance of Mr Julius Aubrey's friends. Of course people have called, as you well know, but there has been a . . . reluctance in that direction which I do not now know how to overcome.'

Mrs Graham nodded. Servants talked, of course they did, and Wilkinson and she had been scandalised by Mr Aubrey's intransigence as far as the receiving of calling cards was concerned. Wilkinson, indeed, had been a most reluctant participant in the whole charade: going to the door, and then having to conceal from his young mistress the fact that someone was doing her the courtesy of calling on her.

'You leave all that to me, Mrs Aubrey. I will find out exactly who will be more than happy to come, visitors from the old days who knew the family and will be flattered to be asked to such an event. After all it is important, as the mistress of Park House, that you become acquainted with them.'

'Could you really, do you think, Mrs Graham? I should be ever so grateful, if you could. I am sure you can appreciate that I live in dread of perhaps asking someone for whom, unbeknownst to me, my husband has no liking.'

All the staff, now well ensconced at Park House, had by now made friends or established acquaintance with many other servants in the neighbourhood, people they had met in the daily traffic of their own lives, or in the taverns or cafés they frequented when enjoying the little time off they were allowed. The underground network of employees was part of their daily lives, keeping tabs on the gossip, and knowing the secrets, scandalous or otherwise, of their masters' lives.

Mrs Graham, however, had the best contacts in the persons of the postmen of Bamford. One in particular, a cousin of hers by the name of John, was in possession of a positively encyclopaedic knowledge of the names and addresses on the invitations he had so often delivered to smart parts of town, invitations that bore the familiar family emblem, a falcon with outspread wings, of the Aubrey family. So it was that Mrs Graham and her network of spies soon had in their possession not just the names and addresses of the few who had visited the house since Mr Julius had married, but also those of the many who had been frequent visitors to Park House when Mr Aubrey senior had still been alive.

'Why, Mrs Graham, this is so clever of you and Wilkinson. You have put a list of possible guests together for me, and so quickly too.'

Mrs Graham smoothed down her black dress. She hoped that she did not feel immoderately proud of her connections, but she did feel she had good reason to feel mildly euphoric. This was what experience brought, a knowledge of human beings and how to use it to its best effect.

Within a short space of time Emmaline and Mrs Graham had compiled a list of people they hoped would make up a suitable party to celebrate the master of Park House's forthcoming birthday. All that now had to be done was to make sure that everyone concerned was aware of the need to maintain the all-important secrecy, and to pray that Julius Aubrey, esquire, was not going to be away from home that evening, either on business or on undisclosed pleasure, for, as they both knew, his habit of appearing and disappearing at will could well destroy everything.

Emmaline and Mrs Graham had been keeping an eye on the time for what seemed to both of them to have been hours and hours. At last they heard Julius's key in the lock, and stared at each other in wordless relief before Emmaline fled up the stairs to change into her best evening gown.

Wilkinson greeted Julius in his usual way, but even to his nervous eyes Mr Aubrey appeared to be taking for ever to climb the stairs to his dressing room, where, as was his custom, he would change into evening dress. As soon as the butler heard the dressing-room door closing, he gave the signal and the rest of the servants surged up from below stairs. Vases of flowers were put out in the drawing room and dining room, wines were decanted, and every other last-minute touch that could be made was made.

Oh, the hurrying and the scurrying that had to be effected as the guests, having left their carriages further down the street, crept into the drawing room, and Wilkinson closed the door after them. Emmaline too hurried down the stairs, her heart seeming to be literally in her mouth as she did so, dreading that Julius would either decline to come down to dinner, or decide on a whim, and without reference to her or anyone else, to go out for the evening. Happily she reached the drawing room and was able to close the double doors behind her without being either called back by her husband, or warned by Wilkinson that he was about to leave the house again.

The line of happy faces that stood about the room was so warming that Emmaline instantly forgot all about her lack of social confidence and went from one person to another introducing herself, and shaking hands, and altogether giving such a wonderfully warm and merry display that everyone present, having speculated before they met her as to her character, and the reasons behind her hasty and secret marriage, decided that Julius's choice of wife was absolutely perfect.

'What is this?' Julius wondered in unconcealed

astonishment when he opened the drawing-room door that fateful evening, thinking only to find Emmaline waiting for him with a glass of sherry before dining and instead being greeted with a sea of welcoming faces, everyone clapping lightly with gloved hands, and murmuring, 'Happy birthday, dear Julius.' Emmaline immediately hurried forward to welcome him, the clamour of the rest of the guests erupting happily around them. 'What is this?' Julius repeated. 'This is a surprise, a great surprise – an extraordinary surprise.'

'Happy birthday, Julius,' Emmaline repeated, coming to stand by his side and reaching up to kiss him on the cheek. For a second it seemed to her that he had paled with the sudden shock of seeing all the faces around him.

'Happy birthday, Julius,' his guests chorused, circling round their host. 'And many congratulations.'

'As I just said to my wife,' Julius replied, with a nod of courtesy to the assembled company, 'this *is* a surprise. A complete and utter surprise.'

Since everyone took this as an expression of delight and satisfaction, general conversation was happily resumed, well fortified now by a steady supply of champagne served by Wilkinson, George and Alan, all of whom looked delighted as they realised that the first part of the evening had gone without a hitch. As Wilkinson remarked later, '. . . and miracle of miracles, Mr Aubrey actually fetched up at the right moment, when all the time we was all certain that the party would be sure to go ahead without him.'

'Do look, Julius,' Emmaline said, gently steering her husband by one arm to a table set in one corner, which was laden with birthday gifts. 'Look how many presents you have been given. Including . . .' Emmaline looked carefully at the pile of beautifully wrapped gifts, and, finding what she was looking for, handed her present to Julius. 'Including one from me,' she finished.

'Emma, you are too kind, truly you are,' Julius muttered to her, opening the gift, tearing at the pretty paper with nervous hands. 'You shouldn't have asked all these people to wish me joy of the day. I don't deserve it.'

'Perhaps not, Julius,' Emmaline said with a calm smile, 'but then perhaps you might enjoy it. Or at least try to find it in yourself to do so, since everyone else is here for your pleasure.'

Julius glanced at her, surprised by the strength of her tone.

'A book of poems,' he remarked, having finished his unwrapping. 'Longfellow. But I think I might already have this one, might I not, Emma?'

'I don't think you do, Julius,' Emmaline said. 'I took the precaution of checking your shelves while you were away. Now come along and talk to your guests – there are many people here who knew your father and would like to make your acquaintance.'

Perhaps due to his wife's calm demeanour, Julius seemed all of a sudden to be more than willing to relax and enjoy himself, moving with growing ease from group to group, talking, listening, laughing. Emmaline watched with increasing pleasure as the enjoyment mounted in the drawing room until, after checking with Mrs Graham that everything was ready, she gave instructions for her guests to be summoned to table.

After the ladies had retired, the gentlemen remained at table to drink the vintage cognac on offer and smoke the fine cigars, leaving Emmaline to attend to the needs of her female guests, none of whom she had ever met socially, although a few of them were known to her by sight.

'My dear Mrs Aubrey,' one tall, handsome older woman said to her, coming to sit by her on the small sofa on the landing as they waited for the rest of the ladies to finish their toilet. 'We have not had the pleasure of meeting either you or your husband until tonight, although of course his father was well known to all of us. I did call on you shortly after your marriage and leave my card, but it seems that you might not have received it?'

'I must apologise for that,' Emmaline said quickly. 'There was a quite unnecessary confusion as to where the calling cards should be placed, and as a consequence quite a few became mislaid. It was a consequence of my only having been newly arrived in Bamford.'

'Perfectly understandable in the first flush of marriage, my dear, let alone arriving in a new

193

neighbourhood. In case you haven't yet put names to faces, I am Marguerite Bateson, Sir Henry Bateson's wife. We live in Sutton George, a few miles beyond the town. Perhaps you will be kind enough to come to one of my At Homes? I shall have my maid call and leave a card.'

'Thank you,' Emmaline replied. 'I would be more than happy to accept such an invitation.'

'Good. Now tell me what part of America you are from. Henry and I intend to visit your country next year, not extensively, there will not be the time, just New York, and then a visit to some relatives in Pittsburgh which I understand is in Pennsylvania.'

'I was born and raised further north, in Massachusetts, in a small town outside Greenfield, about a hundred miles from Boston.'

'Ah, Boston.' Marguerite smiled, tapping Emmaline on her knee with her closed fan. 'Where you held that naughty old tea party.'

Emmaline smiled. 'A pity you will not be visiting Boston,' she said. 'It's a fine city, with a great deal to see.'

'I am quite sure I would appreciate it greatly,' Marguerite agreed. 'But not dear Henry. If I took Henry there I am sure I would have trouble restraining him from burning the place down. It was all the fault of George the Third, of course, but nevertheless Henry is very imperialistic, far too much so in my opinion.'

Emmaline smiled politely once again, and then, seeing that all the ladies were now ready, she led the way back into the drawing room to wait for the gentlemen to join them, which they did almost immediately. All parties, it seemed, had been both well dined and well wined, the gentlemen especially, if the colour of their heightened complexions was anything to go by.

'If I may say, Emma, indeed I must tell you,' Julius said to her as he came to stand by her side, 'you are looking really very pretty this evening, very pretty indeed. The prettiest young woman in the room, I would say.'

'Thank you, Julius,' Emmaline replied, trying not to sound surprised.

Julius nodded appreciatively as Emmaline fanned herself gently. 'That colour, truly, that colour, well, it certainly suits you.'

Emmaline now allowed herself to look more than pleased, for she had been careful to choose both the colour and the style of the gown with Julius very much in mind, hoping that the warmth of the deep red silk would show off her pale skin, and that the cut of the top of the dress, with its ruched edges, would flatter and accentuate her breasts. Once or twice during the evening, when she was sure he did not know she was looking his way, she had thought she had caught him staring at her, as if he had not quite noticed her femininity before, or perhaps because for once there were other men present who seemed really very happy to appreciate both her looks and her young rounded shape. Whatever the reason, Julius was quite definitely more aware of her than he had been since they first danced together in America.

'Yes, Emma, you are looking ravishing, if I may say so.'

'Thank you, Julius,' Emmaline said again. 'I am sorry to interrupt you, but I have to announce the entertainment.'

'Yes, of course.'

He bowed, and Emmaline moved away from him, nodding a signal to Wilkinson to call for quiet.

'If I may have your attention for a minute, ladies and gentlemen?' Emmaline requested once the conversation had died down. 'It being my husband Julius's birthday, as you are all aware, I have arranged a small entertainment in his honour – and of course for your pleasure as well. First of all Mr Arthur Chesterman is going to sing for us, accompanied by Miss Elizabeth Caldecott at the pianoforte, his first song being "Who is Sylvia?" by Franz Schubert.'

Mr Arthur Chesterman, a noted local amateur tenor, and the pianist, an earnest young woman who was the singer's usual accompanist, took their places at Julius's fine Blüthner grand and sang Schubert's already world-famous *Lieder,* followed by Mendelssohn's 'On Wings of Song', both rendered to perfection and much to the delight of the company. Two of the guests, Mr Alfred Booth and his fiancée Miss Constance Stokes, then sang a medley of songs from Gilbert and Sullivan's *HMS Pinafore* accompanied this

196

time by Emmaline herself at the piano, and finally Mr Arthur Chesterman returned to conclude the recital with a fine rendition of Schubert's 'Wandering'.

After she had thanked the singers and the bespectacled Miss Caldecott for their wonderful efforts, Emmaline, looking not just pretty but quite beautiful, filled as she was with the warmth of the evening that she had created for her husband, then addressed her guests.

'The entertainment is not quite at an end,' she told them. 'If I may crave your indulgence for just a few moments more, I would like to give my dear husband, Julius, a special present on his birthday.'

She smiled across at Julius, for once feeling confident of what she was about to do, while the audience, their attention having been gained, waited with great interest to see what was coming next.

'Ladies and gentlemen, as you are no doubt aware, I am new to England, but have been at great pains to try to adapt to your charming ways, as I have to those of my husband. With this in mind I have recently learned of Julius's great love of poetry, which is something I think I share with him, although in no way do I see myself as any kind of equal, I hasten to add!' This earned Emmaline some appreciative laughter from her guests. 'I was going to recite some Robert Browning, who I know is a particular favourite of my husband's, but although I have learned to admire Mr Browning's great verse, I could not find anything in his works that was appropriate to this occasion. So instead I have chosen a poem written by his wife, Elizabeth Barrett Browning. It is entitled "If Thou Must Love Me".'

At this moment Miss Caldecott, having seated herself once more at the piano, as previously arranged, played a charming little introduction she herself had composed for the occasion. As the chords died away, Emmaline began to recite.

'If thou must love me, let it be for naught
Except for love's sake only. Do not say,
"I love her for her smile, her look, her way
Of speaking gently, for a trick of thought
That falls in well with mine, and certes brought
A sense of pleasant ease on such a day",
For these things in themselves, Belovèd, may
Be changed, or change for thee, and love, so wrought,
May be unwrought so. Neither love me for
Thine own dear pity's wiping my cheeks dry:
A creature might forget to weep, who bore
Thy comfort long, and lose thy love thereby!
But love me for love's sake, that evermore
Thou mayst love on, through love's eternity.'

As Emmaline finished the recitation she realised that so involved had she been, so intense had been her wish to convey the right emotion, that she had closed her eyes. Now she opened them and saw her audience applauding her with genuine enthusiasm, the gentlemen in particular.

She bowed several times in response, feeling as happy as she had ever felt, and it was only as the applause died away that she noticed that there was one pair of hands that had not been applauding. Julius's chair was empty, and as she took this in she realised that the people who had been seated either side of him were looking not just embarrassed for her, but mortified.

'Julius?'

'He went that way,' one of the women said. 'My dear, I think he was overcome by such a pretty sight – just too affected.'

Emmaline shook her head, and taking her lace-edged handkerchief she dabbed her forehead with it, feeling suddenly both sick and faint.

What can I have done now? she wondered, trying to catch the breath that seemed to have frozen in her throat. *Why ever should Julius get up and leave the room in the middle of the poem – what can I have done now?*

She slipped out into the corridor, hoping to find him standing outside, perhaps, as the older lady had remarked, overcome by the sad, sweet nature of the poem, but there was no one there, the corridor was empty. She searched further, longing to find him doing anything, anything at all, rather than have to admit what she and Mrs Graham, and indeed Wilkinson, had dreaded all along – that Julius had disappeared.

Drawing a blank, and reluctant to absent herself for too long from her guests, Emmaline leaned against the wall in the corridor, breathing deeply in an attempt to stop her head from swimming. Beyond the door she could hear the heightened buzz of conversation, talk that sounded animated and inquisitive, and it seemed to her that every-one in the drawing room was busy discussing Julius's disappearance.

After a minute or two, possibly as a distraction, someone began to play the piano again, some introductory chords, after which a new female voice arose singing another of Sir Arthur Sullivan's popular ballads, 'The Moon and I'.

Feeling sufficiently recovered to rejoin her guests, Emmaline straightened her dress, took one last deep breath and prepared to re-enter the fray, but was prevented from doing so by the sound of voices in the main hallway.

'You have to wonder what kind of man would apparently take such exception to his wife's re-citing a perfectly beautiful poem like that?' the first light female voice was saying. 'The dear little creature was so obviously directing the senti-ments most firmly his way. What a compliment to a husband, and what a little beauty she is. Julius doesn't realise how lucky he is, I would say.'

'I only wish I had the courage to do something quite as enchanting,' the second voice replied. It was a deep female voice that Emmaline immediately recognized as belonging to Marguerite Bateson. 'Can you imagine if I stood up and recited a love poem to Henry on his birthday? He'd probably take a horsewhip to me.'

'The man must have no feelings,' the first

voice said. 'He must have an iceberg for a heart. Of course his father was an old rogue, deserted the mother in France, left her with the children, caring naught for any of them and coming here.'

'I have heard how terribly difficult he is, have you not?' came Marguerite Bateson's response. 'But then, given the family history, I suppose there is reason. Even so, such behaviour! Poor little Emmaline, poor, poor Emmaline.'

'I do hope you mean poor as in unfortunate, Marguerite,' the first voice chided her companion drily, 'because as we all know she certainly did not come poor to England in any other sense, not poor at all. Are you sufficiently cool now to return to the party? Because I think I am.'

Wishing to get back into the drawing room herself before the two women she had just overheard, Emmaline hurried towards the door at the less crowded end of the room, so that she was able to slip back into the room unobserved. She herself, however, was well able to observe that there was still no sign of her husband.

'Have you seen Mr Aubrey?' she asked Wilkinson some time later, when she had the chance to do so. 'I do not seem to be able to find him anywhere.'

'No, madam,' Wilkinson replied, but from the look in his eyes Emmaline knew at once that he meant the very opposite. 'Would you like me to see if I can locate him? He might have gone upstairs.'

'In that case, Wilkinson,' Emmaline replied,

understanding the butler's meaning, 'let us leave it until later.'

'I feel that might be wise, madam,' Wilkinson agreed. 'Under the circumstances.'

Shortly afterwards a general exodus began, carriages having been called for eleven. Everyone thanked Emmaline for a most entertaining evening, many expressing the wish that they would be seeing her at their own houses sooner rather than later. Their obvious sincerity had the effect of making Emmaline feel for the first time that she was actually welcome in Bamford. Not one guest referred to Julius's absence, which seemed to Emmaline most definitely odd, but then, on the other hand, perhaps that was the way the English went on. Noticing but not saying.

At last the drawing room was empty of everyone except the servants. Dolly had reappeared clothed in a great black apron, ready to damp down the fires and re-lay them, while Alan and George set about helping Mr Wilkinson to clear up.

'Bedtime, madam?' Agnes said, hovering around her mistress. 'I've turned your bed down and laid out your things, so if you would care to go up now . . .'

Emmaline nodded, turning from staring into the re-laid fires.

'I want to thank you all for helping me to give this lovely evening for my husband. I am quite sure that he will wish to thank you himself, in time, but for the moment I am here to tell you that I could not be luckier in you all, truly. I only hope that you enjoyed yourselves too.'

Wilkinson looked quite affected by this little speech, and gave a short bow, glancing round at the rest of the staff.

'We did, Mrs Aubrey, and, if I may say so, we were all more than happy to see that all your guests enjoyed theirselves so very much, and that the evening went with such zest, and no one could or did go home feeling anything except happy.'

Emmaline smiled. 'Thank you, Wilkinson, thank you very much. Now I am sure we are all plumb tired out, as we say in America, so I will wish you all the best of nights and hope for many more such pleasant experiences.'

She turned away, trying not to notice the compassion in the eyes directed towards her. They all knew that her heart was fairly broken by the night's events, and that the last part of the evening had been a nightmare, saying goodnight to all her guests, seeing how embarrassed they felt for her.

She climbed the stairs to bed, too proud even to glance towards Julius's dressing-room door to see if there was light coming from under it. She couldn't care less where he was, indeed she cared so little that for a second, as she entered the bed-room, it seemed to her that she would be quite happy if he stayed away all night.

Once Agnes had helped her undress and had

brushed out her hair, chattering away about the evening and asking her mistress how everything had gone, Emmaline thanked her and dismissed her, but remained at her dressing table for a moment, not wishing to get into bed until she had composed her thoughts.

'You sure you're all right, madam?' Agnes asked from the doorway, as if sensing something was wrong.

'I am perfectly fine, Aggie, thank you,' Emmaline replied. 'Now run along. You must be asleep on your feet, you poor child.'

She waited for Agnes to disappear down the corridor, listening for the sound of her squeaking footwear to recede, and then she quietly turned the key in the bedroom door before sitting down at the dressing table again. She had not yet been married in the biblical sense, and ignorant though she might be of such matters, she was not so stupid, nor so humble, that she would ever again entertain the idea of letting Julius into the room until he had apologised for his behaviour towards her. He had behaved abominably, and while he might think this was perfectly acceptable in an English husband, it was perfectly unacceptable to Emmaline. She would stand up to him, even if it meant leaving England. She had finally had enough, she was sure of it.

And then too there was the matter of the overheard conversation. The woman who had referred to Emmaline's dowry. How had she known of such a thing? Very well, it was not unusual for an American girl to have a large dowry, indeed it was currently quite fashionable for American heiresses to marry Englishmen, and so endow their husbands' ailing estates with their new-found wealth. Onslow Nesbitt was a very rich man, and unlike many rich men liked to spend his money. This, coupled with his quite outspoken desire to have the eldest and plainest of his daughters married off, meant that he was more than likely to have erred on the generous side when deciding the exact sum he would hand over to Julius Aubrey.

Nevertheless, it was puzzling to Emmaline that anyone other than Julius and his bank manager could have any idea of what the English called her *dot*. Yet it would seem that it was actually common knowledge among the gentlefolk of Bamford that Miss Emmaline Nesbitt had been an heiress of some considerable means.

Emmaline's spirits sank still further as she realised that the source of such knowledge must have been Julius himself. She started to see him in a new, darker light. Perhaps the night he so infamously mixed his drinks – their wedding night – had been the night when he disclosed such facts, perhaps at his club? Or perhaps he had been frequenting some downtown bar and had boasted of Emmaline's dowry? Once they had had too much to drink men were so often indiscreet, and with women, it sometimes seemed to her, it only took a cup of tea.

Her thoughts turned to the matter of Julius's

walking out during her recitation of that lovely verse.

What could have been more suitable to celebrate a husband's birthday than the recital of a poem such as that? Why had he walked out? If he had been temporarily unwell and had to be excused she could have understood, yet from the emotions reflected on the faces of her guests it seemed that he had walked out in embarrassment, which was, in itself, unbelievable. Certainly, surely, it could not have been because he didn't like the poetry of Elizabeth Barrett Browning, because she knew for a fact that he did, for she remembered quite exactly that he had, at some point, made some casual reference to doing so. Perhaps he did not hold her work in as much reverence as that of *Robert* Browning, but far from dismissing it as sentimental, or simply the scribblings of a woman, he had given Emmaline the distinct impression that he had great admiration for some of her verses, in particular the *Sonnets from the Portuguese*, of which the poem she had chosen was, as it happened, the fourth.

Nor could he have found the *content* of the poem offensive, since its emotion was so tenderly expressed. Yet *something* must have upset him so much that he had found himself quite able to stand up and walk out, very publicly, when his wife of only a short time was presenting him with a flattering and generous moment, dedicated to him alone.

There was the sound of a scratch at the door.

Emmaline turned from her dressing-table mirror and stared at the locked door.

She would not open it to anyone, let alone someone.

She decided on pretence.

'Aggie, thank you, but I have no need of anything more. You may go, thank you,' she called, and having blown out the candles on her dressing table she crept to the bed, and slipped into it.

Again a scratch at the door, this time followed by a male voice.

'Emma?'

She remained silent.

'Emma?'

She still said nothing.

'Emma? Please open the door. It is Julius.'

Emmaline pretended to yawn. 'Goodnight, Julius.'

'Emma, open this door, please.' He knocked harder.

Afraid that one or two of the servants might still be up, and would overhear them quarrelling, Emmaline lit her bedstick and went to the door. She unlocked it, making sure at the same time to hold up the candle in front of her so that it acted as a shield.

'Can you not sleep after all your birthday excitement, Julius?'

Julius walked into the room, and going up to her dressing table he lit the candles on it.

'One day I will convert the upper storeys to gas,' he remarked absently. 'But truly I prefer candlelight – it is so much more flattering to women, don't you think?'

Emmaline walked quickly down the room, still holding her bedstick in front of her. 'I am sure, and to men too, Julius, particularly older men, I would have thought.'

He started at that. It was the first time she had mentioned his age, and the fact that she did so implied that she knew he was older than her by a good few years.

'You know more about me than I realised, Emma,' he said, looking thoughtful.

'Yes, perhaps I do,' Emmaline agreed coldly. 'Is there something you wanted, Mr Aubrey? I am quite tired. It has been such a long evening. All the worry of it, you know, is very fatiguing.'

'Yes, yes, of course, I perfectly appreciate that,' Julius agreed. 'But I felt I should come and see you to explain my behaviour tonight, which must have seemed a little odd to you.'

'Please, you may behave as you like. You are after all in your own country. An Englishman's home is his castle, they say, and it seems that his wife is also his chattel.'

'That's not quite fair, Emma.'

'I am very sorry, but I find it quite fair, Mr Aubrey, if I may so address you despite there being no servants present? No, I find it very fair. Try as I do to be an exemplary wife to you, Julius, it seems I can only end up by embarrassing you.'

'That is certainly not quite fair. I was very pleased with the early part of the evening. You looked charming, and the idea of surprising me in that way, well, it was quite touching, really. No, the early part of the evening was most pleasing.'

'I am very glad to hear it. Now, perhaps, having conveyed your sentiments so honestly, perhaps you would like to leave *my* bedroom?'

'No, I would not like to leave . . . your bedroom, Emma, not until I have explained myself to you.'

'Very well, explain where you went when I was reciting.'

'Where do you think I went? I went out. I left the room. Because—' He stopped. 'Because I . . .'

'Because you?'

'Because I was very moved. I had to leave the room, as you were finishing. I was intensely moved. There is no other word for it. More than anything I was touched by the pains you had taken, by your – sweet ways, but I didn't want anyone else to see how moved I was, I thought it might prove embarrassing for both of us.'

'I was saying a poem for you, Julius!' Emmaline protested. 'What can possibly be embarrassing about that?'

'It is sometimes embarrassing for people to witness other people – in this case another person – making known their personal feelings in public. That is considered embarrassing in England.'

'What in heaven's name can you mean, Julius? What *are* you allowed to do in this country? You can't mention someone's belongings – you can't show feelings – what *can* you do?'

'This is England, Emma, in case you haven't

noticed,' Julius told her in a tired tone. 'This is not America.'

'That is something of which, believe me, I am becoming rapidly aware, thank you. What is the matter with people in England? What is the matter with *you*, Julius?'

'The matter with me?' Julius looked shocked. 'Why should anything be the matter with me?'

'You are so different from the man I met in America, so, so different. There you seemed – you seemed so . . .' She stopped, shaking her head at the memory of the enchanting man who had rescued her from that wretched gilt chair, danced with her, walked with her, waited for her.

'I am not so very different, Emma, truly I am not. I *truly* am not. I know that married life can be very difficult—'

'Difficult!' The word burst from Emmaline. 'It is not *difficult* to be married to you, Mr Aubrey, it is impossible.'

'Can you lower your voice a little? The servants, you know.'

'I could not care less what the servants hear or don't hear!' Emmaline retorted. 'It might have escaped your attention, Julius – and if it has it is surely because you would wish it to do so – but we are married. We are husband and wife.' She stopped, looking at him, wondering how best to put Julius's failings as a husband to him. 'You haven't once shown me any affection, Julius, not once,' she finally said. 'The way we live, why, we could be brother and sister, really we could.'

'You have full charge of the house, we talk, we dine together, I go to business. That is what marriage is about, surely?' Julius pleaded.

'Of course,' Emmaline agreed, although finding herself momentarily confused by Julius's strange expression and tone. 'You know it to be so, and I know it to be so, but there should be other things that men and women do together.'

'Please, don't let us talk of those things. It is not suitable. You are a nicely brought up young woman, and it is not suitable to talk about what men and women do together.'

Emmaline coloured, and turned away quickly, because she had the feeling that he was mocking her ignorance. She sat down at her dressing table, her back to her mirror, unable to bear to see what she knew would be the quite evident distress in her face. She must not cry, she must not give way, she must not let her emotions show, she was in England.

She let a long pause go by as she composed herself, and then she started again.

'When I was at that ball, in America, what now seems a century ago, a handsome Englishman came over and requested a dance. I was so pleased. Not just because I had been an all too obvious wallflower for the whole evening, up until that moment, but because the man who was asking me to dance with him was tall and elegant and good-looking. The next day when that same man called on me, and talked to me, and walked with me round the lake, I knew he was—'

211

'Emma!' Julius said, holding up his hands in an attempt to stop her, but Emmaline would not be stopped.

'I will not be quietened, Julius! I simply will not remain silent any more. It is because I have been silent that I was almost forced to – no, I was *determined* to show you this evening! To show you! I wanted to show you.'

'Tonight? This evening? What precisely was it you wished to show me? And why, Emma, should you want to show me anything? Do we not live together? Do we not share everything here together? I certainly do, and I am only sorry to hear that you do not feel the same way about our sharing, about our life together.'

Emmaline gazed up in astonishment at the man standing in front of her. 'Very well. All I wanted, all I wanted tonight at your birthday evening, was to show you . . . my feelings,' she finally stated. 'That is all, Julius. That is all I wanted to show you.'

'And you did, Emma, you did.' Julius turned suddenly on his heel, and wrenching open the bedroom door he left, shutting it behind him with commendable quietness.

Emmaline did not stir from her dressing-table stool for some time, and then she drifted hopelessly towards the door that Julius had closed, and slowly turned the key in the lock. Too sad for tears, she lay back against her pillows and stared down the room until finally the candle beside her spluttered and went out, and the birds outside her window began to sing, and she could see the pink light of dawn between the gap in the curtains. Shortly, Agnes would arrive, and she would take tea, and they would talk, and her mind would be taken off her present misery.

Chapter Eight

It seemed the subject of the recitation of the poem was not to be raised again by either Julius or Emmaline, but that did not prevent Julius from making sure that Emmaline was fully aware of her good fortune in being his wife.

Perhaps feeling that in light of their quarrel she had need of the point's being driven home to her, he soon found an opportunity to closet himself with her in the drawing room, where he was at pains to reassure her.

'You have a good home in a fine house. You have security and stability, and now that you have effected your introduction to all my father's old friends and acquaintances you have a place in Bamford society, so if you take my advice you will cease to fret, or to give a poor imitation of a bird locked up in a gilded cage, and start to be happy, as a good wife should.'

Emmaline looked up at him in despair. How could he imagine that a person could be *ordered* to be happy, could be *ordered* to be grateful. It was absurd. You might as well order someone who was happy to be miserable!

'What, Emma, you have to learn is to be accepting of the way things are here. This is the way of things, this is how they are, and we must accept that as a fact and not think that by questioning it we can change the status quo. You are in England, you are married to an Englishman, and whether or not you understand me, or indeed agree with what I have to say, is entirely your own business, since what you say or what you feel will have no bearing at all on how I view such matters, you understand?'

'Yes, Julius,' Emmaline said in a voice utterly drained of emotion.

'I trust, Emma, that you will be happy from now on, that you will try to be happy,' he pleaded.

'Yes, I will try, Julius,' Emmaline replied, clearing her throat, and at the same time determining to pull herself together. 'Thanks to your frankness I now understand my position, and I shall take time to examine it before I conclude how best I may live here as your wife.'

'Forgive me, Emma,' Julius begged. This time it was he who cleared his throat. 'So, where was I? Yes, it is perfectly clear, I think, to both of us, we have a clear understanding, do we not, as to how best you may live here as my wife, as you put it? As a matter of fact, if you think back, it was made abundantly clear in the wedding service how best you may live here as my wife.' Julius smiled down at her, the look in his eyes suddenly tender. 'You promised, if you remember, to love, honour and obey me.'

'To love, honour and obey you?' Emmaline's heart sank as she remembered what now seemed to her to be such strangely medieval words. 'Is this what you intend our marriage to be about, Julius? About loving, honouring and obeying each other?'

'Naturally. Why else would we have been married in a church and repeated those sacred words? Now, shall we go in to dinner? You must know I am going away tomorrow, so I will need to retire early. Thank you, Emma, for being so good as to listen to me as you have. Perhaps you will be sweet enough to play to me after dinner. You have a fine touch, a very fine touch.'

Emmaline knew she had been unhappy before, but in the ensuing days, with Julius thankfully absent, she found out something quite different, she found out the true meaning of the word misery. It was not just the confusion that unhappiness brings, it was not just the loneliness, it was the despair that accompanies all those emotions that turns unhappiness into utter misery. All of a sudden she thought she knew what it was like for Pilgrim to fall into the Slough of Despond.

Day after day, as she forced herself to pretend to take a continuing interest in the domestic affairs of the house, she found herself wandering the corridors or the garden, turning everything over and over in her mind. Why had she come to England? Was it because she had wanted to marry a man she had been deeply attracted to, or was it to get away from her family? Or had she come for the sake of her younger sisters – had she made of herself some kind of willing sacrifice so that they would be freed? Or had she married just to, as the saying went, get a ring on her finger? The answer to all those questions was a most definite no. She had married Julius because he pleased her, because he was elegant and handsome, and from the moment he had danced with her she had quite lost her heart to the idea of his being her husband-to-be.

Day after day she had also to ask herself whether she loved Julius now as she had done, as she perhaps should. The answer to that was also a most definite no. She could not now love him, surely? It was not possible. But, knowing that to be true, she had to admit to herself that she had once loved him. Therefore, for whatever reason, perhaps he too had once loved her, before she came to England? Therefore, had she done something – not the poem, long before that – had she said or done something which in the mind of a reticent Englishman could have destroyed that love? Had she committed some unknown social sin that had made him unable to go on feeling as he might once have felt?

And yet.

And yet it was Julius who had said repeatedly

on the night of their wedding, *How could I do this? What have I done?*

Was it something to do with his business? Was it that to which he had been referring? Or had she remembered it all wrong? Perhaps he was referring to something terrible that he had done that night. Had he committed a crime? Done something so terrible that he could not even tell his wife?

Finally, unable to sleep or eat to any degree at all, Emmaline came to the only decision that she thought was possible. She would have to leave her husband and bury all the misery he had brought so unnecessarily into her life in a past which, however painful, would at least be short-lived.

She had every reason not to stay. Although they were married in name, Emmaline knew that this was no marriage because there had not been what her mother sometimes referred to in a vague voice as *the marriage act* – and although, most unfortunately, Emmaline did not understand as yet what the phrase embraced, she was well aware that it, whatever it was, had not happened. She had also gathered, if only from novels, that if a man took a wife and then treated her as Julius seemed to be treating her, as a sister, the union could be declared invalid, leaving the innocent party to retain her innocence, and finally regain her freedom.

She decided to write to her father and explain that she had made a terrible mistake, and that she would be coming home just as soon as she could book a passage, but then, facing the reality of the letter, day in and day out, she found herself strangely unable to pick up her pen. Finally when she did it was in words that made her ashamed of her inability to express herself in an original manner.

Dearest Father, I do hope this letter does not find you as it finds me – most terribly unhappy . . .

Emmaline put down her pen, suddenly hearing imagined words in her head, seeing her father reading the letter, hearing in her head just how he would mock her in front of her mother and sisters.

Oh dear, Anthea, oh dear, girls, just as we all thought we'd got rid of her, back Emmaline comes, like a bad penny. Shall we suggest we change her name to Penny, Anthea? It would be appropriate, as well as amusing.

Emmaline was well aware that everyone at home would laugh at her behind her back, while sympathising to her face. A few weeks would pass, but only a very few, before they would start reminding her that they had told her not to trust an Englishman, that they knew such a marriage wouldn't last – that it had been doomed from the start. They would claim that they all knew she was doing the wrong thing, rushing headlong into marriage with a stranger, but they had not dared to tell her. After which they would set about privately pitying her, because they would know that her chances of marrying again were nil. She would be on the shelf, an old maid, a spinster, unfulfilled by either life or marriage. They would also say, behind her back, that they had known all along that Julius was just another English adventurer who was simply after Emmaline's money, that there could have been no other reason why he had suddenly turned up on the family doorstep and set his cap at someone as plain as Emmaline.

And that was all before they began to feel bitter and uneasy, thinking, no matter what their current circumstances – Charity already engaged, Ambrosia about to be the same – that she had brought shame on the family, and that their own future establishment would be threatened.

Despite all these imaginings, once again Emmaline began her letter to her father.

Dear Father, As you may know I am safely married, safely, yes, but unhappily. Oh, Father, please may I come home? If only you knew how miserable I have been made by Mr Julius Aubrey . . .

Emmaline stared at the words she had written, and saw at once that they were self-pitying, and that, as old Mary their Irish maid had always said, *if you feel sorry for yourself, dotie, there's nothing for anyone else to do.*

So she tore the half-started letters up, and put them on the fire. And as she watched them burning, burning as fiercely as her spirit was grieving, she became aware that she might as well be burning her marriage, her time at Park House, because, aside from the servants who were all now her friends and, she was well aware, pitied her situation, she could see no one and nothing that had any point for her.

'Here I go again,' she scolded herself. 'Here I go feeling sorry for myself. I must stop feeling sorry for myself, and think.'

This was really where her innate misery lay. Her mind had become incapable of seeing things calmly, of finding a way out of the despair in which she had allowed it to be enveloped. She would, if she were her own best friend, be able to accuse herself of indulging her emotions to a ridiculous degree. She must pull herself together and make the most of whatever it was that life was presenting to her. To do less than that would be shaming.

First things first. She would make a list. This had always helped her with her school work, and now more than ever it could help her again.

She wrote *Emmaline Aubrey – her sorrows,* but that too looked so self-pitying that she scratched it out and wrote *my sorrows* out fifty times, as a punishment, and then threw that page too in the fire.

Very well, Miss Emmaline Nesbitt, now is the time to sing, to play, but not to feel sorry for yourself.

Oh, my Lord! She had called herself by her maiden name, not by her married name. Perhaps that was the trouble? In her own *mind* she was unmarried, not just in her body.

What I must do is try to win Julius back by my own faith and diligence. I must win back not only Julius's respect, but finally also his love, for I know he has felt,

*might still feel, something for me. Why otherwise do I
find him looking towards me suddenly as if he would
love to love me? Why has he on occasion stroked my
hair with such a tender touch?*

She determined on one final effort, while recognising in herself an understandable reluctance
to face any of the people who had witnessed her
humiliation at the party. Carriages came and
went leaving elegant engraved calling cards, but
Emmaline gave it out through the servants that
she was unwell, unable at the moment to attend
At Homes, or return calls. Meanwhile, with Julius
still away on business, she lay on a chaise longue
in her dressing room, staring into the fire, and
struggling with her despair.

Happily the weather continued to be fine and
warm, even as summer began to edge towards
autumn, with the colours fading in the borders
and on the roses as the garden started to go over.
In the borders the herbaceous plants grew too
tall to stay upright, their heads turning to seed
pods and their leaves browning and curling at
the edges, advertising in advance nature's general
move towards winter.

Sometimes, although only at Agnes's urging,
Emmaline would snatch up a shawl and leave
her room to wander round the grounds, picking
the best of what was left of the roses, which she
would then be encouraged by the ever faithful
Mrs Graham to arrange into magnificent displays
to be enjoyed by herself and the servants.

At other times she would just sit in the shade

of a large umbrella on the terrace watching blackbirds pulling worms from the lawns, and swallows building up their strength for the coming migration to warmer climes.

It was as the first leaves of autumn began to fall that Emmaline started to write poetry, and unlike her tentative forays into letter-writing, she did not tear up the pages that she started to work on in her generous sloping hand.

So easily did the first verses come that it was as if she had always done it, and so mystified was she by the process that when she had put down her pen she was startled to realise that she had no recollection of how or when she had begun. She found herself sitting on the terrace as was her wont, a fine lace shawl round her shoulders and a glass of freshly made lemonade on the occasional table Wilkinson always set out for her, with the notebook she used as an *aide-memoire* for household matters open in front of her, but instead of lists of household necessities, and suggested menus, she saw she had written a four-verse poem.

She stared at it, reading it and re-reading it, each time understanding it less, incapable of judging its merit. The verses seemed to rhyme and they appeared not to be doggerel, yet, as she immediately realised, she could not possibly be the best judge of that if she was unable to judge the poem at all. Even so, just as the verses seemed to rhyme and to be written in the correct rhythm, they also seemed to express some of the emotions

Emmaline had been feeling, although when she realised just how much of her soul she had exposed she quickly shut the notebook and left it locked in the bureau in the bedroom for several days, even imagining that when the time came to retrieve it she would find the pages to be blank, leaving her to imagine that she must have fallen asleep in the warm September sun and dreamed the whole experience.

But when she did come to unlock her desk drawer and take out the notebook, there indeed the poem was, just as she had remembered it. So the following afternoon, once again left to her own devices, Emmaline wrote another – a longer poem that she was nowhere near finishing when Dolly clattered out on to the terrace with a tray of tea, and some delicately made watercress sandwiches.

'I'm sorry, Mrs Aubrey, but Cook sends to tell you that you're to eat up all the sandwiches or she will want to know the reason why. She don't like the sight of so much of her food coming back down to the kitchens again, so be a good lady, Cook says, and eat up good and proper.' Dolly stood back. 'Cook is worried about you, and so is Mrs Graham, and so is I, Mrs Aubrey. We all want you to be happy and smiling same as you were before the master's birthday dinner.'

Emmaline looked up, startled. She had had no idea until that moment quite how much the servants were all worrying about her. She felt guilty, as if she had brought them down by her misery-making and self-pity. She reached forward for a plate, and of course a sandwich.

'Tell Cook I will try to eat the whole plate of sandwiches, and they are perfectly delicious,' she instructed Dolly as the maid poured the tea for her. 'And tell her that I will make more of an effort at dinner too. But tell her too that it is just a little difficult for a woman to eat on her own.'

'That's just what I said, Mrs Aubrey. I said since you are always on your own, the master away so much at the moment, your appetite is bound to drop off of you, same as it always does my mother, at certain times in particular.'

Emmaline glanced up at Dolly. She had no idea what the young girl was talking about, but she was such a dear little girl she knew she must respond.

'I shall eat like a horse from now on,' she said, and Dolly quickly noted that her mistress was already sounding a great deal more herself.

'I will tell Cook, right away I will. I will tell her that you will be eating for – that you will be eating more, eh?'

There was silence after Dolly had clattered off, looking happily bright and perky. Emmaline ate as much as she could, and drank some tea, before once more picking up her notebook, fully expecting, yet again, to find that the poem had disappeared and she had merely dreamed it. But it was not so. The poem was there.

Seeing her words again Emmaline felt oddly excited, as if she had been taken over by some invisible force that had become part of her and was now allowing her to express herself in a way she would never previously have thought possible. The more she read through her two finished works the more she longed to be able to show them to someone, just to see if they were passable.

Of course! she suddenly realised as she sat sipping her tea in the pale glow of early evening. *I could show them to the young man in the bookshop – to Mr Ashcombe!* It was indeed a possibility, since of all the people she had now met at Bamford, there in Mr Ashcombe was someone who not only loved and appreciated poetry, but had achieved a first-class degree in English, which would more than qualify him to comment on the merits, or demerits, of her own verses. Naturally she would not be able to show him the poems as her own; they would have to be said to have been written by a *friend*, and because Emmaline herself had thought rather highly of them she had brought them into Mr Hunt's bookshop for not only a second opinion but a far more qualified one.

It seemed to Emmaline, as she carefully locked her notebook away in her Davenport desk, that hers was a perfect plan, and what was more a feasible one too. With Julius still away on his business travels she had no worries about being spied upon. Moreover, while she was in town, she might even call and leave her card on Mrs Henry Bateson, who had done the same to her only the day before, calling and leaving another card with a message that expressed concern that Emmaline was unwell, and hoped she would soon be sufficiently recovered to be able to grace one of Mrs Bateson's At Homes.

It was colder the next day, with a chill wind blowing down from the north, hinting of bitter weather to follow. As her carriage drove Emmaline into town, she remarked to Agnes on the number of leaves that were now falling, and how soon winter would be upon them.

'But then that'll be a good thing for you, madam,' Agnes replied, watching the branches of the trees in the park being shaken by the rising winds. 'Getting married in the winter, like, means at least you'll have something to look forward to: your anniversary. Thought of that should cheer you up during them long winter evenings.'

Emmaline glanced at her maid, wondering whether the words had been said in true innocence or not, but seeing young Agnes's open and unspoiled expression she realised that the girl was incapable of any sort of malice.

'I do hope it's not going to be a long, cold winter, Aggie. Not like the last one.'

'Winter's always long, madam,' Agnes sighed. 'Not always cold, but it's always bloomin' long, especially in England. If we was Spanishy winter'd be over in a second.'

As instructed, the carriage stopped at the top of the street where Mr Hunt's bookshop was situated, in order that Emmaline could pay a visit to her dressmaker in Lower High Street. Emmaline and Agnes hurried into the house, holding their bonnets down with one hand against the swirling wind. Here, while Agnes looked longingly at the silks and satins stacked in rolls on the counter of the crowded room, Emmaline was fitted for some new winter dresses.

'Next, I have to go to the bookshop, so you might as well wait in the carriage, Aggie,' she said. 'I shan't be very long.'

'I don't mind coming to the shop if you don't mind,' Agnes replied. 'I never been to no bookshop.'

'Can you read, Aggie?'

'No, ma'am. But that's not really the point, madam.'

'We must teach you to read, Agnes,' Emmaline told her with a gentle smile. 'That is something I can spend my time fruitfully doing this winter. Teaching you how to read.'

'Would you, madam?' Agnes looked at Emmaline as she thought of the excitement of what her mistress was proposing. 'I wouldn't half like that, madam.'

'It will be hard work, Aggie,' Emmaline warned her, turning to head for the street that besides Mr Hunt's shop also led to Julius's works. 'But it will be so very worthwhile. And of course you may accompany me to the bookshop – just so as long as you don't get under my feet.'

As they were passing a private house four doors down from the dressmaker's, through an open window they heard the unmistakable sounds of raised voices, of an argument between a man and a woman, their words criss-crossing each other while the woman could be heard to be crying. Unable to resist, both Agnes and Emmaline turned to look and saw a man in a dark red frock coat standing with his back to the window and both his hands to his head of curled flaxen hair, holding it as though in pain, faced by a blonde young woman whose pretty face was running with tears as she continued her protest against him.

'Come along now, Aggie,' Emmaline said to her maid, taking her by the arm. 'This is no business of ours.'

'He's not having much of a time of it, is he, though, madam?' Agnes wondered, wide-eyed. 'She's letting him have it good and proper.'

'It's no business of ours, Aggie,' Emmaline repeated. 'So come along. You may sit in the window seat of Mr Hunt's shop, but do not, I beg you, touch any of the volumes, however tempted you may feel.'

The bookshop was busy, giving Emmaline the impression that it was one of the more successful enterprises in the town. Mr Hunt saw Emmaline as soon as she entered the shop, and came across to welcome her at once, wondering what he might be able to help her with on this particular visit.

Emmaline dropped her eyes momentarily, remembering the initial reason for her last call before telling the charmingly unflappable and very discreet Mr Hunt, bookseller to the gentry, that what she really wished to do was have a quick word with his young assistant, Mr Ashcombe.

'As long as it is no trouble, Mr Hunt,' she added. 'For I can see how very busy you are.'

'We are never too busy for any of our customers, I assure you,' Mr Hunt replied. 'That is why we never close our shop till the last customer has finished his or her business. But I am afraid you might have to wait a moment or so for young Mr Ashcombe. He had to pop back home for something he had forgotten, but since he lives nearby I imagine you will not be delayed very long. In fact, here is the very gentleman in question, even as we speak.'

Mr Hunt indicated with a hand in the direction of the shop door, and as she turned Emmaline saw the now familiar sight of a flaxen-haired young man in a dark red frock coat hurrying through the customers to his desk at the rear of the shop.

'Why, Mrs Aubrey!' he cried with genuine pleasure, extending his hand. His cheeks were flushed with the effort of hurrying back to the shop. 'I am so *very* glad to see you – delighted, in fact. Have you come to talk about poetry again? How pleasant if you have!'

Overhearing this as he passed by to go upstairs to the printing room, Mr Hunt nodded at him.

'I can allow you the time, young man, if that is what you are worried about.'

'Thank you, sir,' Bray replied. 'And what might

it concern this time, I wonder, Mrs Aubrey? A quest for a significant new poet, perhaps?'

Emmaline smiled politely at him before telling Agnes to go and sit in the window at the front of the shop until she had finished her business. Then she turned back to Bray Ashcombe and wondered if there was somewhere they could have a private word.

'I will not take up much of your time, Mr Ashcombe,' she assured him as he walked her to a book-lined but deserted annexe in a corner of the shop. 'In fact I will be very brief, because I am sure you have much to do.'

'Mrs Aubrey, were you and I to spend all today and tomorrow in conversation, I should not notice one minute of the time, I do assure you, and that is the truth.'

'You are most charming, sir.' Emmaline smiled at the compliment, unable to rid her mind of the picture of Bray standing holding his head while being publicly berated by a hysterical young woman. 'Sadly I do not have that sort of time at my disposal.'

'But let us say that you did?' Bray wondered with a boyish smile.

'I am sure I too would enjoy a long and expansive conversation with you,' Emmaline replied. 'About poetry, its rhythms, its rhymes and its inner meanings, but as I said, alas, I do not have that luxury. What I was wondering was whether you would be kind enough to read a couple of poems for me.'

231

'You wish me to read a couple of poems to you? How very flattering, Mrs Aubrey. I have had many requests from our customers, but never that one, I do assure you.'

'No, no, Mr Ashcombe.' Emmaline smiled. 'I would like you to read them privately, when you have a moment, and let me know what you think of their merit.'

'Are we to know the identity of the poet? Or are they by the always and ever famous *Anon*? Who it seems has penned more lines than William Shakespeare himself.'

'They are by a friend of mine, Mr Ashcombe. We have long been friends, since we were tiny children, but we both have always enjoyed reading poetry. But now, due to an unhappy turn that her life has taken, it seems she has started writing it, and for reasons which I find very flattering has sent me her first efforts, which I think are – well, in my opinion, I think they are most interesting. But then I am no real judge of verse, Mr Ashcombe, as you have no doubt gathered.'

'I think you may have forgotten what I said to you on our first acquaintance, as why should you not?' Bray replied, politely holding up one hand. 'The only person who knows whether or not a poem is good, whether it strikes the right chord or emotion, is the reader. I may think some poetry a nonsense, yet someone else might have strong feelings for it immediately, might hear the music to which I am, alas, quite deaf, might see the truth lying behind the words. By all means, I shall read these verses as you request, but always remember that I will never be the ultimate judge. However, I am perfectly willing to give you my opinion, always providing that you bear in mind that my artistic ideal is someone else's dross, and vice versa, of course.'

'I already value your opinion, so if you do think they have any merit I should be very interested to hear your conclusions.'

'Suppose I conclude they are worthless?' Bray wondered. 'Will you tell your – your *friend*? Or will you simply be kind and say that you found them interesting and she should certainly continue with her efforts?'

'I like to think I shall be as honest with her as you will be, Mr Ashcombe. I see no merit in pretence, do you?'

'None whatsoever, I do so agree.'

For a second they held each other's gaze before Emmaline handed over the large envelope she had been carrying, having carefully copied her poems out from her notebook on to single sheets of paper.

'Doubtless your friend will want to hear my reaction to her work quite soon?'

'No, no, absolutely not, no. I have not told her I am showing them to anyone else. She would be mortified. She is very shy, very retiring. I would not dream of telling her. It might make the muse go away if you saw no merit in them!'

'Depend upon it, I shall read them as soon as I have finished my supper tonight, if not sooner.'

'I am quite sure that after a long hard day's work, the last thing you will wish to do when you get home to your wife is sit and work after you have dined.'

'I have no wife, Mrs Ashcombe,' Bray replied, laughing. 'Why – do I look married? Never tell me I look married. Married men always look flustered, driven by demons, carriage horses pulling their families behind them, while I, being single, gallop round the fields, pitying them!'

'Forgive me.' Emmaline tried to cover her tracks. 'I think I must have misunderstood Mr Hunt – or simply made the wrong assumption. He said you had been called home suddenly and for some reason I assumed that it must be to your family – please forgive me.'

'There is absolutely nothing to apologise for, I do assure you,' Bray said. 'And even though my day will probably be a long one, to judge from the number of customers we seem to have attracted, nothing will give me more pleasure than to sit down and read your verses this evening.'

'My friend's verses.'

'Yes, of course – your friend. Please forgive me.'

'There is nothing to forgive,' Emmaline assured him. 'She will be most grateful for your kindness. If you wish to communicate with her perhaps you would address your letter to me at Park House, Park Walk, Bamford, if you would be so good?'

Emmaline then took her leave, collecting Agnes from her perch in the window without looking back, yet somehow knowing that all the time Bray was watching her. Despite the crowded shop, despite the fact that she had been so careful to talk to him in objective terms, nevertheless she felt his eyes on her as she passed the window of the shop, and continued on down the street. For herself, it wasn't until they were halfway to the carriage that her heart started to beat faster, and she had to stop momentarily to recover her breath. What had she done? She had given her precious verses to a virtual stranger, a young man whom she hardly knew, and who hardly knew her. It was, she realised, an act of great intimacy. Never mind that she had pretended that they were by her 'friend': she had given Bray Ashcombe a part of her soul to read.

'It must be wonderful to work in a bookshop, all those books that you can read once the shop closes, all those words that someone has written so you can read them,' Agnes sighed as they made their way back to the carriage. 'I shall most certainly work extra hard at learning to read now I have been in Mr Hunt's shop.'

Emmaline laughed, and taking Agnes by the arm was about to cross the road when she heard someone running down the street behind them. It was a boy carrying a small brown-paper-wrapped parcel done up with string, which he handed to Emmaline when he caught up.

'Sorry, mum,' the boy said breathlessly. 'Mr Hunt said you forgot this, mum, and that I was to give it to you with his compliments, mum.'

'Really? Well, thank you very much.' Emmaline looked at the eager expression on the young person's face, and knowing at once what was wanted she reached into her handbag for a threepenny bit, wondering what the wrapped-up book might be. Then she hesitated. 'You are quite sure he meant me?'

'Yes, mum,' the boy replied. 'Mr Hunt pointed you out from the shop as you crossed in front of the window, mum.'

'Thank you.' Emmaline handed the boy the threepenny bit.

'Crikey, mum,' the boy whispered. 'You don't have to do that.'

'Maybe not,' Emmaline agreed, closing her bag. 'But I'd like to.'

'That is far too much for the likes of you, young man,' Agnes told him, cuffing him lightly on the side of his head.

He grinned at her. 'I know, but just wait till you see how quick I spend it, miss!'

He ran off, thrilled with his tip, watched for a moment by the two young women. It was a cheerful sight, his tousled head bobbing in and out between the people on the pavement, his coat flapping.

'He'll buy something at the baker with that,' Agnes said, nodding at nothing in particular, 'and then he'll sit down on the side of the pavement and scoff it, that's what he will do. Least ways, that's what I would do, in his place.'

Emmaline smiled at the image. It suggested

something to her, although she could not quite think what.

When she got home and unwrapped her parcel in private, Emmaline found her gift from Mr Hunt was a leather-bound volume of *Haynes General Biology – a basic textbook, fully illustrated*. At first, because for no good reason she felt as though she might have been the subject of shop gossip, she wasn't sure whether to be affronted or grateful, feeling more of the former at first but then gradually much more of the latter as she realised both the kindness and the tact behind the gift. It was as if Mr Hunt had read her thoughts and known that Emmaline could not return to his shop with the same object she had in mind as she had on her original visit, and while initially she thought that any study of matters biological might be coming a little late in the day to have any bearing on her marriage, nevertheless when she retired to bed that evening she decided at least to try to dip into the book.

In spite of the scholarly prose style she managed to read through the first few chapters before finally falling asleep, although the scientific language was such that despite her best efforts at understanding it she found it utterly confounded her at times. Besides, so much of what it described really did seem dreadfully exaggerated.

The following day there was some startling news.

First an invitation arrived by post addressed in a formal hand to *Mr and Mrs Julius Aubrey*.

Emmaline stared at the envelope, but since it was clearly an invitation and addressed to both of them, she felt no qualms about opening it. The large engraved card announced that in approximately six weeks' time the Earl and Countess of Parham requested the pleasure of their company at a private banquet to be held for Her Majesty Queen Victoria at Hartley.

Emmaline stared at it, unable to think why she and Julius should have been included on the list of guests, since Julius had been nothing but disparaging about the huge house whose state rooms he had been commissioned to redecorate. Not only that, but he seemed to delight in mocking Lord and Lady Parham, not to mention their eccentric household.

'For some reason I cannot understand, Lord and Lady Parham are convinced that I am not in trade, although why I do not know, since they are employing me. But there, English aristocrats have a way of going on that no one else is allowed to question, and if they are happy to have me in their house, and happy to seat me at their table, then who am I to reject them?'

'I think they see you as an artist first and foremost. Certainly Lady Parham mentioned several times that Lord Egremont had had Turner to stay, and referred to many other painters in the same vein, so I think that is how they see you, Julius,' Emmaline had offered,

238

but it had been, as always, to a fast disappearing back.

She kept on staring at the invitation. There was no doubt in her mind that the moment he saw where they were being summoned, and whom they were being summoned to meet, Julius would have some more interesting views on Hartley, its décor, the Parhams and perhaps even the Queen herself, whose popularity, Emmaline had been told by Wilkinson, had now returned after a long time in abeyance.

Emmaline's next piece of news, however, excited her even more. While she was having her breakfast in the dining room, Wilkinson brought her in a letter on his silver salver.

'Thank you, Wilkinson, you may put it there, if you would.'

Wilkinson placed the letter by her plate, and retired. Emmaline went on eating.

She kept staring at the envelope as she sat sipping her tea, before picking it up and taking it with her into the informal sitting room where she liked to sit now that the autumnal weather had turned cold and blustery, bringing sharp squally showers in on buffeting westerlies.

Settling down by the fireside, she looked once again at the name on the card which accompanied the small envelope: *Mr Bray Ashcombe*, care of Hunt's Book Shop. Finally, summoning up her courage, Emmaline opened the letter, smoothing it carefully flat on the book that was on her knee before allowing herself to read it. Not that she could read it, for at first the words did not seem to make sense.

Forgive my seeming rush to judgement, the note read, *but having read the verses you left with me as soon as I could do so last evening, I could no longer contain my enthusiasm and so felt I really must convey my feelings about these poems immediately. I hope, first and foremost, that you will be pleased with what I feel and I also hope that you will allow me to tell you in person. If you will allow me such an honour, would you perhaps visit the shop again soon so that we may talk at greater length about them? Perhaps, if it will please you to agree, we could meet when I have a little more time at my disposal, possibly during my lunch hour when we could talk at much greater length than is possible during working hours in the shop. For now, all I can say to you is that these verses are in my opinion truly remarkable. They are original in thought and substance and in vision, the feelings are most beautifully expressed and the sentiments very moving. I found myself carried along by them, as if I was riding a great emotional wave, loving both the imagery and the very boldness of the strokes that the poet has used to convey her sentiments (for obviously the writer is a woman, from the expression of the sentiments and the subject matter of the two poems). But enough – this is just to let you know that, for whatever my opinion is worth, I not only admire these verses, I was astonished by them and I must confess at times more than a little jealous! I very much look forward*

to hearing your own reaction to these few scribbled
thoughts about your friend's work.
    I am, yours truly,
        Bray Ashcombe

Emmaline put the note down, and then picked it up again, quite unable to believe that what she had just read was true. She read it again, and then again. Still unable to believe what Bray Ashcombe had written about her poems, her feelings were so turbulent that she stood up and paced the room, his letter in her hand, her heart beating at such a rate it made her feel breathless. It was as if she had received a love letter out of the blue from someone she would have to describe as a *soul mate*, somebody who had seen into her thoughts and her heart and had responded with a passion of his own. She had at last, it seemed, met another being who saw and recognised the person inside her, who had taken note of her spirit and appreciated it.

Still clasping his note to her, she stood by the window looking out at the wintry landscape wondering what she should do, and how this moment might have changed her life. Of course she must keep her feelings to herself, or at least to her poetry, yet she could not bear the thought of not returning to the bookshop to see Bray and hear him talk more about the poetry of her *friend*.

But how best to go about it? If she wrote a note back to him, she thought it might well give him the wrong idea, and while Emmaline knew that she had been thrown, perhaps understandably, into an emotional turmoil she was still sensible enough to realise that she must under no circumstances give the young man any false impressions. For a start, she was a married woman, and even had she not been, she was not and never would be the sort of young woman who indulged in flirtations. Furthermore, she was determined to keep their relationship artistically objective, for had she not seen him with a young woman, and one who was less than happy?

Remembering that Julius was due home by the end of that week – although knowing her husband, as she thought she was beginning to know him, he could just as easily arrive back two days earlier, this afternoon, or not until the middle of the week after next – Emmaline thought she would do well to get the meeting with Bray out of the way as soon as possible. And if there were any danger of Bray's considering her too keen, it would be easy enough to appear only eager on behalf of her friend, for her friend was not enjoying the happiest of times, and that would surely excuse her precipitate behaviour. So once she had composed herself, and had locked the note away with her verses in her little bureau, Emmaline summoned Agnes once again to accompany her into Bamford.

As always Agnes was only too happy to accompany her mistress, since even if she ended up once again sitting alone in the carriage, it would be greatly preferable to having to perform the innumerable domestic tasks which Mrs Graham would find for her if she suspected that the young girl had time on her hands.

Instead of leaving Agnes behind to wait for her in the carriage, however, Emmaline, knowing how much she had enjoyed sitting in the window of Mr Hunt's bookshop, decided to treat her again. Having instructed the driver to wait for them in the Market Place, Emmaline led Agnes once more towards the bookseller's.

As they approached the end of the High Street and the house where they had witnessed what appeared to be an argument between Bray and an unknown woman, by chance they saw the woman approaching them. Emmaline recognised her at once, not just by her striking looks but by her long blonde hair, which was no longer loose but heaped up under a small piece of lace. As the parties approached each other, the young woman began to walk unsteadily, putting one hand to her mouth and reaching out with the other one to lean against the nearby wall. By the time they met she had come to a stop and was standing with her eyes closed.

Emmaline went to her aid at once, enquiring whether the young woman was all right, and if she was not, might there be something they could do for her? The young woman opened her eyes to look at these kindly Samaritans, while the hand that had been at her mouth stayed put. After a moment she shook her head slowly.

'Thank you, no. I am fine, thank you,' she said in a low voice. 'A slight fit of dizziness, that is all. It will pass.'

'You look very pale, madam, if you don't mind me saying,' Agnes remarked crisply.

'What we really need is to have you sitting down,' Emmaline told her.

'You're American, aren't you?' the young woman asked, looking at Emmaline with sudden intensity.

'Yes, I am indeed, and very clever of you to notice,' Emmaline replied, taking the woman's arm. 'Not everyone in Bamford recognises so readily where I am from, probably because there are so many newcomers, so many different accents, since the new factory opened on the edge of town.'

'Few people here in Bamford have ever heard an American accent, let alone met an American,' the young woman said. 'What are you doing so far from home?'

'I live here. And you live . . . ?' Emmaline enquired tactfully, knowing very well that she was but a couple of doors from the stranger's house.

'I live here in town,' the woman replied. 'Only along the street, a couple of houses down. Please – I shall be perfectly all right now. You've been most kind.'

'Let us see you to your door,' Emmaline insisted. 'I think it's the very least we can do.'

Agnes and she escorted the young woman the few remaining yards to her house, which indeed was the very one in which Emmaline and Agnes had witnessed the vehement argument. Thanking them for their kindness once more, the woman let herself in.

'Are you sure you'll be all right now?' Emmaline pressed before the door was finally shut on them. 'You have someone to look after you?'

She had of course asked the question in the hope of shedding some light on the reason for Bray's presence in the house on their previous visit to Mr Hunt's shop. It was none of her business, yet she could not contain her curiosity as to the relationship between this striking young woman and her poetic friend who sold books and took such an interest in Mr Hunt's customers. But the young woman was obviously not going to provide any information of a personal nature, assuring Emmaline that she was quite recovered, despite the fact that she was still looking ashen-faced, and making sure to thank her most warmly before finally closing the front door.

'She's probably sickening for this thing everyone's getting here in Bamford,' Agnes offered once they had resumed their progress to the bookshop. 'Everyone's going down like skittles with some ague or other. Mind you, it's no different to last winter – and winter afore, come to that. Soon as winter comes seems everyone here in Bamford takes to their beds like bunnies to their burrows.'

'Let's just hope we're not to be counted among

their number, Aggie,' Emmaline said as they reached the door of Mr Hunt's shop.

'We got a bit close to her, madam,' Agnes remarked sagely. 'You did, certainly. Closer than what I did, I couldn't help noticing.'

'Thank you, Aggie,' Emmaline replied with a smile. 'That has now filled me with the happy expectation of being felled by some dread disease known only to folk who live in Bamford.'

As she left Agnes once more in the window of the shop, Emmaline went to where Mr Hunt liked to stand to survey the world and its doings, the position he always adopted when he was not directly involved with one of his customers, on a small dais towards the back.

'Good day to you, madam,' he said, with a short bow. 'Here to browse? Or have you come for another tutorial from our Mr Ashcombe?'

'I am here to buy a book, I do assure you, Mr Hunt,' Emmaline replied firmly, determined to give the right impression of what she was pretending was her objective. 'I wish to buy a speller and a first reader, if I may.'

'Of course, Mrs Aubrey,' Mr Hunt agreed, turning to lead the way to the relevant shelf. 'You should find everything you are looking for in this section here.' He gave Emmaline an odd look. 'A speller and a first reader for yourself?' he asked, his head on one side, looking diplomatically indifferent.

'These will be for myself, yes.'

'I see. Were you not then putting the cart a little

before the horse when you were here the other day?' he asked, careful to adopt a kindly tone.

'Not really. You see, Aggie can at least *say* her ABC, so she has had a little education, but I intend to start her reading lessons as soon as possible. Not to be able to read is a terrible thing, is it not, Mr Hunt? What we are deprived of if we cannot read is something that you and I can only guess at. Ah – *A Child's Book of the Alphabet.* The very thing to get Aggie started.'

'Aggie being your daughter?' Mr Hunt asked, looking both relieved and amused.

'Oh, no, Mr Hunt. No, Aggie is my maid. She is seated there by the window. She has fallen in love with your shop, Mr Hunt. Mark my words, it will soon be Aggie to whom you will be sending books. Which reminds me that I have to thank you for the volume you sent me yesterday. I am very grateful and much appreciate both your tact and your generosity.'

Mr Hunt laughed appreciatively, and turned away as Emmaline looked around innocently for help. Well, innocently as far as any stranger could have told, but not as far as she was concerned, for without looking up she knew that he had seen her. She could sense his gaze, and imagined those intense eyes looking at her, waiting for her to notice him. She found herself making him wait, as if she were playing a fish the way she did on the lake back home, walking round the shelves, taking books down, putting them back on the shelves again, and never once looking in Bray's direction. Finally it became too much for him, and when Emmaline did finally turn her attention to the more general aspect of the shop she found herself all but face to face with her poet.

'Mr Ashcombe,' she said. 'I was hoping I might see you before I had to hurry home.'

'Mrs Aubrey,' Bray returned with a half-bow. 'You are running short of time?'

'This really was intended to be a flying visit,' Emmaline explained. 'I do have quite a few other calls to make.'

'I see.' Bray nodded. 'You did – did you – did you get my note?'

Emmaline noticed that Agnes was watching them from the window, and turned her back to her.

'Your note?' she wondered deliberately. 'Ah, the note you sent round about the verses we were discussing? Thank you, I did.'

She smiled politely at Bray, noting his surprise before returning her attention to the book in her hand.

'Good,' Bray said uncertainly. 'And – and were you – I trust you were happy with my comments?'

'I really only had time to glance at them before I left the house this morning,' Emmaline replied. 'But from what I saw I would say they seem very favourable, so yes – if that is indeed the case then I shall be very happy.'

'There is quite a lot more I would enjoy discussing with you,' Bray continued. 'Whenever you have the time – and of course the inclination.'

'Of course, Mr Ashcombe. But as I said, I have other calls to make and I am not altogether sure when we could – when we could have any further converse.'

'I could perhaps call on you?'

'No, that is not possible, since my husband is away at the moment, Mr Ashcombe.'

'I understand.' Bray, once more seeming to have come to a dead end, stood for a moment in thought while Emmaline browsed through some more reading primers. 'What time would you be free to walk in the park, I wonder? If it was around the time of my lunch hour, and if you could spare me ten minutes, we could walk together and I could quickly give you my further thoughts on – on your friend's poetry.'

Emmaline smiled at him, glanced up at the clock on the wall of the bookshop and considered the matter.

'I have to be back at my house by one o'clock, so I doubt if that would give us sufficient time.'

'I could ask Mr Hunt,' Bray suggested. 'He would probably allow me to take ten minutes from my lunch time now, or whenever it might suit you.'

'Very well, Mr Ashcombe,' Emmaline agreed. 'If you feel this matter to be so pressing, if it really cannot wait—'

'For the sake of your friend,' he told her with sudden passionate intensity. 'I really think the sooner I relay my full opinion on the poems to you, so that you can pass it on to her, the better for all parties concerned. I do have a very positive suggestion to make.'

While Emmaline waited to have her purchases parcelled up, Bray obtained permission from Mr Hunt to take the required time off in advance of his lunch hour, and he accompanied Emmaline and Agnes as they left the premises.

In line with her mistress's instructions, Agnes dropped half a dozen paces behind Emmaline as Bray fell into step beside her.

'I wish you had read my note more closely,' Bray said in a voice he hoped would not be overheard by the maid. 'If you had you would have sensed the excitement I felt on reading these poems.'

'Rest assured, Mr Ashcombe, I read enough of it to get a very good impression,' Emmaline told him, smiling her reassurance.

'Even so, *I* get the impression you are in some way chiding me – for my enthusiasm perhaps?'

'Not in the slightest, Mr Ashcombe. You must remember these poems are the work of a friend. Had they been, let us say for the sake of argument, by myself, why then naturally my emotions would be quite different.'

'Of course,' Bray said carefully, taking a sideways look at Emmaline, who continued to look straight ahead. 'I understand. Since we have very little time to discuss this matter fully, let me just say this, if I may. You might remember I said in my note that I was so struck by the style and content of the verses that I found myself feeling quite jealous – of your friend.'

'Indeed?' Emmaline gave a slight frown as she turned to glance at him. 'I really do not recall that statement, but then I was interrupted before I could reach the end,' she added, raising her eyes to ask God to forgive her such an untruth.

'Well, that was exactly how I felt when I had concluded my study of the poems,' Bray continued with a sigh. 'Perhaps I should not say this, but compared with the verses I myself am trying at this very moment to create, your poems made me feel, well, there is no other word for it, I am afraid – they made me feel envious.'

'My *friend's* poems, Mr Ashcombe,' Emmaline corrected him. 'I showed them to you on her behalf.'

There was a slight, perhaps inevitable pause.

'Yes, of course – so now let me come to the point. The point is, Mrs Aubrey, from what I have read—'

'The *little* you have read, Mr Ashcombe.'

'In this instance a little is quite enough, I do assure you. It is quite sufficient for me, or for anyone, for that matter, to realise that the author of these verses has a truly singular voice, and one I really feel quite passionately should be heard. Which is why I would suggest, if you will permit me, that these verses should be shown to a professional publisher – one, naturally, whose field is poetry – to see whether or not I err in my firm belief that this poet should be published, that these are not verses to be kept by the poet in a drawer. You know of course that there is a new

251

printing works attached to Mr Hunt's shop, and that his friend Mr Tully, who has a great interest in poetry, is making a good business from it?'

Emmaline was aware that she must be careful in her response. In all her imaginings she had never gone so far as to see herself as a published poet – after all, she had only sat down on two afternoons and written from the heart. Why she had done so, she still had no idea, unless perhaps her overwhelming sense of loneliness had led her to stray into a strange, mystical world, a world of images, of paintings with words, of unexpressed feelings that had forced themselves into her imagination, willing her to put them down.

She hesitated, quickly remembering her 'friend', and the undisputed fact that when she had first read her poems back to herself she had had the distinct impression that they had been penned by someone else. It was this feeling that she now kept before her, as she walked beside the handsome young scholar. Someone else had indeed written them, someone not previously known either to herself or to her family, and certainly not known to Julius.

'Mr Ashcombe,' she began, hoping she sounded prosaic, adopting an everyday tone such as she might use when discussing menus with Mrs Graham. 'Mr Ashcombe, this is very exciting for my friend. It is particularly remarkable, since my friend has really only just started writing. She has written nothing other than the verses you have in your possession, so we would have to call her a tyro, a beginner – only at the start of the artistic race for perfection, if you like. This might be all she has to offer the world, Mr Ashcombe. There is nothing to say she will be able to produce more verses of the quality you so admire. We have to bear that in mind in order to forestall any future disappointment. I have read of shocking cases where the first blooms of literary talent have been killed by the enthusiasm of others.'

'What you say is true, but life is for the brave, for the courageous, as we know. Besides,' Bray replied, giving her a sudden appreciative look, 'seen from any point of view, whether yours or mine, surely that is a question that can only be answered when your friend sits down to write some more verse?'

'True,' Emmaline agreed. 'That might well be the only way to find out. I must tell her to take her courage in both hands and pursue her own inner voice, to listen to the muse and not to mind if the result is less successful.'

'For myself, if I can be of any assistance, you must tell your friend that I am here, if she so wishes, but only if she so wishes.' He smiled. 'You have probably realised that I so love the art of verse writing that I am more than interested in trying to help anyone who aspires to pen even one line of poetry, particularly someone who is as obviously talented as your friend.'

'Very well, Mr Ashcombe,' Emmaline agreed. She allowed a few seconds to drift by as they walked on. 'I shall certainly make it my business to convey your enthusiasm to my friend, and, if I may, I will show her your note – with your permission, that is?'

'Certainly. By all means. I wrote it with your friend in mind.'

'After which I shall of course let you know her reaction.'

'You may also tell her that there are a number of publishers to whom this type of poetry has a very strong appeal. My only other suggestion concerns the second of the verses you gave me to read, the longer one without any title. This is to be part of a much longer work, I imagine?'

'I would not know, Mr Ashcombe – but I could enquire of her.'

'Please do, because if it is intended to be a longer poem, then I think it most certainly has every chance of being published as a single work, such is the power of the stanzas I have already read.'

'You have been so kind, Mr Ashcombe,' Emmaline said, coming to a halt. 'On behalf of my friend, thank you. This is where I must leave you, alas – but you have been not just kind but so diligent, and I really do thank you, on her behalf.'

'No, Mrs Aubrey,' Bray corrected her. 'It is not I whom you should thank. It is your friend.'

Emmaline was about to turn away when her attention was caught by the unmistakable sight of the stranger to whose aid she and Agnes had come earlier in the day watching the two of them talking. She was leaning against the same window where Emmaline and Agnes first saw her arguing with the young man who was now standing beside Emmaline. Seeing her, Emmaline raised a hand in greeting, and after a second the young woman half raised her own in return, before dropping it in what seemed suddenly to Emmaline to be a gesture of despair.

Bray, seeing this, frowned.

'You two ladies are acquainted?' he wondered, almost sharply.

'Hardly,' Emmaline replied calmly. 'No, no, we only met this morning when I was on my way to the bookshop. The young woman in question was coming towards us on the street when suddenly she seemed to become unwell, most distressed, so naturally Aggie and I stopped to help her.'

'I see,' Bray replied with a nod, staring back at the window, only to see the young woman now waving and indicating something to him.

'It seems that you two are also acquainted?' Emmaline said, reading into the woman's sign an indication that she wanted Bray to go and see her. 'It certainly appears that she wishes to talk to you.'

'Yes,' Bray said slowly. 'Yes, it does, doesn't it?'

'I do so hope she has recovered from her distress,' Emmaline added, concerned. 'She was really very unwell, even perhaps feverish, when we went to her aid.'

'She has recovered, she is perfectly recovered, I do assure you,' Bray informed her a little too quickly. 'A passing malaise, that is all.'

'So you two *are* acquainted?' Emmaline persisted,

despite the fact that she knew full well the answer to her question.

'Yes, we are, Mrs Aubrey. Miss Ashcombe is my sister.'

Emmaline could hardly contain either her excitement or her apprehension on the return journey to Park House. While Agnes sat religiously studying the alphabet book that Emmaline had bought her, her mistress stared out of the carriage window at the grey winter landscape and wondered what might be going to happen next in her life. She supposed there were two possibilities – when she sat down to write again she would discover that she did possess a natural gift for verse, hitherto unsuspected, or she would find herself sitting at her desk and staring at a blank sheet of paper, unable to pen another word.

She gazed at the neat stone-built townhouses they were passing, houses in which other young women like herself were confined by society and by reason of their sex. How many of them, she wondered, would be sitting staring at a blank sheet of paper, feeling the same as herself? How many of them would be inveighing against the constriction of marriage? For, swiftly following on the possibility that she might have an unfulfilled gift for verse, came a truth. She would not be able to publish her poetry, she would not be able to publish anything, without Julius's permission. It was a fact as unalterable as the colour of the sky, as Agnes's finger moving under the letters of the alphabet, as the blue of her walking dress.

Julius most certainly would not approve of his wife's being a published writer, the sort of person who not only shows her emotions in public but has the audacity to do it in print. He would be outraged. Even the most famous female authors in England used male pseudonyms, or signed their work 'by a lady'.

'Yes, of course!' Emmaline banged her umbrella tip on the floor of the carriage. 'Yes, of course!'

'Beggin' your pardon, madam?' Agnes looked up in surprise. 'Did you say something?'

'Yes, I did, but nothing that need concern you, Aggie – at least not quite yet.'

Emmaline smiled at the little maid opposite her in her black dress, and her black coat, and her little neat lace-trimmed hat. Her 'friend' would publish her verses, if they were indeed good enough to be published, as 'a lady'. She would be so meek and retiring that nothing else would do.

Her thoughts then turned to the conversation she had had with Bray Ashcombe, not that part of their talk that had been to do with the writing of verse, but the latter part, when they had passed the house of the beautiful young blonde woman who had been taken ill earlier.

How strange that it had turned out to be none other than Bray's sister whom Agnes and she had come across feeling so unwell. Yet the fact that it was his sister, Emmaline could not help realising, brought with it a certain sense of relief. If it had been his wife it would have been disappointing, for he had denied being married with such grace and sweetness that it would mean he was a very different sort of person from the man Emmaline thought she knew had he lied.

Emmaline stared at the street outside, trying not to face the undoubted truth. If it had been Mrs Bray Ashcombe whom they had stopped to help, *Mr* Bray Ashcombe would have seemed somehow a lesser man, less the exciting young scholar, less the handsome young enthusiast. It was not that Emmaline wanted him to be a lonely bachelor, by no means. She just did not want him to be married. If her experience was anything to go by, marriage brought all kinds of complicated emotions in its train, which might influence his reading of her friend's verse and colour his reaction to it, whereas if he was merely young and single, and not in the least lonely, then his enthusiasm for her poetry was, as it were, freely given, and could therefore be taken at its face value, which was considerable.

By the time the carriage pulled up in front of Park House, Emmaline was in a particularly good frame of mind. She had met Bray Ashcombe and handled their meeting with decorum, being particularly pleased with the way she had not allowed herself to show how exhilarated and excited she had felt. Any show of emotion might not only have given away the true authorship of the verses, but, worse than that, have revealed to

Bray much more about herself than she would ever wish.

So, when George appeared to help Emmaline down from her carriage, she felt well able to give him a brilliant smile.

'Thank you, George. What a lovely day it has turned into, has it not, after all?'

George, still holding her hand, which in his eyes was no penance, steadied her as she climbed the shallow steps to the house.

'It is a lovely day,' he agreed, wondering whether or not she had heard the news. 'On such a day one feels ready for anything, that is what I always says.' But he looked up at the grey of the sky and shook his head.

Emmaline nodded happily. George was right. She felt quite ready for anything now, anything at all.

'Mr Aubrey has returned, madam,' Wilkinson informed her as he took her coat from her. 'He is in the drawing room.'

Julius was standing by the fire smoking a cigarette, one foot propped up on the fender and in his hand the splendidly engraved invitation from Lord and Lady Parham, but he was frowning at it as if it gave him no pleasure.

'Julius, you are home earlier than expected, are you not?' Emmaline asked, crossing the room to greet him. 'I hope your venture was a success?'

'When did this arrive?' Julius wondered, as if he had not heard her, still staring at the engraved invitation in his hand.

'This morning. Why? For some reason you appear to be aggravated by it, Julius. Was it not a compliment to ask us, for Lord and Lady Parham to ask us?'

'It just isn't something I was anticipating, that is all.' Julius tapped the card against the mantel before replacing it there. 'And yes – yes, my journey was successful, thank you. I suppose we shall have to go to this.' Once again Julius picked up the invitation and stared at it. 'I cannot imagine why we have been asked. We are merely the artisans in the pack, they must have other far more important people they could ask, they *should* ask. But then that is the Parhams. They may be members of the aristocracy, but they make little sense out of their lives, poor souls.'

'Perhaps the Earl and Countess are pleased with your work at Hartley, Julius? Perhaps this is their way of rewarding you, with an invitation.'

'Well, you may be right,' Julius agreed. 'And yes, they were pleased. As so they should be. Mind you, it would not take much to please them as far as decoration goes. I might have advised them to slap whitewash fit only for stables everywhere, and they would have been more than content. They really are the oddest of people. The previous earl constructed a whole system of tunnels under the house for his sole use, the purpose being so he could wander from room to room or whatever without ever seeing a servant.'

'My.' Emmaline smiled, sitting herself down

by the fire in order to get warm. 'And what about the countess? I wouldn't be surprised to learn she also has eccentricities.'

'If it is of any interest, Emmaline, Her Ladyship's main preoccupation is the breeding of ferrets.'

'Ferrets?'

'Yes, ferrets. They are like stoats, or weasels, and they are used for ratting, mostly. I am surprised you didn't encounter any while you were there. On occasion she allows them to run quite wild through the place.'

'I did see something I thought was a squirrel once or twice. So that was a ferret?'

'Undoubtedly,' Julius replied without interest, and yet again he picked up the invitation. 'I suppose we shall have to go, although I cannot imagine why Her Majesty should choose to visit the Parhams. On her way to Osborne, perhaps? Is it not about time luncheon was served?'

'Did anyone tell Cook?' Emmaline asked him, trying not to laugh.

'Is that necessary?' Julius asked in return, looking slightly astonished. 'It's only luncheon.'

Even though it was *only luncheon*, Emmaline rang for Wilkinson to inform him that she and her husband were ready to lunch. Wilkinson nodded gravely and replied that he had taken the liberty of telling Cook this might be the case, so there should only be a slight delay in calling them to table.

'I am so looking forward to eating English food again. I love French food, but there are so many rich ingredients,' Julius confided, looking suddenly boyish and pleased to be home.

'Is that where you have been, Julius? You have been in France?'

'Yes, I was called to a château in the Loire which is the size of Windsor Castle and in total disorder. No one but no one knew where to begin, and in truth it really did not matter where we did begin, such was the state of the place. The Bastille would be cosier, and easier to alter.'

'I wish you had told me that you were going to France, Julius.'

'You do?' Julius replied, giving her a puzzled look. 'Why would you wish to know such a thing?'

'I would like to have given you a list of some small items which you could have purchased for me, in particular some Breton lace, and gloves. French gloves are the very finest. And more than that, it would have been reassuring to know where you were, in case you suffered an accident.'

'No matter,' Julius said, consulting his fob watch. 'I know where you are. I am afraid I have to go into Bamford this afternoon, I must have lunch as soon as is perfectly possible. I hate to be an imposition, but is it possible to eat very soon?'

'We will eat as soon as lunch is ready, Julius,' Emmaline told him in a firm tone, 'and it is too bad of you to turn up as and when you think fit, having told no one of your whereabouts

262

before. It makes life impossible for both wives and servants.' As Wilkinson came into the room, she nodded at him. 'Thank you, Wilkinson, we will go in, and many apologies to Cook from Mr Aubrey for not conveying to her at what time he wanted luncheon served.'

Emmaline swept ahead of Julius, a small and naughty voice repeating in her head, *I have written verses with which a young scholar is much taken, I have written verses with which a scholar is much taken.* And because of them she was able to hold her head high.

Julius followed his wife into the dining room, trying not to look as surprised as he felt. He did not know why, but Emmaline seemed greatly changed. Not outwardly, perhaps – her lovely thick brown hair was just the same, as was her slim figure, and she was wearing a blue day dress which he particularly liked, all that was the same. No, it was something else, something on which he could not put his finger, something of which he felt suspicious.

Julius did indeed hurry through his lunch, not speaking other than to tell her he would be away again the following week.

'Where might you be going this time, Julius?' Emmaline asked, trying not to look relieved.

'Same as last time, I imagine. Although I doubt if even Hercules would have taken on this particular task.'

'I would really like to go to France with you,' Emmaline remarked carefully.

'Have you not been to France, then?'

'I think you must know that perfectly well, Julius.'

'I would love to take you to France, one day, but not on this journey,' he said, half to himself.

'Would you, Julius? Would you really?'

Julius stood up without replying, so that it seemed to Emmaline that his putting his napkin down and walking from the room was a reaction to what she had said. *Would you, would you really?* Had it sounded all too much like a plea?

'Will you be in for dinner, Julius?' Emmaline called, but Julius was gone, replaced by Wilkinson, who had silently appeared through the pass door.

'The master *will* be in for dinner, madam,' the butler informed her, easing her chair out from the table for her as she rose. 'I enquired before lunch, because Cook was becoming somewhat animated on the subject of Mr Aubrey's coming and going, and he told me he will be in for dinner tonight.'

'Thank you, Wilkinson,' Emmaline replied. 'It is possibly just as well one of us knows when Mr Aubrey will be in.'

By the time Emmaline settled herself down once more to write at her desk in the bedroom the rain was flinging itself against the windows as if it was begging her to let it in. The wind was howling round the house, while the fire in the grate smoked and doors rattled in the draughts. Emmaline could not help shivering at the sound of the wind, because it sounded more and more like a person, a person calling insistently and often, someone needing her, someone wanting to tell her something, but who could it possibly be?

To take her mind off such imaginings Emmaline opened her book of writings, and once again it was as if she was reading something from the hand of someone else, a total stranger, someone she barely knew. Yet it was perhaps because the poetry seemed to be written by another hand, in a voice she could not recognise as her own, that within no time at all she found herself beginning to write. At one point it was as if she was watching her pen move without any effort on her part, as if it was being held by someone else, and yet she knew that she was being swept along by emotions that came from deep inside, engulfed by passions and sentiments that arrived with a life of their own. She became so infused with the excitement of what was happening to her that when she stopped for a moment she found she had been writing with her bent forehead resting in her left hand and that the fingers of that same hand were damp with perspiration.

For a moment she stopped, leaving her desk and sitting at her dressing table, where she carefully wiped her forehead with a handkerchief dipped in lavender water, watching the stranger who was staring back at her in her looking glass. Once she was cool again, and her heart had slowed to its normal rate, she returned to her desk and saw that she had written two whole verses of fourteen lines apiece, both of them with hardly a correction – a word crossed out here, perhaps, and another moved two spaces back and another to the next line – and it seemed as if the poem had just flown out of her, until looking at the clock she realised she had been sitting at her desk for well over two hours.

She rang for Agnes and asked her to instruct Dolly to bring her tea up to her room, since she wished to continue writing for the half-hour she still had at her disposal. Then she sat back down at her desk to do some further corrections until Dolly appeared with the tea tray. While the housemaid went about her business, Emmaline stood at the window watching the trees in the darkened garden bending in the force of the wind, their branches waving signals of distress as the gale grew in force and threatened to break them in two. Unswept leaves swirled in eddies at their base, while the rain continued to be driven hard against the panes. Emmaline pulled the curtains and asked Dolly to build up the fire before she left the room, and then she went once more and settled herself at her desk.

She had hardly picked up her pen again when she heard a door bang along the corridor. Thinking that Julius might have returned home earlier than expected, she at once shut her notebook away, and went to peer out of her door and down the corridor.

She could see that the door of his dressing room was open and there was a light burning within, yet the longer she watched, the less it seemed there was any sign of her husband. She waited, listening to the howling wind, that voice crying out for someone, that anguished lonely voice.

All of a sudden the door of the dressing room blew wide open, seeming to acquire a life of its own, before trying to shut itself once more, and failing. It gave out a repetitive dull thud, as if the latch had jammed, and Emmaline hurried forward into the darkness of the corridor to close it. When she reached it she found that the latch was indeed stuck, and she could not free it with the use of just her finger, so she went into the room to search the dressing table and the top of the chest of drawers for some sort of improvised prop that would free the latch and put a stop to such an irritating noise.

First she tried using one of her husband's boot hooks, but the hook itself was too big to fit the latch so she searched for something smaller, finally uncovering a small nail file that she thought would be ideal, which in fact it proved to be. On returning the file to where she had found it on top of the chest of drawers, her attention was caught by something unusual covered with a cloth and half hidden between the back of the chest and the wall. Peering more closely from one side and lifting the cloth, underneath she saw a large picture frame.

Her curiosity now well aroused, she hurried to the dressing-room door and peered out into the darkened corridor to make sure that there was no one down the landing or downstairs in the hall. The storm having stopped as suddenly as it had arrived, the house was absolutely quiet, and seemingly deserted, only the sudden distant sound of someone in the basement kitchen calling to someone else disturbing the eerie stillness.

Emmaline quickly returned to the dressing room, and easing the heavy chest away from the wall she pulled out the frame, which she immediately found to be not just a frame but an oil painting. When at last she had the picture propped up the right way she saw a portrait of a beautiful young woman in a white dress, a dress which seemed suddenly all too familiar.

She stared into the dark eyes of the beautiful young girl, and as she did so it seemed to her that it was this girl whom she had heard calling out above the sound of the howling wind, this beautiful girl who had been calling to her. Who was she, though? She had the air of a foreigner, and in her eyes was the look of someone who knew she was not long for this world.

She had little time for any more conjecture, for she heard a sudden noise in the hall, the sound she thought of someone at the front door. As quickly as she could, being careful not to damage the fine frame or indeed the painting itself, Emmaline slid the portrait back into its hiding place, replaced the cloth that had been covering it and finally eased the chest back into position before hurrying out of the dressing room, gently and silently closing the door behind her.

Someone was coming up the stairs. She could hear footfalls as the treads creaked under the weight of whoever was climbing towards her, and knew she had just enough time to get back into her own room before whoever it was reached the top of the staircase and began to walk down the landing. Hugging the wall as closely as she could Emmaline flew on tiptoes along the corridor, just managing to reach the bedroom and ease the door shut behind her before the unseen person came into view. Leaning against the wood, she heard footsteps approach her door and stop, as if whoever it was out there was intending to come in. Holding her breath, Emmaline remained where she was, her back against the door, her eyes tight shut, until to her immense relief she heard the person walk on down the corridor and open a door, a door which, since it only shut after a few attempts, gave her to understand that it might be having difficulty with its latch.

There was no exact way of telling whether or not it was Julius she had heard without going along the corridor to listen at his door, but once she was sure she was going to be spared a visit from her husband she hurried to her desk, locked the drawer containing her precious notebook and flopped herself down on her bed to try to work out why on earth Julius would suddenly decide to take down that portrait and hide it away in his dressing room. Was it perhaps of his sister who had married and gone to live in Canada? Was the wedding dress a family heirloom, and was that why he had behaved so oddly on their wedding day? Had she broken with some family tradition?

It was more than odd that Julius had not only taken the portrait down and hidden it away, but had also allowed her to believe that the missing painting had been of his father. The more she thought about it the less Emmaline was able to explain his actions, unless he had suddenly, for reasons known only to himself, taken a dislike to the painting and decided to remove it. But then why lie about it? Why, Emmaline wondered, yet again allowing despair to take her over, was he treating her as if they were not married?

Julius had met her – he had seen her, he had talked to her, he had danced with her, he had asked her father for her hand in marriage, then as soon as she had arrived in England, except for the rare occasions when he had caressed her hair, he had treated her in the same way that he treated his servants.

Unless, and this suspicion was starting to seem increasingly likely in Emmaline's mind, unless Mr Julius Aubrey had always been playing out a deliberate and well-planned game, the all too common game of finding a plain little rich girl and marrying her not for love, but for her money.

The awful fact was that this interpretation was making increasing sense to her. After all, it was common knowledge that Julius had been over in America on business, and from the few idle conversations she had overheard between her father and her mother she had gathered that Mr Aubrey was keen for his company to be promoted nationally by Onslow Nesbitt's own business enterprise, in particular his famous catalogue.

Yet Julius could surely have married anyone? For all his strange behaviour, she could not bring herself to believe that he was a fortune hunter. He had a good business, a fine house, paintings, silver, servants – he would not need to stoop so low, surely? She could perfectly understand that Julius had asked her to dance because he felt sorry for her, that she could accept. He might have agreed to dance with her, to pay some attention to the girl who seemed to be the wallflower of the family, for all kinds of reasons, but not that he would marry her as part of some sort of business bargain. Nor could she believe it of her father, for tough as Onslow always had been in business, and worldy and impatient in character, as a father he had never been anything but affectionate and generous to his wife and daughters, putting up with his wife's affliction with as good a grace as he could muster, and with his younger daughters' bumptious ways the same. So yet again Emmaline found herself unable to come to any conclusion about Julius, but this time the comforting knowledge that her verses were secreted away in her small Davenport gave her life a strange new reality.

By the time Agnes knocked on the bedroom door to tell her mistress it was time to dress for dinner, Emmaline had convinced herself that somehow Julius's removal of the portrait, his hiding of it in his dressing room, must all be part and parcel of whatever it was that had happened to him before they met to cause him to act as he did, but as to what it was, she still had no idea.

'I was wondering about what our Christmas arrangements might be?' Emmaline said a few days later during lunch, a meal that once more she found herself taking alone with Julius. Their solitariness was becoming so irksome that she was hard put to it not to turn and ask the servants to sit down with them.

'Our Christmas arrangements? Yes, of course!' Julius seemed to be coming to, as if he had quite forgotten what season it was.

'It is such a lovely time of year, and this will be our first Christmas in this house. Did you ever have Christmas here with your family, Julius?'

Julius looked up from staring at his plate with sudden interest.

'Would you think this fish is fresh, Emma?' he asked, as if he had not heard a word that she had said.

'I would say yes, the fish is fresh, Julius,' Emmaline told him, 'but if it is not, Cook's cat has just had kittens.' George, the under footman, smothered a giggle as Julius continued to frown at the segment of fish on his fork. 'Yes, Cook's cat has just had kittens and will no doubt be most grateful. So why not leave it for Prudence?'

'And what were you saying, Emma? What might it be that you were saying?'

'Leave the fish for the cat.'

'Not about the cat, about something else?'

'Christmas. In America we spend weeks preparing for Christmas. It is a time of great celebration.'

'As it is here, I do assure you, Emma.'

'Is that so? In that case, since it is only three weeks until Christmas, and we haven't discussed the matter once, perhaps we could discuss it now?'

'What is there to discuss?'

Holding on to her patience, Emmaline took a deep breath before replying.

'What we should perhaps discuss, Julius, is what you would like to do over Christmas.'

'Nothing very much. We shall go to church, of course, and then Cook will produce a goose or a turkey, and we will eat it, and a plum pudding, and then we shall perhaps give each other gifts, and that will be Christmas.'

'Not so different from any other Sunday here, from the sounds of it.'

'It is a religious festival.'

'Do you want to ask anyone to lunch on Christmas Day? Or perhaps for dinner on Christmas Eve, which I understand is the Continental way?'

'No.' Julius stopped her. 'I don't want to ask anybody.'

'That is a pity, because I would quite like to invite some people to share Christmas with us, Julius.'

'I would really rather not have guests, Emma.'

'I am sorry about that, because in America it is a time for seeing friends and celebrating.'

Julius stared down the long table at Emmaline with a sudden look of speaking sadness in his eyes. She stood up.

'You may leave,' she told George and Wilkinson. 'No removes from the table at the moment.'

She went up to where Julius was sitting as the servants hurried off, and stood in front of his chair.

'Julius,' she said. 'You know we cannot possibly go on living like this.'

'And what might you mean by that?'

Emmaline saw that it might be necessary to speak to him as if he were a child.

'I have said this to you before. We're meant to be man and wife, and we're not even living together—' she stopped, 'we're not even living together like brother and sister. We're like two strangers.'

'I hardly think so, Emmaline. You are exaggerating here. You must have become infected by reading too much, or playing too much romantic music.'

'We are, Julius, we are like two strangers. And every time I try to make life more pleasant, suggest some sort of social activity – even as in this case at Christmas – you deny me everything, and yet you expect me to stay here with you, to go on living like this, in a nightmarish state, not knowing where you are when you go away on business; and now it seems to me I have no idea *who* you are.'

274

Julius stared past her as if he hadn't heard her.

'I shouldn't have done this,' he said quietly, half to himself, but loud enough for Emmaline to hear. 'I should not have done this.'

'Done what, Julius?'

'I should never have done this,' he repeated in a dazed fashion.

He rose to his feet, screwed up his linen napkin, and quickly left the room. Emmaline was about to get up and go after him when Wilkinson, George and Dolly came in. They appeared so promptly that Emmaline knew they must have heard everything, although no one actually spoke, and as Emmaline sat on, braving it out on her own through the succeeding courses, their faces reflected her own sense of despair.

When Emmaline finally left the table, she knew that what had happened would already be a source of gossip and speculation in the servants' hall. The happy atmosphere that she had been able to engender when Julius was absent had quite disappeared. At home in America, old Mary had always said unhappy marriages made for badly run houses, and that servants did not want to stay where the atmosphere was uneasy. She had said that if the maid who opened the door to you was rude and surly then you should expect the mistress and master of the house to be the same. If the servants left, Emmaline would have no friends, and that was the truth.

Just then, though, Emmaline could think of

nothing except that she was cold, and tired, and trapped. She went back to her little sitting room and seated herself in front of the fire, which, perhaps knowing how she must be feeling, Wilkinson had stacked up once more. She was staring into the friendly flames, wondering whether to leave Park House before or after Christmas, when she realised that she could only see half of the fire, and then less than half. She felt overcome by panic, as if an enormously heavy net had been thrown over her, weighted down at every corner, and she was struggling with it, only to realise that she was fighting for her life while someone on the outside, in the room, stood waiting with something terrible with which to kill her. She was suddenly quite certain that she was going to die.

By some good grace Wilkinson was just passing by the door of the sitting room when he heard the noise, a crash as if someone had toppled into a piece of furniture followed by a thud as whoever it was fell to the floor. He found his mistress lying in a faint by the fireside, her head resting sideways on the brass fender, a trickle of blood seeping from a wound in her temple. Post haste, he sent George for the doctor, while Agnes, Mrs Graham and he carried their unconscious mistress upstairs to the bedroom, where Agnes and Mrs Graham loosened all her clothing, and laid her under the covers to wait for the doctor.

'Do you think we should have moved her,

Mrs Graham?' Agnes wanted to know as they both stood staring down at Emmaline lying on the bed. 'I am not at all sure that we should have moved her, really. I remember when there was this accident at the works, when Mr Ralph knocked himself out, the older women said they should leave him where he was, quite still, that it was better that way.'

'I think the most important thing is to keep Mrs Aubrey warm, Agnes,' Mrs Graham replied, sitting herself down on one side of the bed to keep watch. 'It isn't as if she has broken anything, fallen downstairs or from any sort of a height. My fear is she fainted.'

'She has been looking awful pale of late, Mrs Graham,' Agnes chipped in, standing with her hands clasped tightly in front of her on the other side of the bed. 'I been that worried about her 'cos she has been looking awful pale, like she's not been sleeping or something, and she has acted awful strange since the master came home.'

'She's only very slight, Agnes,' Mrs Graham stated, carefully avoiding the emotive subject of Mr Aubrey's treatment of his wife, while keeping her eyes directed on her patient. 'Mrs Aubrey is not the strongest of souls. And she eats very sparingly.'

'You think it was a faint then, Mrs Graham? She fainted, like . . .'

'And banged her poor head on the fender, Agnes, yes,' Mrs Graham agreed.

'Well, ladies can faint sometimes for all sorts of

reasons, can't they, Mrs Graham? For all sorts and sizes of reasons.'

'I think we should perhaps mind our tongues until the doctor arrives, Agnes, truly I do,' Mrs Graham said quickly, realising that any minute Agnes would be going too far.

'Very well. It was only that I was thinking—'

'Best not to think just now, Agnes, best to just watch and pray.'

The genial, kindly Dr Proctor duly arrived within half an hour, throwing his hat and cape at Wilkinson before climbing the stairs breathlessly, cigar in mouth and Gladstone bag in hand, his stethoscope half hanging out of it. As he was examining the wound to Emmaline's forehead, she stirred and opened her eyes.

'Sound,' he said with some relief. 'Sound. At least we're still alive then. Least we're still drawing breath. How long d'you say she's been fainted, Mrs Graham?'

'Over half an hour now, sir,' Mrs Graham replied, up from her chair and standing at the end of the bed.

'Long business for a faint, I would say, wouldn't you?' Dr Proctor asked himself. 'I would say so,' he replied to himself, clearing his throat. 'We must have actually knocked ourselves out then. Must have knocked ourselves out good and cold.'

He handed his cigar, which too had now gone out, to an astonished Agnes.

'Hold that for me, girl. Or put it down somewhere,' he said. 'I need to examine this head wound. Can you hear me, Mrs Aubrey?'

Dr Proctor bent over the bed and carefully turned Emmaline's head towards him so that the wound on her temple was visible.

'What happened?' Emmaline asked of no one in a dazed whisper. 'I don't remember anything. Why are you here? Who are you?'

'Took a bit of a bang, Mrs Aubrey. A bang to the head – I'm just going to take a look now. Can you move your fingers and toes, that's what I want to know now, eh? Can you feel your digits, Mrs Aubrey?'

'Who are you, please?' Emmaline said, closing her eyes in pain. 'What is happening exactly?'

'I need some warm water in a bowl, girl, and quickly,' the doctor told Agnes. 'Quick as you can, girl – get moving.'

Agnes did as she was told, scurrying off as fast as she could to fulfil her errand.

'I need to know if you can hear me, Mrs Aubrey, there's a good lady,' Dr Proctor repeated. 'Say if you can hear me, that's all.'

'I can hear you,' Emmaline told him in a vague voice. 'Though you seem very far away, and I feel dreadful.'

'That's because of this nasty bump to your head here. Fingers and toes? Move them all right, can you?'

Emmaline moved the fingers of both her hands, which were resting in front of her on the sheet.

'That's the thing, good girl,' Dr Proctor said. 'Toes as well?'

'I think so,' Emmaline agreed. 'Yes. Yes, I can move my toes as well.'

'That's the thing. Jolly good show.'

Once Agnes had returned with the hot water, Dr Proctor set about dressing the bump and bruising to Emmaline's temple, checked her pulse rate, looked carefully into his patient's eyes and then pronounced that all was as well as could be expected.

'Somebody has got word to her husband, I imagine?' he asked Mrs Graham as they descended the stairs. 'Nothing to be unduly alarmed about, but someone had best tip him the wink. Don't want the poor fellow coming home and finding a wounded soldier in his bed.'

Mrs Graham gave Dr Proctor an old-fashioned look before assuring him that she would telephone Mr Aubrey's office with the news immediately. Then she handed him over to Wilkinson, and disappeared below stairs to arrange for her mistress to have a cup of camomile tea taken up to her, a beverage that the housekeeper believed was second to none when it came to calming the nerves after shock.

'I wonder what happened,' Emmaline said to Agnes when her tea had been brought up to her. The maid was sitting as requested by her mistress by her bedside. 'I really do not remember one thing about it at all.'

'All I knows is Mr Wilkinson heard what he says was you falling, madam,' Agnes replied. 'So everyone thinks you must have fainted out.'

'I don't even remember what I was doing.'

'P'rhaps it was your stays, madam. Mrs Graham was only saying the other day how stays have this habit of making ladies faint.'

'I was not wearing particularly tight stays, Aggie – that is not my custom.'

'No, madam, I was forgetting. And I should know really, seeing it's me what dresses you. Maybe you're sickening for something. Like we was talking about the other day, when we met that lady being ill in the street.'

'I hope not, Aggie,' Emmaline sighed, putting her hand on her maid's. 'I do not wish to spend Christmas in bed.'

She heard Julius returning later, heard his melodious voice in the hall as he talked to Wilkinson, then heard what she thought must be the drawing-room door close as she supposed Julius went to partake of a drink before changing for dinner. Except tonight he would be dining by himself, a situation that Emmaline thought he would probably prefer, only to find herself surprised by the sound of a knock on her bedroom door and the appearance of her husband on the threshold.

'Hello,' he said, frowning at the sight of Emmaline lying in bed with her maid sitting on a chair beside her. 'I heard you'd had an accident or something.'

'You can go now, Aggie,' Emmaline said. 'I'm much better now.'

'Agnes doesn't have to go on my account,' Julius said, remaining at the doorway. 'I just looked in to see what had happened and how you were.'

'Aggie has matters to attend to, Julius,' Emmaline replied. 'Thank you, Aggie. If I need you I'll ring.'

Agnes left the room, bobbing to Julius as she passed him, before scurrying away down the corridor as if she was being chased.

'I do wish she wouldn't run round the place like that,' Julius complained. 'I find it most unsettling.'

'Dr Proctor said I have to stay in bed for a few days, Julius,' Emmaline said, sitting herself up on her pillows and tidying the sheet in front of her. 'I hope this won't prove too inconvenient for you?'

Julius frowned, then raised his eyebrows and shrugged in a slightly juvenile fashion, as if unable to make sense of what Emmaline had just said.

'Don't see why,' he replied. 'I shall probably dine at my club, because I really cannot tolerate eating on my own. But otherwise I don't see why I won't manage. You are all right, I think? Just a bit of a bump on the head, Wilkinson said, nothing too bad, nothing to worry about.'

Now he peered at her across the bedroom, making Emmaline feel as though he might be looking for further signs of disease, perhaps a rash, or the heightened colour that would denote the onset of a fever.

'As you say, just a bit of a bump on the head. I fell over and gave my head a bang, that was all,' Emmaline said with what she hoped was a comforting smile. 'I shall be quite the thing very soon, you will see.'

'Wilkinson thought you might have fainted.'

'Why? Why on earth would I faint? I really am not prone to fainting fits, Julius – as you may or may not have noticed.'

'Women are forever fainting,' Julius muttered. 'Least that's what I have been told. I'll look in on you again tomorrow. Meanwhile, I hope you continue well and are able to get a good night's sleep.'

'Thank you, Julius,' Emmaline replied sincerely. 'You are really very kind, do you know that? A great deal kinder than you realise.'

This remark elicited an unexpected response from her husband, who had been making for the door as she spoke. He turned back and stared at her, not in his usual way, but in a way that gave her the impression he was looking at her properly for the first time in a long while.

'What did you say?' he asked.

'Nothing, only that you are a great deal kinder than you think you are.'

'No I am not, Emma, far from it, and you know it. You are the one with the heart of gold, not me. I am, for whatever reason, the very opposite of what you call "kind". Goodnight, Emma. Sleep well.'

Chapter Nine

The next day Emmaline felt well enough to make some notes in her secret notebook. She was working on a poem, and after a light lunch of clear soup and lightly poached fish she sat in bed writing. She must have exhausted herself because she fell asleep mid-task, so that when Agnes brought up her tea her notebook had slipped from the bed to fall on the floor.

Agnes put the tea tray down quietly on the bedside table and picked up the book, which was lying open on its face. She stared at the words, unable to make sense of anything and longing more than ever to be able to read and write, particularly as beautifully as her mistress wrote. She shut the book and replaced it beside the still sleeping Emmaline before pulling the heavy velvet curtains closed, then returning to the bed to wake her mistress.

'I was asleep?' Emmaline enquired. 'I can't have been. I wasn't tired.'

'I'm just the same when I climbs into bed, madam,' Agnes replied. 'I think I'm not even a tiny bit done, then next thing I know it's time to get up. Sleep'll do you good.'

'My notebook.'

'On the bed. By your hand.'

Emmaline took the book and clasped it in her hands as though she had lost it.

'You keeping a diary, madam? That's something I'd like to do, keep a diary, put in things I see and hear. Is that what you are doing?' Agnes wondered. 'If I might ask.'

'What?' Emmaline looked at her, coming back to earth after being somewhere miles away. 'No. No, I'm not keeping a diary. At least I don't think I am.'

She opened her book carefully, wondering if she had written anything before she fell asleep, thinking it most unlikely after receiving a bump on the head, but to her surprise, and quiet delight, there were six lines of a brand-new poem. She read them through as Agnes bustled about tidying up the already immaculate room, refolding Emmaline's discarded lace shawl and picking her dressing gown up to smooth it out before refolding it and placing it carefully on the back of a nearby chair, finding that, at least to her mind, the new lines were pleasing.

She had been concentrating on shorter verses, leaving the composition of the longer poem aside for a while since she found that much more demanding. It would be useless to pretend that she had an overall vision of the long poem, she knew that well; what she did have was a feeling about the theme, a feeling that was so intense, in fact, that she wondered whether another reason why she was backing away from its composition, at least for the moment, was because the power of the sentiment she had so far expressed in the unfinished verses astonished her.

The shorter poems all dealt with various aspects of love and hope and belief, disappointment and regret, and melancholy. While examining the complex conundrum of love between a man and a woman, they seemed in spite of everything to leave the reader with a sense of expectation and optimism, a promise that such wondrous feelings and emotions did exist and when experienced filled the hearts of those so blessed with an ecstasy whose description was beyond words, even sometimes the words of the poets.

The longer poem was much darker in tone, substance and voice. It told the story of a young woman in medieval times – perhaps someone who like Emmaline had promised to love, honour and obey – who waited in the tower of her castle for her love to arrive back from the wars. She had only seen him once, but that was enough to win her heart, and now as she waited for his return she examined the nature of her sentiments, trying to understand them and expressing the hope that her returning love, the hero who would one day be her husband, would come back to her. Finally, she doubted that he ever would. The longer she was made to wait the more doubtful she became, until she began to believe that he did not exist, because love itself did not exist.

That was as much as Emmaline had written of her epic, and although she thought she knew how it must end, she had to be sure. As she lay in bed watching the sky beyond the window, it seemed to her that one of the protagonists must die, and her feelings were directing themselves, insistently, towards the young woman.

Dr Proctor called again late that afternoon to check on his patient. He brought with him some iron tonic which he recommended Emmaline start taking immediately, having noted what he considered was her undue pallor. He enquired if she had been suffering from any other symptoms, but besides the mild headaches to which she confessed she had always been prone, and the occasional feeling of fatigue which she ascribed to the variety and fullness of her new life in a new country, she considered herself to be in good health.

'And you say you have never been prone to fainting fits before?' the doctor wondered. 'Not even as a young girl? Or when you – when you matured?'

'If anything, doctor, I was considered to be a bit of a tomboy when I was a girl,' Emmaline replied. 'My three sisters were always what you would, I suppose, call more girlish than I, and I have to say that when they were maturing they were forever fainting – although there were some among us at home who suspected that their faints were more often than not to draw attention to themselves, since they always occurred in front of the opposite sex.'

Dr Proctor smiled and began to pack up the contents of his Gladstone bag. 'So definitely not a genuine family malaise then, Mrs Aubrey?'

'I would say not, doctor. When may I get up? I'm really not very good at lying in bed.'

'One step at a time, young lady. Now, I must just ask you one question, which as your doctor I not only have to ask but am permitted to ask. Might you be, by any chance, in an interesting condition?'

Emmaline stared at him. 'In an interesting condition?' she faltered, her mind racing round this English euphemism, wondering if Dr Proctor could possibly mean the only thing she could imagine he meant.

'Are you by any chance with child?'

For a moment Emmaline felt indignant at the impertinence of the question, laying bare as it did the barren nature of her marriage. Looking up into the good doctor's face she realised that of course there was every reason why someone of her age and marital standing might be supposed to be expecting a child, yet she still could not help being shaken by the enquiry. It was not the question that had upset her but the dilemma she now faced as to how to respond to it. She could answer with a flat rebuttal of there being any chance of such a thing, but even though Dr

Proctor by nature of his profession ought to keep any such information to himself, there was always the possibility that doctors talked in confidence with their wives, and too flat a denial of any expectation of a child would cause comment. Since Emmaline was perfectly sure that the more mature servants at Park House must know that she and Julius did not share a bedroom, let alone a bed, it seemed to her it would not be long before the whole of Bamford would also be in possession of this fact. Faced with these considerations, rather than issuing a denial, or looking in any way affronted by such a question, Emmaline plumped for looking bashful.

'As a married woman I have no idea how to answer that, Dr Proctor. We ladies must live in hopes of great things to come, must we not?'

She actually managed to blush as she spoke these vague words, although her heightened colour was due more to the fact that she was trying to deceive the good doctor than to any maidenly modesty.

'I understand, perfectly understand. You ladies are always bashful on these points, and quite rightly so. Why, there are some young ladies I have attended who are so reticent that it is only when I lay their offspring in their arms that they care to admit to having been in an interesting condition. And I am here to tell you that if and when what we suspect does become the case, you will get the best attention from your doctor. No mother I have attended has ever had cause to complain. In fact, several of them have named their babies after me – there are three young lads in the town even as we speak named Dennis.'

'How charming, Dr Proctor, how perfectly charming,' Emmaline said. Determined to maintain her character of a modest young woman, she put one hand to her mouth and lowered her eyes, while the good doctor smiled paternally down at her.

'I have to say something further here, Mrs Aubrey,' he continued, preparing to leave her. 'If there is a possibility that you might be expectant, then, given your current medical condition, it might be best to remain confined to your bed for a little longer, just to ensure that if this is indeed happy news, then that is the way it is going to stay. I will wish you goodnight, Mrs Aubrey, but before I do I have some light sleeping powders that I think you should take. They will not induce anything more than a drowsiness that will help you rest better at night. My wife takes them whenever her mother has been to stay.'

They both laughed, and Dr Proctor placed the small packets on Emmaline's dressing table. When he reached the doorway he stopped, as something else obviously occurred to him.

'Apropos of the matter of bed rest,' he said, 'my wife has been most anxious to call on you, but without success so far, it would seem. Might it be possible for her to arrange a visit now that you are confined to barracks, so to speak? She would be delighted if you could make time.'

'Of course, doctor,' Emmaline replied, remembering that Julius was due to leave on his travels first thing the next morning and so in theory anyway she could entertain what lady friends she liked. 'If it's possible, perhaps she would like to call tomorrow afternoon around tea time. If she doesn't mind visiting a sick room.'

'Hardly a sick room, Mrs Aubrey,' Dr Proctor reassured her. 'Hardly that at all – not if things map out the way we would all like, eh? Eh?'

With a smile the good doctor was gone, leaving Emmaline quite content with the way she had conducted herself. Her thoughts turned back to her poetry and how she could best get it delivered to Bray Ashcombe, a man whom she now found occupying a far larger share of her thoughts than she had previously realised.

Julius put his head round the door on his way out to dinner.

'Might you be feeling a little better?' he asked her, after his usual initial stare.

'Yes, thank you, Julius. I really am feeling much more the thing.'

'The doctor wants you to stay in bed, I hear.'

'A precaution. Just to be on the safe side.'

'Hmm.' Julius regarded her, one hand resting on the side of the door. 'I'm off very early tomorrow. So I won't disturb you.'

'I don't mind being disturbed, Julius. I don't mind if you wake me – I shall have all day to catch up on my sleep.'

'We'll see,' Julius replied. 'Goodnight, Emma.'

'Goodnight, Julius.'

During the evening, after she had finished a light supper taken in her room, Emmaline worked some more on her poems but found herself tiring very quickly, more than she would have thought possible, in spite of all her bed rest. So, locking away her notebook, she settled down to sleep a great deal earlier than her usual hour. Later, she woke when she thought she heard someone on the landing, and sure enough when she looked she could see light seeping under her door. Moments later she heard the sound of Julius's dressing-room door closing. She lit a candle and saw it was nearly half past four in the morning, and for a moment she felt like getting out of bed and going to ask Julius what he had been thinking to stay out until such an unearthly hour.

'Really,' she said to herself, half in and half out of bed and still half asleep. 'This really has now gone far too far. Far too far.'

Whereupon her door opened and with a small shriek of fright Emmaline hopped back into bed and pulled the covers over her head.

'Who is it?' she said from beneath the bed-clothes. 'Have you any idea what the time is?'

'I thought you said you didn't mind being disturbed,' came a laconic voice from the doorway, and when Emmaline peered out from the covers she saw Julius standing there dressed in his morning clothes and carrying a large suitcase.

'Oh,' she said. 'It's you.'

'I told you I was leaving early. I have to be at the port by seven o'clock because we sail at eight, and Weymouth isn't exactly a stone's throw from here.'

'Sorry,' Emmaline said, sitting up in bed and trying to tidy her hair, which had fallen loose. 'I was fast asleep.'

'Don't worry about your hair, Emma,' Julius muttered, frowning at her. 'Looks very nice down. I'll see you next week.'

'Goodbye, Julius,' Emmaline called out after him, but he was gone.

By midday Emmaline had finished copying out her short poems in her best hand. When she had done so, she put them carefully into a large envelope which she sealed with wax and addressed *Personal: Bray Ashcombe, Esq. By hand.* Then she summoned Agnes and bade her take the package into Bamford and deliver it personally.

'Shall I wait for a reply, madam?'

'Kind of you, Aggie, but I think not,' Emmaline replied. 'It will take some time for Mr Ashcombe to read what I have sent him.'

'Very good, ma'am.' Agnes nodded. 'I'll get Alan to take me into town in the pony and trap.'

Having nothing to do now that she had delivered the set of short poems, Emmaline took a bath and changed her nightdress and dressing gown for fresh ones, ate a light lunch by her bedroom fire, and then read and slept until Agnes woke her to tell her that Mrs Proctor was downstairs waiting for permission to come up and see her. Once she was fully awake and Agnes had tidied her hair, her visitor was shown upstairs. Dolly served them tea, Emmaline sitting up in her bed against a pile of down pillows, and Mrs Proctor sitting between the bed and the fire.

By the time the small talk had been dispensed with, such as how Emmaline was enjoying life in England, what she thought of Bamford, the latest fashions and what they were both reading, the two women were at their social ease, and Mrs Proctor steered the conversation round to a more personal level.

'Your husband is away, I gather,' she said, putting down her teacup, and carefully wiping any trace of cake crumbs from her mouth with her napkin. 'France again? His mother bad again, I dare say.'

'You seem very well informed, Mrs Proctor,' Emmaline replied, trying not to look shocked that her visitor knew more about Julius than she did, but quickly recovering, not wanting Mrs Proctor to guess that she knew so little about her husband that she did not even know that he had a mother in France. 'Although I imagine your husband must have said something to you?'

'My husband hardly ever says anything to me, Mrs Aubrey,' Mrs Proctor replied a little tartly. 'And you must not be surprised about what people know in this town. It is a small society, and most of the talk even smaller. No, I heard your husband was going to France from the wife of someone who has a relative in the medical profession there. He is advising Mr Aubrey, and all is being done for your poor mother-in-law that can be done, I gather.'

'That is very good to hear,' Emmaline said, with caution.

'It is just as well that Mr Aubrey is so conversant with French ways, for their treatments and attitudes are quite different from ours, but then since he lived there for so long, before he inherited this house from his father, it is hardly surprising.'

'My husband lived in France before he came here?'

'Did you not know that?' Mrs Proctor looked at Emmaline, and seeing her inadvertently startled expression added: 'Perhaps not.'

'He may have mentioned it to me, Mrs Proctor,' Emmaline replied, trying to dissemble even though she realised her reaction must have given her away. 'But I didn't think of it as having very much significance. What happened before we met, you understand, is something I am still discovering.'

'You are so unlike me, my dear.' Mrs Proctor smiled, keeping her eyes well and truly on Emmaline. 'I have to know everything about everyone even if it is nothing to do with me. I would simply have to know why my husband apparently grew up in France and only returned here when his father died.'

'He only arrived to live in Bamford then? Just after his father died?'

'Oh yes, indeed. Before that the works, and everything to do with them, were some way from here, I gather. It was only when Mr Aubrey senior passed that they were brought to Bamford, and I understand are better for it.' She took out a lace-edged handkerchief and dabbed her forehead with it, suddenly finding the room very warm. But then, she reflected, sickrooms always were. 'You know nothing of the family history, obviously – perhaps by choice?' Emmaline just shook her head, suddenly tired by the fact that everyone seemed to know more about her husband and his background than she did as his wife. 'Mind you,' Mrs Proctor continued with a sigh, 'I knew very little about *my* husband when I married him. That is just how it was then. A match was considered for you by your parents, and if it was deemed to be a good one, the next thing you knew you were married – to a perfect stranger most of the time, so who am I to say? Of course because my family arranged my marriage they found out all about my husband's background and upbringing and his status in society and passed it on to me much later, I forget exactly when. I just would have thought that in this day and age . . .' Mrs Proctor stopped to consider her words and to shake her head, indicating her bewilderment with yet another sigh before continuing. 'However, as I was saying, your husband's return to Bamford following the gathering of his father was possibly the first time he had set foot in the town since he was a tiny boy.'

'He can't have been educated in France, surely? He has no trace of an accent – although he does speak French, and his accent sounds impeccable.'

'I have no idea where he was schooled, my dear. In fact, like most of us around these parts I have very little idea about the family as an entirety, other than the fact that I gather Mrs Aubrey – your husband's mother – disappeared with the children, back to France, which was hardly surprising since she was, I understand, French. Certainly in all the time I have lived here – I'm not a native of Bamford, do you see? I moved here from Gloucester after I was married – there has never been a Mrs Aubrey here in Park House until you arrived. Mr Aubrey senior had – he had a housekeeper who looked after his needs. She was a Mrs Watson. A very striking woman, you could say beautiful, and not at all one's conception of a housekeeper. Yet she kept Mr Aubrey's house and he must have been a very pleasant and interesting man to work for because when he died they say the poor woman was utterly distraught. She left here very shortly after the funeral and I suppose one must imagine she took a similar post elsewhere.'

'I see,' Emmaline said, trying to make sense of all the new information being given to her. 'So Julius returned to Bamford – or rather came to Bamford – quite recently?'

'When his father passed on there were rumours

that the business was foundering, and that was why he brought it into less expensive premises here. As you can imagine, in a town as small as this, a town that is dependent on its industries and businesses, people's ears are kept very close to the ground, and word had it that there was financial trouble at Aubrey & Aubrey. Yet now we gather things are looking up there, although we know no details as to the whys and wherefores, other than the fact that it might well have something to do with the firm's being adopted by one of those American postal catalogues that are so popular over there, as well as all the new business that your husband has brought in through his connections to our large country houses. He is a most gifted man, as you know, so different from his older brother.'

Once again Emmaline found herself trying not to look astonished. Julius had an older brother? If that was the case, why had he not mentioned it before? Why had he only mentioned a sister? The same young woman who was perhaps the subject of the beautiful hidden portrait? If she had been able to close her eyes at that moment without exciting Mrs Proctor's curiosity, she would have.

Having reached her conclusion, or at least her final supposition, her last throw of that afternoon's cards, Mrs Proctor folded her hands carefully on her lap and regarded Emmaline, waiting for a reaction.

Emmaline knew better than to give her visitor the satisfaction of seeing her astonishment, but she was nevertheless able to ask her, most politely, if she could call another day. Mrs Proctor was the first visitor she had received since her indisposition, and she would be very grateful if she could now be allowed to rest.

Mrs Proctor agreed at once, tendered her apologies if she had overstayed her welcome, squeezed Emmaline's hands in farewell and left, leaving Emmaline to try to make some kind of weary sense of all she had learned about the Aubrey family that afternoon.

Two days later the postman brought another letter to the house for Emmaline, and once again Emmaline found herself in the sitting room excitedly reading a note from Bray Ashcombe concerning her poetry.

In no way can I convey to you the intensity of my feelings at this moment, the letter read. *I have just heard from the gentleman of whom I spoke to you regarding the possible publication of the verses you have so kindly sent me in order to seek my opinion, and I trust my help. Although I am excited beyond measure at his response I must say that it comes as no surprise, for having read the now finished verses written by your anonymous friend I know it is only meet and right that someone should be as keen as Mr Herbert Tully is to publish this poetry. He is of the opinion that the short verses he has now read (and I must tell you read again and again and over again) should be published at once as a collection. You being* such an admirer of modern poetry will appreciate what a readership there is for publications such as this; we sell countless copies of small poetry collections here in the bookshop, as well as long single poems such as the ones you have now read which have been the subject of our discussions, as indeed do booksellers all over the country.

How we set about this I am not sure, and I must leave it to you to discuss with your friend her wishes and her intentions. If she is agreeable there will be negotiations to be undertaken and a contract to be signed. In the understanding that your friend wishes to remain anonymous, I can of course act as agent for this agreement, consulting if not directly with your friend then at least with you, if I may. The poems would be printed here in Bamford in the printing works attached to the bookshop, works that were built expressly to print and publish works directly commissioned or encouraged by the bookshop. Mr Tully will act as the publisher, as he has done on many previous occasions, and will ensure the proper distribution of the booklet. Once an agreement has been arrived at it will only be a matter of a few weeks before we shall be able to see, read and buy your friend's poems from such places as Mr Hunt's bookshop.

I do hope this gives as much pleasure to your friend as it does to me, and that we may meet soon and discuss this wonderful news.

Yours sincerely,
Bray Ashcombe

This time Emmaline realised she must be more measured in her immediate reaction, so, putting the letter aside, she remained seated in her place by the warming fire. Closing her eyes, she tried to keep at bay the excitement she felt welling up within her at the thought that her verses were going to published, and not just published, but published, distributed and read – *read*, she kept telling herself.

These poems that came to me out of the very blue – who knows? They might bring solace and comfort to those in the same sort of emotional distress as the author. They might enlighten and soothe souls in trouble and torment, they might ease the minds of those who think their plight is unique, and help them realise that this is something that many of us undergo – and that as long as we keep love and faith intact, there is always hope, because somewhere there is always love to be found.

Once she felt she was calm, and her thoughts collected, Emmaline opened her eyes and began to consider how best to go about all the arrangements that would be necessary if the verses were to be published. She wondered if she should disclose the true identity of the author, or merely pretend that the proper authority had been settled on her so that she might act as her friend's representative and sign the papers for her, her friend being in America.

No! she told herself. *There is such a thing as a postal service and doubtless Mr Tully as publisher would insist on getting the signature from the original artist, in case of fraud or deception, even if it meant a long delay while the contract was shuttled to and from America.*

At last she recognised the pitfalls of her situation. In whose name would the agreement be made, and to whom should it be sent? Some mythical person, or was it necessary to bring someone else into the deceit? Whichever way she looked at it, it seemed that she was in an impossible position. Emmaline very soon realised that the only way was to make a clean breast of the matter, to confess to Mr Ashcombe and Mr Tully that she was in fact the author, having of course naturally sworn them both to secrecy, a confidentiality that could be legalised in any agreement they might draw up.

Inevitably, along with that decision, came a new concern – if she needed such a clause in a contract then she also surely needed a solicitor, or similar, to ensure that everything put before her was properly legal? Yet to engage such a person in a town as small as Bamford, and for the engagement to remain unnoticed, must surely be next to impossible? While the fact that a lawyer must protect the confidences of his clients was indisputable, there was nothing to say he could not disclose the *identity* of any client. Julius was known to everyone in Bamford, and it would surely only be a very short time before tongues in the clubs and bars were wagging, and the news would be out that Mrs Julius Aubrey had written and was having published poems that were, to say the least, of a very personal nature.

For Emmaline that reflection was almost enough to deter her from doing anything more about getting her poems published. It seemed to her that the very action of engaging a lawyer could easily be misconstrued by the town gossips, and she could come to be seen as a woman whose marriage, already rumoured to be unsuccessful thanks to that disastrous birthday party, was now exposed as being quite pitiably unhappy.

But then the excitement of the thought that she might see her verses in print overcame her, and pushing aside any feelings of modesty she determined that she would visit Bray Ashcombe and take him into her confidence.

She knew she must not write to him on the matter because, as her father had always advised her, if you wanted to keep life simple it was best not to commit anything to paper. So, summoning up all her strength, she determined to fix appointments to see Mr Ashcombe and Mr Tully as soon as she was physically able, and to initiate the negotiations by confessing to the authorship of the poetry. With that in mind she wrote a brief note to Mr Ashcombe to the effect that she would like to arrange a meeting with him and Mr Tully to discuss the matter of her friend's poetry as soon as it was possible. She despatched Agnes into town to deliver the note in person, and then sat happily in front of the fire sewing a new purse intended as a present for Mrs Graham.

*   *   *

While Agnes was away on her mission the telephone bell rang. It was a most unusual sound, since they currently received more communications via the Post Office and callers to the house than they did by telephone.

Since Emmaline was passing the telephone room at the time she went to answer it, even though normally this was something she preferred to leave to Wilkinson who greatly enjoyed this privilege, answering the few calls they had had since her arrival at Park House with military precision. But this time there was no sign of her butler, so Emmaline closeted herself in the small room dedicated to the making and taking of telephone calls, lifted the receiver, and held it to her ear.

'Yes?' she said.

An American voice answered, somewhat startling Emmaline.

'How do you do? I wish to speak to a Mr Aubrey, if you please. A Mr Julius Aubrey?'

'Yes,' Emmaline replied, feeling awkward as she always did when using the telephone. 'This is Mr Aubrey's residence, but I am afraid he is not present at this time.'

'When might I speak with him, please?' the caller asked. 'I am not going to be in this country long and I need to speak with him most urgently.'

'Mr Aubrey is in France at the moment, sir,' Emmaline said. 'We're not altogether sure when he means to return because he likes to leave such matters open, but he did mention something about the day after tomorrow.'

'I see.' The American paused, then, after clearing his throat, continued, 'Am I speaking with Mrs Aubrey?'

'Yes, sir, you are. And whom might I be addressing?'

'My name is Dwight Freeman, Mrs Aubrey. I am a business associate of Mr Aubrey.'

'I see. Would it not be more advantageous for you to telephone Mr Aubrey's office? Not only is it a better place to catch him, Mr Freeman, but someone there might have a more precise idea than I when to expect him.'

'Very kind of you, ma'am, but this is a confidential matter. A personal one, really, and I thought it more prudent to telephone his home. Perhaps you would be kind enough to convey a message to your husband from me, in case I fail to make contact with him or he returns earlier than expected? I am on my way to stay at the Grand Hotel, Cheltenham – and I would like to meet with him there on a matter of some urgency before I have to leave the country once more. Perhaps he would be good enough to telephone me at the hotel when he returns? Thanking you kindly, ma'am.'

'I shall do exactly as you request, Mr Freeman,' Emmaline replied. 'And I must say it's very nice to hear a fellow American. What part are you from, sir?'

'Me? I'm a New Yorker, ma'am, born and bred.'

'Really?' Emmaline said, in some surprise. 'It must be the telephone line, but I would have said you were from somewhere much further south.'

'Is that so, Mrs Aubrey?' the man replied after a slight pause. 'And where might you be from? No – let me guess. I would put you down as a Bostonian.'

'You are absolutely right, Mr Freeman.' Emmaline laughed. 'Completely so.'

'Then forgive me for saying, ma'am, that perhaps my ear for an accent is even better than yours.'

With that he hung up, as did Emmaline, still convinced, as she wrote a note for Julius, that what she had heard was most certainly not a New York accent.

She was sitting at her desk in her room checking her household lists after lunch when Wilkinson knocked and informed her that Agnes wished to see her.

'Can it not wait, I wonder, Wilkinson?' Emmaline replied, looking up from her notebook. 'I am rather busy.'

'She said it was urgent, madam,' Wilkinson replied, standing in front of the closed door. 'She seems more than a little upset.'

'Very well, Wilkinson,' Emmaline told him, not having the sort of heart that could exclude someone as nervous and sensitive as her young maid. 'Show her in, please.'

Agnes entered with a frown so deep that

Emmaline was alarmed. The girl was chewing her lower lip with anxiety and twisting her hands.

'Yes, Aggie? Has something upset you?'

'Yes, madam,' Agnes replied, all but under her breath. 'But I don't know as how I should tell you.'

'Forgive me, Aggie. Do you mean you don't know how to tell me, or whether you should or not?'

'Yes, madam,' Agnes muttered, frowning even more deeply and staring down at the carpet. 'Both really.'

'Only tell me if you wish to, Aggie. You must never feel obliged.'

'It's not that, ma'am. I never as feel obliged to you, 'cos you're always so kind, like. To me. To everyone really.'

'That's very sweet of you, Aggie – yet here am I and we haven't even started on your reading yet.'

'You been ill, ma'am. Not the sort of thing you wants to do when you're ill, like.' The girl fell to silence, continuing to chew her lower lip and frown at the carpet.

'So what is it then, Aggie?' Emmaline asked gently. 'It's obvious something is troubling you deeply.'

'P'rhaps I should have told Mrs Graham first. And asked her if I should tell you, madam.'

'You can go and do so now if you wish, Aggie.'

'I seen Mr Aubrey, madam,' Agnes blurted out instead. 'Least I'm as sure it were him.'

307

'You saw my husband, Agnes?' Emmaline suddenly straightened her back, as if she knew this presaged bad tidings. 'And when would that be, may I ask?'

'Please don't be cross, ma'am,' Agnes begged, her eyes suddenly full of tears. 'It's not my fault.'

'I'm not cross with you, Agnes,' Emmaline assured her. 'It's just – you must understand this comes as a bit of a shock. Seeing that my husband is in France.'

'No, ma'am. I mean I know, madam, but I'm sure I saw him, honest. Cross my heart and hope to die. I swear it were him.'

'Perhaps you saw him on his way home. If you saw him – I take it it was when you were out?' As Agnes nodded, without looking up, she went on, 'Then the possibility is that he is back in England and either on his way to his offices before coming home, or even now on his way back here.'

'Yes, ma'am,' Agnes muttered.

'That would be very typical of my husband, Aggie. I don't think even he knows where he is going to be from one minute to the next.'

'It wasn't like that, madam,' Agnes said, now looking her mistress in the eye as if she had just determined that the truth must and should be known. 'It was really peculiar, see. I was walking back to the trap, up the High Street, see, 'cos Alan had parked it where we usually does, and this carriage was coming through the town, like. Then this dog runs out and the driver swerves the horses to avoid it and runs on to the pavement, see. Right where I'm standing. I mean it near as anything crashes into me and I don't know what, I was as close as that to getting hit. And the carriage has tipped over a bit, see – the driver falls off his seat and as the carriage tips over the gentleman inside gets thrown off his seat as well. He falls against the window, sort of on his knees – and as he tries to recover hisself he looks up at me and – and I'm pinned up aginst this wall, see – and he looks at me and he's only this far away, madam – and honest I swear, madam, honest I swear it was Mr Aubrey.'

'Yes, Aggie.' Emmaline smiled. 'And as I said, the probability is that he was on his way either to the office or—'

'There was someone else with him, ma'am,' Agnes blurted. 'Beggin' your pardon.'

'Someone else?'

'There was this other person in the carriage, see. There was this – this woman, like. With Mr Aubrey.'

Emmaline said nothing. She just looked as steadily as she could at her maid, because she could not think of anything suitable to say, and also because she could hear her heart pounding in her ears, a thrumping sound. She took a deep breath, held it, then nodded at Agnes to indicate that she should proceed.

'She had this red silk coat on and an 'at with a big yellow feather,' Agnes continued. 'She in't seen me as yet, like, but as I can't get past to get to the trap because I'm stuck up against the wall

I'm standing there staring at Mr Aubrey and she says – 'cos she's fallen off her seat too, like – she says something or other then I hears her say, "*You all right, my darling?*" She's leaning up against him, holding her hat, and she's saying—'

'Yes, yes,' Emmaline said quickly. 'Yes, I heard what you think you heard her say. This woman.'

There was a silence now as they both considered what had been said. Finally Emmaline, having taken another deep breath, nodded and clasped her hands tightly on her lap.

'They are probably friends in business, Aggie,' she said. 'I don't think we need to – to – er – read too much into this.' She tried to smile. 'After all, my husband lives and works here, and I really don't know very many of the people he knows, so I don't think we need to think there is anything untoward in this situation.'

'Well, it weren't just that, madam,' Agnes continued, swallowing hard and wiping the back of her mouth quickly with her hand. 'The thing is, obviously, with me this close, the thing is Mr Aubrey sees me, see. He's looking out of the window and straight at me.'

'Mr Aubrey saw you,' Emmaline said slowly.

'He couldn't as help it, ma'am. He was that close to me, see. But when he sees me he just stares. That's all. He gives me this look, just as though he's never seen me before. I'm doing me best not to stare at him 'cos I know I shouldn't, but I can't help it, madam, 'cos of the way he's staring at me. He just looks at me. He looks at me as though I wasn't there. Then as the carriage tips back upright he gets back on his seat and he leans over – and he pulls the blind down at the window.'

'Thank you, Aggie,' Emmaline said after a moment. 'But I think you were probably mistaken, don't you? I think you thought you saw Mr Aubrey, but if he didn't recognise you, then it cannot have been him, can it?'

'No, madam,' Agnes said, colouring deeply. 'But I mean it was, madam. What I mean is, I'm sure it was, madam.'

'But it can't have been, Aggie. Not if he didn't recognise you. And before you tell me that when he saw who it was looking at him he then pretended not to know you, I think you would have seen that, would you not? You would have seen some glimmer of recognition or even surprise on his face when he saw you – if it was my husband, which I now doubt that it was.'

'Yes, madam,' Agnes muttered. 'I shouldn't have as told you, should I? Least not till he come home. Your husband – Mr Aubrey, I means. 'Cos then if he was home now I'd have known it was him, wouldn't I?'

'No, Aggie,' Emmaline said. 'You did right to come and tell me. You were upset because like me you thought Mr Aubrey wasn't due home for some days yet. And you thought he might have been hurt – in the accident – and then when he seemed not to recognise you – it's perfectly natural for you both to be upset, and to come and tell me. Thank you.'

'You're not cross then, madam?'

'No, Aggie. Just a little puzzled, like you. Rather, I was a little puzzled, until it became obvious from what you said that you were mistaken, and that it wasn't my husband.'

But when Agnes left, she was still convinced that the gentleman she had seen at such close quarters was indeed her employer, since Mr Aubrey was a man of such distinctive looks that he would not be easily mistaken. Emmaline was equally certain that the man in the carriage with the woman in red could not possibly have been her husband because to her way of thinking it would have been impossible for him not to have recognised someone as familiar and in her own way as distinctive as Agnes. None the less, she asked Wilkinson to telephone her husband's offices to see when they might be expecting him to return.

'Not for two or three days, madam,' Wilkinson reported back to her. 'Apparently Mr Aubrey told his secretary quite specifically he was not to be expected back in the office before Friday at the very earliest, and due to some considerable setbacks, some difficulties the other side of the Channel, it was more likely that he would not be back at his business until the beginning of next week.'

'Which is not going to give us a great deal of time to prepare for Christmas, Wilkinson.' Emmaline sighed. 'Not that there seems to be a great deal to prepare for.'

'Things are a little inclined to be left until the last moment sometimes, madam, I do agree,' Wilkinson said. 'But never fear. When the orders come it will be all hands to the pumps, I assure you.'

Although initially more shaken by Agnes's supposed revelation than she liked to admit, Emmaline, who was at last beginning to feel better and a little stronger, resolved that she would follow up her note to Mr Ashcombe by arranging the meeting with him and Mr Tully for the following morning, and so she slipped discreetly into the telephone room in order to leave a message with the secretary in Mr Hunt's bookshop that she would be calling in to see Mr Ashcombe at eleven o'clock. She spent the rest of the afternoon in the bedroom, working on her longer poem, before dining alone and retiring early to bed with a book.

When she thought it was time to blow out her light, she found that sleep would not come. Attributing her insomnia to the fact that she had rested so much over the past few days, she went to her dressing table and took one of Dr Proctor's powders mixed in water. It was the first time that she had taken one, and she was surprised to find that in only a short time, with her precious notebook still on her knee, she felt her eyelids growing heavy. Turning to blow out her nightstick, she lay back on her pillows feeling strangely light in mind and body, not even stirring as the notebook filled with her poems slid to the floor.

But the sleep she finally fell into was fitful, as if the powder had brought on some sort of fever. She knew she was asleep, and that she was dreaming an ugly uncomfortable dream filled with images of strange people, faces that were not quite faces, forms that were neither human nor animal, but she couldn't wake up – and then there were the noises.

When she at last forced herself to sit upright, she knew something had woken her because she had heard it in her half-dream: the sound of someone in the house, a door or a floorboard creaking, or perhaps not even a noise, she thought as she sat listening – perhaps it had just been a sense of disturbance. She had taken to the habit of sleeping with the bedroom door a little ajar when Julius was away, half because she found she had become afraid of the dark when she was alone and half because she believed that somehow it was safer, as if it left her a ready exit to flee from whatever nocturnal terror might befall her, or would permit her more readily to call for help and afford one of the servants a better chance of hearing her cry. And now, through the half-open door, she could see a faint ray of light coming from somewhere, not from anywhere on the landing it seemed but from another source, one downstairs. For a moment she sat there, the bedclothes pulled tightly round her for security while she listened and waited, but in vain, because there was nothing to hear. There was just the light, a light that had grown brighter now she was completely awake and fully conscious. Emboldened, she decided to climb out of bed, and take a look over the banisters to see if she could identify its source. Pulling on her dressing gown, and hooking her long hair back over her shoulders, she tiptoed out on to the landing and looked down into the hall.

The light was coming from Julius's study. There was no doubt about it. Emmaline could see that the door was slightly open and a strong ray of light was seeping out into the otherwise darkened house. She was about to call out Julius's name but stopped herself just in time, realising that if it were not her husband, any intruder would be alerted and know that he had been spotted. Instead, she went to the top of the staircase and slowly eased her way step by step down the stairs until she was opposite the study door, in a position to see into the room, hoping to identify the person within. As she stood waiting, holding her breath and frowning into the gloom, she heard the sound of someone moving about inside the room and then by sheer good chance caught sight of him in the large, ornate mirror that hung on the wall opposite the door. It was a tall man in a long dark coat.

It was Julius, she was sure of it.

Unable to contain herself, Emmaline called out his name as she ran quickly down the rest of the stairs and into the study, where sure enough she found Julius standing at the desk going through some papers apparently taken from an open drawer. She also realised when she saw the curtains billowing above the desk that for some reason the study window was open.

'Julius?' she repeated drowsily. 'Julius – you're back.'

Even as she said the words she knew how foolish they must have sounded, but such was her state that she could think of nothing else to say. She remembered that earlier in the day she had been reliably informed that her husband was not to be expected back until the end of the week at the earliest, perhaps not until the beginning of the following week, yet here he was at home in the early hours of the morning, in his study, going through a pile of documents.

He stared at her in the half-light, clearly startled.

'I'm sorry, Julius,' she said vaguely. 'What are you doing home so . . . so . . .' She struggled to complete the thought.

'My dear—'

'What are you doing home?' Emmaline repeated dreamily. 'I thought – I thought . . .' She searched in her mind for the words, ' I am sure we were told—'

'Urgent business,' he said quickly, cutting in on her.

'I see. I do see. Forgive me, but I feel a little strange – it must be the time of the night . . .'

'I really am sorry.' Julius smiled, and when he did Emmaline thought she noticed a different look to his eyes, a look that she could not remember seeing before.

'Julius,' she began again, still not knowing quite what she was going to say.

'I must say, you look . . .' he said quietly, 'your hair looks – I do so love it when women wear their hair down like that.'

'Julius . . .'

'Go back to bed, do.'

Emmaline watched him, watched him smile, then looked into his eyes, once again seeing something that seemed to remind her of something, but what?

'Very well,' she replied drowsily, sensing her heartbeat racing, feeling it as if it was in her mouth. 'I'll go back up the stairs as you say. And get into bed.'

She held the look between them for a moment and then turned to go, but as she did so she felt a hand take her arm, and when she turned back he was standing very close to her. He put his other arm slowly but firmly round her waist, drawing her to him.

'Except, you see, I can't let you go just like that,' he murmured. 'Certainly not without kissing you.'

Emmaline's eyes opened as wide as they would go as she realised what was about to happen, and then they closed and everything was dark, everything went black as he held her tightly to him, kissing her firmly. And the more he kissed her, the longer and tighter he held her, the more she wanted to struggle. This was the moment for which she had waited, for which she had longed, holding back her ever-growing impatience with the man who neglected her so cruelly, waiting because she knew she loved him – she *thought* she loved him, for now in the very act of him kissing her she felt that *something was wrong* and she put her hands on his chest and tried to push him away, but he just increased his hold on her and kissed her again. She could not match his strength. The light was dim and her heart was pounding so fast that it made her breathless, suffocating her until she was unable to draw breath, to keep awake, to stay conscious.

Since his eyes were still open he saw her fall away from him, and immediately felt what was now a dead weight in his arms. He put one hand to her neck and felt a pulse still beating, and turning quickly he carried her up the stairs and into the bedroom, where a bedside candle was still burning.

He laid her on the bed and stood for a while looking down at the slender unconscious young woman lying on her back. He removed her dressing gown, and very soon the clinging white linen of her nightdress revealed the roundness of her young breasts and the slender shape of her waist and the curve of her hips. He began to loosen his tie and the studs in his shirt, smiling to himself as he thought of how much he was going to enjoy this particular turn of events, and of the confusion and the mayhem he was going to cause. But in that moment of imagined delight he became careless, stepping backwards as he began to undo his shirt and walking straight into the low round table on which Dolly and Agnes placed evening biscuits and milk.

The tray crashed to the floor, as did the heavy decanter and glass, the noise seeming all the more startling in the sepulchral quiet of the house.

He waited for a moment, listening, before going to the door to check on the corridor outside. Just as he imagined it was safe to return to the bed he saw a light go on on the other side of the pass door at the end of the landing and at once he was gone – down the stairs and into the darkness beyond, leaving no trace of his presence, only an odd sense of disturbance.

By the time darkness had enveloped him Mrs Graham, pulling her dressing gown tight around her, was bustling along the landing in the direction of Emmaline's bedroom, where she too saw a light still burning. When she came into the room Emmaline was still unconscious, flat on her back with an arm thrown to the same side as the upturned table and spilled tray.

The housekeeper hurried to her mistress's side, kicking aside the notebook by the bed, hoping that her mistress had not blacked out but was merely suffering from some sort of nightmare, or had perhaps taken to sleepwalking, in the midst of which she had knocked over the piece of furniture which had been so close to her bed. Having righted the table and picked up the pieces of broken glassware, Mrs Graham turned back to Emmaline. Putting a hand on the still outstretched arm, she tried to rouse her mistress as quietly and undramatically as she could.

At first there was no response, Emmaline continuing to lie inert, and seeming to be hardly breathing, so that Mrs Graham found herself leaning forward and taking hold of one of her hands.

'Mrs Aubrey?' she said, sitting on the edge of the bed and stroking Emmaline's hand in hers. 'Mrs Aubrey? Wake up, dear. Please wake up.'

To Mrs Graham's great relief there was a slight sign of life, Emmaline's eyes moving and then opening, although when the older woman leaned over her she seemed to see nothing and no one.

'Mrs Aubrey?' Mrs Graham repeated. 'Madam? Madam – are you all right?'

Now Emmaline turned her head and looked at her, but the housekeeper wasn't sure she recognised her. 'What happened?' she said faintly. 'Where am I? What happened?'

'You had a dream, dear,' Mrs Graham said quietly. 'It would appear you were sleepwalking for a moment, for you knocked over your night table.'

Emmaline frowned, but continued to stare at her housekeeper rather than look for the sign of any such accident.

'Mrs Graham?'

'It's all right, dear,' Mrs Graham assured her. 'You must just have had a nasty dream, that's all.'

'I was dreaming, was I?' Emmaline asked in a low voice, slowly looking round the room as if expecting to see someone. 'But what? What could I have been dreaming?'

'I don't know what you were dreaming, dear,' Mrs Graham said, standing and carefully pulling the bedclothes back into place. 'But it must have been something very frightening, or perhaps, as I say, you were sleepwalking, Mrs Aubrey. I am the lightest of sleepers, but the noise could have woken the dead.'

'Julius,' Emmaline said suddenly, sitting up as she seemed to remember something. 'My husband.'

'He'll be back soon,' Mrs Graham said, tucking in the bedclothes then plumping up Emmaline's pillows and patting them into a comforting pile behind her. 'Won't be long before he's home.'

'He's not home?' Emmaline turned to Mrs Graham. 'But he is home. I know I saw him, I saw him in his study, I am sure I did.'

'That was what you were dreaming, was it?' Mrs Graham straightened up and looked round the room. 'Not long now. As I understand it from Mr Ralph at the works, he is expected to be home by the weekend. Just you rest there while I fetch something to clear up all this mess. Will you be all right for a moment, while I fetch a bucket and an old towel from the airing cupboard and finish clearing up this mess?'

'Yes – I am feeling a little better, Mrs Graham, truly I am,' Emmaline assured her. 'I'll be quite myself soon, thank you. I am so sorry to put you to all this trouble.'

When the housekeeper had finished clearing up, and had disappeared once more to her own room, Emmaline lay back on her pillows in a daze, trying to remember, trying to recall anything from the night before, trying to make her hazy mind concentrate on what it was she had dreamed. Why had she woken up saying her husband's name and thinking that he had returned? But try as she might, she could recall nothing of any note other than going to bed and falling asleep.

'Mrs Graham must be right, I must have been dreaming,' she assured herself quietly, yet putting a hand to bruised lips as though the touch might help her recall. But nothing came to her, nothing other than a feeling of dread and of intrusion, and a sense that Julius had somehow returned. 'It must have been a nightmare. After all, Mrs Graham has just told me that Julius isn't coming back until the end of the week.'

But there *was* something else, she was sure of it, something in all that darkness. She could see something – there, in her mind's eye, she was sure she had seen a light. She remembered a soft flickering ray of illumination somewhere, and her sense of foreboding increased. Had she been dying in her sleep? Was the light that brightness that the dying were said to see, towards which their spirits were pulled as they eased out of this life and into the next?

'To sleep, to dream . . . what dreams may come must give us pause . . .'

She found herself filled with an irrational panic, so much so that it seemed to her that to stay in bed would be to court death, although why she could not have said. She put her feet on the floor. The coldness of the old wood was reassuring, and she straightened up, but the moment she did so a sudden spell of dizziness overcame her, forcing her to grasp one of the sturdy oak bedposts. She stood still by the bed, taking two or three long deep breaths, which together with the cold of the floor beneath her feet seemed to steady her, so that, taking hold of a candlestick to light her way, after a few seconds she was able to set off for the door, just making it before she had to seek the support of the wall. She took more deep breaths, and then, determined on her mission, she opened the bedroom door, and walking slowly along the corridor, supporting herself with one hand tracing along the wall, she went to her husband's dressing room and opened the door. The room was empty, the bed still made up and undisturbed.

'Mrs Graham!' she called out, once she had returned to her own room. 'Mrs Graham!' As the housekeeper came hurrying into the room, she said, 'I am afraid you are quite right, I have been dreaming, no doubt because of the sleeping powder. Of course you are quite right, Mrs Graham, it was all just a dream – unless of course I have been awake all the time, and I am not dreaming but going mad.'

'Now, now, Mrs Aubrey, we must not have such talk. A more sensible young woman I have seldom met, and that is the truth. No, no, dear, do not trouble yourself, because you are only young, and there is nothing here that we cannot put right, nothing less and nothing more than a little accident, although I do say to you, you might well have been sleepwalking on account of the powders, it is not uncommon, really it isn't.'

'I have never done such a thing before, but then I have never taken a sleeping powder before.'

'Best thing I always find to get rid of bad dreams,' Mrs Graham told her in a comfortingly practical voice as she steered her back towards her bed, 'best thing is to do what I do. You get into bed, shake your head, turn over six times, and when you go to sleep you sleep dream-free. Always works for me, I have to say.'

Emmaline smiled faintly at her housekeeper's well-intentioned suggestion.

'I don't know that I have the strength to turn over six times in my bed, or even three times,' she confessed.

Mrs Graham didn't answer her for a few seconds, watching Emmaline with concern in her eyes. Then she said, 'That's right, now you just climb into your bed, dear, and we'll soon have you back to rights.'

Emmaline slipped into bed, thinking that with her mind as disturbed as it was there was no chance she would get back to sleep again that night.

'Now come on, dear, turn over, that's it, and again, and again, and again! Well, four times will do. Now let me fix your nightstick, and then I'll be off. Not far from here if you want me, remember?'

Not long after Mrs Graham had tucked her in and blown out her light, and perhaps because of the housekeeper's insistence on her turning over in bed, Emmaline fell into a dreamless sleep.

So deep was Emmaline's sleep that when Agnes came to wake her mistress in the morning she lay so unmoving that for one awful moment the little maid found herself imagining that her mistress was dead.

As she watched Emmaline wake up, she was hardly more reassured, for even when awake she seemed to be unusually withdrawn and silent, as if she was actually in some sort of trance.

'You all right, Mrs Aubrey?'

'I am, Aggie, although I must tell you I had a somewhat disturbed night, thanks I think to the sleeping powder that Dr Proctor prescribed. I think I dreamed so powerfully that I was induced to sleepwalk, or some such; at any rate, hearing all the disturbance, Mrs Graham came to my rescue. Nothing like that has ever happened to me before.'

Agnes looked round. 'I thought there must have been a bit of to-do here,' she said, staring at the marks on the floor, and seeing a bucket in the corner of the room. 'What with the tray gone, and all.'

'I wonder if you could lay out my dark blue walking dress this morning, Aggie? I, er – I plan to go into town today.'

'Are you sure you are quite yourself, Mrs Aubrey? Do you imagine yourself to be well enough?'

'Of course. Once I have breakfasted I will be quite myself. These sleeping powders make a person feel a little dreamy, make me sound the same I dare say. That is all that is the matter with me, Aggie.'

Agnes laid out her bath things in front of the hip bath which was placed in front of the fire for her convenience, and afterwards helped her to dress, and they both tried to pretend that Emmaline was not doing everything at half pace, only seeming to become less dazed when her hair was put up. She stared in horror at her pallor in the dressing-table mirror, and promptly smacked both her cheeks hard, which made Agnes giggle.

'Best way to get colour in your cheeks, don't you think, Aggie?'

The maid nodded, and Emmaline went down to breakfast, leaving her to clear up. When the meal was over, Emmaline moved to her little sitting room and sent for Wilkinson.

'Ah, Wilkinson.' She looked up from her piece of sewing. 'I was wondering if anyone called late last night.'

Wilkinson frowned. 'No one called while I was around, Mrs Aubrey, most definitely not.'

'No one at all?' Emmaline echoed, wondering why she did not believe the butler. 'No one called, say, on business, someone for Mr Aubrey?'

'I closed the curtains and lowered the lamps at precisely the usual time of ten o'clock, madam,' he said, leaning forward and putting a log on the fire. 'I did my rounds of the house shortly after that to make sure everything was locked, and to the best of my knowledge the house was secure by the time I went to bed shortly before it showed eleven on the kitchen clock.'

'Very well, Wilkinson, thank you. I am sure you are telling the truth, it is just that I dreamed I heard someone downstairs, in Mr Aubrey's study, later in the evening. But as I say, it was probably only a dream.'

'As you say, madam. If I may take the liberty, you have been somewhat unwell, Mrs Aubrey, and sometimes a fever-induced sleep can bring about all sorts of hallucinations.'

'You are perfectly right, those are my thoughts too. Thank you, Wilkinson.'

Emmaline watched the butler letting himself out of her sitting room, and frowned. He had always seemed so kind, and so loyal, but was she mistaken in him? Was she mistaken in everyone at Park House? Were they all, newly in Julius's pay, sworn to keep some secret?

Later, making sure that there were no servants about, Emmaline let herself into Julius's study.

The desk was as tidy as it always was in Julius's absence, and everything seemed undisturbed, the window fastened shut, the curtains tidy.

'You see?' she said to herself, turning round and checking the room once more before leaving. 'You were dreaming. It is as simple as that.'

Her spirits were raised, however, by her visit to Mr Hunt's bookshop, which was crowded out with people buying books as presents for the forthcoming celebration of Christmas. Bray Ashcombe made himself immediately available to escort Emmaline through the packed premises into a small but comfortable office at the back where she was introduced to Mr Tully, the man proposing to be her publisher, a thin-faced, bespectacled and completely bald man with a pronounced tic that made him tip his head to one side every five seconds, giving the impression of a cheerful wink.

He stood up from his desk when Emmaline entered and was introduced, at once expressing in an oddly high monotone his admiration for the poetry he had read and read again, and was hopeful of publishing in splendid style.

'I have already envisaged a cover for the booklet,' he added, dropping his two thumbs into the pockets of his waistcoat and waggling the rest of his fingers rhythmically as he continued. 'Being verses of a contemplative and melancholic nature I see the binding having a distinct purple tint, lettered in a Gothic style – the poems perhaps entitled *O Love! My Heart! – Poems by a Lady.* I have also imagined some decorations that might be suitable to be printed above and below each verse – nothing ornate, just simple linear streamers along these lines.'

Receiving a nod – along with a wink – from the publisher, Bray showed Emmaline a page with printed embellishments, at which Emmaline expressed polite but muted enthusiasm, wondering if it would not be better to discuss the actual agreement before deciding how the book of poems might look. To judge from the smile of delight Bray gave Emmaline it was obvious he was in complete agreement with her, and he picked up another set of documents. He was about to show them to Emmaline when she stopped him.

'If you wouldn't mind, Mr Tully,' she said. 'I need to have a word in private with Mr Ashcombe. It does concern these negotiations, so I assure you I will not be wasting your time.'

Mr Tully retired to browse in the bookshop, leaving Emmaline alone with Bray, who brushed some long locks of hair out of his eyes and smiled at her as if he had never seen her before.

'I think I know what you need to tell me, Mrs Aubrey,' he said. 'And mind now, I only say this to spare you any undue embarrassment or awkwardness, although there is no need for either.'

'Really, Mr Ashcombe?' Emmaline replied with a slight rise of her eyebrows. 'And what do I need to tell you?'

'I think you need to tell me the authorship of the poems, Mrs Aubrey. If this were not the case,

329

I'm sure you would have felt free to talk in front of Mr Tully.'

'I do not think that is necessarily the case, Mr Ashcombe.'

'Very well, Mrs Aubrey – then please prove me wrong.'

He looked at her directly, and in the kindness and compassion of his look Emmaline saw that he had always guessed the true authorship of the poems, and she immediately felt awkward. For if he had always known who was the true author, then he would always have known of her distress and unhappiness, which she supposed might mean that he pitied her in some way.

'Please, Mrs Aubrey,' Bray prompted her. 'Put me out of my suspense.'

'Very well, Mr Ashcombe,' Emmaline conceded, unable to resist the gentle plea in Bray's voice or the look of sympathy in his eyes. 'I am the author of the poems, if that is what you are thinking.'

'I so hoped you were!'

Before she could stop him he had taken her hands, which he held tightly while staring at her with passionate earnestness.

'Mr Ashcombe—' she began to protest, although she left her hands in his.

'I really did so hope you were the author,' Bray was continuing. 'I don't think I could have stood it had the author really been a friend of yours, someone I would never meet, someone with whom I would never be able to commune – another soul who understood the anguish and agony of life but would turn out to be a distant stranger.'

'Mr Ashcombe,' Emmaline said, as gently as she could while finally easing her hands away, 'Mr Ashcombe, I am very flattered by your zeal, and by your enthusiasm for my work. But I would remind you—'

'You do not have to remind me, Mrs Aubrey. I only have to say your name, remember your name, to be reminded of your state. But while you may be married—'

'While I *may* be, Mr Ashcombe? Married I *am*, Mr Ashcombe.'

'Please, Mrs Aubrey, please,' Bray pleaded. 'Not now. This is not the time to discuss such matters, believe me.'

'I am not really sure what that time may be, Mr Ashcombe.'

'We have to deal with your agreement with Mr Tully,' Bray continued, ignoring the caveat. 'And I shall have to explain to Mr Tully about the authorship, you do realise that?'

'Of course. But it must remain confidential. And I want it to be agreed that the author remains anonymous.'

'I understand, naturally,' Bray agreed. 'I too shall keep it entirely secret.'

'I shall require you to sign such a guarantee as well, Mr Ashcombe.'

'Naturally. Now I think we must call Mr Tully back in.'

The publisher having duly been summoned,

the three of them sat down to finalise the agreement contracting to publish the poetic works of a Lady, entitled not *O Love! My Heart!* as suggested by the publisher, but simply *Reflections of a Faithful Heart.*

Every morning and every afternoon, to make sure she was not mistaken and that what she vaguely remembered from that night really had been imagined in her sleep and had not happened in actuality, Emmaline requested Wilkinson to telephone Mr Aubrey's offices to find out the latest news of his return, but nothing more was heard until Friday when a telegram arrived to say that everyone was to expect him back in the works on Monday morning since he was due to cross the Channel on Saturday midday. True to his word a tired and travel-weary Julius arrived back at Park House early in the evening, in time for a much needed bath and then an equally necessary dinner.

Thinking the best time for a proper conversation would be at table and not while Julius was getting washed and changing into evening dress, Emmaline waited, dutifully, until they were settled at table.

'How was your trip, Julius?' she asked.

'As trips to France invariably are,' Julius said, carefully spooning some soup up and away from him. 'Very French.'

'Have you spent much time in France, then?' Emmaline wondered, ignoring his facetious reply.

'I have spent some time in France, yes. How is your health, Emma? I am sorry to see that you still look a little wan.'

Emmaline stared down the table at him, knowing that he was putting up emotional barricades, but remembering Mrs Proctor's teatime visit, she persisted.

'I am a little better, since you ask.' She finished her soup, wiped her mouth carefully on her napkin and smiled down the table at her husband. 'You were in France all the time you were away, were you not, Julius?'

'What a strange question to come from one's wife, what a very odd question.' Julius looked up from his place with a frown, and stared past Emmaline. 'No, as a matter of fact, I went to the North Pole for dinner one evening and Australia for luncheon the next day. Other than that, yes. Yes, I was in France.'

'I was merely curious,' Emmaline replied, ringing the bell on the table for the servants to make the next remove. 'You never tell me any details of your travels. I am just trying to show my interest, that is all.'

'My travels are dull, sometimes tiresome, and that is why I don't discuss them with you. If there was anything interesting in them, I would share it.'

'You are often in France. Do you visit Paris while you are there, because if so I should so appreciate it if you brought me back some gloves, as I have asked you to before.'

'I hardly set foot in Paris, hardly at all. If I visit a city on business, it is Lyons, not Paris. That is where the best silks come from, not Paris, but certainly, if you wish me to bring you back some French gloves, I will do so.'

'And do you always go to this place called the Loire?'

Julius started playing with his napkin. 'I really do not enjoy being questioned in this manner, Emma. It is not seemly.'

But Emmaline, with Mrs Proctor's conversation still foremost in her mind, would not let the matter drop.

'Where did you go to school, Julius? Was it in England?'

'I am not sure why you need to know. It is not interesting, Emma.'

Emmaline stared at him. He was still folding and refolding his napkin. As she watched him she once more felt as if she was suffocating. Was this what her life was to be, endless meals with Julius playing with his napkin?

She thought of Bray, of his warmth and kindness. He spoke of poetry, not of wine or food, as Julius was now doing, asking about some choice of wine, asking yet again if the fish was fresh. The servants hurrying forward and backward, dishes being placed, endlessly and it seemed to her so often pointlessly, never finished, except downstairs in the kitchens where they were enjoyed a great deal more than they were above stairs, even by Cook's cat.

'Very well, Julius, if it is not interesting we will cease to talk about it.'

There was a long silence broken only by the sounds of knives and forks on plates, of servants moving across the carpet, of the long-case clock striking eight o'clock of a long, long evening. Emmaline thought of her poetry, of her notebook, of the excitement of the bookshop and all that had happened there, and she sighed inwardly, longing to be back there, away from the grandeur of Park House, with Bray and his eager looks, with Mr Tully and his plans, longing to see those words *by a Lady*.

'You're still looking very pale, Emma,' Julius said when he finally joined her in the drawing room after dinner. 'I think we should ask the good doctor to visit you again in the morning. You really have very little colour.'

'I have always been pale, Julius. I was pale as a child, and so I suppose I shall always be a pale person, wouldn't you say?' She put down her sewing. 'May we continue talking about your past, Julius, or would that still be irritating to you?'

'Did I say that?'

'You might as well have done, Julius.'

'Then there you have your answer.'

'So where did you grow up, Julius?'

'I think you already know,' he said finally, after an absurdly long silence.

'So let me see if I am right . . .'

'I was brought up in France,' he said. 'I was born in Sussex, where my father had his studio, and then – then my mother moved to France and took her children with her. She lived in the Loire valley not far from Vendôme, which is where I grew up.'

'And which is why you speak French?'

'Every educated Englishman speaks French.' Julius shrugged his shoulders and sighed, as if the whole subject of himself was so tedious that he could hardly bear to go on talking about it. 'Apparently my father insisted that we were not to be educated in France so I was sent to a school in Surrey, and then another in Dorset, and used to come home – used to *go* home to the Loire valley in my holidays.'

'And your father? He wasn't living in France, then? Or was he? Or did he—'

'No, Emma.' Julius sighed again. 'You know better than that.' He looked down the table at her and shook his head. 'How could my father be living in France when his business was here?'

'Not when you were a little boy, surely?'

Julius looked up, and from his expression and tone of voice Emmaline knew she had touched a raw nerve.

'My mother left my father. She walked out on him, taking her family with her, back to France. My father was a very unfaithful man, a philanderer. He was always unfaithful – with his models – when he was painting. Then when he started up his business he was unfaithful all over the place, with his clients' wives, with their daughters, with their mistresses.' Julius suddenly looked straight at Emmaline. 'My father was a rascal,' he said. 'And yet because he had charm, everybody loved him.'

'And you, Julius? Did you love him?'

'I tried my best not to. It was difficult when I saw how lonely my mother was. I suppose as a small boy I hated him a great deal of the time, his profligate ways, his selfishness. I particularly hated him when he said I wasn't to be a painter. That I was to go into the business with him and take over after him – but I didn't. Not for a long time. When I finally left school I stayed in France and painted. It was only after he died that I found he had left me the business – all of it – and money was a bit short. I needed money quite badly to make sure my mother was properly cared for. I wanted to ensure she had the very best doctors and care that could be afforded, which is what she has had.'

'And I suppose the journey to America, to visit us in Massachusetts—'

'The journey? Oh yes, it was business. First and foremost. Apparently we are beginning to do very well over there. In America. The business.'

'Have you not thought of bringing your mother to England?'

'My mother is French, Emma. She was born in the Loire. She doesn't like England. She certainly didn't want to die here.' For a moment he was silent. 'I think that's understandable.'

'So that is what has happened?' Emmaline ventured, seeing the look in his eyes.

There was a silence, and then Julius stood up.

'You really do look pale, Emma. I think I will tell Mrs Graham to ring Dr Proctor in the morning – no, as a matter of fact, I will go to the telephone room and ring him myself. I don't like to see you looking as you are just now.'

Emmaline stared up at him, and even as he finished speaking it seemed to her that she was growing weaker, and paler, and that in some way that was what he wanted.

After a while Julius went to the telephone room to make the call to Dr Proctor. As he was waiting to be connected he went through the notes left by the telephone about incoming calls received in his absence, noting particularly the one from an unknown gentleman staying at the Grand Hotel, Cheltenham, one Mr Dwight Freeman.

Having booked a visit from the doctor for the following morning, Julius telephoned the Grand Hotel in response to the stranger's request.

'Yes, sir,' the receptionist at the other end of the line said in answer to Julius's opening enquiry. 'Mr Freeman was staying here but he left late this morning – no, sir, he left no forwarding address – and as you possibly know, sir, it is not the policy of this hotel to disclose any personal details about our guests, including any home address.'

'Thank you,' Julius replied, thinking it odd that someone who was visiting on business and apparently calling him for the same reason should up sticks and depart without leaving details of where he might be contacted, although on reflection, as he closed the door of the telephone room behind him, Julius supposed that if indeed this Mr Freeman was serious about contacting him then contact him he would from his next place of residence.

Having examined his patient thoroughly once more, carefully checking the texture and colour of her fingernails, her tongue, and her gums, and the strength of the pulses in her neck, wrist and ankles, and having listened closely with his stethoscope, Dr Proctor then produced a machine that Emmaline had never set eyes on before.

'Goodness me, doctor,' she said, looking at the large clock-like dial attached to a length of rubber tubing to which in its turn was affixed some sort of rubber bulb. 'And what in heaven's name might this be?'

'This, dear lady, is an instrument very grandly called a sphygmomanometer, this particular type having been thought up by some chap called Samuel von Basch, and it is for measuring the pressure of the blood in the patient's body,' Dr Proctor explained as he prepared to use it on Emmaline. 'Recent findings have indicated that there is a regular and correct pressure for the blood in our bodies, and if this becomes excessive it can lead to progressive illnesses, such as damage to the spleen and to the brain and also to the heart itself, while if it falls too low the patient can be prone to severe lassitude and indeed regular fainting fits – and now you probably understand my reason for trying to get a reading of your own pressures, Mrs Aubrey.'

In order to take the reading, Dr Proctor pressed the bulb on to the radial artery in her arm, explaining that he intended to hold it there until the pulse disappeared. A moment or so later he consulted the large round dial on the machine which he was holding in his other hand and nodded sagely.

'As I suspected, my dear lady,' he concluded, taking the bulb off Emmaline's arm and putting the machine away. 'Your pressures are a great deal lower than I would like to see, and this would go a long way to explaining your constant faintness, and indeed your pallor. So.' Dr Proctor stood up from his bedside chair to roll his sleeves back down, put his jacket back on and pack up his Gladstone bag. 'So I think all in all, given that your general health seems otherwise unimpaired – your chest is absolutely fine, your heartbeat as regular as the workings of a clock.' He waved his stethoscope at her before packing it away in his bag.

'In the old days, of course, one had to do it by ear, don't you know,' he said. 'And it was as uncomfortable for the doctor as it was for the patient, disgust in itself making it impracticable in hospitals. It was hardly suitable where most women were concerned, and with some – well, without going into details I'm sure you can well imagine the difficulties. So thank goodness for Samuel von Basch's great invention. Good. Good,' he repeated. 'So now I shall go and find your husband to have a word with him as to my recommendations – which mostly will be to make sure you get complete rest and some fresh sea air. And plenty of iron, young lady – I want you to eat lots of liver and take the iron tonic I have prescribed. If you follow my directions we shall have you as right as rain in no time at all. Good day to you.'

Finding Julius waiting for him in the drawing room, over a glass of excellent sherry wine the doctor informed him of the diagnosis he had reached at the end of his most extensive examination of the patient.

'She is not of a very strong constitution, Mr Aubrey, alas,' he said. 'But please do not let this alarm you. There is nothing physically awry – no specific illness or disease that I can identify – other than a weakened pressure of the blood system, which as I have explained to you both can cause these various unpleasant and unsettling symptoms. However, if we feed the patient up with victuals that have a high concentration of iron and make sure as best as we can that she suffers from no undue tensions and concerns, because I do feel very much that patients who are subjected to unnecessary or excessive worry do themselves no good at all, no good whatsoever, I am sure we shall prevail. So peace and quiet and as much of it as possible, but above all a good dose of ozone, please! A good long dose of ozone, which in cases such as your wife's we know to work miracles. So off to the seaside with her as soon as possible.'

'Not now, surely, Dr Proctor?' Julius replied. 'In the middle of December?'

'Sea air is good any time of year, my dear fellow!' The doctor laughed. 'And often in the winter, when it is particularly bracing, we in the medical profession find the ozone to be even more efficacious. Have you not found yourself that standing on the sea shore with a winter wind blowing a storm around you makes you almost intoxicated with the goodness of the air? I most certainly do, which is why I recommend any of my patients who are in need of a good physical boost to their systems to get themselves to the seaside with as little delay as possible.'

'I see.' Julius nodded, placing his empty sherry glass on the chimneypiece. 'As it happens the Aubreys do have a place in Cornwall.'

'Excellent,' the good doctor opined. 'Could not be better. The Cornish climate, while kinder and softer than ours, is still an immensely healthy one, so if you have a place there, so much the better. Mrs Aubrey could rest there as long as it takes her to recover.'

Julius eyed the doctor and nodded before going to the door. 'I shall see what can be arranged, doctor,' he said. 'Thank you for coming out so promptly.'

'As you know, the health of all my patients is paramount, Mr Aubrey.' Dr Proctor picked up his hat. He walked to the door, his expression commanding, his tone serious. 'So please do be advised by me. This is not a condition that is going to clear up by itself, and let us hope there are no future complications. Good day to you.'

He left Julius frowning after him.

So it was decided that Emmaline should be sent to Cornwall to benefit from the ozone, in the hope that in due course a seaside convalescence would help to restore her health and strength.

'Are you to come too, Julius?' she asked her husband when the decision had been made. 'Or am I to be sent there by myself? I would find that a little difficult seeing I do not even know where Cornwall is, I am ashamed to say.'

Julius smiled at her, produced a large atlas from the bookcase and showed her the lie of the land.

'It's less of a county and more of a small kingdom really,' he told her. 'A duchy, as it happens. Owned by the Prince of Wales, when he has a mind to remember it. Or the time – the time away from the racecourse or the card table – or the boudoir.'

'I know nothing of your prince, really,' Emmaline confessed, 'other than what I read in your newspaper.'

'I would not consider that a hole in your education,' Julius said, lightly. 'Now – see here.' He pointed to a spot on the map of Cornwall.

'My father built a house here. Nothing grand, you understand, just a place where he could go on holiday from his work, and paint if he had a mind to do so. This is an area called the Roseland Peninsula and it contains very fine stretches of coastline, very fine indeed. I used to go there sometimes as a boy for a few weeks in the summer.' His face softened. 'Good beaches, amazing cliffs, wonderful walks – the perfect place for a good dose of ozone. The house is about here – with a wonderful view of Veryan Bay and out to Dodman Point. Even in winter you'll like it.'

'Will you be coming down as well, Julius? Or am I expected to take the sea air alone?'

'I shall come down as soon as it is possible, Emma. I shall certainly be there for some part of Christmas. When work permits – we have just had a couple of very sizeable orders that must be filled first – but when work permits I shall get down there, rest assured. A Mrs Carew keeps house. Cooks as well. Utterly reliable woman and a very pleasant one as well. You can take that maid of yours, and there are housemaids who come in daily.'

'Agnes might not want to come. I have not asked her,' Emmaline reminded him with a look.

'Oh, Agnes will come, I promise you. She will not be parted from you. She is your little pug dog, is she not? And Mrs Carew will organise any other help that's necessary. It's a bit of a walk to the village, but since you're going there for the air and the exercise that will all be to the good. And please – please do not look so disconsolate. Dr Proctor would not have advocated this convalescence unless he thought it absolutely necessary.'

Confined to the house until all arrangements had been made for her journey to Cornwall and her stay at Gorran Lodge, Emmaline began to fret about what was happening to her book of poetry and what the exact plans for it might now be. Unfortunately, it was not possible for her to invite Bray Ashcombe to the house without giving rise to unnecessary speculation . . .

'Of course!' she exclaimed out loud, halfway through the reading lesson she was giving Agnes, and causing her maid to jump.

'Course what, madam?' Agnes wondered. 'I ain't said nothing.'

'No, no, Aggie, don't give it a thought,' Emmaline said with a smile. 'I have just remembered something I must do, that is all – and I want you to help me. I want you to take a note into town.'

'To Mr Hunt's bookshop again, is it, madam?' Agnes enquired with a small rise of her eyebrows.

'I think it better if you carry in a note, rather than my using the telephone, because I am not altogether sure that at this very busy time of year messages will get passed on with the greatest of speed.' Emmaline finished writing her short note, placed it in an envelope, sealed it and gave it to

Agnes. 'You will need to take it in when we have finished this lesson, if you will.'

She had suggested to Bray that he should call between the hours of 2.30 p.m. and 4.00 p.m., making it as clear as she could without giving the message any added sense of drama that she was expecting him in company. She suggested that if his sister was well enough now then she would be pleased to see her at Park House. When he received the note Bray understood perfectly well that he could not and would not be received as a solo visitor, but since he could not do exactly as suggested for a very particular domestic reason, he invited a friend of his, a Miss Lamb, to accompany him as if she were his secretary. He was of course delighted to be asked up to Park House, not only because he had some page proofs of Emmaline's poems that Mr Tully had given him the day before hot off the presses next door to show her, but because he would be seeing the young woman who had already begun to haunt his dreams, and whose handkerchief he still kept hidden in his desk at the shop.

Arriving on the stroke of half past two in the afternoon, Bray introduced Miss Lamb to Emmaline by way of a message on the card he handed to Wilkinson, and waited to see if they would be allowed admittance.

After what seemed to Bray to be an uncomfortably long wait, a hiatus that was in fact no more than a matter of a minute or two, Wilkinson returned to say that Mrs Aubrey would be happy to receive them in the drawing room.

'Forgive me,' Emmaline said, after shaking hands with her visitors. 'I was expecting to see your sister again.'

'And most kind of you too, Mrs Aubrey,' Bray replied, 'to have invited us both up to see you. But sadly Arabella, my sister, is still not fully recovered, and has retired to the country, where I shall shortly be joining her. Miss Lamb here is to take my place, temporarily, in the bookshop.'

He gave Miss Lamb an affectionate glance, which she returned in full.

'Miss Lamb is a particularly assiduous reader of poetry. You might say she is a muse to every passing poet.'

'A muse, truly?' Emmaline gave Miss Lamb a considering look. She had quiet good looks, and such a shy manner that it occurred to Emmaline that there must be more to her than was perhaps revealed at first acquaintance.

'She inspires so many of us . . .'

'Well, that is charming, I am sure, but, Mr Ashcombe, what a coincidence that you should be leaving Bamford.' Emmaline laughed lightly, indicating to her visitors that they might be seated. 'I have also been ordered to leave Bamford for reasons of health, and to take the sea air.'

'I had no idea you were not well, Mrs Aubrey,' Bray said with concern. 'I trust it is something from which you will soon be recovered?'

'A passing affliction, Mr Ashcombe,' Emmaline

replied. 'One I am assured will be cured by rest and sea air.'

'Before you go away, Mrs Aubrey,' Bray said, 'I wonder whether you would have time to look at these and let me know what you think of them. I'm sure they are the sort of thing that will appeal to you.'

He handed her a sealed envelope which contained the page pulls of her verses, an enclosure about which, Emmaline devoutly hoped, his muse, Miss Lamb, did not know anything.

'Thank you, Mr Ashcombe,' she said, putting the envelope safely beside her. 'I shall look forward to reading these – they are short stories?'

'Indeed, Mrs Aubrey. You will find them most entertaining. And you have not yet told me whether you will be going away for very long?'

'I am to go to Cornwall, Mr Ashcombe, to a house belonging to my husband's family. It is called Gorran Lodge, somewhere on a place called the Roseland Peninsula,' Emmaline replied, and immediately wondered why her visitor had changed colour. 'Now, what is wrong? You look as though you have seen a ghost. Is this the effect Cornwall has on people? If so I think I shall change my mind, and stay at home.'

'Forgive me, Mrs Aubrey,' Bray said hurriedly, recovering his composure. 'It – it is just that that is exactly where my – my sister has gone to recuperate. And I have every intention of going down to Cornwall to visit her at Christmas.'

'That really is a coincidence, Mr Ashcombe,'

Emmaline replied, herself considerably heartened by the knowledge that there would be at least one good acquaintance of hers staying not very far from her in the unknown county of Cornwall. 'Who knows?' she added. 'Perhaps we may even meet during the holiday. Now, if you will excuse me, Mr Ashcombe, I am in the middle of preparing to leave.'

Emmaline rose to show the meeting was at an end, at which both Bray and his companion did the same.

'Just one other thing, Mrs Aubrey, before I take my departure,' Bray said. 'These – these stories I have brought for you to read. I hope you do not mind them in proof form – but if you would rather wait, the first copies of the published book should be in the shops in a matter of days.'

'I see,' Emmaline replied, getting the message. 'Of course I would eventually like to see the stories in their final form, so perhaps when you come to Cornwall you might bring a copy then – and somehow I am sure we can contrive to make sure I see it.'

She smiled, and Bray smiled back, taking her words as an invitation to go and visit her on the Roseland Peninsula – which indeed, in view of the time she was probably going to be spending there, was precisely how Emmaline had hoped Mr Ashcombe would take them.

Chapter Ten

It was a long and a tiring journey, first by coach from Bamford to Bath and from there by Great Western locomotive to the busy stannary town of Truro, a town which had grown so prosperous from tin and copper mining that in 1877 it had been accorded city status, even though the cathedral was only very recently completed. The journey by rail from Bath to Truro took over six hours, since the train stopped at every station along the line, so to help pass the time Emmaline gave Agnes the reading lesson of her life, before reading out loud to her from the book on Cornwall that Bray Ashcombe had sent up to Park House for Emmaline just before they left.

'It seems it was Truro's position close to the convergence of the Truro and Fal rivers that made it so important both as a river port and a tin-mining centre, Aggie. That and the fact that it was one of the stannary towns, which I gather means tin had to be brought to the city for official testing and stamping until the last century. Anyway, by all accounts it has been a very prosperous and indeed fashionable town, so we are not going to be stuck away in a totally uncivilised neck of the woods, thanks be.'

'I never been so far from home, madam,' Agnes said, looking wistfully out of the window as the train slowly passed through a vast cutting made of long unbroken banks of sand and clay. 'It's like I imagine a foreign country might be, is this, it really is.'

'It will possibly seem even more foreign once we get into the countryside itself. From what I have seen from our carriage, it is somewhat under-populated. It seems so strange to me to see so few people on stations, or in villages and towns, as you can imagine.'

However, Truro itself was busy enough, they noted, as they alighted from the train and searched the long line of carriages waiting outside the station for one bearing the Aubrey crest on its doors.

Sure enough, near the head of the queue, Agnes soon identified a hansom drawn by a single tired-looking and aged grey gelding which had turned shock white with age, the animal dozing in its shafts with its nosebag still in place while an equally tired-looking coachman sat also half asleep on his box, most of him buried beneath a thick green wool rug.

Once woken by Agnes and reminded of his task, the driver took his passengers on the last fifteen-mile leg of what turned out finally to be an eleven-hour journey, decanting the two by now

351

utterly exhausted young women at the front door of a house set at the end of a long tree-lined drive at the top of a winding lane that led nowhere else. There was an oil lamp stuck on a pole outside the door, blazing a welcome in the darkness of a moonless night, while Emmaline could hear the pounding of waves on sand far below them, and smell salt on the stiff sea breeze.

The door was opened to them at last by a large red-cheeked woman with a shock of hair as white as the coat on the carriage horse and a smile as broad as a half-moon.

'Well, you poor dears!' she exclaimed. 'You must as be a-cryin' out aloud for some'at to eat and some'at warm to drink, my poor dears, after your journey – so come you in, come you in and be welcome at Gorran Lodge. We got a fine supper waitin' on you,' she continued as she bustled them into a hallway lit by a roaring log fire, the coachman following behind with the luggage. 'And we got stones in your beds and fresh linen to sleep in so don't you worry about one more thing now, you hear me? After a journey like that, what you'll want is some'at good and warm inside of you and somewhere good and warm to rest your heads.'

In a dark-panelled dining room warmed by yet another roaring fire, blazing with bone-dry whitened logs that had drifted up on sandy beaches, and lit by a dozen thick-waxed candles that stuttered and fluttered and danced in the draughts that sneaked round heavy dark red velvet curtains, Emmaline and Agnes sat and ate a supper of thick pea soup and home-made bread, fresh chicken roasted in butter and herbs with big floury potatoes and large succulent carrots, and the most delicious home-cooked apple pie dotted with thick Cornish cream of which two weary travellers could have dreamed. Across Emmaline's button-booted feet a large rangy lurcher with a salt-and-pepper coat slept, his tail occasionally flicking and his whiskers twitching as he dreamed, while on Agnes's knee, out of sight and much to Agnes's delight, sat a large and deeply contented cat, entirely black except for the very end of its tail, which was as white as if it had just been dipped in a paint pot. Mrs Carew, their welcoming cook and hostess, hovered between the table and her many ovens.

When they had finally finished their dinner, Emmaline felt as if she must be already a little better, for not only did she feel restored physically, but ever since she had crossed the threshold of Gorran Lodge she had felt better in both her head and her heart, as if a weapon that had been stuck in her side and constantly twisted had been inexplicably removed and the wound miraculously healed.

'Have you always lived in Cornwall, Mrs Carew?' Emmaline asked as Agnes helped the good lady to clear.

'Always have, never been anywhere else and never want to, my dear, not ever. When you have the good luck to be born in Cornwall, that is where you stay, my dear, and that is God's own truth.'

Emmaline stared around at the brass pots hanging on the walls, at the large cream jugs in different sizes ranged across the wooden surfaces, together with the vast cream-coloured baking bowls. From the ceiling hung herbs in bunches, swaying slightly when the draught from the fire made itself felt, or when a larder door was opened as Mrs Carew went to fetch some fresh butter, or some newly prepared dish that had to be put back into one of several ovens.

Here was a room where fishermen, their wet things removed, could sit and talk of months away at sea, months when they must have dreamed of just such a winter evening when it seemed that neither wind, nor rain, nor storms, could come between them and the joys of home.

'My husband, God rest his soul, was taken at sea, some ten years ago, and so it was that I came to work for Mr Aubrey senior here. It is a sad fact that I would rather have worked for a family that had made Cornwall their home, but beggars can't be choosers, and certain it is that widows can't be either. Now, my dears, would you help yourself to more of my apple pie? There's cream there, and plenty of it too.'

Emmaline smiled up at Mrs Carew, and in that moment it seemed to her that the housekeeper was an angel dropped from heaven. The last thing she wanted was another helping of apple pie, but seeing the hope in Mrs Carew's face she could not disappoint her, even if it meant leaving off her stays the following morning.

By the time Agnes had helped her undress, both of them concealing yawns, and neither of them able to keep their eyes open, Emmaline knew she was about to fall into probably the deepest sleep she had ever known. It did not seem possible that her life could be transformed in such a short time, in a matter of less than a day, that in that moment of night-time arrival it had seemed to her that all her troubles were not simply forgotten, but quite disappeared.

She brushed her hair one last time, and then, mindful of nothing but the peace of the house she now found herself in, the sound of the sea almost inaudible in the distance of the night now the tide was running out, and the gentle zephyr that carried on its breath the salty tang of the ocean, she slid down beneath the warm, fresh linen sheets, even as Agnes blew out the candle beside her sweetly smelling bed.

For a minute or two, as Emmaline lay in the darkness, she thought she had left behind all the anxieties of Park House, the concerns of the town, the disquiet of her mind. Then she suddenly sat up, remembering.

She had left her precious notebook behind. She leaned forward to light the candle beside her bed, and watched the dancing lights from the small bedroom fire making patterns on the ceiling. Why did it matter that she had left the notebook behind? The poems were copied. It mattered not a whit. Julius would be going away soon, he would not bother to look about the bedroom. Besides, Mrs Graham would have tidied the room, and she knew that it belonged in Emmaline's desk. She would lock it in there, as always, and place the key in the spills vase by the chimneypiece. Emmaline blew out the candle once more, and settled herself to sleep, comforted by the memory of Mrs Graham's meticulous habits, convinced that that was what she would do.

But Mrs Graham had done no such thing. Indeed, since it was the end of the year, Emmaline was hardly gone before the housekeeper began to help Cook to prepare for the many complications that Christmas always brought, not to mention finishing all her own small hand-made gifts in time to post them off to all her nephews and nieces.

In fact, as always with the departure of the mistress of the house, Emmaline's absence gave the servants time to catch up on all those other tasks which they had not been able to accomplish in the aftermath of her illness, when their time had been taken up with the comings and goings of bringing and fetching trays, answering doctor's calls, and other small duties that nevertheless accumulated in such a way as to leave other matters outstanding.

As for Emmaline, it was understandable that in all the confusions and tribulations, and the turmoil and disorder of the days preceding her departure, she had not noticed that she had dropped the notebook, that no one had picked it up. It was all very understandable, just as it was understandable that in the chaos of packing, of things put in and things put out, of suitcases opened and suitcases shut, no cleaning or dusting had taken place. Mrs Graham judged that the dust and the dirt coming from suitcases stored in attics should be given time to settle, just as the servants needed time to settle once the carriage had finally driven off with the invalid and her maid.

Besides, in her mind's eye Emmaline had put away her notebook for the moment, as a pupil once term is over will put away her school books. Writing the poems had been a way of getting her through what had seemed to be the endless maze of her misery. Now that she seemed to have found her way out of that maze to a new country, in a new house, away from Julius and all the torment that lay between them, she never gave it another thought.

Emmaline's departure from Park House brought a feeling of relief not just to her, but also to Julius, for it seemed to him that her illness had changed her character. It made him feel guilty to see her so pale and listless, to see how the servants looked at him with accusing eyes as if they blamed him for everything that had happened to her, for her unhappiness, as if they knew that the only happiness that had come into her married life had been brought by them. So with Emmaline no longer present, he fully expected a lifting of his spirits, a diminution of the guilt that washed over him in the presence of the object of his dishonourable behaviour.

After a solitary dinner that night he retired to his study, where Wilkinson, unprompted, brought him a large brandy and a cigar.

'Ah, thank you, Wilkinson. Put them down there, would you?'

Wilkinson did as indicated, placing the glass and the ashtray at Julius's elbow, and cutting the end of the cigar before holding a match for his master.

'Is there anything more, sir?'

Julius looked up at him briefly. 'I don't think so, Wilkinson.' He stared into the fire, sipping his brandy, and wondering that he could see nothing of interest in the shapes and sparks of the fire. When he was a little boy he had been able to see the universe.

There was a small silence.

'So I take it that will be all, sir.'

'Yes, yes, of course, Wilkinson, unless you can think of something?'

'No, sir.'

Wilkinson made a small bow, and went to the door. As he reached it, Julius turned.

'I don't suppose they have the telephone in Cornwall yet, do they, Wilkinson?'

'No, I believe they do not, sir. I am sure it will come in time, but Cornwall is rather far away, sir.'

'Yes, it is indeed, another country,' Julius agreed, wondering why he did not feel the expected relief that Emmaline and Agnes were there, far away, instead of upstairs doing whatever it was that women did when they were in their bedrooms with their maids all the livelong day. 'So we should not expect to hear from Mrs Aubrey, except by post.'

'No, sir.' Wilkinson cleared his throat. He was only too glad for the poor young woman's sake that she was away from Park House at last. 'Will that be all, sir?'

'Yes, Wilkinson, thank you. Thank you, Wilkinson. Dinner was excellent tonight, please tell Mrs Field.'

'Thank you, sir. Cook will be gratified.'

Wilkinson closed the door. Cook would not only be gratified, she would be astonished. It was the first time for all too long, she had announced to no one in particular, that all the removes at dinner had not come back down again virtually untouched. Of course it was not true, but it was certainly true that Mrs Aubrey had only a light appetite, and what with Mr Aubrey being away, or in a bad mood, there was no doubt that the food had not been appreciated the way it should.

In his study Julius sighed, finished his drink, and threw his half-smoked cigar into the fire. It did not taste as it usually did, and it was not bringing him any kind of relief or relaxation. He poured himself another brandy, and started to drink it too fast, realising from the way the windows were rattling that the weather had turned. He put down his drink and, feeling claustrophobic and in need of fresh air, he went to the front door. Pushing it open, he stepped outside to see for himself how strongly the winter wind was blowing, and how the rain that had begun to fall had now turned to driven sleet, before shutting himself back in the house and wandering upstairs, where he eventually found himself standing outside Emmaline's bedroom, staring at the door as if he expected her to be on the other side, or that she would suddenly open it to find him there smelling of brandy and cigars, his hair awry from being outside.

Afraid that for some unknown reason there might be a servant inside, he knocked on the door before he opened it. So strong was her presence about this part of the house, about the room where she slept, he half expected her to be sitting up in bed, her lustrous brown hair brushed out, outlining her always pale, sad and beautiful face, her hands folded in front of her on her sheets, her eyes holding his as he stood at the door – but the bed was empty, although untidy from the packing and the chaos of departure, a shawl still hanging casually from the bedpost, a hat box on the floor beside it, obviously abandoned at the last minute.

Candlestick in hand, Julius looked round. It was a gloomy room at the best of times, made gloomier by his father's refusal to bring either gas or electricity to the upstairs rooms, but somehow her character had coloured and inhabited it, her things set about it as if in defiance of the heavy furniture, the dark red curtains, the endless coverings of chimneypieces and tables that his father and his generation so favoured. Julius wanted to rip everything in the room out and start all over again, make it as she would have surely chosen, light and elegant, with delicate feminine touches.

He sat down on the bed and draped the shawl around his hands, staring down at it. It was filled with her scent, one she used sparingly but which he now realised had a hint of sophistication in it, as if in Emmaline's choice of fragrance there was another hidden part of her character that he had never noted, or wanted to note.

He pulled off his shoes and lay back against the pillows on the bed, closing his eyes, the shawl close to his face, and before long it seemed to him he was drifting on a sensual barge, a place where life in its proper sense could not reach him, where there were no anxieties, only relief.

He must have slept for quite some time, because he awoke with a start, feeling ice-cold. He sat upright, startled. Too much brandy! He swung his feet to the floor and started to scrabble about for his shoes, and as he did so his hand caught at something half hidden under the bed. He stopped, and bent down. It was a notebook. He picked it up from the floor and placed it on the bed, and having slipped his shoes on he stood up and prepared to leave the room, notebook, shawl, and hat box left as they were.

But something drew him back to the notebook, as if he knew that, unlike the rest of the contents of the room, the notebook was something that would normally be forbidden to him.

He opened the book and saw Emmaline's handwriting. He stared at the writing, admiring its generous elegant form, looking only at the words and their formation, so that it was some time before he realised he was reading poetry, but what he read was like a blow to his chest, so full of pain and longing were the verses. He sat down on the bed again, and read on, and when he had finished he closed the book, put it on the bed, and covered his face with his hands.

When Emmaline awoke the following morning to nothing but the sound of the sea and the mewling of the gulls she wondered for a moment where she was. Soon she rose from her bed, put on her gown and crossed to the window in her bedroom. Pulling the curtains back she saw a sight that made her catch her breath. It was a perfectly cloudless day with the sun well risen and shining on a flat calm sea, a stretch of water no more than a couple of hundred yards away, down the slope of the fields in front of the house and across a stretch of golden sand. So calm and fine was the day it seemed to Emmaline it could have been spring rather than late December; and although the sun was winter pale it still had strength enough to make the water of the Atlantic Ocean glint and shimmer as low-crested waves lapped the beach.

Emmaline stood entranced, imagining she could spend the rest of her days in such a beautiful place, a house set in meadows back from the shore, in a bay of tranquil beauty and form, with high forelands at either end affording protection from the worst the wind could do, enfolding this particular stretch of beach as if to make it a private heaven.

Nor was there a soul in sight, the only sign of life being a fishing boat making its slow progress out to deeper waters as it set off on its day's work.

Mrs Carew greeted Emmaline at the foot of the stairs as she descended. 'I done the liberty of setting your breakfast in that room to the side of the main kitchen which has a fine view of the strand, so I's a thought it fine for you if you took your meal there, madam. Sun shines direct in as well, being a southern aspect, and lord let's say it, 'tis like a spring day now, is it not?'

The ample Mrs Carew led the way along the polished wood-floored corridor through a large wooden door fitted with shining brass furniture into the kitchen area where off to the right, just as described, was set a breakfast room, with a large oak table big enough to seat eight people placed under a large window with a direct prospect of the sea. The kitchen itself was immaculate, with a polished iron range with gleaming brass fixtures, rows of shining copper pans on shelves and lines of plain white china jars with their contents labelled in blue lettering. The floor was flagstones and all the working tops had been made from slate, with two large ceramic sinks set immediately under another large picture window also affording a sea view to whoever was washing up or preparing food at that station. Emmaline was deeply impressed by the beauty and order of the kitchen, something for which she had longed at Park House, but at Park House she was rarely allowed downstairs, that being Mrs Graham and Mrs Field's preserve.

"Twas all the late Mr Aubrey's doing, madam,' Mrs Carew said. 'Afore my time, course, since I only been here the ten years now. Mr Aubrey made the whole place, d'you see – from basement to rooftop. Drew it all out of his head, thought up every fitting and every gadget you see here. He loved coming here, so he did, him and Mrs Watson. She was a lovely soul and beautiful too. Summertime they'd sit out there on the terrace, Mr Aubrey with his paints or his sketching book, and Mrs Watson in some booful gown made of what look like goss'mer – and this big straw hat she'd sometime have to hold one-handed on her head in the wind, see. There's a big painting of that in the drawing room, madam. You can see it after you've had a good breakfast, and a good breakfast is what I'm to make for you, 'cos I unnerstand you need to build up your stren'th.'

'Where's Agnes, Mrs Carew?' Emmaline asked

as she settled down at the table in the sunshine. 'Do you know where my maid is?'

'Your girl's out a-walkin', madam,' Mrs Carew replied, nodding her head seawards. 'She's had her breakfast and said she just had to go down and see the sea. There she be now.'

Sure enough, down on the beach Emmaline could see the diminutive figure of Agnes, sauntering along at the very edge of the shore, with the ocean lapping over her feet. She wondered what it was like for Agnes, this first sight of the sea, her first experience of being at the edge of such vastness, of a seeming eternity of water that disappeared over the horizon on its way to cover two-thirds of the earth's surface. Every time she saw the sea Emmaline felt as if she had never seen it before, unable to understand how such an endless, immeasurable amount of water simply did not rise up out of control, particularly when whipped by fierce gales, and flood the entire world, washing away all populations and burying them in fathomless graves at the bottom of what would then be one enormous, biblical ocean.

'Hope you didn't mind, madam,' Agnes apologised when Emmaline joined her on the beach after she had finished her breakfast. 'It's just like – well. It's just – I don't really know what to make of it, see. I seen pictures, like, course. But pictures just don't give a notion, not at all. It just goes on for ever, like, and it's so beautiful. I never seen anything so beautiful as this place, and the sea, and – I just in't ever seen nothing like it.'

'It does quite take your breath away, Aggie, doesn't it?' Emmaline agreed. 'Even on a flat calm day like this, the sense of eternity, the sense of vastness, mystery, the feeling that this is where all life began – that in the oceans life was formed and from out of their waters all life came.'

'I don't understand. I thought we all come from the Garden of Eden?' Agnes puzzled.

'In a way we do, Aggie,' Emmaline said, taking her maid's arm to turn and walk back along the long deserted beach. 'Although, as I understand it, a gentleman by the name of Mr Charles Darwin would now have us see things very differently.'

As they walked westwards towards the distantly glimpsed fishing village of Portloe, with mighty Nare Head clearly visible in the background, Emmaline explained to a rapt Agnes the theory of evolution as she had understood it from reading a shortened version of Charles Darwin's great work. It somehow seemed a particularly apt thing to do.

They were gone all morning, just as the morning was gone before they knew it. In Portloe they found a small inn with a dining room where they were served a lunch of freshly caught mackerel served with more large floury potatoes soaked in butter and black pepper and followed by Cornish ice creams, a delicious repast that they then walked off along the sands ahead of the now incoming tide.

All of a sudden the weather was changing fast, the tide racing, with a strong wind picking up and blowing in a south-westerly, building waves that had been no more than six inches high into frothing breakers twenty times that size. Unsure as to how high up the beach the tide came the two young women decided to abandon their walk along the strand well before they got back to Porthollan, taking to the foothills first then clambering up on to the lane that ran back due east in the direction of Gorran Lodge, a destination they reached just in time for a tea of hot scones filled with Cornish cream and Mrs Carew's home-made strawberry jam.

After such a day and such a walk, the longest walk Emmaline could remember taking, she fully expected to fall fast asleep in front of the roaring fire. She did not, finding that although she was physically tired her mind was fresh and awake, full of so many new sights and sounds. So instead of either taking to her bed for a rest, as advised by Dr Proctor, or even cat-napping by the warmth of the log fire, Emmaline sat with a pencil and a pad of paper and began to write down just some of the many colourful images that the day had brought her.

Back in Bamford, at just about the time Emmaline had been sitting down to breakfast on her first morning at Gorran Lodge, the telephone had rung in Park House. Wilkinson took the call in the telephone room, before going to inform Julius that a Mr Freeman was on the line waiting to speak to him.

Julius followed Wilkinson across the hall and quickly shut the door behind him.

'This is Julius Aubrey speaking.'

'And this is Dwight Freeman speaking to you,' someone with a strong American accent replied. 'I telephoned you before, Mr Aubrey, but sadly you were not available.'

'So I understand,' Julius replied, wishing as he always did when on the telephone to get straight to the point. 'What might I do for you?'

'No – what might I do for *you*?' Mr Freeman laughed. 'I would very much like to put some business your way, Mr Aubrey – having seen your wares in the new Nesbitt & Nesbitt catalogue.'

'That is very good to hear, Mr Freeman,' Julius replied. 'But whatever you see in the catalogue you can order by mail. Nesbitt & Nesbitt run a first-class postal service.'

'What they don't supply is advice, Mr Aubrey,' Mr Freeman returned. 'I'm a widower, do you see – and without the help and advice of the gentler sex, I find myself at a bit of a loss when it comes to the matter of purchasing what I need for my new house. Now, my understanding of the matter is that you have a very fine business here in England, a business that includes advising clients on matters such as this.'

'That is correct,' Julius replied cautiously.

'I won't waste your time, Mr Aubrey, I assure you, sir. I won't waste it now and I won't waste it when we meet. I have a very fat wallet and I am anxious to take the best advice as to what I should purchase before I return home. So if you would do me the kindness of coming to meet with me and talk with me, I do assure you it really will be well worth your while.'

So, reluctantly, Julius agreed to meet with the mysterious Mr Freeman the following day at his hotel in London, reluctantly because he was busy packing up and making ready to go and join Emmaline at Gorran Lodge in time for Christmas. But he knew it would be foolish to miss what sounded like a very sizeable order. He comforted himself that if he concluded the business swiftly in the morning he might still be able to catch the midday locomotive from Paddington to Truro, which meant he could be in Gorran Lodge and with Emmaline shortly after midnight.

And so, having given Wilkinson new instructions for the packing of a small overnight case for his trip to London as well as the bags he would need for his time in Cornwall, Julius repaired to town to leave instructions for his workforce to cover the time he would be away.

That night he played cards again. He could not resist it, and again it was that most illegal of card games – baccarat. It was the third game in the sequence and towards the end of the evening he was nicely ahead, a position he intended to keep given the appalling run he had just suffered, a series of games where for once both his luck and his judgement had deserted him. But not this evening, not this time, when he rode his luck and used all his skills. All was fine so far – the game was running smoothly, the conversation was friendly and the atmosphere was congenial, even though among the card players was a gentleman of the very highest rank.

When time was called and all debts and promises were honoured, he found he was £423 to the good, which by any standards was a sizeable win for an evening at the table. Accepting the congratulations of several of his fellow players, mainly he noted those who had also been fortunate, although none as fortunate as he, he drank two glasses of champagne, and once the most distinguished of their number had departed he also took his leave to return to his hotel.

After he had gone, the host suggested to the half-dozen gentlemen still remaining that they have a brandy and discuss the evening's play. When drinks had been poured and fresh cigars had been lit, the host, a member of the aristocracy, announced that they had entertained a cheat at the table.

Silence fell as those remaining looked round at each other as if one of them might be the culprit. When they were assured by their host that the suspect had already left the relief was palpable, but the shock was still toxic. Who could possibly have cheated in such company – company graced by a gentleman of the very highest degree? What sort of cad and bounder would risk life, limb and reputation by cheating at cards one of the best-connected gentleman in London if not the land?

'The gentleman in question is the gentleman who was the last to leave us,' their host finally disclosed. 'There is no doubt about it. Evesham here and I,' he continued, indicating the tall distinguished man on his right, 'have been keeping close watch. We were alerted

370

to the possibility after his first visit here, so during the last game and tonight we watched him very carefully. It would appear that the gentleman in question cheats by altering the size of the bets he has on the table after he has won or lost a hand. It is done with the utmost skill – one could even say legerdemain – and I vow that had he not made one very small but visible mistake on the very first night – one which aroused Evesham here's suspicions since he was on the receiving end of the bet – my guess is that he would have got away with it. That this chicanery of his would have gone quite unnoticed.'

'If this is so, Tommy,' one of his friends enquired, 'then what to do?'

'Given that we have access to no other resources than ours, seeing that what we are doing here is illegal.'

'Why the playing of baccarat should be deemed illegal passeth all my understanding,' a corpulent gentleman in one corner grumbled. 'I certainly don't think our esteemed guest thinks much of the proscription.'

'Beside the point, Percy,' his host replied. 'This is something we have to handle ourselves, because it is to do with ourselves and those like ourselves only, which is why we have to take care of the cad.'

'How?' the one called Tommy wondered. 'Not like racing. Can't exactly warn him off.'

'Yes we can,' his host assured him. 'In our own way we can do precisely that – which is why I have despatched our two bulldogs off to follow Mr Aubrey to where he is staying, and there to take care of him. That is all. Now I think we should have one more drink and call an end to the evening.'

The two so-called bulldogs – a small but effective

partnership that consisted of the heavyweight Thomas Martin and his former runner who were regularly employed by the toffs of the town to take out anyone who overstepped the mark – dutifully followed their quarry back to his hotel in Mayfair, in the lobby of which once he had been admitted they took it in turns to keep watch.

In the morning, after he had breakfasted in his room, Julius went down to the reception area and asked the concierge to tell Mr Freeman that he was here and ready to attend their prearranged meeting. Oddly enough the concierge, who had not been on duty when Julius had arrived, seemed to know him immediately, addressing him by his name, an odd fact which Julius was about to comment on, when the man was called away, leaving Julius to lean against the reception desk to read the headlines of the Morning Post, all the time watched by a thin-faced man sitting beside a pillar half hidden behind his own copy of the same newspaper.

On being told that Mr Freeman was ready to receive him, Julius went up to the first floor and knocked on the door of Room 4 to announce his arrival.

'Enter!' an American voice called from within. 'Come on in, please, sir!'

Julius did as bid, entering the main room of the suite, which he found to be a good-sized and well-furnished room with a large display of flowers on the sideboard, beside which stood two suitcases, apparently packed and ready to go.

'Hello?' Julius called after a moment. 'Mr Freeman?'

'Hello, my dear fellow,' an unmistakable voice said

from the bedroom behind him. 'How very nice to see you.'

'Good God,' Julius exclaimed when he saw who was standing in the doorway. 'You? What in the name of God—'

'I became disenchanted with the idea of Australia, alas,' the man said, laughing at him. 'You know how it is, no real racing, missing Ascot, all that.'

'You bastard! You bastard! We have a legal agreement—'

'Had. We had an agreement, but alas we do not any more. I burned my copy and yours too.'

'What are you talking about?'

'I stole your copy and burned it as well.' The man smiled, lighting an oval-shaped cigarette. 'You really should have kept it in a safer place than your desk.'

Julius stared at him, wondering how the man smiling at him could possibly have gained access to his house and to his private papers.

'Don't bother trying to work that one out,' the man suggested, reading his thoughts, tapping the ash of his cigarette into the fireplace. 'You'll just waste time. You were away somewhere, I was in the vicinity, so I took the opportunity to pay a visit to Park House and see if I could perhaps, let us say, annul that wretched document.'

'You destroyed my copy of the agreement?'

'It would never have stood up in court anyway, my dear fellow. Not worth the paper it was printed on. Now we have much more urgent business to conclude. I need some money.'

'When do you not?' Julius said angrily.

373

'Since the agreement no longer exists—'

'An agreement was made between us. You accepted the proposals, which were fifty per cent of any sales made through the catalogue, a capital cash payment and your fare to the country of your choice, which was Australia.'

'I chose Australia, my dear fellow, because it was the place farthest away and therefore would cost the most to reach!' The man laughed, throwing his finished smoke away.

'You never had any intention of going there at all, did you?'

'None whatsoever. Took meself to Ireland instead for a bit of sport, and didn't do too badly for once. Sadly the luck turned when I came back here, as it so often does, although I did win myself a tidy sum last night at the table.'

'In that case why do you have need of money?'

'Because, my dear fellow, I have a very expensive lifestyle, and there is some trouble with a lady, doncher know?'

'How much?' Julius enquired, sinking down into a chair. 'How much this time?'

'This will be the very last time, I promise you.'

'I feel somehow I have heard and lived through all this before. Very well.' Julius eyed him and then stared at his own right foot, which he was tapping anxiously on the floor. 'Very well,' he said again, now staring up at the ceiling. 'I will advance you what you need. I'm not going to give it to you and you are not going to pretend that you are going to pay me back because what I am going to do is advance it to you out of the catalogue money.'

374

'My dear fellow—' the man began in protest.

'That is final,' Julius cut in. 'How you live from now on, what you exist on and how you earn it is your affair, because I am having nothing more to do with you. How much do you need?'

'Seven hundred pounds.'

'No, you don't. You are probably hoping for five hundred, so I shall write you a cheque for three hundred and fifty and that is an end to it.'

'I cannot possibly survive on a measly, pathetic three hundred and—'

'You are going to have to, and that is an end to it,' Julius said abruptly, rising to write a cheque for the nominated amount. 'And I want nothing more to do with you, do you understand?'

'If that is what you want, that is how it shall be,' the man sighed. 'Tell me – how is that delightful little wife I brought you from America?'

Julius said nothing. He just tore the cheque from his cheque book, handed it over and prepared to leave.

'This time I would advise that you do go to Australia,' he said, turning back from the doorway. 'Or you may well regret it, truly.'

He returned to his room to lie down, for there was some time before he was due to catch his train, and besides, the force of his emotions had brought on a splitting headache, a nausea, as all dealings with the man calling himself Dwight Freeman, Arnold Bonniface, and many other names, always had done. God knows he did not wish him dead, but please God, he did not wish to ever, ever see him again. He was surely born with the sign of the devil engraved on him.

Sighing, Julius closed his eyes, longing for sleep to ease the pain.

At the same time that Julius was resting on his hotel bed, the man who was currently calling himself Dwight Freeman was hurrying past the bulldogs and disappearing into the telephone room, where he put in a telephone call to Julius Aubrey Ltd to see if and when Mr Aubrey was expected.

Bray Ashcombe had arrived in the house he was renting just outside Portloe the day after Emmaline had arrived. He had done so quite deliberately, having found out on the Bamford grapevine through a friend of Arabella's who worked at Julius Aubrey Ltd that Mr Julius Aubrey had been delayed by business both in Bamford and now in London, and was not expected to be able to travel down to Cornwall until Christmas Eve at the earliest.

Desperate to see Emmaline, and using the excuse of now having copies of her book of poems to show the author, Bray persuaded Mr Hunt to allow him to leave a day early on his Christmas holiday and hastened down to Cornwall, feeling that time and luck were on his side.

As further luck would have it, on the fine sunlit morning when Emmaline and Agnes walked from Gorran Lodge to Portloe and had lunch, Bray had seen the two solitary figures on the strand from his rented cottage window, had watched them arrive in the port and observed them disappearing into the famous old inn for refreshment.

Bray was able to see all this through an old telescope, one of the fittings in the whitewashed cottage which he just happened, coincidentally, to have rented for Arabella.

The moment he saw the young woman in the dark red coat and tightly fitting fur hat and cape he knew at once, despite her head's being bent against the wind, that it was the divine Emmaline. And here she was walking towards him along the golden sands by the undoubtedly sparkling blue sea. It was as much as Bray could do to stop himself from rushing out of his cottage to surprise her.

Instead he forced himself to wait until later in the day, until after he had seen the two young women retracing their steps, once again following their progress intently with his telescope, so that he could ascertain exactly where they were headed, losing them for a while as they disappeared off the beach in order to escape the tide, but then picking them up on the track as it rose up from behind the dunes, and then following them all the way to where they turned up the lane that finally led them to their own destination.

Now he took a horse from the nearby livery stables, and, with a copy of Emmaline's book of poetry carefully tucked into his coat pocket, he rode as fast as the horse would go, which for most of the ride was little more than a sloppy trot followed by a sporadic and idle canter, during which activities the animal still managed to snatch mouthfuls of hedgerow *en passant*, a snack which he then managed to chew over the heavy bit in his mouth, ignoring all Bray's kicks and slaps and tugs, delivering his rider finally in a dishevelled lather at the gate of a handsome square house built of dark granite and roofed in fine slate that stood in a windswept meadow overlooking the glorious bay of Veryan.

'Bray Ashcombe to see Mrs Aubrey, and the matter is of the utmost urgency.'

What with his disordered appearance and his precipitate arrival, one foot over the threshold, Mrs Carew had no intention of letting the visitor in.

'Wait here, sir, please, wait here. Mrs Aubrey is not a well young woman. She has been most unwell, she is here to rest, not to endure visitors,' Mrs Carew protested, but it was useless. Bray burst into the sitting room with Mrs Carew calling to Emmaline from behind him that she was sorry but he had demanded to see her.

'Mrs Aubrey, forgive me, please. The point is I had to see you, and I had to see you now!'

'Mr Ashcombe, I think you must agree this is no way to arrive, is it?' Having thanked and dismissed Mrs Carew, Emmaline resettled herself once again by the fireside where she had been quietly reading. 'I gathered you were going to be in the vicinity, but not so soon, and you do look most frightfully disarrayed. Have you had bad news of some kind? Not your sister, I hope?'

'I think you can put down part of my dismaying appearance to the wretch of a hireling that carried me here,' Bray groaned, mopping his brow with a bright red handkerchief. 'What you cannot see, although you can perhaps sense, is my inner consternation. And as for my unannounced arrival – I saw you on the beach today, so I knew you too had arrived, and I simply had to see you, Mrs Aubrey. It is simply no good, do you see? I cannot go on living like this without giving some expression to my feelings, because if I wait it may be too late.'

'My word,' Emmaline said, staring at the handsome young man who she now realised did look strangely pallid, dark shadows under his eyes, the expression in them one of such intensity that he looked feverish. 'Are you unwell, Mr Ashcombe? Please, you had better sit down here.' Emmaline indicated the chair beside the fire, but instead of sitting down Bray seized first one of her hands, and then the other.

'Yes – yes, you could say I was unwell, Mrs Aubrey, but it is a sickness only you can cure,' he said wildly, fixing her with a look of such longing that it could not fail to astound her. 'No – no, you must not look like that! No, please do not look at me like that.'

'How am I looking at you?'

'As if I am mad!'

'Hush, Mr Ashcombe, please. Please do not raise your voice,' Emmaline urged him, glancing at the sitting-room door. 'I truly don't think it quite right, quite proper, that you should visit me like this – and there are other people here whose sensibilities you must consider, truly there are, to say the least.'

'No, no! Please forgive me for disagreeing with you,' Bray begged her, interrupting, 'but it is long past the time for being right and proper! Long, long past! You see – oh, how can I best explain? Without making a complete and abject fool of myself? This is about our feelings, Mrs Aubrey – what you feel – what I feel – what you write about! This is about love – the love you crave so much – the love you need, the love you *deserve*. When first I read your verses, you must know that I lost my heart to the author?'

'Mr Ashcombe,' Emmaline began. 'You must understand poetry is one thing, verses are another, life is *quite* another.'

'You do not deserve to suffer, Mrs Aubrey,' Bray continued. 'I know how sensitive you are. I have seen the depths of you, and I love every inch of your shimmering soul. I have loved you from the moment I saw you. I fell in love with you in the time it takes for a man to look at a woman and see a fellow pilgrim – another soul – the woman for whom he has always been searching. Please do not say that you feel nothing for me. I have seen it in your eyes, on your face, in your sadness and – and in the few brief moments of happiness we have had together – I can see you care for me. You cannot continue as you are, you know you cannot.'

'That is my choice, Mr Ashcombe. Now, please, I have not been well, as you know, I must not—'

'You have been made ill by your unhappiness, can't you see that?'

Emmaline stared at him. Of course it was true. She had been made ill, but not by unhappiness – by despair.

Bray, seeing her hesitate, reached forward to take her hands once more, but Emmaline moved away just as Mrs Carew knocked on the sitting-room door and, giving Bray a look that should have turned him to stone, replenished the logs on the fire before retiring once more.

'You really must go, Mr Ashcombe. It is not right that you stay here, least of all in the mood you are in.'

Realising that he had shocked her with the intensity of his emotions, Bray pulled back a little from what he finally understood was an emotional brink, and began again, in a less emotive tone.

'Mrs Aubrey, what you must believe, first and foremost, putting aside all that I have said – although all that I have said is the truth – is that I am your friend. I have watched how much you have been made to suffer in a loveless marriage, I have seen how a beautiful young woman can be brought to the edge of despair. I can see more clearly than anyone else you know, because I am not part of society, not someone with whom you must observe the niceties, with whom you must follow protocol. You, of all people? You, like me, are a poet – and poets are not bound by these conventions! We are the wordsmiths – the dreamers of dreams – the painters of feelings that will be quoted for ever more! With a soul like yours, you cannot be imprisoned by such a man as your husband! He will kill the artist in you – if he has not already killed you by slow degrees with his neglect.'

'Mr Ashcombe, you mustn't frighten me in this way. You must go, before you upset me further.'

'How can your heart tell you anything about a man as cold and cruel as your husband, except that he is not worthy of your love?'

'I don't know, Bray,' Emmaline answered. 'That is what I am waiting to see.'

'Will you be all right?'

'Yes. Yes, I think I will. Now go – please. Back to Arabella. She needs you. Go.'

Bray stopped, turned, and looked back at Emmaline. 'You know?'

'Yes, I am afraid I guessed the day Aggie and I met her fainting in the street.' She smiled a little sadly. 'I have seen too many of my friends back home in the early stages of her condition not to recognise her sickness for what it was.'

Bray sighed sadly. 'Poor Arabella. She has no one but me, and I am not a practical person, but I have done my best to protect her from all the insults that an unmarried woman in a town like Bamford has to endure. I finally gave in to the realisation that her suffering at the hands of others was unendurable, and brought her away here, to await the great event in this place of temperate climes and seaside walks. There is a doctor I know, an old friend I knew at university, who has promised to attend her. She has been greatly reassured by him and is already much calmer.' He shook his head. 'To think that some families put women in her state into mental asylums, and take their babies from them. What a world we live in, so cruel, so heartless.'

'Society judges us when *we* should be judging society, surely?'

Bray looked at Emmaline with another of his looks of deep understanding. 'There, you see! Once again we are twin souls. That is how I feel. And seeing how much Arabella has suffered at the hands of hypocrites – that is why I brought her away.'

Emmaline smiled at him, happy that he seemed to be calmer.

'Forgive me. In the turmoil of my feelings I almost forgot this,' he said, putting the slender book he had brought with him into her hands.

Emmaline stared at the little volume. Was it true, was this her book in print? It did not seem possible.

'I think it looks very handsome,' he told her, and before she could say anything he leaned forward and brushed her lips with his.

Emmaline was startled, but not surprised.

'Bray . . .'

'Emmaline.'

He touched her lips, but this time with a light finger, and then tapped the book in her hands. 'Just remember you are here, always, and you have the soul of an angel.' Before she could say anything more he hurried out of the sitting room, past Mrs Carew, who needless to say had hardly left the hall even to see to her cooking pots, so shocked was she by the precipitate arrival of Bray Ashcombe, and so curious as to the cause of his flinging himself into Gorran Lodge in a manner hardly befitting a gentleman.

Emmaline glanced down at the book again. It was a wonderful moment, so wonderful that she quite forgave Bray the kiss. After all, a kiss was just a kiss, unless of course you were married to Julius. She turned away from the memory, the excitement that one particular kiss had aroused in her, and sat down to leaf through the little book written by a Lady.

After they had finished their dinner, Emmaline insisted on helping Mrs Carew and Agnes clear away so that they could all get on with decorating the Christmas tree that the Gorran Lodge gardener had cut and brought in for the festivities. Mrs Carew had boxes full of decorations from previous years, so with a huge fire blazing in the fireplace they set about hanging the tree with a glittering, shimmering assortment of ornaments. As they did so, Emmaline remembered Christmas time back home, with the enormous tree they would all help decorate in the hall and the handpainted paper chains and bells they would hang everywhere to gladden the house, and in that moment she felt a tidal wave of homesickness, until she saw the look in Agnes's eyes and the smile on Mrs Carew's bonny face as they all stood back from the tree to admire the enchantment, and it was then that Emmaline knew that whatever happened she now belonged in England.

Still unsure quite when to expect Julius, since they had received no definite word, the now pleasantly tired Emmaline went up to bed shortly after ten o'clock. There was a new moon that night, so Emmaline asked Agnes to leave the curtains open, and before she finally retired she and Agnes stood in happy silence looking out at a sea lightly dusted with moonlight under a dark velvet sky, and watching the fast-scudding clouds that flitted intermittently across the face of the crescent moon.

'This is a really beautiful place, don't you think, Aggie?' Emmaline said, still standing at the window. 'There's just something about it that seems to centre right back where it belongs. It's ridiculous, but I feel like the person in that story – what was it? About someone who's unwell, and they go up this mountain, which has magic properties, although she doesn't know it. And when she comes down the other side she's cured. Sure, it's a fairy story, I know – but then so many of those wonderful stories come from old legends, and so many of the old legends are based on some sort of fact. And I really feel as though I have climbed a mountain, a journey that started in a rocky barren place, and now I'm beginning a descent into a valley full of sunshine and spring flowers. I don't know why – don't ask me, Aggie – I just have the oddest feeling that everything is going to get better.'

Agnes crossed herself. 'Well, let's hope so, Mrs Aubrey, for you certainly haven't had much luck lately, what with one thing and another.'

Agnes walked off to put away Emmaline's gown. What she couldn't say was that none of the servants at Park House had been able to understand why her mistress had stayed in a marriage which was clearly not a marriage at all. However, now that they were down by the sea, in Cornwall, and Mr Aubrey nowhere in sight, and that poet chap calling, perhaps things would soon look up for her, poor soul. As Mrs Graham had kept saying to anyone who would listen, 'It's the abandonment that I would find hard to take, the never being at home, only us for her to talk to, and then her health so poorly lately, the sweet creature.'

Agnes's confidence in a rosy future might however have been soon shattered, for within an hour of Emmaline's snuffing out her bedroom candles and lying in her bed propped up on her pillows to watch and finally fall asleep under the spell of a new moon, a tall, dark, elegant and handsome man, whose face and figure would be all too familiar to the servants at Park House, could be seen disembarking from his train at Truro station, and looking for a cab to carry him on the last leg of his journey to Gorran Lodge.

'Greetings, Mr Aubrey, sir!' the stationmaster

called, hurrying up to him. 'Your wife be already arrived – Mrs Carew, my cousin, sent someone to collect her here, several days back. You'm come down to see us for Christmas? I dare say you'm might prefer to spend the rest of the night at the Railway Hotel rather than rouse them at the Lodge you'm be thinking, better you not?'

'No, no, I shall continue on. I would not wish to disappoint Mrs Aubrey. You know the ladies, always so suspicious of us!'

Both men laughed appreciatively, and a cab was duly called up.

By the time the cabbie swung his hansom off the main carriageway heading due west and on to the first of a series of much narrower roadways that would finally lead to Gorran Lodge, its passenger had become aware of the clatter of another set of hooves not far behind him. Taking a look over his shoulder, he saw in the distance another cab travelling in the same direction as his own.

'Busy night, eh?' he called to the driver, who didn't respond.

The following cab was still there as they passed through Tregony and then down into the lanes leading through a lonely stretch of deserted countryside before reaching St Michael Caerhays, the last village of any note before the final destination nominated by the fare, a fare who in spite of the bone-shaking ride had fallen asleep several miles back.

The lanes were quiet except for the sound of

the hooves of his own horse, or so it seemed to the cab driver as he slapped the ribbons on his horse's rump to urge him up the steep hill rising beyond the village, and that was the way they remained until just before he slowed to locate the lane which, without lights, and nothing but the brightness of the moon overhead, he had managed to overshoot.

'You passed it, I think!' the now awake passenger called up to the driver as the cab stopped once again. 'The turning's marked by a white post on one side and a water trough on the other. Hard to see at night – but we should be able to pick up the post all right!'

After another brief search, this time made by the cabbie on foot, the right lane was located and the last stage of the journey completed. As the cabbie walked his horse slowly up the rise and through the named gates of Gorran Lodge he heard the clopping of the other carriage horse disappearing into the night as the following cab made its way along the coast road, leaving his passenger to alight from his transport in utter peace and quiet under a star-spangled sky. He stood there for a moment with his luggage at his feet taking in the night view and listening to the sound of a sea that from the distance seemed to be at low tide. An owl in a tree somewhere at the bottom of the gardens hooted tremulously, but otherwise all was silent, until he thought he heard someone behind him. Turning, he found himself confronting the bulldogs.

'What the hell—'

'We been sent to teach you not to cheat at cards.'

'My dear fellow, I don't cheat at cards, and whoever has sent you must know that. No, certain rather well-connected and even royal persons do cheat at cards, but not me. I am too good to need to cheat—'

Brave words, perhaps, but not enough to save him from what followed.

Up at the Lodge something had woken Emmaline. She sat up, listening. She had often had cause to curse being a light sleeper, but never more than now as she thought she heard a dull thud, and then someone, or several people, walking on the gravel outside the front door.

She was sure it could not be Julius, because if it had been he would merely have put a key in the door and walked into the Lodge to make himself at home until morning. After all, he knew the house well enough.

She lay in bed, feeling less than brave, realising gradually that there was nothing she could do. Uneasily, she remembered Mrs Carew telling Agnes and her, with some relish it had to be said, of the pirates that still plagued the Cornish coastline, and, according to her, always would. Since both the housekeeper and Agnes slept in a different part of the house, Emmaline knew that she was, in all senses, quite alone.

For a few seconds she remained frozen with

fear, her teeth chattering, and then she pulled herself together. She could not confront pirates or anyone else on her own: self-preservation was called for. She slipped out of bed, and as quietly as was perfectly possible she turned the key in the lock, and promptly went back to bed, where she lay once more listening for something further. There was nothing. Not a sound, not a footfall to disturb the gravel, not a sighing of the wind in the trees, only an owl calling out almost laconically, as if it was becoming mightily bored by its own sound, and soon, with daylight upon it, would be falling thankfully asleep.

Emmaline closed her eyes. The Lord only knew, and the Lord was the only one who did know, it had been a bad enough day, what with coping with Bray Ashcombe and his passionate outpourings, and trying to pretend to Mrs Carew that it was normal for gentlemen like him to push their way into people's houses armed only with a small book of verses.

She lay for the next few minutes straining to listen, but there was definitely no other noise to be heard, so whatever it was had gone away, if it had ever been there. She sighed with relief, and was woken, many hours later, not just by the bright daylight of the south-west, but by Agnes pulling her curtains, and the sound of Mrs Carew calling in a carefully modulated manner.

'Agnes, could you come down here, my dear, for a little minute?'

Agnes excused herself and went downstairs,

but the look of happy expectancy on her face was soon wiped off.

'My dear! It's Mr Aubrey! Out here!' Mrs Carew pointed to the open door. 'Not 'imself at all, he's laid down in the drive not moving, laid down in the drive, like one dead. I think he *is* dead.' This last she said in a whisper, at the same time putting a hand over Agnes's mouth to prevent the inevitable scream.

The heaviness of a mature man became all too apparent to the two women as they attempted to half carry, half drag the body into the hall, and from there into the darkened drawing room, where they laid him out as best they could, given the circumstances, on the rug in front of the dead fire.

'Is he alive, Mrs Graham? Is Mr Aubrey alive?' Agnes begged in a whisper, covering her face, because she could hardly bear to see what a state he was in.

Mrs Carew stared down at the body. 'I am very much afraid not, my dear,' she confessed, having knelt to put a hand to his wrist and temple, and as Agnes started to sob she said in gentle tones, 'Come away now, Aggie my dear, this is not for the likes of you and me, this is for the doctor. If the poor man is gone there is nothing to be done, and we have moved him as far as we could.' She beckoned to the terrified Agnes, who was staring down at the corpse on the floor. 'Here, girl, you look after your mistress. Say nothing until I go for help. Leave her be in her bed, make to show that the water is taking a time heating up for her bath, see, my dear? If she do come down, burnt feathers under the nose, and a teaspoon of brandy, but no need, we hope.'

Agnes did as she was told, and after taking a deep breath and letting it out somewhat noisily she walked up the stairs to the upper rooms.

Meanwhile Mrs Carew ran to the cottage to send her nephew on his pony to the doctor's house a mile away, and on the way back, having the luxury of being able to slow to a walk, she found herself shaking her head.

'Lord have mercy on his poor soul, the poor man has been beaten black and blue. And that this should happen at Christmas time, too.'

The boy saddled his pony and rode as fast as the plucky little pony could take him to the doctor's house. Happily the doctor was in, unhappily he was drunk.

'I can't make out a word you're saying, my boy. Where is it I am meant to be go-in?'

His wife arrived at their front door, and dragged him back into the house. The boy heard with some interest the sound of water being run, and protests being made, and more water being run, before the good doctor reappeared at the door, his bag in his hand, and a look of startled concentration on his face. He leaned against his gatepost and sighed.

'I know I have forgotten something,' he said to no one in particular. 'But what it is I'm confounded if I know, confounded if I know.'

'The pony and trap, sir, to take you to Gorran Lodge? I'm much afraid my pony won't take both of us, sir.'

'Yes, of course, pony and trap, yes, of course.' The doctor turned very slowly from the gate to see his groom bringing up exactly that, and waiting for him to climb in, which he did with little dexterity, and much swaying and sighing. 'It's Christmas, d'you see,' he said, finally seating himself at the back of the trap. 'I allus gets drunk at Christmas, it's my prerogative, along with the rest of the world, and all my patients. Carry on now, carry on, to wherever it is, lives must be saved, it's Christmas after all!'

Everyone at Julius Aubrey Ltd left the works on the last dot before the clock struck midday on Christmas Eve. They knew they were lucky to get two days for Christmas, there were many in the town who only enjoyed one, and everyone was looking forward to the feast to come, their appetites sharpened by weeks of happy expectation. Not only that, but Mr Ralph had been instructed by their benevolent employer to give them all a Christmas tip, which meant that the buying of the Christmas bird and all the other necessary arrangements were all the merrier for having been paid for in advance.

They all wished each other the joys of the season and ran through the rain-darkened streets to the marketplace, where there would be hard bargaining to be done. Birds would be held up and rejected, vegetables would be felt and weighed, and neighbours would eye them with envy if they saw they were carrying home more to their families than they themselves could afford.

Mr Ralph shut up the works with a feeling of quiet satisfaction. He was glad that Mr Aubrey had gone to Cornwall. Of late the poor man had appeared as being most unhappy, and his return from London had merely served to heighten this feeling. To say that Mr Aubrey had looked shattered was to say the least: he looked done in, almost oblivious of everything that was happening at the works, so distracted had he been. But happily, now he would be in Cornwall with Mrs Aubrey, and everything would start to seem better once he was reunited with his new young wife. Poor man, he had suffered so much in his life, most particularly at the hands of his older brother, the son and heir to whom Mr Aubrey senior had hoped to be able to entrust his business affairs, but who had turned out to be a wastrel of the worst kind. But never mind that now, that was all in the past, along with Mr Julius's poor dead first wife, and all the other sadnesses that had darkened his life, turning him from being a happy soul to the introvert he had become.

Mr Ralph stopped and stared in the window of a delightful shop displaying fans of the prettiest kind. He was sure that he knew someone very close to him who would like a fan for her Christmas gift. He leaned forward, staring at one in particular. A prettier piece no one could wish for. He pushed his way into the shop knowing that this Christmas, unlike so many before, thanks to the prosperity of the works, he could afford to spoil his wife, and he only hoped that Mr Aubrey would be doing the same to his.

At Gorran Lodge Mrs Carew and Agnes were standing beside Emmaline's bed staring down at her in distracted fashion.

'That is right, now, you just sip on this brandy, my dear, and Mrs Carew will stay with you. The good doctor has come and we can safely leave all the practicalities to him. Oh, you poor soul, that this should happen to you at Christmas time.'

Emmaline stared at her. What did she mean? What did it matter when it happened? Julius was dead, and she was a widow. She was too stunned to cry, but pushing away the brandy spoon she turned her tear-stained face into her pillow. What kind of life was it that could take Julius from her when they had had no life at all?

'I loved him, but I never told him. I never told him that I loved him,' she kept saying to Agnes, until both women could be forgiven for wanting to shake her to stop her saying the same words over and over again.

There was the sound of a carriage in the drive, and, later, muttered voices.

'I must go to him before they take him away,' Emmaline protested, but Agnes tried to restrain her.

'You go to whoever it is. I expect the doctor has sent for help to remove the poor man to hospital,' Mrs Carew said in a low voice, not wishing to say more, knowing that there would be a need for an examination.

Agnes nodded, and walked slowly down to the hall. Seconds later the women upstairs heard a prolonged scream, whereupon they both flung themselves downstairs to see Julius Aubrey standing at the front door, a shy, hopeful smile on a face that said he was very much alive.

Chapter Eleven

Emmaline stared up at Julius. Everything was making sense, but a great deal of the sense that it was making was as upsetting as it was bewildering.

'He was my elder brother by an hour,' Julius was saying.

'He was your twin—'

'He was a blackguard, a liar, and not a little depraved, and although he should have been heir to everything, he was heir to nothing but his own sins.'

Emmaline waited as Julius walked down the drawing room and stood looking out. He was glad that Theodore was dead. He found only relief in the fact.

'My father was a hopeless businessman,' Julius continued. 'He was an artist – and a very fine one too. A man with a great imagination but not a man born to run a business, that was why he left it to Theodore to run. It seemed ideal. He loved to travel, enjoyed being in America, which was so alive to new ideas, new businesses. It was when he was in New York that he met these so-called entrepreneurs who had all sorts of schemes. You had to buy into them, of course, which Theodore did, with company money – and that was where all the trouble began. In the end, when it became necessary to buy him out in order to give the company any chance of survival, I agreed that if he concluded an agreement to have Aubrey & Aubrey recommended in Nesbitt & Nesbitt's catalogue, I would sign over to him fifty per cent of any sales made through the catalogue, and a very handsome cash settlement. So that is what he did. He made a bargain with your father, and your father made a bargain with him.'

Emmaline rose to her feet.

'My father – my father – don't tell me—'

Julius looked at her, shrugging his shoulders helplessly. 'What could I do? I had no idea that marrying you would be part of the contract made with your father, but I have to say that when I saw you that first time, I felt no regret. Why should I? I thought you were beautiful.' Emmaline was holding on to the mantel, probably whiter than he had ever seen her. He sighed. 'The truth is I fell in love with you, Emma, but it was only when I had married you that it came to me what a terrible thing I had done, and I couldn't make love to you as I should, because I doubted that you could possibly love a man so base as to go through with such an agreement.' He stopped and went over to Emmaline, then guided her gently back to the sofa and stood opposite her to continue his story. 'There is more, I am afraid. I began to feel that no one could accept me as I was, that I was unacceptable, because – because my first wife died only a week after we married, and once you were in the house it seemed to me, time and again, that I might be betraying her by loving you, which is why I—'

'Which is why you hid her portrait.' Emmaline shook her head. 'And the wedding gown – that was hers too, wasn't it?'

'No! That was my mother's wedding dress, it's been in her family for over fifty years. I am not that – no, I *am* that callous, of course I am. I fully admit it, but I wouldn't do that.'

Emmaline was silent, and Julius continued.

'The works had dwindled to nothing by the time I picked up the reins, which was why I took up advising and helping with restoration work. The two combined very well, and Ralph, you know, he is an excellent fellow, he looked after that side of it, but we would have been scuppered without this business agreement, and your father, you know, he was all for it, and now it seems he is more than pleased with the way things are going, orders are flooding in—'

'And my sisters can all marry now *I* am married. What a very happy ending,' Emmaline said in a flat voice. Then she looked up at Julius as something came to her.

'Tell me the truth, Julius. Did you imagine that I had fallen in love with the man who had wooed me in America, and that put you, in your mind at least, out of the running?'

He nodded miserably. 'Naturally. Why wouldn't I imagine it? Theodore was always more captivating than I was, rogues so often are. He had inherited my father's charm, and his way with women.'

Emmaline threw up her hands in despair.

'I hardly knew him, I hardly had time to get to know him before he was gone, and all I knew was that he sent me a mirror with a sweet message—'

'No, it was I who sent you the mirror. He had told me this cock and bull story that – well, that your family considered you plain, and thought you would never marry – I felt so sorry for you. I wanted to give you courage, and I was, I must confess, expecting just that, a plain little American girl who had never been able to capture a husband. But what I met was so far from that, I was bowled over. For me you were, and still are, just beautiful.'

'How do I know?' Emmaline demanded after a long silence. 'How do I know that you are not as big a liar as your twin brother?'

'You don't, Emma. Alas, you do not.'

Emmaline stood up suddenly, and leaning forward she kissed Julius on the lips.

'Oh, dear Lord,' she said, moving away from him. 'So it was him that night. It was Theodore who kissed me, and I fainted – I knew there was something different, so terribly different.'

As Julius stared at her, she went on to explain.

'I had taken a sleeping powder on Dr Proctor's orders, but even so I awoke thinking that I had heard you coming in. I went downstairs and thought I saw you in your study at your desk, going through some papers, and you kissed me, but everyone told me that it was not possible, that you were away, which of course you were—'

'That must have been the night that Theodore broke in and stole my copy of our agreement. Fool that I was, I should have locked it in a safe. Had I known that he was still kicking his heels in England I would have done, but I was so sure that he was in Australia.'

Emmaline sat down slowly, shocked, remembering how frightened she was, and how repulsive the feel of that mouth on hers had suddenly seemed. She looked up at Julius. Was there so much in a kiss? There must be. She had just kissed Julius and it had been different from anyone else's kiss. It had been the kind of kiss that leads to another and another, the kind of kiss that needs no biology book to explain what might happen next. She frowned. Was this then what love was? She looked up at him in understandable bewilderment.

'What will happen next, Julius?'

Julius looked away. 'I don't know,' he said, moving towards the drawing-room window. 'What should happen next is Christmas, but that is not possible now, is it?'

Emmaline frowned, and then, to the

astonishment of both of them, she heard herself say, 'I do not for the life of me see why not.'

So Christmas was celebrated in some style at Gorran Lodge, if only for the benefit of Mrs Carew and Agnes, although it seemed to both Julius and Emmaline that, forced as they were to pretend, for their sakes, that it was a joyous time, it was far merrier than they could have thought possible. The roast goose was one that Mrs Carew had fattened herself, the many side dishes were delicious, and even Emmaline, who could not have supposed that after so many shocks she could have swallowed even a mouthful, enjoyed every morsel.

The following day Julius took his leave of her. 'You will stay here to get better,' he said, and it was not a question.

'Yes, Julius.'

He cleared his throat, one eye on the waiting carriage outside. 'I have made all the arrangements for my brother to be buried in France, going from here at the first opportunity. He will be buried beside our mother, whose fault it was that he was as he was.' As Emmaline looked up at him, surprised, he went on 'I was not expected, you see. My old nurse told me I arrived an hour later, to the great and horrified shock of my mother, who had to go through the same labour again. I do not think, in all candour, that she ever forgave me, nor was she able to share the first love that she had felt with the first son with another.'

Emmaline went to put a hand on his arm, so affected did she feel by this revelation, but Julius had moved away from her towards the drawing-room door.

'I do not expect you to forgive me for the suffering I have caused you, Emma, but I do so hope that in time you will come to understand that I have been more the victim of sin than the sinner. Goodbye, my Emma.'

He was gone before she could reply, and for a few seconds she remained where she was before going to the window and watching the carriage leaving the short carriage drive and turning awkwardly into the country road beyond.

Julius was right. She could not be expected to forgive him. He had made her suffer too much, but in time, if he was right, perhaps he could be expected to receive her understanding?

A few days later Mrs Carew came to the drawing-room door with an announcement.

'It's that madman again, Mrs Aubrey. You don't want him coming in here, do you, my dear? Seeing that he is mad, and come on that dreadful hireling of his too, and unannounced I'll be bound!' She frowned at Emmaline, looking more like a member of the Praetorian guard than a housekeeper.

'Oh dear, if he has come to visit, perhaps I had better see him,' Emmaline said, after a pause, sighing.

'Well, don't let him tire you. You are tired

enough, heaven only knows, my dear, heaven only knows.'

There was the sound of a scuffle in the hall, as if Mrs Carew was holding back a large dog, and in a moment a dishevelled-looking Bray Ashcombe appeared at the drawing-room door.

'I do declare,' he said, looking back at the closing door, 'I do declare that your goodly housekeeper does not think much of me, Emmaline – Mrs Aubrey.'

He stopped, shocked by Emmaline's appearance.

'You look dreadful,' he said tactlessly. 'Were you made ill over Christmas?'

'No, no, it is not Christmas that has made me ill, Bray,' Emmaline told him in a weary voice. 'It is life, my life in particular.' She indicated for him to sit down. 'You have always been most sympathetic to my circumstances, and, as it turns out, with good reason.'

Bray leaned forward to take her hands in his, but Emmaline shook her head.

'No, please, you must understand that there is a certain decorum to be followed. I am a married woman, even if in name only.'

Bray stared at her, not understanding. 'There must be something I can do to help you,' he said in a genuinely compassionate voice.

'Oh, there is,' Emmaline admitted. 'There is. You can listen to me, be my friend. I am so much in need of friendship. Indeed, if it were not for Mrs Carew here, and my dear little Aggie, and this beautiful place, I think I might have taken my own life, so despairing have I become.'

'But this is terrible—'

'Oh, it is more terrible than I can admit, even to you.' Emmaline sighed. 'It all began, you understand, with the misfortune of being the oldest of four sisters. I had an obligation to marry, or rather my father had an obligation to marry me off, and so it seems he did, to Julius Aubrey, and that is how I came to England, and that is the start of all my unhappiness.' She shook her head suddenly. 'I cannot tell you more. It is too distressing, and too shaming.'

She had never looked more ethereal, as if a light breeze would take her off. Bray felt desperate. He was not used to dealing with real emotion, only the poetic variety, and now he was faced with the real thing he wanted to get back on his hireling and gallop off. Instead, he took up the book of poems by a Lady.

'See what you have here? You have a work of great beauty that will be read by many, a work of such beauty that no one who reads this slender volume can ever come away unaffected. You must see.' He leaned forward, trying to take her hands again, but once again Emmaline rebuffed him. 'You must see that your suffering has not been for naught. Here is something good that has come out of your misery, here is something deep and true. I have told you – these are enviable. I envy them!'

Emmaline stared at him. He was such a boy still, so transparent.

'You have been a guiding star to my own creativity, a muse to me these last months. Seeing how much you suffered has deepened me, I am sure of it.'

Emmaline nodded. It might be true.

'There is something more that could deepen you further, Bray,' she said in a kindly voice, after a short pause during which he looked at her questioningly. 'You could marry your "sister" and put her out of your misery. You could marry Arabella, before the birth of your child, and make an honest woman of her. It would be a happy outcome for one of your many muses.'

Bray stood up, quite put out.

'I, er – I, er – I cannot marry Arabella,' he said. 'It would be wrong to marry.' He walked down the room. 'After all, if I marry her, she might spend the rest of her life thinking that I married her for the sake of the baby.'

'I can think of many circumstances that would be much worse than that,' Emmaline told him in a suddenly lightened voice, and then her tone changed, and she too stood up. 'Can you not understand that all the misery I have suffered comes, as the Bible has so often told us, from the sins of the past? Will you not understand that I am the victim of my husband's past, of my father's past, of everything that has gone before, ancient shibboleths to do with the subjection of women, old familial customs to do with traditions that should long have been shaken off? Is Arabella to be spurned and your child not even allowed a baptism because of illegitimacy?'

Bray sighed long and hard. 'Must I become a carriage horse? Must I draw the carriage for the rest of my life? Must I give up my muses?'

Emmaline stared at him. 'Yes, Bray, I am afraid you must.' She picked up the book of poetry and flung it into the fire. 'What is this compared to human life? Nothing!'

To say that Bray looked as if he had been hit would be to say the least of it, but very shortly afterwards he became Arabella's husband in a short service in a little nearby chapel, and, the union having been blessed, Mrs Carew, Agnes and Emmaline held a small wedding feast for them back at Gorran Lodge. It was a happy occasion, made a great deal happier not long afterwards by the safe delivery of a baby boy, brought into the world by the now sober doctor who had so reluctantly attended Julius's unmourned dead brother.

Every morning and every evening Julius looked at Wilkinson with the same pretence of not caring whether or not there was any post from Cornwall, and every evening and every morning Wilkinson looked back at him with the expression of someone who was as bad at hiding that he had bad news for his master.

'Nothing from Cornwall, I don't suppose, Wilkinson?'

'Nothing from Cornwall, no, sir. But there is a letter from Canada.'

Julius nodded. His sister. She wrote to him sometimes. It was always the same letter. The weather. The children. Her husband. Or, sometimes, her husband, the children, and the weather. She had not been able to travel to France for any of the family funerals, so now it seemed she was overcome with guilt, and felt that Julius needed cheering up, which he did, but not for the reasons that she imagined.

Dining alone, night after night, having to appreciate Cook's efforts, going to his club some nights, drinking more than was good for him. It had been the same for weeks now. At least the weather was getting better. He stared out of the window. And Ralph was more than happy with the orders coming in from America, and the Parhams were more than happy with the state visit of the Queen, and she had been more than gracious about the improvements to Hartley. All in all, he should have been a happy man, but a lovesick lonely man was not a happy man, and he was all of that, and everyone around him knew it.

If only she would write to him, let him know something of how she was feeling, how she was going on, but he heard only from Mrs Carew, and her letters were about as illuminating as those of his sister.

Mrs Aubrey was going along very well. The spring weather was warm. Agnes was going along very well. She had made a cake for Easter, which being that it was so early this year they had celebrated with spring lamb, and all the daffodils were out.

Julius found he was treasuring Mrs Carew's letters with the same assiduousness with which he might have cherished the letters of his beloved Emma, if she had written to him.

How the days dragged, when he was not at business, and the nights when he was not at his club. He occupied himself at these times with reorganising the house, banishing all the paintings that had been his father's, repainting the drawing room in Emmaline's chosen apricot, watching the eight coats of paint being put on, as if he was a little boy again and fascinated by workmen, talking to the painter all the time as he watched him, as lonely people do.

'It will take time, sir,' Mrs Graham told him, once or twice, and they both knew what she was referring to. 'Time is the great healer.'

But time had not healed Julius of his love for his Emma, so why, he wondered, should it bring her back to him?

And then one day just as he had returned to Park Lodge resolved to sell the place, to start all over again in some out-of-town country house where he would have no memory of anything except the present, Wilkinson presented him with a letter, and it was from Cornwall.

Wilkinson immediately plunged down to the basement with the news.

'Well, thank the Lord for that,' Mrs Graham exclaimed as she sat at the top of the servants'

409

table serving soup, and Mr Wilkinson took his place at the bottom of the table opposite her. 'Any more misery upstairs and I was about to hand in my notice.'

She had hardly finished speaking when a voice bellowed downstairs.

'Wilkinson! Wilkinson! Come up here at once!'

Wilkinson stood up, reluctantly, his napkin tucked into his collar, and ran up the servants' stairs to the hall.

Julius was standing in the hall. His face was alight with emotion.

'Wilkinson, she is coming home! She is coming back, for her birthday! June,' he said distractedly. 'Her birthday is in June. The roses will be out. We must start at once, to make everything as beautiful as is perfectly possible for her!'

Wilkinson was at pains not to look moved by the news.

'Very well, sir, but might I first finish my soup?'

Everything that was ever known to be a favourite of Emmaline's now came into play. Her favourite colours for the bedroom. (Her favourite colour in the drawing room was already present.) Her favourite scents, her favourite flowers – white roses – her favourite books of poetry, sent in by Mr Hunt of course. Miss Lamb, no longer a muse to poets, but a publisher's wife, brought the books in specially, and set them about

Emmaline's bedroom with a reverence that was most speaking.

'This is particularly her favourite,' she told an attentive Julius.

Julius opened the slim volume by a Lady, and then quickly shut it. He knew those verses all too well.

'I will put that downstairs,' he said. 'On the centre table in the drawing room. They are very beautiful, too beautiful to leave up here.'

The new Mrs Tully nodded. 'I am so glad you think that,' she told him. 'I have learned some of them by heart. They speak so movingly of the human condition.'

Julius moved quickly away. There was still so much to do. The musicians to be hired, her favourite music to be played, the drawing-room furniture to be set about in such a way that dancing could happen quite naturally after a splendid dinner set about with her favourite dishes.

And then there was the new worry. Would her carriage arrive on time? Would the train bringing her from Cornwall crash? Would she be quite well?

'Dresses! What dresses does she like?'

He stared distractedly at Mrs Graham, who was trying not to look tired out with his endless flustering.

'Leave that to me, sir. Mrs Shannon helped her with everything before the wedding. I am sure she will be of a great assistance now.'

Mrs Shannon could not wait to be of assistance. Together with Mrs Graham, she sent for the top dressmakers and their models, and for several afternoons the good ladies were shown the most fashionable day gowns and evening gowns of the season, the most delicious-looking confections produced for their delectation. Gowns of silk and lace, the cut of which were positively faint-inducing.

'I don't know what it is but I have only to see such beautiful gowns and I feel in need of sal volatile,' Mrs Shannon confessed.

'Yes, indeed,' Mrs Graham agreed, and having made a list of the chosen gowns, and their prices, she presented them to her master.

Julius gave the list a peremptory glance, hardly taking in anything, so distracted was he by choosing Emmaline's favourite music with the leading musician.

'Yes, yes, of course, have them all sent up.'

'All, sir?' Mrs Graham asked, astonished.

'Yes, of course, all of them.'

There was a short pause.

'But is there room upstairs, sir?'

Julius looked at her. 'Well, if not, we will just have to make room, Mrs Graham. Mrs Aubrey must have everything. Everything!'

He went back to choosing music with the musician, and having done so he hurried out to the telephone room to telephone through to the jeweller that Ralph had recommended. And so to Park House came the jeweller with his large leather boxes, and Julius who had impeccable taste chose a sapphire and diamond set to go with Emmaline's eyes, and that was all before he ordered her a new carriage and a matching pair of greys to pull it.

'It will be a motorised vehicle soon, mark my words,' Wilkinson opined, trying to look disapproving, while all around him flew in every direction to make ready for the great arrival.

Emmaline was now not just healthy, she was blooming. The Cornish spring coming early as it did, as early as the weather in the south of France, and quite as clement, had meant that her skin had taken on the colour of a peach, and her figure had filled out most becomingly – a fact which in view of all the new gowns gave Mrs Graham a momentary attack of nerves, which fortunately proved to be unnecessary, for as it transpired she had only regained her weight.

'Julius.'

Emmaline looked round at all the smiling faces. It had been a long journey, broken by an overnight stay, arranged by Julius, so that she could arrive as he called it 'bandbox fresh'.

'Emma.'

Now it was Julius who was the pale one as he showed her round all the alterations, and took her upstairs to see all that he had accomplished there, before leaving her to choose a dress to go with the birthday necklace, which he presented to her with a shy bow, and for which he received a long and quite public kiss.

Julius tore himself away from her to make sure of all the arrangements, and then leapt up the stairs to his dressing room, no longer the gloomy place it had once been, with Wilkinson in attendance to help him do up his white tie, and pull on his tail coat, for his nerves were such that he could hardly brush his hair with his silver brushes, his hands were trembling so much. Eventually he emerged, thankfully before Emmaline, only to rush downstairs again so that he and Wilkinson could make sure that everything was as it should be.

Emmaline had been truly shocked by the changes in the house, so much so that it was a few minutes before she could say what she felt, which was that everything was more beautiful than ever. Agnes finished dressing her hair, did up the sapphire necklace and stood back to admire the deep blue and silver of her evening gown, which with its back interest and its flounces showed off Emmaline's graceful figure.

'You have never looked lovelier, Mrs Aubrey,' Agnes told her, sighing.

It was no good pretending, as they both stood looking at her reflection in the cheval mirror, that there weren't tears in their eyes, for both mistress and maid were all too aware that they had come on a long journey together.

Julius was standing at the bottom of the stairs

waiting for Emmaline, with the servants behind him, as he had requested. They all clapped their hands as their mistress descended the stairs, and the musicians struck up the first of many of Emmaline's favourite songs. It was a magical moment and they all knew it, but there was something more to come, something which Emmaline herself had requested in the letter to her *dearest Julius* in which she asked not only that they put the past behind them, but that they came into the present together.

Emmaline went into the drawing room and sat down on a gilt chair, as the music played on.

After a moment Julius came up to her.

'Good evening, Miss Nesbitt. May I say how beautiful you are looking this evening?'

'Yes, you may,' Emmaline returned, fanning herself and looking round at the rest of the company for appreciation of her performance. 'And who may you be, sir?'

'I am Mr *Julius* Aubrey, and I would very much like the pleasure of your company all evening, and every evening, for the rest of our lives.'

'You may have it, Mr Aubrey. You may have it.'

She reached up to Julius, and not caring one jot about the servants, the musicians, or the arriving guests, she kissed him very prettily, after which she stood back and said thoughtfully, 'Yes, you see, how silly of me not to have known all along, it *is* all in the kiss!'

Postscript

To say that Mr and Mrs Julius Aubrey lived long and happy lives would be to say the least of it. They prospered as people who love each other and have learned from their past mistakes so often do. What they could not forget, and did not want to forget, was that each had come to know the other with a knowledge and admiration that perhaps only living through much suffering and many vicissitudes can bring. The strange outcome of such contentment was that Emmaline's poetic inspiration left her, and no amount of encouragement from her husband would bring it back. Emmaline herself harboured no regrets, seeing her verses as a part of her past that she no longer wished to visit, and recognising that however beautiful a description of a waving daffodil might be, it could never really better the flower itself.

THE END

If you enjoyed THE LAND OF SUMMER, look out for Charlotte Bingham's next novel, THE DAISY CLUB

Charlotte Bingham would like to invite you to visit her website at www.charlottebingham.com